# BRANDED

C.T. DANIELS

DOUBLE EDGED PUBLISHING

*To my beautiful wife, without whom, this novel would have never happened.*

# CONTENTS

# ACKNOWLEDGEMENTS

This work would not have been possible, first and foremost, without Jesus Christ. He was my inspiration and kept me going throughout all of the trials and struggles that came with writing this novel and putting it out for the world to see. I am extremely grateful for all of the blessings that He's bestowed on me over these seven years.

I also want to thank my amazing wife, Laurilee Anne Tracy, who gave me the idea, after years of writing, editing, and marketing this story as a play and screenplay, to write it as a novel. She has stood by my side since day one and helped me in more ways than I could have ever asked. This novel is as much hers as it is mine.

This book also would have never happened without all those who were around for the initial creation of the play, Falkland Road. To Harley Erdman, your tutelage in the writing was invaluable. To Savannah Van-Leuvan Smith, you have been one of my biggest supporters and put in so much work to make the play a success. To Camee Manderfield, you have been such a blessing, from your amazing dedication to the play to your unwavering support to your invaluable assistance with the audiobook and book trailers. Of course, none of this would have been possible, as well, without Julie Digiusto, Samantha Creed, Tiahna Harris, Leah Bugden, Daveth Cheth, Dillon Crocket, Stephen Lajoie, Rachael Hobson, and Jordyn Albert. You all were brilliant in every way.

I also want to give special thanks to everyone who worked on the book trailer, which has helped make this possible: to Christina Chenier, Bobby Morse, Ally Hebert, Tyler Handford, Camee Manderfield, Mariah Waite, Dan Hurd, Kayleen Gerow, Jennifer Decristopher and Savannah, Denise McLaughlin for use of your house, and Michael Normand. You all were instrumental.

And to everyone else who ever helped me out along the way: Shane Adams, Dan Johnson, Donna Saloio, Jasmine Marino, Demi Bernice Eslit, Will Power for teaching me playwriting, Hannah Cushman, Ashley Cummino, my parents Brian and Cristie Tracy, Julie Norval, and everyone else who has ever encouraged me or supported my work. I could not have done this without any of you.

Finally, I want to thank my beautiful children, Karstyn and Tristyn, who have been my inspiration. May you both always follow your dreams, like I finally did.

# PREFACE

This novel started back in 2011 as an idea. I was sitting back-
stage as a stage hand for a brilliant production of The House of
Bernarda Alba at the University of Massachusetts. I was
working on some writing and poems at the time, so naturally, I
had my laptop with me. One thing about the play stuck out to
me: the exploitation of women by another woman. This got me
thinking about human trafficking. What would it be like for a
woman to run a sex trafficking ring?

So, I pulled out my laptop, in the middle of the production,
and started writing. At this point, my knowledge of the cold
realities of human trafficking was limited. However, over the
next year, I started to develop a heart for the women affected by
this scourge. It was truly heartbreaking. This was a story I
needed to write, and the story needed to revolve around the
trafficker.

There's something special about stories that are told from
the perspective of the villain. In my theatrical career, I have
played a number of villains and antiheroes. You might even call

it my specialty. The most important thing that I learned through that experience is that a villain never thinks of themselves as a villain. Oftentimes, they aren't terribly different from the rest of us.

This is the reality of serial killers, terrorists, and child molesters that we are so often faced with in media. We hear interviews from friends, family and neighbors about how they had no idea that this person was doing such awful things behind closed doors. Because of this, we believe the truth that terrorism, murder, and abuse could be around any corner. However, we don't treat human trafficking the same way.

We look at prostitutes, porn stars, and strippers as women who made a choice, and we see traffickers as inhuman monsters who, if we're being honest, could not possibly be real. Maybe this is why we don't understand the gravity, reach, or reality of the problem. I worked for two years at a truck stop where prostitutes were said to work out of the motel next door, and I thought nothing of it. Years later, I found out on the news that those girls were victims of human trafficking. My heart was broken. How could I not have seen?

What would happen if we realized that human trafficking is bigger and more insidious than we know? And what better medium than fiction? When I sat down to write this novel, at my wife's suggestion, I also had to ask the question of how much horror I wanted to hit people with. Through prayer, I decided that people need to see the full reality of what these women go through.

This is a work of fiction. Names, characters, organizations, places, events, and incidents are either products of the author's imagination or are used fictitiously.

TRIGGER WARNING: Due to the graphic reality of the subject matter, this story deals with graphic descriptions of physical and sexual abuse. Reader discretion is advised!

# PREDATOR

## DETROIT, MICHIGAN

*Illuminate: Brighten Your Night.*
The sign that hung outside the Illuminate Night Club certainly lived up to its billing. Its silver and blue flashed so spectacularly that it could be seen from miles away; that is, it could have been had it not been located smack-dab in the middle of pure urbanity. Nestled in the bosom of the once thriving Motown, Illuminate unquestionably stood out from its neighbors as the sole representation of modernity in a sea of dilapidated, brick architecture. Anyone who opened its doors was immediately met by a deluge of radiating light, a testament to the club's namesake. This was because, along the walls, hidden beneath rows upon rows of translucent panels, was a grand succession of neon lights, which rotated periodically through a range of colors so extensive that one could spend an entire night in the club without feeling like they had seen the same shade twice.

The club floor extended so far back that a whole football field could run along its length and width. With the exception of the bar, kitchen, and bathrooms, the entire floor functioned as a singular space, the focus of which was a concert-grade stage at its rear. On either side, thirty feet from the main stage, stood several, staggered, circular stages with small, ivory tables and chairs surrounding them, standing in stark contrast to the shadowy floors. Erected in the center of each stage was a glowing pole, side lit by blue and purple lights mounted into the stage floor.

That night, the club was lively. The rhythmic, pulsating sounds of EDM resonated from every corner of the building, which was, as usual, filled to capacity with a veritable rainbow of humanity. From the dance floor to the bar, no race, creed or people group was forgotten. Everyone was full of drink and full of life. Beneath the pounding beat of the music could be heard chatter from groups of friends around their tables and laughter from the girls at the bar who were trying a bit too hard to impress the handsome bartender.

On the club floor, gorgeous, shapely waitresses carried food and drink back and forth to each customer, wearing little more than eggshell-colored tops and navy-blue shorts. Truly, they were a sight to behold in and of themselves, but almost every eye in the building was transfixed, unwaveringly, on the side stages. There, dazzling dancers slid their bodies up and down the luminescent poles, caressing them gently with each pass. Their movements were masterful and tantalizing, as though they had studied under the masters of the exotic arts them-selves. Occasionally, one of the dancers would leave the stage and take one of the more generous patrons into a private room, hidden behind the translucent panels, for a private dance, only to be replaced by another, equally hypnotizing dancer.

Above ground, life was bright and full of life. However, if one was to venture underneath, they would find exactly the inverse, for Illuminate held a dark secret beneath its neon lights.

It was one that should have been plain to anyone if they were to truly take a look at the girls who serviced them. Every sly smile and flirtatious wink masked pain. A cloud of darkness raged behind their eyes, slowly draining the life from them with each passing day. However, no one could see the pain in their eyes because they were simply too busy looking at their asses.

In the depths, where darkness dwelt, pale, grey cement covered everything, and there was barely enough light from above to see the ground. A long hallway stretched across the basement with indents on either side of the walls that functioned as small rooms where the workers slept and did most of their dirty work. At the end of the passage stood the only door, which led to the office of Lena, the club manager.

Lena was a stern and imposing woman whose very essence provoked fear and mystery. Her skin was neither dark nor light, making it difficult to nail down exactly where her family hailed from. She stood five-foot-five but carried herself as though she was much taller on account of the five-inch heeled, dark, leather boots she wore everywhere she went. Her hair was perfectly straight, which highlighted her harsh, yet stunningly attractive, features. Her employees often shared stories of how they believed there to be pure ice hiding behind her crystalline eyes. This mythology was only aided by her demeanor, which was demanding and abrasive. Many wondered how exactly she came to manage the type of business she did, but none dared ask for fear of her wrath.

As she did every night, she sat behind her desk, studying personnel and financial files. This was her preferred hideaway on busy nights because being upstairs meant having to socialize with throngs of customers who only brought her more work and frustration. In her office, she could focus on the things that were truly important: the numbers. As she pored over the documents, the door creaked open, revealing a large, imposing man behind it.

He was a monster of a man, standing six-foot-three, but the way he held his shoulders back, like a Pufferfish trying to scare away any and all potential predators, made him look at least two inches taller. His hair was pure shadow, save for a few streaks of grey that marked his age. Though he was not a particularly religious man, his puritanical dedication to his weight-lifting routine was obvious, evidenced by his chiseled frame, which the skin-tight, black T-shirt he wore every day only served to accentuate.

"Redd, we have a situation," Lena stated without so much as a glance up from her files.

"And here I was thinking you called me here for pleasure," Redd said with a confident smile that verged on arrogance. "What do you got for me, Lena?"

Lena looked up from her files with a glare so intense that Redd imagined she was trying to turn him into an ice sculpture. He knew better than to address her by her first name.

"Redd," she said authoritatively.

"Right," Redd replied. "What do you got for me, *boss*?"

"It seems Nicholas has forgotten the importance of securing our product. I need you to remind him."

As if on cue, the door burst open, and a young woman stumbled inside so forcefully that she nearly fell headlong over the top of Lena's desk. Her appearance was anything but clean. She was dangerously thin, covered in blood, cuts and bruises, and her hair was tattered and layered with dirt. Upon seeing Lena, she immediately recoiled into the center of the room and stood with her head down, as though she was awaiting execution.

Behind her, a confident, younger man entered and planted himself in the corner of the room with a smug grin across his smooth, unimposing face. Despite his age, he carried himself as though he already knew it all. Though he wasn't as physically intimidating as Redd, everyone who met him treated him with the utmost respect, believing that, even though he had never witnessed the horrors of war, somehow, he could still handle it: an impression he often used to his advantage.

"Thank you for returning our merchandise in one piece, Paul," Lena said, her eyes focused on bursting the young woman's head into flames. "And as for you, Ivanna, get out of my sight until I decide what to do with you."

As Ivanna scurried out of the office and into the nearest room like a frightened mouse returning to its hole, Redd glared at Paul. The disdain that exuded from his eyes was palpable. As always, there was a hatred between the two of them that everyone could sense but few could describe.

Most assumed that Redd viewed Paul as a threat to his position as second-in-command, an heir apparent to everything he had worked so hard to achieve. Others figured that Redd was jealous of Paul's looks, cunning and business sense. Though he was only twenty-five, Paul had an understanding of the world beyond his years. On top of that, he had a wife, a daughter and a house of his own, all things Redd had still failed to achieve in a much longer amount of time. He was also the only person Lena allowed to call her by her first name, though he rarely exercised this privilege.

"That bitch caused me a lot of trouble today. Almost ruined everything," Paul muttered.

Earlier that day, Ivanna, in her attempt to escape, had run to the only place she could think of for safety: a homeless shelter. Luck had not been on her side that day, however, as the shelter she had run into was managed by Paul's wife, Rebecca. Adding to her misfortune was the fact that Paul was there at the time, serving food to the homeless.

"It took everything I had to keep Rebecca from finding out, but thankfully, I'm quick on my feet," he continued. "Now that that's taken care of, how's the club running? I noticed we're short-staffed tonight. I thought this was supposed to be Florian's night behind the bar, but I saw Nick bartending instead. Did Florian call out?"

"He left early. Kept saying something about being late for a night out with his new 'project,'" Lena answered.

ACROSS TOWN, FLORIAN WAS OUT ON A DATE, AS HE WAS AT LEAST once a week. He was the type of guy who never seemed to have trouble getting a girl: tall, suave and handsome with jet black hair as smooth as silk. That night, he was dressed in his best suit and tie, seated at his favorite seat at his favorite ristorante, a spot he frequented so often that servers often joked that his name should be permanently engraved on his chair. On the other side of the table for two, his date scanned nervously over her menu. Her deep, brown eyes darted indecisively across its pages. As she pored over her options, he found himself unable to look away from the glow that surrounded her glistening, caramel skin.

"Is everything alright, Janelle?" Florian asked.

"Of course it is! Well, obviously – I mean, yes. Why wouldn't it be?" Janelle stammered.

"Because you're a couple bites from chomping that poor straw's head off."

"Oh… sorry," She giggled, setting the straw back in her glass. "I guess I might be a little nervous."

"I should be the one who's nervous. I'm out to dinner with the brightest star in the galaxy," he said.

Janelle blushed as she tilted her head to the side and gazed into his bright blue eyes, absolutely mesmerized. After a moment spent staring into the depths of his soul, her trance was suddenly broken by the voice of the waiter, asking what she wanted to order.

Immediately, she panicked. "Oh my gosh! I haven't even figured out what I wanted. I'm sorry. Could you give me a minute?"

Throwing his shoulders back confidently, Florian said, "I've got this. I'll have the Eggplant Parmesan and a house salad, French dressing, and for the lady, could we get the Chicken Scampi, hold the garlic?"

The waiter turned to Janelle, looking for confirmation, only to find her jaw affixed to the floor, so stunned that the only thing she could do was nod her head in approval.

"Okay, that was incredible. How did you do that?" she asked, her eyes still wide with amazement, as the waiter left to place their order.

"I knew this would come up sooner or later. There's something you should know; I'm psychic," Florian joked with a suave subtlety.

In reality, he had known what she was going to order since before she started chewing on her straw. While she studied the menu, he used a simple trick he learned from a mentalist friend of his. He read her eyes, looking for the times she paused, even for the briefest of moments. Then, he took note of every spot she stopped and how many times she returned to each one. Having long since memorized where every item sat on the menu, it was quite simple to ascertain what someone really wanted to order, even if they didn't yet know themselves.

"Fine, don't tell me," she said. "But at least tell me how you knew I didn't want garlic."

"I didn't," he said with a wink. "I was gauging my chances for the night. How am I looking?"

Janelle smiled coyly and gave no answer, but Florian knew; his chances were looking very good.

After dinner, the couple made their way to a nearby motel. The door to the room had hardly been closed for a second before she kissed him passionately on the lips, leaving Florian breathless and bewildered. The shock wasn't so much that she desired him but the ferocity with which she pursued him. It was as if a switch had flipped inside her brain, releasing a primal desire that had, before that moment, lay dormant.

And now, nothing could hold back the flood.

Before he could react, she ripped off his shirt and began to kiss him all the way down his torso. He fumbled in his pockets for a moment, searching for the protection he always carried with him for moments such as this. As his fingers finally grazed the plastic, Janelle's hand latched onto his wrist.

"Screw that," she protested as she thrust him onto the bed. "You're all I want to feel tonight."

With the agility of a cheetah, she leapt on top of him, taking his hands and placing them on her ass. As he felt his way down her silky-smooth legs, she slowly removed her shirt, revealing nothing underneath. He ran his hands up her stomach, caressing her breasts, and she let out an orgasmic sigh. Shivers ran up and down his spine as she drove herself into him.

Her warmth was intoxicating, like a fine Merlot. He didn't know how she did the things she was doing, but he wasn't about to complain. After five minutes, it was over, which came as a surprise to him because he prided himself on being able to last as long as forty-five minutes.

She was unlike anything he had ever known.

Once she finished, she collapsed next to him on the bed, breathing heavily. "Damn, that was hot," she sighed.

"I know," he replied, unable to muster up any other words.

"I think I'm in love with you."

Florian looked at the clock. It was midnight, two hours later than he thought. He panicked. She leaned over to kiss him, but he was already standing at the side of the bed, half-dressed.

"I'm sorry, but I have to go to work. I told my boss I'd close up tonight," he apologized hurriedly.

"You're not leaving because of what I said, are you?" she asked with an anxious chuckle. "I was joking. I promise."

"No, honey, don't worry. I really do have to work. Besides, I thought it was cute."

Florian leaned over the edge of the bed and gave Janelle a soft kiss on the lips. Then, like a flash, he was out the door and in his car.

Lena would have his head if he was late.

~

"SHE NEEDS TO BE TAUGHT A LESSON," REDD QUICKLY FIRED at Paul.

"I don't disagree, but your lessons are always too barbaric," Paul replied.

"No lesson is learned without pain. What would we be teaching the others if-"

"We don't have to be animals!"

"Listen to yourself!" Redd said. "Have you taken a look at the world lately? My god! What the hell do you think we do here?"

Paul growled, "That's the most ignorant, self-absorbed-"

"Waste of my time!" Lena said. "Do what you will. Settle it amongst yourselves. One way or another, I want you to take care of it by sunrise."

With those words, Lena stood from her desk and left the room, leaving Paul and Redd to continue their pissing match by themselves.

"Don't worry. I will," Redd promised.

Before Paul could utter a word, Redd was gone. Paul tried to yell after him, but the commotion drowned out his plea. It was closing time at the club, and the girls were heading downstairs for the night. With ease, Redd maneuvered through the pack, pushing aside anyone who got in his way. Paul, however, got caught up in the cluster and was unable to keep up with Redd's pace.

Outside the club, Nick was having a smoke in the back alley, as he did every night after closing. He had been looking forward to this moment all day. It was the longest and most stressful day he'd had in more than a month, but not even five seconds after his first hit, Redd came bursting through the back door with his eyes set on Nick.

"Hey Redd, how's it going?" Nick chuckled anxiously, reaching into his pocket for another cigarette. "Want a smoke?"

Without a word, Redd snatched the cigarette from his hand, lit it and leaned against the wall beside him. He stayed there for a moment, sucking in every last spec of tobacco he could fit into his lungs, with his right hand against his jean pocket. Soon after, the alley door burst open with Paul trailing not too far behind.

"Are we having a party out here or something?" Nick asked as he reached into his pocket for another cigarette, hoping a shared smoke would calm the rapidly brewing tension around him.

"Why don't you tell him, Paul?" Redd asked, tilting his head back and calmly blowing a thin puff of smoke into the night sky.

Paul sighed, "Tell us about Ivanna."

Flicking his cigarette to the ground, Nick closed his eyes and inhaled. For a moment after it fell, the cigarette flickered on the ground, appearing as though its embers would continue to burn. Sadly, however, it was not meant to be, as Redd's steel toes squashed out any hope it had of continuing to burn. One last billow of smoke rising from the ground marked its last breath.

"Shit," Nick began, anxiously tucking his long hair behind his ear. "Listen, it wasn't my fault. We were going out to Levis Square, just like every-"

"This is bullshit," Redd whispered under his breath.

It was at this moment that he revealed the knife in his right hand. It glimmered in the alley lights as he raised it in the air, catching Paul's eye. Before Paul had a chance to react, however, Redd removed the cigarette from his mouth and blew a huff of smoke into Paul's eyes, blinding him. Then, he plunged his blade upward into the space under Nick's ribcage. Nick's eyes widened as the piercing pain hit his chest, and just like that, it was over. Redd ripped the knife from Nick's chest, freeing the river of blood that had built up on the other side of his cutlass.

Paul's sight returned to him just in time to see Nick's body on the ground, the life slowly draining out of him. He rushed to help, but in a matter of seconds, cold steel was at his jugular and warm, dank blood oozed down his neck like sweat. His throat tightened. He tried to swallow, but he couldn't.

"Try to help him, and you're next," Redd threatened.

"What are you doing?" Paul asked, trying not to make any sudden movements.

"What you're too much of a pussy to do. You can't be everyone's friend. Sometimes, you've got to get messy. Sometimes, the only way to survive is to get a little blood on your hands," Redd said as he forced Paul through the alley door and dragged him down the basement stairs. "Sometimes, you have to be an animal because that's the only way anyone listens. If someone betrays you, you pay him back double. If someone steps out of line, you put him in his place."

"You don't have to leave Nick to die. He learned his lesson."

"Maybe the lesson isn't his to learn."

As they reached the bottom of the stairs, Redd flung Paul against the cement wall and picked up a metal rod that was lying on the ground. Then, hoisting the shaft into the air, he struck the water pipes in the ceiling. Immediately, the echoing clang of metal on metal, a cacophony of ear-piercing noise, filled the entire basement. Worried, Paul looked up at Redd, whose eyes had turned an other-worldly shade of vermillion. Smoke billowed from his eyelids with every swing of his wrist, and Paul now understood what Redd meant when he had spoken of the animal inside. There was a terrifying emptiness behind his eyes, as though he held nothing there except an eternal emptiness, not even a soul to mark his humanity.

The pipes tolled like a reverberating gong, drawing the girls from their rooms. They knew what that sound indicated, and it wasn't good. The last to emerge was Ivanna, who looked like a nervous wreck as the sweat poured from her face like a babbling brook. She tried to stop her hands from shaking, but the terror overwhelmed her senses. Intently, Redd surveyed the field of women in front of him, like a predator stalking his prey. After a moment, his eyes met Ivanna's, and he pounced. He clenched his hand on the back of her neck so firmly that blood started to flow. Then, he threw her into the center of the room for everyone to see.

"Listen up!" Redd snarled. "I'm really tired of having to do this shit. I really am. I wish I didn't have to, but unfortunately, stupid bitches like Ivanna, who decided she thought it was smart to try and run away before she'd paid off her debt, keep forcing my hand. Well, let me tell you something; it is NEVER smart to try to run away from me. If you do, I will find you, I will bring you back, and I will teach you to never run away again. Pay close attention! Because this is what happens when you cross me."

As Redd swung his arm back to strike her down, Paul's resolve became clear; he couldn't let the animal win. He wouldn't. Leaping up like a wild hare, he took hold of Redd's arm with every ounce of strength that remained in his body. Immediately, Redd's head jolted back, and he grinned. He twisted his wrist violently, breaking free from Paul's grip. Then, he spun around, and hard metal smashed against Paul's skull, sending him soaring into the cement wall.

Paul tried to open his eyes, but the world around him melted into a haze. He pushed with all his might, attempting to force himself back up, but his arms buckled beneath him, sending him face first into the cold, concrete floor. Through the fog, he saw the outline of what looked like a massive bear, rearing its claws back to strike the helpless gazelle that had fallen beneath it. He reached his hand to stop the fiend, but darkness overtook him.

And all he could hear were the screams.

When Paul finally regained consciousness, all he could see was a grey blur. His head was pounding, and his ears were ringing, as though someone was repeatedly hitting his skull with a hammer while simultaneously blowing a whistle into his eardrum. Slowly, the world came back into focus, and all was quiet and dark. So, he started back home, tail between his legs. Paul's anger burned hot inside of him as he drove home, locking the steering wheel in a death grip. He told himself he needed to let it go, that if he dwelt on it, Redd would get exactly what he wanted. He couldn't allow that to happen, but even still, he couldn't move past it.

The thoughts still flowed like an avalanche as he entered his home. Hanging his keys on the ring, he took off his coat and placed his shoes on the mat, hoping that a good night's sleep would clear his mind. As he made his way through the living room toward the stairs, a soft, sweet voice tickled the back of his ears.

"Aren't you going to say, 'hello?'"

He had been so caught up in the moment that he hadn't even registered that he walked right past his wife, Rebecca. Turning around, he took one look in her warm, sapphire eyes, and everything else melted away.

He was home.

"Shouldn't you be in bed now, young lady?" he asked.

"I was waiting up for you, my love." She smiled, placing a bookmark in her book, closing it, and standing up from the couch.

As she walked over to him, he couldn't help but think she was the most beautiful woman in the world. She wasn't wearing any make-up, but that didn't matter. If anything, she looked more ravishing without it, like a hot, young librarian with her long, dark hair pulled back into a ponytail and her reading glasses on. It was as though she had been pulled out of a teenage fantasy Paul never even knew he had. Her face was so soft that it could drown the rest of the world away and make him forget every care he had in the world, even when every-thing was crumbling around him. She wrapped her arms around his neck, and his body melted into hers. Looking deep into his eyes, she rubbed her hand across his temple. As she reached the spot where Redd had struck him, he grimaced.

"What did you do?" Rebecca giggled. "I can't leave you alone for one minute, can I?"

"Maybe you shouldn't," he replied with a flirtatious grin.

Biting her lip, she smiled seductively, but, almost as quickly as it had come, her smile disappeared, replaced by concern. "Do you think that girl's going to be alright?" she asked. "She was so scared when she burst into the shelter. I can't even imagine what had happened to - I wish I hadn't been so busy so I could have gone with you both to the hospital. That way - you know - I could have made sure she was okay. Do you think she's going to be okay?"

"Don't worry, honey," he said, preparing himself to tell her yet another half-truth, which, over time, had become almost routine. "I went back to check on her after I got out of work. She was much... calmer when I saw her."

In that moment, Paul wished he could tell her everything, the whole, unfiltered truth, but that wasn't an option. Rebecca would never understand the things he had to do so she could spend her days doing what she loved: helping people. Regretfully, she was too caught up in the Good Book to see things the way he did, to realize that she was the yin to his yang or to believe that sometimes, in order to survive, one has to balance the good with the bad. After all, light can't exist without darkness. They have to live together in harmony.

Instantly, the worry left Rebecca's face, and she looked into Paul's hazel eyes and stroked his dirty blonde hair. Meanwhile, she slid a hand slowly down his chest and unbuttoned his jeans. Then, she ran her hand down his pants. As she turned and walked away, leading him toward their bedroom, Paul lingered for a moment, gazing longingly at her perfectly shaped hips that swung seductively from side to side. She looked radiant in her white tank top and shorts that hugged her cheeks so tightly that he could see every curve. As she turned the corner toward the stairs, she loosened her hair from its ponytailed prison, letting her wavy hair flow. Then, she batted her eyes and shot him a flirtatious wink that could only mean one thing; he had to have her.

## 2

## PREY

NEW YORK, NEW YORK

*T*he air hung like death over the lamp-lit street. Though the rest of the Big Apple spun around at a dizzying pace, this particular corner of civilization seemed to exist at a perpetual stand-still. Passers-by could sense their hearts sink deep inside their chests as soon as they crossed the corner lamppost. No one understood exactly why they felt this way, except for those who lived there, forced to endure with their hearts embedded in their spines.

For Natasha, however, that night was little more than business as usual. Her emaciated frame rested against the same dirty, rough brick that she'd leaned against so many times before, so often, in fact, that even when she was gone, the faint impression of her body still lingered in the smudges of dirt on the wall. Gazing out into the darkness before her, she felt herself, once again, drown in the familiar emptiness that had hounded her for the last four years. Though she wasn't the only girl on the streets that night, she still felt utterly alone.

Suddenly, a black Mercedes pulled along the curbside, breaking her daze. As its window descended, she wanted nothing more than to ignore the suit that sat behind the wheel. However, that wasn't a choice she was afforded, so she lifted her body from the brick wall, tossing her tangled, black hair behind her, and slowly approached the passenger's side door, swinging her hips hypnotically from side to side. She wasn't more than twenty feet from the car when the trance she held on the suit was broken by an opportunistic girl who saw Natasha's deliberate gait as a chance to fill that night's quota.

As Natasha turned away, she felt cold, rough skin grab a tight hold of her backside and calloused fingers caress her beneath her mini-skirt, which stopped well before her thighs began. When she spun around, she met the gaze of a wife-beater who ogled her, his gaping mouth dripping with lust. He looked her up and down, admiring her bare stomach as he ran his hands clumsily up to her breasts, which were only half-covered by a lacy, black, tube top. The wife-beater smiled, revealing his gold-plated teeth, which looked almost as cheap as his knock-off watch.

"You're looking fine tonight, mama," Gold Teeth said with a mischievous grin.

"Fifty dollars, or I walk," she retorted, coldly.

"Fine," he scowled. "But you better be damn good."

Taking his hand, Natasha led him through a scarlet, iron door and into the warehouse where she turned all her tricks. As they entered, they were immediately met by a crimson sea of curtains, which stretched out for what seemed like an eternity, sectioning off rooms that were only big enough for twin beds to fit inside. Despite the apparent enormity of the operation, only a couple dozen girls lived in the warehouse, cordoned off in the middle rooms while the rooms toward the front and back were used mainly for storage and warding off any curious policemen who wandered inside. During the days, all was quiet in the warehouse, but that night, like every night, groans and sighs echoed off the cement walls, filling the whole space and making it sound as though the whole city was having an orgy inside.

Natasha led her client into her room, which was fifty feet from the entrance, and closed the curtain behind them. Backing up against the bed, she dropped her clothes to the floor and beckoned him to have his way with her. The lust exuded from his pores as he bit his lower lip and loosened his belt.

She laid down onto the bed and closed her eyes, trying to drown out the shrill squeal of the bed as the wife-beater climbed on top of her and forced open her legs. As he drove into her, her body grew as stiff as a board. Every thrust of his hips made her feel like she was a ship that was lost at sea, riding wave after wave. She could even feel her stomach churn from seasickness. After four years, it should have been easier to ignore, but it wasn't. Though she should have been able turn herself on auto-pilot, she couldn't. Her body refused to work. Instead, it simply rode along with the crashing waves until suddenly, they stopped.

Surprised, Natasha opened her eyes, and Gold Teeth stared down at her, furiously.

"Are you even doing anything?!" he exclaimed, driving her shoulder back into the bed as he stood.

Gold Teeth was seething. He bolted through the curtain door and stormed down the hallway. Natasha followed closely behind, hoping to catch him before her pimp, Alexei, could. Alexei was a large, stern-faced brute, who Natasha was convinced had been the original inspiration for the myth of the cyclops: large, bald and unbelievably ugly. As if his frame wasn't terrifying enough, he also bore various, red and black tattoos like vines that snaked all the way from his wrists to the top of his head, marking each of the seven stints he had done in the local penitentiary. The last thing Natasha wanted was for him to find out she had upset a client, but regretfully for her, that was exactly what happened, only five seconds later.

"What is problem?" Alexei asked in a thick, Russian accent.

"This bitch right here 'is problem,'" Gold Teeth mocked, pointing at Natasha. "I paid good money for this whore, and she ain't doing shit! I want my money back!"

"We work out deal," Alexei said. "I give you two for one, yes?"

"I could swing for that."

"Good. Katrianna! Emilia!"

Within seconds, two girls emerged from different rooms and lined up next to Alexei, both only half-dressed in nothing but their skirts. Ashamed, Natasha hung her head, shifting her eyes up and making eye contact with the younger of the two girls, the one they called Katrianna. Under the warehouse lights, Natasha's blue eyes glimmered as though they were made of pure tears. She mouthed the words "I'm sorry," but Katrianna shook her head, as if to say there was nothing for which to be sorry.

"Show this man good time," Alexei ordered, as Katrianna took Gold Teeth's hand and led him and Emilia into a nearby room.

Once they were gone, Alexei glared at Natasha so sternly that she felt a searing pain rise up in her shoulder. She backed away slowly, hoping that would be the end of it, but he followed. As they entered Natasha's room, he raised his arm into the air, every vein and muscle in his body tensing and pulsating violently. Then, with lion-like ferocity, he unleashed his anger, the back of his hand connecting sharply with her cheek and sending her reeling onto the bed.

"You will do as told, whore," he said as he raised his hand to strike her again.

"Please don't!" she pleaded, raising her own hands in defense.

"You're right. I will not hit you again," he replied, lowering both hands to his side.

A wave of relief washed over Natasha. The truth was; she didn't know if she could handle another beating. Her thighs were still bruised from the last thrashing she had received from his clenched fists. However, as she looked into his dark, unforgiving eyes, it became obvious that he had something different and infinitely more horrible in mind. Slamming the curtain closed, he began to loosen his belt. With each loop that the belt snapped past, she grimaced with ever-increasing pain. Then, he mounted her, pinning her to the bed. As he forced her legs apart, every muscle in her body clenched.

"No!" she cried. "Please stop!"

With all her might, she tried to hold him back, but it wasn't enough. He was too strong. Then, like a wounded animal, fighting solely for her own survival, she snapped. She clawed ferociously at his chest, trying to rip the skin from his bones, and swiped at him as hard as she could, but for every blow she delivered, the intensity of her punishment only escalated.

The bed buckled beneath them, squealing as its legs scraped against the concrete floor. Natasha screamed in pain, for there was no other sound her voice could make. She dug her nails into Alexei's shoulder, but this only made him angrier. With one, furious motion, Alexei dismounted her and flipped her onto her hands and knees. Then, grabbing her firmly by the ass, he forced himself through her defenses once again.

Suddenly, excruciating pain seared through her entire body. Her knees buckled, and the fight left her entirely. She tried to think about anything other than the pain that resonated from every molecule in her body, but she couldn't. The pain was too much, like daggers digging into her flesh. It seemed as though an eternity passed before the pain finally ceased. Then, she was alone. Curling into the fetal position, she wept silently, unable to breathe, unwilling to move. If she moved, it would only mean that she was still alive. In that moment, existence was the last thing she wanted.

After some time, there was a rustling at the curtain. The bed sunk beside her, and a warm body and a soft arm wrapped her in a tender embrace. She didn't have to turn to know who it was. It was her only friend in the entire world, the one they called Katrianna but Natasha knew only as Blair.

Blair was the most beautiful soul, inside and out, that Natasha could remember having ever met. Despite all the pain, all the suffering she endured every day, she knew that she could always confide in Blair. There was something hiding behind Blair's jade eyes that was inviting, something in her wide smile that made Natasha feel like everything was going to be okay. There was hardly a free moment that they didn't spend together in Natasha's room, enjoying each other's company. Their friendship was the only pure thing either of them had left in that God-forsaken place. As they lay there, with Blair's arm wrapped gently around Natasha's waist, every muscle in Natasha's body relaxed, though that only served to also release the torrent of emotion she had been holding behind her dam.

"It was terrible," Natasha choked through the tears.

There was a moment of silence. Blair took her hand and wiped away the tears that had fallen from Natasha's eyes.

"I know," Blair replied.

"I'm sorry," Natasha said. "I didn't think that he'd…"

"Don't worry about me," Blair insisted.

"How can I not?"

"I just want you to be okay."

Natasha turned and looked Blair in the eyes. "How do you do it?" She asked. "How do you stay so strong?"

Blair shook her head. "I'm not strong."

"Stronger than me," Natasha said.

"You're the strongest person I know."

Natasha chuckled. She wasn't strong. It took everything in her to keep from ending her own life every day. The only thing that kept her going was having Blair to talk to at the end of every night. That wasn't strength. A strong person could have withstood the pain, made it through the day without making a mess of it. A strong person wouldn't need to depend on someone else in order to survive. Natasha didn't feel strong. In fact, she felt the opposite, like a baby bird that had fallen to the ground, flapping its wings with all its might but never leaving the earth.

"You're still alive. That makes you strong," Blair assured her.

"I couldn't do this without you."

"Nor I without you."

Blair tightened her arms around Natasha and hugged her for as long as she could stand. In an instant, all of the tension and anger melted away, and she was home. Slowly placing her arms around Blair, Natasha held her tightly to her heart, where she remained for the rest of the morning, until the rising of the sun, which marked the end of one, full day in the warehouse. As night fell, Alexei's voice echoed above the curtains, calling for everyone to go to bed. With pain in her eyes, Blair let her arms fall from around Natasha and returned to her own room, leaving Natasha alone once again.

Over the weeks that followed, Natasha felt more broken than usual. Most days, she couldn't sleep. Her mind wouldn't allow her to rest. Even though Alexei was no longer inside her body, he was still in her mind. And there was nowhere she could hide. She saw his face when she was alone and when she worked the streets, in the faces of every suit and every pair of acid-washed jeans she screwed. She even saw him in her dreams. The only peace she ever found was when she was with Blair. However, those moments felt fewer and farther between those days, and the only way Natasha survived was by shutting down entirely.

> *On and on, this pounding drum beats as the*
>   *story goes.*
> *All night long, the terror comes; defeat as the*
>   *story goes.*
> *The curtain falls. The lights dim deep as the story goes.*
> *Every day, a performance grim repeats as the*
>   *story goes.*

"You must get lonely."

Those four words broke Natasha's self-imposed stupor. She stared at the suit that sat in front of her on the bed, speechless. He wanted to talk, but she just wanted to get this over with.

"I have plenty of company," she replied un-ironically.

"You're a beautiful girl," he said. "You don't have to sell yourself to feel loved."

Natasha's heart almost leapt out of her chest to choke the life out of him. He looked at her with the one look she couldn't stand: pity. She could handle the disgust. She could stand being objectified, silently judged, even openly mocked, but not being pitied. Pity wasn't real. It was merely a thing people offered because they felt sorry for her. It made them feel righteous despite their inaction.

"Get out," she ordered as flame built behind her eyes.

"You can let people in."

"Get out!"

"Why won't you-"

"Either screw me or leave!" she screamed as her fist

clenched and flew into the suit's skull, knocking him flat on the bed.

Within seconds, Alexei appeared in the doorway. "Is there problem?" He asked, his eyes fixated on Natasha with a furious glare.

In that moment, however, she wondered if she would rather be punished again than spend another minute in therapy.

"No, no problem, sir," the suit replied. "Just a bit of foreplay."

His anger placated for the time being, Alexei nodded and left the room. Once he was gone, the suit stood and approached Natasha. She could feel his pity cover her like sludge. Every hair on her body stood on end as he reached out his hand to console her. Immediately, she recoiled away from him, afraid that if he touched her, she would pity herself too. Slithering past him, she sat on the edge of the bed, leaned back on her hands and opened her legs, hoping he would drop the therapist charade and get it over with. In an instant, the pity fell from his eyes, replaced by desire. As he climbed on top of her, it was clear; this suit wasn't any different from the others.

Later that morning, after all the work had ended, Natasha sat alone in her room. Cautiously, after looking around to ensure that she was truly by herself, she reached her hand underneath the back corner of her mattress, pulled out a small, silver necklace and held it in her hand. There was nothing overly special about its appearance. It was little more than a simple, silver cross, whose once sterling luster had faded over the years. For Natasha, however, hope still shone off its stained silver, and peace still rained down the small loops of its chain that cascaded down her palm like a quiet waterfall. It was the most precious item in the world to her, the only thing she had held onto from her previous life. Natasha gazed at it so intently that she didn't even notice Blair enter the room.

"It's beautiful," Blair said as she sat down next to her. "Can I see it?"

Natasha smiled and handed the necklace to Blair, who took it and immediately moved behind Natasha. Gently re-positioning Natasha's hair to her left shoulder, she hooked the necklace around her neck.

"There, now it's perfect," Blair beamed. "Where'd you get it?"

Natasha smiled. "Some lady gave it to me. Not long before I came here, actually."

"Why do you keep it?" Blair asked.

"It reminds me that there's still good in the world, that there's still light in the darkness and angels amongst the demons."

"You're beautiful."

Natasha turned away. She wanted to believe Blair. Really, she did, but every atom in her body felt dirty and disgusting. She had been called many things: spicy, hot, sexy, but never beautiful. Blair placed her hand under Natasha's chin and turned her face so she could look her in the eyes.

"No," Natasha said, shaking her head sadly. "I'm not."

"Yes, you are. You're the most beautiful person I know."

Natasha looked into Blair's eyes and saw nothing but absolute sincerity, a warmth behind her shining, emerald eyes. Even though Natasha could never hope to believe Blair's words for herself, she believed that Blair meant them. And for her, that was enough.

Just then, Alexei's voice echoed, once again, through the warehouse, calling for everyone to go to sleep. As Blair stood to leave, she kissed Natasha on the forehead before starting slowly for the curtain.

But, Natasha grabbed her by the hand. "Stay with me," she said.

Blair hesitated. Natasha knew it was risky for Blair to sleep outside of her room, but in that moment, being with her friend was worth the risk. Taking a deep breath, Blair closed the curtain and laid down next to Natasha, wrapping her arm around her waist. Then, they closed their eyes and drifted off into the best sleep either of them had in years.

# 3

# STOLEN

LOS ANGELES, CALIFORNIA

"No one said your last day would be uneventful."

Those words hung ominously in the air as Officers Bradie Lam and Loman Darvey tossed the crumpled remains of their extra spicy, Sriracha burritos into the back of their police car and sped off. Bradie had hoped that his last day would be easy, full of reminiscing with his partner of the last five years and saying goodbye to the city that had raised him. The last thing he wanted to do was talk a jumper off the roof of the First National Bank, but that was life in the LAPD.

Eight years in the department had seen Bradie flourish beyond expectation. While many of his classmates from the Academy had aged well beyond their years from the stress, Bradie still looked as fresh as he did at graduation, mostly due to the meticulous effort he put into looking his best.

There was rarely a wrinkle or stain on his uniform. He was always neatly shaven, and his hair never seemed to grow longer than a simple, military buzz-cut. Loman, however, seldom appeared so fresh. He was several years older than Bradie, and it showed. The grey streaks in his hair gave him a dignified, yet frazzled appearance, accentuated by the wrinkles under his eyes from many sleepless nights. His years on the force had not been friendly to him.

As they approached the east side of the bank, Bradie couldn't help but feel like he was driving onto a movie set. Approximately fifty feet from the bank entrance, a perimeter had been set to contain the crowd that had gathered to watch. Their car slowed to a stop along the back of the crowd, and Bradie and Loman pushed their way through the mass, followed by their typical dosage of ire and resentment. Recent events in Ferguson and New York, among other places, had soured public opinion toward the police. But, as African American policemen, Officers Lam and Darvey received the hatred of both sides.

At the front of the building stood a rookie officer, fresh out of the Academy. He stared up the building, megaphone in hand, trying to talk the jumper down.

"Please, just think about what you're doing!" he pleaded.

"What's the sit-rep?" Bradie asked as they approached the front.

"Oh, thank God you're here!" the officer exclaimed, dropping the megaphone to his side and wiping a river of sweat from his forehead. "Jumper's been up there for a half hour, argumentative as hell. Says she'll jump if anyone goes up there."

"Good work, Rook," Loman said. "We'll take it from here."

The officer nodded and handed the megaphone to Loman while Bradie studied the scene. From his angle, the jumper appeared to be a young woman. She stood at the edge of the roof directly overhead, overlooking the crowd. Curious, he turned his back to the bank and held his arms out to his sides in an attempt to see things through her eyes. When he did, all he could see was an endless sea of faces that wrapped entirely around the police perimeter. As he watched, he saw the rookie officer they had just spoken to pass through the front of the crowd. Immediately, he was enveloped by the multitude and disappeared, becoming one with the crowd. This gave Bradie an idea.

"How long can you keep her talking?" he asked.

"I'd give it five minutes," Loman estimated.

"I'll be up there in four."

The crowd acted as ample cover, successfully camouflaging Bradie as he made his way to the back of the building. Within a minute, he had navigated through the horde. Then, before rounding the building's right corner, he checked back to gauge how much time he had to get to the roof. At that point, the jumper stood with her toes on the roof's edge and simply stared into the distance, as though she was taking one last look at the horizon before leaping into the unknown. Beneath her, Loman held his arms toward her in a desperate attempt to keep her on the ledge.

He had to hurry. There was no time to waste.

Thirty seconds later, Bradie burst through the maintenance door at the back of the building. He bounded around the corner and up the first set of stairs. After another forty-five seconds, he stood in front of the roof access door. Closing his eyes and taking a deep breath, he calmed his nerves and gathered his thoughts. Once he opened that door, there could be no mistakes. One wrong move could literally send that girl over the edge.

The door slid open and closed again without a sound. Then, he began his approach.

He took a step.

Loman's voice echoed across the rooftop. "You don't want to jump!"

"With all due respect, Officer, you don't know me. You don't know what I want," the girl insisted, her platinum hair gleaming in the midday sun.

Another step.

"No one wants to see you die today," Loman said.

"Then how come everyone is lining up for the show?" she asked.

Bradie took two more cautious steps, leaving him fifteen feet from the ledge.

"Because they want to see a happy ending," Loman answered.

Another step.

*Only ten feet to go.*

"I think that's far enough, Officer," she announced, throwing her head over her shoulder and looking in Bradie's direction.

He froze.

She continued, "It was clever to use the crowd as camouflage. I even lost sight of you for a second or two, but you stick out like a white crow in that uniform."

"You don't want to do this," Bradie said.

Without warning, the girl whirled around to face him and laughed, "Why does everyone keep telling me what I want?"

"Okay, you're right. I don't know you or what brought you here," he said, his voice calm and unwavering. "But, I'd like to. My name's Bradie. What's yours?"

"Interesting," she replied as she turned around, her bright blue eyes fluttering back-and-forth, as though they were studying him. "You're more observant than the other one. Okay, Bradie, you've got yourself a deal. Let's talk. But, since I have the higher ground, I'll be asking the first question. Answer correctly, and I'll tell you anything you want to know."

"Sounds fair."

"Why haven't I jumped yet?"

Bradie closed his eyes. Taking a deep breath, he shoved his emotions deep into the recesses of his mind, packed them in a chest and locked them away. If there was anything he had learned at the Academy, it was that emotional connections limit objectivity and taint observations. Then, after conjuring up a picture of her in his mind, he carefully placed it against a blank canvas, like a picture in a text book. He could bear no distractions in this moment. There was too much at stake.

*Inhale. Exhale.*

*This is a case study. Use what you've observed to determine her motivation.*

*Her skin is fair, almost porcelain in appearance. It doesn't shimmer in the sun like most, meaning it likely hasn't seen the light of day in quite some time. She is young, somewhere between sixteen and eighteen, but she isn't scared or emotional like a typical teenager would be. Rather, she appears calm, calculated, which means she's already decided her fate. But why?*

*Her clothes are ragged, covered in dirt, and look like they haven't been properly washed in weeks. Underneath the torn sleeves of her t-shirt, I can see bruises, fresh ones. Is she from an abusive home? No, she can't be. The bracelet on her right wrist is made from small, colorful blocks and barely fits around her wrist, meaning it's likely from her childhood. If I look closer at the blocks in the center, I can see that they read "Mom & Dad." Why hold on to such a keepsake if her parents are abusing her?*

*Because she has no parents, no family to go back to. Her bracelet is a reminder.*

Suddenly, a deep pang of sorrow settled inside Bradie's gut. When he was twelve, his own father was killed in the line of duty. In fact, his father's memory was the reason he joined the force in the first place. Like her bracelet, the uniform he wore was his keepsake, his reminder. His eyes began to well with tears.

*Shake it off. This is not the time to get emotional.*

*Her eyes. There's something she's hiding behind her calculated exterior. But what? Her eyes are searching, like they're expecting something. Or someone. I've seen that look before, in kidnapping victims. But if she was taken, why escape just to end her own life?*

*Because she's afraid, terrified that, no matter where she runs, her captor will find her and take her back to wherever she came from: a fate worse than death. But that still doesn't tell me why she hasn't jumped. It's not as though she's undecided.*

*In fact, it's almost as though she was waiting for me...*

"You want an audience," Bradie answered.

"Very good," the girl said with a sly smirk. "They made a good decision promoting you to detective."

"How did you know about that?" he asked.

"You make your observations; I make mine," she said. "But, why an audience? What could that possibly gain me?"

"Nothing."

"Go on."

"This isn't about you. You think it's too late for you to be saved. Someone took you, someone powerful, and you're afraid, terrified even, that you'll never get away, no matter what you do. But, there's someone else, possibly more that he's taken. The audience is for them. You think they might still have a chance."

She nodded and looked at him, her eyes wet with dew, as she took a deep breath and told him her story.

At birth, her name was Anna Idona. She was born to a beautiful, young couple from a small, farming town in Northern Quebec. For the first thirteen years, her life was a good one, full of love and happy memories, until one day, her parents got sick. Three months later, she was alone, orphaned and thrown into foster home after foster home, none of which were good. Finally, she'd had enough and ran away, deciding to take her chances on the street instead of in the hands of families who only saw her as a dollar sign. Soon, however, she found herself, once again, broke, alone and living in a homeless shelter downtown. That was when *he* found her. At first, the arrangement he offered sounded beneficial: a place to stay and food to eat. All she had to do was work, and for a while, it was fine.

Then, he started asking her to perform special favors for his higher paying customers, and for a time, even that was preferable to being starving and homeless on the street. Then, they moved to Los Angeles. That was when the beatings began. Soon, they were happening daily, and she couldn't take it anymore. She tried to escape once, twice, seven times, but every time, *he* found her. Eventually, it became clear; she was doomed forever to that perpetual torment, and the only way out was to jump.

"That's just *my* story," Anna explained, wiping the tears from her eyes. "The others have their own tales, most worse than mine and of no fault of their own. Can you promise me something, Detective?"

"Anything," he answered.

Turning back to the ledge, she raised her arms to either side, like an eagle preparing to fly, and said, "Get them out."

"Wait!" he pleaded. "Let me help you!"

"You said it yourself, Detective. 'It's too late for me.'"

"Come with me to the precinct. Tell us what you know. We can keep you safe, away from him."

"I know you mean well," she sighed, pain in her voice. "But with him, there is no safe. As long as I'm alive, as long as I'm here, he will always find me. There's no other way. I have to do this."

"But I can't help anyone if you jump!" he cried.

She shook her head. "Give yourself a little more credit," she said. "You're a smart man. You'll find a way."

She leaned forward. Bradie's hands shook as tidal waves of fear crashed over him. In the few moments they had spent together, he had witnessed more strength, more resiliency, in Anna's petite frame than he had in any officer he had ever met. For such an amazing, young woman to be lost to the world, it would be nothing short of a travesty.

"Come with me to Detroit!" he blurted out in equal parts desperation and sincerity. "You can stay with my family, and I'll make sure he never finds you again."

Instead of responding, Anna remained motionless for a moment, as though she had frozen in a solid block of ice.

Then, her voice shook with doubt. "I know what you're trying to do. You're trying to talk me off the ledge, hoping I'll change my mind once my feet hit the ground. You don't mean what you're saying."

"Listen to my voice," he said. "And tell me if you think I'm lying."

Shaking, her arms fell to her side. She turned to him, streams of tears rolling down her cheeks, and choked, "You would do that? For me?"

"You'll never know unless you take the leap."

Anna looked him in the eyes, trying to uncover the slightest hint of insincerity, but there was none to be found. With a deep, fluttering breath, she stepped off the ledge and onto the rooftop. Immediately, he rushed to her side, wrapping his arm around her shoulder before her feet even hit the ground.

Once they reached street level, Anna hardly uttered another word for the rest of the day. Even in the interrogation room, as Bradie tried to convince her to tell her story on record, she remained silent, choosing instead to train her eyes, intently, on the dim lights that reflected off the table's surface.

"Anna," Bradie implored. "I'm going to need your help if we're going to save the others. Why don't you tell me about the man who took you?"

Anna didn't respond. Instead, she ran her finger along the polished wood, tracing the light's reflection.

He tried to reassure her. "No one's going to hurt you. You're safe here. You can talk to me."

Looking up at him, her eyes narrowed, their laser-like focus trained directly on him. She leaned forward, staring into his eyes for much longer than was comfortable. Finally, he realized; she wasn't tracing the light. She was writing a message, a message that read:

*Not Safe.*

Later, Bradie stood outside the interrogation room with Loman, watching Anna through a one-way mirror. On the rooftop, he thought he had her all figured out; she was strong, confident, immovable. Here, however, he didn't know what to make of her. She seemed weak and scared, like a helpless animal playing dead amongst a pack of predators. No matter how hard he tried, he couldn't figure her out. She was a conundrum, one that he was determined to solve.

"What do you think she means?" he asked.

Loman shrugged. "If what she told you is true, at least in her mind, whoever took her must have an almost unlimited reach, like some sort of god."

"More like a devil," Bradie said.

"And if it's not true," Loman replied. "She might be afraid of getting found out. It's a lot easier to fool one cop than the whole department."

"You didn't see her up there," Bradie said. "She was so calm, so, dare I say, levelheaded. She knew, absolutely knew, that she was going to die, and all she wanted was for one person to believe her before she jumped. She had nothing to gain by lying and even more to lose by stepping off that ledge and dying for a lie."

"Sometimes, people's reasons for doing things aren't quite that obvious."

"I just wish I was going to be able to see this one through."

"Her case is in good hands. I promise."

"Thank you," Bradie sighed. "That means the world to me, partner. I guess this means I have to call the state and make sure I can keep *my* promise."

"I don't see why." Loman shrugged.

"What do you mean?" Bradie asked.

"As far as we know, she is exactly who her ID says she is: Marina Mientkiewicz, twenty-one. According to the state of California, 'Marina' has full right to do pretty much whatever she wants."

"And there's no proof that Anna Idona ever existed."

"Not unless you want to go to Northern Quebec to find her records."

"Thank you, Loman. You've been a really good friend to me. I'm sorry we had to cancel my going away dinner tonight. It's just with everything going on…"

"Don't be sorry. You're about to enter a big, new world. Don't worry about the old one you're leaving behind."

In that moment, Bradie couldn't help but feel that Loman was right in more ways than either of them could possibly understand.

Anna's apparent vow of silence continued all the way from the precinct to Bradie's house. Once again, she didn't move, choosing instead to sit in the back of his car with her head resting uncomfortably against the glass and stare out the window. Through the rearview mirror, however, Bradie could see that she wasn't passive or pensive, as he had assumed. Instead, her eyes darted back and forth as though she was learning, studying, taking in every detail. From his vantage point, he thought she looked like either a freed prisoner who hadn't seen the outside world in far too long or a kidnapping victim, plotting her escape. He just couldn't tell which one she thought she was.

The car pulled up to the curb outside his house, and, opening the door, he stepped out onto the pavement. Anna, however, remained stoic, her gaze frozen upon the tan, two-story Colonial that stood before her. Bradie walked over to her door, opened it and knelt down in front of her, placing his hand on her shoulder.

"There's nothing to be afraid of," he said. "She's going to love you. I promise."

She hesitated for a moment, looking past him at the front door, before saying, "I'm not afraid. I'm just trying to take it all in."

Smiling, he repeated a phrase his mother had told him a million times growing up, "If you never take that first step, you'll always be where you've always been."

With closed eyes and baited breath, Anna took a tentative step out of the car, supported by Bradie's sturdy hand on her shoulder. As they approached the front steps, passing the lit lamppost that stood sentry ten feet in front of the house, a change inhabited the air. It was as though the orb of light that encompassed the lamppost marked a passageway to another realm, and they were entering uncharted territory.

After exchanging a reassuring glance with Anna, Bradie rang the doorbell. Within seconds, the door swung open, and in the doorway stood the most beautiful woman he had ever laid eyes on. She was flawless in every way, from the top of her blazing, black hair to the bottom of her perfectly manicured toes. She was perfection personified and had been, ever since the day they said, "I do." Though she glared at him with eyes that could have liquefied silver, they were still the warmest, chestnut eyes he had ever seen.

Throwing her hands dramatically on her hips, she said, "You do realize the reason they give you a key when you buy a house is so you're able to, you know, open the door yourself."

"But Stacy, my love," he flirted with a wink. "If I did that, then your gorgeous face wouldn't be the first thing I saw when I got home. And that's something I can't have."

As Stacy rolled her eyes with a hearty laugh, her eyes fell on Anna, who immediately tensed up, like a deer in headlights, and stuttered as formally as she could, "Hi... uh, Ms. - I mean Mrs. Lam. I - I'm..."

Before Anna could finish, Stacy threw her arms around Anna's neck. Immediately, every emotion Anna had buried beneath the surface erupted like a long dormant volcano, and she wrapped her arms around Stacy's waist, drowning in the rivers of tears that were now flowing from her eyes. Her knees buckled, and she fell into Stacy's arms. Then, without letting Anna go, Stacy pulled away and, rubbing her thumbs along Anna's cheekbones, wiped every, last tear away.

Stacy promised, "You don't need those anymore. You're home now."

And for the first time since Bradie had met her on the rooftop that morning, Anna smiled.

# 4

# FENCED

*T*o everyone who met him, Kayde Meade was the typical "boy next door." In high school, he was spoken highly of, whether it was for being the class treasurer and salutatorian, president of the poetry club or the first person to sign up for any and every community service project. His senior yearbook even listed him as the "most likely to succeed," a title granted him by his graduating class. He was the type of guy that fathers wanted their boys to become and mothers dreamed their daughters would marry.

Physically, Kayde was no Adonis, unremarkable in every way, from his average height to his frame that was as thin as an artist's canvas. Likewise, his personal style was far from legendary, instead teetering on the precipice between half-pipe legend and starving artist, and his scraggly, light brown hair ran well past his ears, halting a centimeter above his eyebrows. Out of all his features, he had two, redeeming qualities, the first of which was his jawline, which was defined and strong, sharply chiseling out what, in anyone else, would have been attractive features. However, it was so well-hidden beneath his jungle of hair that few ever noticed.

His other redeemable quality, the one people actually noticed, was his ocean-blue eyes, which he was told meant that he had a beautiful soul. And although it was meant as a compliment, it always felt like an insult, especially considering he had never had a girlfriend in his life. That fact was insignificant, however, as everyone assured him that he was a catch, the type of guy any girl would be lucky to marry.

There had even been a time when Kayde believed them. But that time had long passed, ever since *that* day.

It happened the year after he graduated from high school. He was nearing the end of his first year at Butler University, working toward an English degree. While Butler may have not been the most prestigious of the schools he had been courted by, it was the closest to home, which gave him the chance to commute to school and stay close to his family, particularly his sister, Blair. That year was also to be her freshman year of high school, and he couldn't imagine leaving her to face that labyrinth alone. Although he had managed to end high school, by all accounts, on top, he had entered with built-in social standing, thanks to the community theater, from which he had acquired friends from every grade before his first day. Unfortunately for Blair, she had been afforded no such luxury. Thankfully, however, she would have her big brother.

At first, commuting to college wasn't so bad. His class schedule allowed him to be in Zionsville to pick Blair up from school every day. In fact, it was the part of the day he often looked forward to the most. He enjoyed hearing about her classes, friends and even the inevitable high school drama. As time went on, however, Kayde found himself becoming more and more involved around campus. Running back and forth from Butler to Zionsville became a chore, and soon, he was asking his mother to pick his sister up from school more often until it was seldom that he even made an appearance at Zionsville Community High. That was when it happened.

It was a Wednesday afternoon, and The Sonnet Society, a campus poetry club of which Kayde was president, was in the middle of a riveting discussion about one of the lesser known works of his favorite poet, John Milton. After thirty minutes of vigorous discourse, they had finally worked their way through the poem's first stanza when his phone rang. It was Blair. Their mother had been forced to work late, leaving Blair with no way to get home. She begged him for a ride.

"Just this one time," she said.

"I can't," he replied. "I wish I could, Sis, but my club's in the middle of an important meeting. Can't you take the bus? I'll pick you up next time. I promise."

As Kayde hung up the phone, he felt a pang of guilt, heavy as an albatross, nest atop his shoulders. He quickly shook it off, figuring he would make it up to her when he got home.

But he never got that chance.

In fact, he never saw her again.

From that day forward, there was hardly so much as a moment that he didn't feel that albatross on his shoulder. He tried everything he could think of to shake it off, as he had done before, but with each day that passed, its talons dug deeper into his shoulder blade, causing blood to trickle from his wound and run down his arms until his hands were stained red with guilt.

*Why couldn't I have picked her up? What was so damn important about poetry club that I would sacrifice my own sister?*

The police said she ran away. Of course, they would never officially inform a family member that a missing person's case had been closed, but the lack of new information, persistent suggestions that she might have run away, and constant, if not bordering on incessant, assurances that everything possible was being done to find her only confirmed that they had stopped looking. Despite every assurance they gave him, Kayde no longer believed a one. If a breakthrough was going to happen in Blair's case, he was going to have to be the one holding the sledgehammer.

It was this realization that brought him to Theresa Henderson's door. She was Blair's best friend and, at this point, the only other person in the world who hadn't given up on her. Sometimes, on the hard days, Theresa's steadfast belief in Blair was the only thing that kept Kayde sane. He usually looked forward to the time he got to spend at the Henderson home, but that day, the door of their home loomed threateningly over him like an executioner in front of the guillotine.

*How do I tell her that the police have stopped looking?*

*How do you break someone's heart without breaking them?*

As Kayde raised his hand to the door, he ran through every conceivable scenario. None of them, however, were promising. His hand trembled before the door's surface. With each rap-tap-tap on the door, shock waves of anxiety rippled from his knuckles to his shoulder, all the way to his heart. Slowly, the door opened, revealing a thin, raven-haired girl with matted hair that was pulled back into a tight bun with two strands of hair that fell in front of her forehead on either side behind it.

There had been a time, before Blair's disappearance, when Theresa's amber eyes shone like a wildfire, when she wore a myriad of colors as extensive as the rainbow. Now, however, she wore nothing but black, and her eyes were soulless and her skin pale. She was a shell of her former self.

When Theresa saw him, the right corner of her mouth lifted into a slight smile but immediately fell upon sensing Kayde's anxiety. "Did they find her?" she whispered nervously.

"No," he sighed.

"Do they have any leads?" she asked.

"No," he repeated, shaking his head sullenly. Then, he peered around him anxiously before asking, "Do you think we could talk about this somewhere a little more private?"

Theresa nodded, opening the door wide, and Kayde followed her inside. They made their way through the kitchen, up the stairs and into her room at the end of the hall. Before closing the door behind them, she took a final, surveilling glance over her shoulder. Then, without a word, she turned her stereo up loud so no one, especially her mother, could listen in on their conversation.

Over the past few months, Mrs. Henderson had become increasingly averse to any and all conversations regarding Blair's disappearance. Like Kayde's own parents, she wanted, as perverse as it seemed, for Theresa to move on and return to some semblance of a normal life. This, of course, had no effect whatsoever on her desire to find Blair. If anything, it only strengthened her resolve. After all, what is a command to move on if not an invitation for obsession?

Theresa's room was a reflection of this fixation: scattered, messy and searching for identity while never truly finding one. The back wall was bright pink, flowery and dedicated as a shrine to Blair, filled to the brim with memories and mementos. In the back, right corner of the room, nestled against wall, sat her bed. Above and across from it, the walls were striped pink and grey, littered with posters of metal bands from every sub-genre. Against the wall opposite her bed, there was an art desk with various drawings hung on the wall above, ranging from colorful and light to dark and riddled with despair and destruction. The final wall nearest to the door was completely empty, save for the grey that covered every inch of its surface, and completed the transition from light into darkness.

"So...?" Theresa asked. "What did they say?"

"They said..." Kayde choked, praying that a meteor would crash through the wall of the house so he wouldn't have to finish his sentence. "They said that sometimes you can't find someone who doesn't want to be found."

"Bullshit," she barked.

"They said they're still looking, though."

"Which means they're not doing a damn thing."

"I know."

"What the hell have they been doing for the last year?!" Theresa shouted as she paced around the room, frustrated. "God, it feels like we're the only people left who give a shit anymore!"

"I'll find her," Kayde said. "I'll find something to make them listen. I have to."

"Not alone, you won't," she insisted, sitting down beside him and placing her hand on his shoulder.

He shook his head. "This is my fault. I was supposed to protect her. You're already risking your mother's wrath by talking about it. I can't ask you to do anything more."

"Then, don't ask," she said.

With a sigh, she fell back onto the bed, laying her head on her pillow. Quickly, Kayde followed suit.

Theresa stared up at the ceiling and recalled, "I don't think I ever told you this, but after Blair disappeared, I saw her everywhere: the mall, the store, on the street corners. She never moved, never spoke. She just looked at me with these cold, dead eyes, and every time I tried to run to her, she disappeared. Every time, the same thing, until one day. I was walking into The Eclipse for a concert, and I saw her, across the lawn, out of the corner of my eye. Our eyes met, and I swear I saw her lips move. She mouthed, 'I miss you.' I know it sounds crazy, but that's what I saw! And after that, she was a phantom, just gone. I never saw her again."

His ears perked up. "What concert?"

"Um..." she said. "I think it was Fifteen Minutes to Pluto."

"I have to go," he apologized as he jumped to his feet and hurried out the door. "I'm sorry. I just remembered something I have to do."

Then, like a flash, he was gone. As Theresa had been recounting her sightings of Blair, he remembered something; he had seen Blair too, at the same concert. Those arctic, comatose eyes had haunted him incessantly ever since that night, boring through his flesh and making their home in his soul. The cops, his parents, everyone told him that he was only seeing things, that he was projecting his desire to see Blair onto some bystander who bore similar features. However, he never saw her again after that night either. He had even gone back several times, hoping to catch another glimpse of her, but she was never there. Deep down, he knew he had seen her. He just didn't have any proof.

Until now.

Before he realized it, his car was skidding to a stop in front of The Eclipse Music Center. He hopped out of the car and slammed the door behind him, filling the otherwise ghostly parking lot with its resounding echo and emptying a nearby tree of its feathered inhabitants. Storming through the main doors, he marched straight to the box office, where a tall, thin man with glasses was in the middle of a duel with a ballpoint pen. He nervously stabbed over and over again at a piece of paper, trying to get the "damned incompetent pile of refuse" to write. Once the teller had completed his job as paper executioner, he nearly jumped out of his skin at the sight of Kayde.

Collecting himself, the teller raised his right hand to his brow and fidgeted with his glasses as he stammered, "Oh! Sorry, I - I didn't see you there! I was just having a few - some issues with... I'm sorry. Hi! Welcome to The Eclipse Music

Center, where *your* pleasure is *our* pleasure. What can I help you with today?"

"Have you seen this girl?" Kayde asked as he slid a picture of Blair across the counter.

The teller took one look at the picture, and his face fell. "Are you with the police?" he whispered.

"No," Kayde replied, dumbfounded by the accusation. "I'm her brother."

"You'll need to speak with my manager," the teller said before bee-lining into the back office.

Within seconds, a shorter man, dressed in a solid, black suit and silver tie, waltzed out of the back office, took a quick glance at the picture that was still sitting on his side of the counter and said, "I'm sorry for the trouble, Officer. I can assure you that the department will have my full cooperation. What can I-"

"Why does everyone keep assuming I'm with the police?" Kayde asked.

"I'm sorry, sir," the man said. "It's just that usually no one else seems to take much interest in girls of her position."

"Her position?" Kayde repeated.

The man nodded. "Ah, so you're a member of the family, I take it? Family is often the last to know about these sorts of things. I'm sorry you have to find out this way."

"What are you insinuating?"

"Whenever we have a large concert or conference, which admittedly is quite often, we attract a number of girls that like to mingle with the crowd in order to profit off of men's... baser instincts."

"Blair would never do something like that."

"Family's a funny thing. You spend every day with them, but you don't ever really know them, do you?"

"You're not listening to me!" Kayde roared like a lion

defending its pride. "I know her better than anyone. She would never choose this."

"I understand your anger. This must be quite the shock for you," the man replied curtly.

At this point, Kayde couldn't stand to hear another word come out of that man's oversized mouth. So, he left. He stormed out of the doors, enraged, and slammed his fist into the concrete wall of The Eclipse. As he did, he caught a glimpse of something out of the corner of his eye. Just to the left of where he was standing, there was a poster advertising a Metal Heads' concert at the end of the week.

*If he's right, Blair might be there, or at least someone who might know where she is. I have to be there. I have to know for sure.*

The night of the Metal Heads' concert, Kayde parked his car at the back of the lot, overlooking The Eclipse. From that distance, the concert crowd looked like an army of ants, funneling, one by one, into its colony, every one of its members faceless in the mob. He watched them for a moment, from outside his car, hoping to find someone, anyone, who might be able to lead him to Blair. That was when he saw *her*.

Immediately, he was drawn to her, an absolute vision in black, adorned in a half-shirt, fishnet stockings and mini-skirt. Her hair was lusciously thick, wavy and made of such a fine color that it blended seamlessly with her outfit, save for a single streak of purple on her left side. She looked as though she had been carved of the finest marble before being brought to life by some beautiful sorcery, absolute perfection in every way.

In that moment, everything else faded away. He could hardly even remember what he had even come there for, if not to watch the way she glided across the earth, filling the air around her with a glorious glow. Before he knew what had come over him, he was standing mere feet from her. Their eyes met. Hers were like crystal. She smiled, and butterflies made permanent residence inside Kayde's stomach. With a skip in her step, she strode over to him. When she reached him, her shoulder grazed against his, sending shivers cascading down his spine.

"Hey there, Cutie," she greeted him. "What's your pleasure?"

He wanted to say, "To take you away from this place and lay next to you for hours, contemplating whether or not anything other than a supreme being could have created a creature so heavenly."

But, all that came out was, "Uh... you."

She smiled, softly biting the bottom corner of her lip, ran a single finger along the curvature of his arm and laughed flirtatiously, "So forward! I like it. I can certainly arrange a little something like that."

"Oh! Uh - I mean," Kayde stammered, turning an uncomfortable shade of pink. "I want to talk to you."

"I don't get paid to talk, honey. But, if it's foreplay you're after, I can definitely oblige, for a little extra."

He pulled the picture of Blair from his pocket and handed it to her. "Do you know this girl?" he asked.

She looked at the picture quickly, a pained expression painting her face, before saying, "Katrianna isn't here anymore, but Violet's just as good, baby."

*Violet. What a beautiful name. So fitting.*

"Aw, thank you! I rather like it myself."

*Did I say that out loud?*

"Please, I need to find her," he said.

Violet hesitated for a second, furrowing her brow anxiously. Then, she turned away and said with a cringe, "I can't help you."

"She's my sister," he implored, latching onto her arm and refusing to let go.

Just then, a strong hand grabbed his shoulder. He spun around, and his eyes were met with the dark glare of a sinister-looking man. In and of himself, the man didn't look particularly intimidating. He stood only a half an inch taller than Kayde and looked more like a college, frat boy than an enforcer, but there was something in his eyes, inches beneath the surface, that made Kayde shudder. An empty madness made its home there, unlike anything he had ever seen.

"Do we have a problem?" the man asked sternly, as though the tone of his voice held the answer to his own question.

"No problems here, Eric," Violet answered quickly, shooting a subtle wink at Kayde. "Just a little foreplay."

"Sorry," Kayde said, following her lead. "This is the first time I've done anything like this."

Eric, still glaring in Kayde's direction, stated, "Foreplay is extra."

"Okay, okay," Kayde said as he fumbled through his pockets for every spec of loose change he could find. "Just give me a second."

Finally, after a few too many moments of searching, he handed fifty-seven dollars and forty-seven cents over to Eric, who, once every last penny had been meticulously counted, ordered, "You have ten minutes."

With Eric's wrath placated for the time being, Violet took Kayde by the hand and led him into the parking lot. As they walked, Kayde couldn't help but marvel at the weightlessness with which she strode, as though she was an angel, fluttering from cloud to cloud, only making contact with the ground for a split second between ascents. Arriving at his car, he walked her over to the passenger's side door and opened it, allowing her to float down into the seat.

She giggled, "Such a gentleman! I think I might have to keep you."

As Kayde walked around the front of the car, he couldn't take his eyes off her. She was intoxicating, breathtaking, magnetic. She was majestic, radiant, angelic. In that moment, there were no words to describe the spell she had him under. With every move she made, he was drawn further and further into her ocean. She pulled her hair behind her ears; he was on her shore. She smiled at him; he was wading in her waters. She winked at him, and he drowned beneath her waves. It took everything in him to keep his mind focused on his goal. Slipping into the driver's seat, he took a deep breath. However, before he could utter a syllable, Violet flipped her hair over her shoulder, bent over and placed her head in his crotch. His entire body stiffened.

"Wh-what are you d-doing?" he stuttered.

"We have to make this appear natural," she answered. "And for me, this is as natural as it gets. Would you rather we talk while having sex in the backseat?"

He shook his head.

She chuckled, "Besides, it's not like you aren't happy to see me. Don't get too distracted though, slugger. You're down to seven minutes. What do you want to know?"

"Why'd you call her Katrianna?" he asked.

"That's the only name of hers I ever knew," she answered. "None of us get to keep our names when we come here."

"What's your real name?"

"You didn't come all this way to talk about me."

"That doesn't mean I wouldn't like to."

"Six minutes," she deflected.

"So, Blair's a prostitute?" he asked.

"We all are, honey," she said with a light chuckle that sounded more like pain than amusement.

He sighed, "I can't believe that she would sell herself like -

I'm sorry. I didn't mean that you were making the wrong decision. I just meant-"

"None of us chose this life," she explained. "It was chosen for us."

"What do you mean?"

"You may not see our chains, but that doesn't mean we walk unbound."

"Why don't you go to the police?"

At this, Violet sat up, tears welling beneath her eyes, and scoffed, "You think we haven't tried that? That story always ends the same way; no one believes us, and we end up in the same place we started, except this time, with bruises on our thighs."

He pleaded, "But I believe you! Maybe if we went together, it'd be different. Maybe I could get you out."

"You're cute," she said sadly, placing her hand on his cheek and stroking it slowly. "But you can't save me. No one can."

Then, as quickly as Violet had entered his life, she was gone. The car door slammed, and all that was left of her was the dull ringing in his ears. He sat there for a moment, hands fixed to the steering wheel. All he wanted to do was march up to that buffoon, Eric, and give him a piece of his mind, but all that would earn him would be a swift strike to the cheek. His next move needed to be smart, calculated. An impulsive decision would simply doom them both to destruction, but he finally had something he hadn't had in a millennium: hope.

And maybe that was enough.

## 5

# HERDING

### DETROIT, MICHIGAN

*T*he morning after his confrontation with Redd, Paul awoke, feeling like a hundred howler monkeys were using the inside of his head as a jungle gym. They rattled, rebounded and ricocheted against his skull so raucously that the resounding pain was more than he could bear. He turned over and checked the clock. It was a stroke past five. All he wanted to do was roll over and go back to sleep, but he couldn't. The monkeys wouldn't let him. Besides, there was work to be done.

Cautiously, he rolled out of bed and stumbled into the bathroom, stopping in front of the mirror to make sure he didn't look as bad as he felt. He turned his head to the side, examining the spot where Redd's pipe had struck him. In one night, it had gone from being as noticeable as a needle, apart from the blood that trickled down his face, to a haystack.

The gash on his forehead had turned into a dry, crusty scab just above his eyebrow, and in every direction around it, his skin was painted a vicious shade of black and blue, extending from below his right eye to well above his hairline. He looked like the perfect beginning to a killer, Halloween costume, but regretfully, the ghost of prison inmate number five wasn't the character he would be playing that day. For this performance, he had to look perfect.

Paul rifled through Rebecca's make up bag, pulling out a batch of concealer. Thanks to the hundreds of hours he had spent working in his high school theater department, as actor, director and stagehand, he knew exactly how much to apply in order to sufficiently camouflage his wound. With his look complete, he crept down the stairs, being careful not to wake Rebecca, and into the kitchen for a fresh pot of tea to go with the twenty-five aspirins he would inevitably need to take in order to satiate the barrel of monkeys that had declared all-out-war on his cranium. As he waited for his tea to brew, a tiny thud slammed against his left leg.

"What was that?" he gasped. "I could've sworn I felt a little leprechaun brush by my leg. I hope it's not after me gold!"

The thud giggled, "No, Daddy! It's me!"

"Me?" Paul asked, bending down and whisking the thud into his arms and swinging it around wildly. "I don't know any 'Me.' Who are you, Me? And why do you look like my daughter?"

She laughed, and, instantly, every ounce of pain dissipated. He looked up at his little, pigtailed painkiller who, that morning, was wearing her favorite, $E=MC^2$ pajamas, complete with a picture of Einstein plastered on her chest, and couldn't help but think she was the smartest, most beautiful nerd the first grade had to offer. As he spun her around, her blonde hair, which was pulled back in two, uneven pigtails, sprang and bounced back and forth, nearly knocking the glasses off her head.

Once he had dizzied her to his satisfaction, he set her down. After steadying herself, she clamped onto his leg and said, "I love you, Daddy!"

"I love you too, Eleanor," he replied.

"Daddy!" she protested, stamping her foot angrily on the floor. "My name is Elle!"

"Nine months of name planning, and I can't even use the one I picked."

"Then you should have picked a better one."

"Duly noted."

"Can I ask you a question?" Elle asked as she broke away from the hug, her bright, blue eyes growing to doe-like size.

"Is this about your pencil?" he asked with a chuckle.

Rebecca had warned him the night before that Elle might be in mourning after the tragic kidnapping of her favorite pencil, Thomas Pencilson. Ever since she received him as a present from her grandmother that past Christmas, she had loved that pencil like it was her own child. It never left her side. The day before, Thomas had been pilfered by Elle's arch nemesis, the nefarious Susan. In a dreadful series of unfortunate events, Elle dropped Thomas Pencilson without realizing it. Moments later, when she returned to retrieve him, she saw Susan pick him up off the ground. Elle tried to confront her, asking her politely to give it back, but Susan refused, cackling villainously, "Finders, keepers." It was a horrendously heinous crime, the likes of which the world had never seen before.

"She knew it was my favorite pencil, but she took it anyways," Elle pouted.

"I know, honey," Paul said. "Regretfully, people don't always do nice things."

"But why, Daddy? Why does people do bad things?"

"Sometimes, people do bad things because they're selfish. They see something they want, and they don't care if it's somebody else's, or if they hurt someone to get it. But other times, it can be a little more complicated. Sometimes, people are bad because they think it's the only way to help a friend or someone they love. Does that make sense?"

She scratched her head. "I think so. Like, if I really wanted to make you happy by doing well in school, but I forgot to study. So, I cheated on a test. I did something bad, but I did it to make you happy. Like that?"

He laughed, "Sort of. Why? Did you cheat on a test?"

"No!" she exclaimed. "That was just a hyper–medical situation."

"Good. Now, why don't you run back upstairs and snuggle with Mommy while Daddy goes to work?" he said, bending down to her level and stroking her cheek with his thumb.

"You're leaving? But you can't leave. It's Saturday! You're going to miss our show!"

"I'm sorry, honey," he sighed, his heart aching. "Daddy has a very important event today, but I promise I'll be home as soon as I can. And next week, we can have an extra-special, double feature of our show. How does that sound?"

"I suppose that sounds acceptable," Elle said.

She leaned in and kissed Paul on the cheek before turning to head back to her room and prancing up the stairs like a show pony who had just won first prize. In that moment, as she smiled from ear to ear, he couldn't imagine anything in the entire world that could give him more joy than that sweet, little girl's happiness. Then, stopping at the top of stairs, before she disappeared into the second story, she turned and blew him a giant kiss. Quickly, he reached out, took hold of the kiss, and placed it in his pocket for safekeeping.

She always knew how to make him melt.

Then, the curtain rose.

All it took was a brush of the hair and a flip of the collar, and Paul became Leon Tarsus: the flamboyant fashionista, who was responsible for discovering some of the most famous models in the world, or at least that was what his InfoPedia page portrayed. Leon was the finest character Paul had ever brought to life. Over the years, from Boston to L.A, he had meticulously hand-picked every detail of his personality, wardrobe and eating habits. No aspect went unaccounted for, even his favorite ice cream flavor, which was pistachio.

After a few, quick sips of Earl Grey tea, Leon hopped into his car and drove to a nearby, abandoned warehouse in the heart of the city. The stage was set, and the crowd was waiting for the performance of a lifetime.

Every inch of the warehouse had been polished to pure perfection, exactly as Leon had designed. Nearly a week's effort had gone into covering over its broken windows and decorating the exterior. Another week had been spent masking the smell of mildew that had previously been the building's sole inhabitant. Finally, however, everything was perfect.

As he entered the warehouse, velvet, red carpet ran the length of the room. Along the sides of the carpet, potted, bay trees stood, staggered, running down the aisle until they were met by rows upon rows of white, ornate chairs, which were filled with beautiful, young faces, all of which brimmed with hope and excitement. At the end of the carpet, there stood a stage, completely layered in crimson, atop which, a table and three chairs stood. There, Redd and Lena sat in front of a shadowy curtain that extended along the stage's width, a stark white background hanging to their right.

Leon sauntered onto the stage, inspecting every millimeter of his design. Then, once everything had been given his seal of approval, he stood dead center, basking in the spotlight.

After clearing his throat dramatically, he announced in an outrageous, foreign accent, "Good evening, ladies! I am absolutely thrilled to be in the presence of such goddesses this afternoon. I am Leon Tarsus. Today, you are being given the once in a lifetime chance to work with me and showcase your beauty to the world. You already know what this chance could bring you. Most of you have read about my achievements in the industry, and all of you have seen at least one of the models I've mentored over the years, even if you don't yet know it. Play your cards right, and you could be next. This is the moment you've been waiting for all your lives, ladies, so let's bring the fierce!"

He then took his seat beside Lena and Redd as Florian stepped forward to call the first name.

"Alexandra Applewood," he announced.

One after another, tall, beautiful girls crossed the scarlet sea and took their place before the snowy backdrop, where Florian took pictures of each one in various poses, which were relayed to a monitor in front of Leon. The opening hours of the casting call passed like watching paint dry. Though every girl that came forward was stunning, none of them were unique or had that special spark that would sell. Then, there was Alice Harper.

From the moment Leon entered the warehouse, she stood out, like Helen of Troy in a Grecian marketplace. Her long, golden locks shone as bright as Jason's fabled fleece, and her skin was like smoothed marble, without spot or blemish. When her name was called, she walked confidently up the stage and, with every picture Florian took, painted the room with extraordinarily vivid colors, each pose taken straight out of an editorial. It was clear she had done this before.

"She's perfect," Redd whispered through drool-drenched lips.

Leon shook his head.

"Don't shake your head at me, you fake prick," Redd snarled. "She would kill, and you know it."

Leon shook his head once again, but this time more out of

disdain than disagreement. If Redd had been sailing the Titanic, Leon was confident that history would have repeated itself. Alice Harper may have had everything going for her: the beauty, the confidence, the talent. And in any normal casting call, she would be a shoe-in. However, this was no normal casting call. In the absence of any talent requests from the few, legitimate contacts Leon had in the modeling industry, this recruitment was being done in-house. Where Redd saw sexiness and swagger, Leon saw years of training, the kind of which could only be taught by a professional. He saw a young girl with a dream, whose parents loved her enough to pay for modeling classes, parents who wouldn't give up searching for her until she was found. In this case, she wasn't perfect. She was an iceberg.

The next name Florian called was Monica Hatfield. In many ways, Monica was Alice's opposite. Where Alice was Helen of Troy, Monica looked more like a peasant girl, with her muddy hair pulled back into a tight bun and her snowy complexion nearly camouflaging her in front of the stark white background. Dressed plainly, she wore a red, collared blouse with sleeves that were folded back at her elbow and a jean skirt that fell past her knees. As soon as the camera flashed, her entire body became as stiff as a board. Though she tried to paint the canvas with the same colors Alice had used, all that came out was grey. She was drowning in the spotlight, swallowed up by the blizzard behind her.

After several shots, Florian set the camera down and walked over to Monica. Removing her glasses, he freed her wavy hair from its shackles and undid the top two buttons of her blouse. At this point, Redd and Lena had given up watching out of boredom, but Leon remained fixated on the scene that played out before him. For a brief moment, when the camera flashed again, the canvas lit with a faint shade of blue, only lingering for a moment before fading back into the grey. But it was there. As Monica exited the stage, the bottom hem of her skirt raised an inch, revealing a deep bruise beneath. Immediately, she pulled her skirt down to cover it up, but Leon now understood why she was so self-conscious; she was being abused.

"She's perfect," Leon said.

Redd clenched his fist like a snake coiling back before it strikes and hissed, "You're so full of shit, Paul."

Leon glared at Redd.

"Leon... Whatever." Redd rolled his eyes. "She'll break the first day."

"She'll do whatever we say," Lena said with realization.

"Why the hell do you even bring me to these things if neither of you are going to listen to a damn word I say?" Redd contested as he shook his head and returned to his notes.

The final hour passed as the others had, unremarkably. Outside of Alice and Monica, none of the other girls stood out. They simply blended into the canvas, like rabbits in a snow-storm. Once the final girl had taken her photos, Leon stood from his seat and addressed the girls from center stage. Thanking them for their time, he sent them on their way and assured them that he would be in contact those who were chosen. While the girls returned to the concrete jungle, Florian tapped Monica on the shoulder, asking her to stay for a moment. Then, as Florian locked the warehouse door, leaving them alone, Leon left the stage to meet her in the center of the aisle.

There, he said, "You were absolutely brilliant up there today, my darling. I would be absolutely delighted to offer you the opportunity to work with me in the beauty-entertainment industry. Would you like that?"

Monica looked at him hesitantly.

"Of course, you would!" he answered for her. "Now, I'll

never understand why you were so self-conscious up there today, Monica. You are a gorgeous young lady! You have no need to be so shy. However, sometimes, a model needs to learn confidence, and I'm going to help you do just that. So, here is your first lesson, free of charge; you need to be confident in your own skin, to know your beauty and own it. Would you mind taking off that blouse and skirt for me? I promise, you have nothing to be ashamed of."

Monica's eyes widened like a deer in headlights. Smiling genuinely at her, Leon touched her shaking, left hand, as if to tell her that everything was going to be okay. Then, he moved closer to her, slowly unbuttoning her blouse. As it fell to the floor, he noticed even more bruises, running all the way up her arms and across her waist.

He asked in a soothing voice, "Has your daddy been hitting you?"

Monica nodded, ashamed.

"Well, we cannot allow for that!" Leon exclaimed, as he removed her skirt. "Here's what we're going to do; if it's okay with you, we are going to take you with us tonight so you don't have to go back home, only to get hurt again. We'll have you write a note to your parents, telling them that you've decided to travel the world and become a big star. I'll even have Florian drop it off in the mailbox at your house so you never have to go back there again. Would you like that?"

She looked away for a moment, mulling her options over. Then, she looked back at Leon, and he saw it again: the flash of blue. Her eyes sparked with color, and she was in.

"I'm going to need you to trust me, Monica," Leon explained. "There are going to be some things you will have to do in this business that you may not be comfortable with, but remember how you feel right now. Make it your anchor and don't ever let it go because that is what will get you to the top.

Now, if you would please go with Florian, he will get you dressed and bring you to the car."

Then, the curtain fell.

Paul's gaze lingered as she walked away, painting the ground beneath her feet a brilliant shade of cerulean. The shy, little girl that had walked so nervously onto his stage was now a masterpiece, and it was all thanks to him.

AFTER DROPPING MONICA OFF AT THE CLUB, FLORIAN DASHED LIKE a cheetah to make it on time for his date with Janelle, stopping momentarily by his apartment to make himself look presentable for a night out. As he pulled outside of Janelle's parents' house, his heart began to beat at a frenzied pace. He was nervous, which felt strange, considering he had never been nervous for a date in his life. After quickly burying that feeling six feet deep within his subconscious, he approached the front door, rang the doorbell and waited.

A moment later, Janelle, with a schoolgirl grin on her face, sped out the door like a bolt of lightning and closed the door tightly behind her. As she stood there, radiating in the porch-light, Florian searched for the perfect word to describe how amazing she looked: beautiful, gorgeous, ravishing. However, nothing that came to mind seemed to accurately capture the full breadth of her beauty.

"You look stunning," Florian said, moderately disappointed in the incompleteness of that statement.

Janelle blushed as he took her by the hand, leading her to her chrome chariot. That night, the itinerary for the evening wasn't terribly different than many of their other dates. First, they went to dinner at Vinny's before heading to the Franklyn Theater for the seven o'clock performance of Ghost in the Playhouse, which was, far and away, Florian's all-time favorite piece of theater. However, as the production moved through its first act, he found it difficult to fully focus on the spectacle due to the constant fluttering in his stomach. Everything about Janelle was intoxicating: the scent of her hair, the touch of her skin, the warm breath escaping her lungs. It was enough to send shivers down his spine.

After the show, which he had only managed to pay attention to for half of, they left the theater, hand-in-hand. As they walked, Florian slid his hand gently along the small of her back, lifting the bottom of her shirt and placing his hand on the supple skin underneath.

He pulled her close to his side, kissed her hair tenderly, and asked, "So, what did you think of the show?"

"I thought it was good," she replied, nestling her head comfortably into his shoulder. "But I think I like the movie version better."

Florian's mouth dropped. He was speechless. In the countless scenarios he had played out in his head, those were words he never expected to hear about a production at the Franklyn. It was akin to saying that Jaylon Jones was the best Kung Fu Child or that they should make more Vamp Night movies. It wasn't something that sane people said.

Janelle giggled, "I'm kidding! I just wanted to see the look on your face when I said it!"

"Good, because I was starting to wonder if we should even be dating anymore," he joked.

Then came the part of the night Florian was worried about. Many hours had been spent in front of the mirror, rehearsing every fragment of this moment. He had picked the perfect location, carefully penned his words and painstakingly chosen every detail, down to his micro-expressions, but he couldn't shake the feeling that somehow, he would still ruin the pure poetry of this moment.

Inhaling deeply and trying, once again, to close the coffin on every grain of trepidation, he began, "Janelle, the moment I first saw you, I forgot how to breathe. Light shone from the heavens, and angels sang in glorious chorus. At first, I feared that I was hearing the fabled siren song, doomed to pursue a beauty that I could never, though I live forever, dream of holding in my arms. But, despite my inadequacies, you somehow found it in your heart to choose me, flaws and all. Therefore, hear my soul. Hear the very beating of my heart. Hear the longing of my spirit. You-"

"I love you too, baby," she said, giggling.

"You didn't let me finish."

"Okay, my love. You may continue."

"It's just that I wrote this whole speech and everything..."

"I'm sorry. Go ahead," she laughed.

"And I was really hoping you would hear all of it," he went on.

"Then get on with it!" she implored, playfully pushing him into the street.

Stepping back onto the curb, Florian cleared his throat dramatically and said, "Therefore, hear my soul. Hear the very beating of my heart. Hear the longing of my spirit. You are my breath. When my lungs forget how to breathe, your smile fills them with air again. You are my strength. When these bones are so weighed down that they cannot move, your voice sets them in motion. You are my song. You are my muse. I can no longer imagine how I even existed prior to knowing you. Janelle, I love you."

"I love you too."

As she uttered those words, Florian heard a panicked voice

coming from the adjacent alley. Immediately, he rushed to its entrance, trying to locate the source of the cry, but the alley was empty and dark, lit only by a single light that flickered dimly next to a dumpster that stood, alone, at the far end of the corridor. Then suddenly, from behind the dumpster, a figure emerged from the shadows, covered in a layer of dirt and grime that masked its form. From that distance, it was difficult to tell whether the figure was a man or a beast. After a few, labored steps, the being collapsed to the ground, motionless. Without even taking a second to process the situation, Florian started down the alleyway but was stopped by the outstretched arm of Janelle.

She looked at him with fear in her eyes that begged him not to go, but he said, "I have to. He could be hurt."

"It's too dangerous," she pleaded.

"If I do nothing, he could die," he replied. "I couldn't live with myself if I let that happen."

With a sigh, Janelle let go of Florian's arm, electing instead to follow behind him. As they neared the dumpster, the mysterious figure came into full view. It was a man, lying face down on the ground. He appeared to have been beaten severely, but it was difficult to determine the extent of his injuries due to the dirt-covered blankets wrapped around his body. Every breath he took sounded immeasurably painful, as though he was barely clinging to life.

"Babe, call nine-one-one," Florian implored. "I'm going to try to help him."

As Janelle dialed, Florian placed his hands on the man's shoulders, pulling back the blanket. Then, as if brought to life by his very touch, the man whipped back his head. Startled, Florian fell backwards onto the ground, and Janelle's phone plummeted to the concrete below, cracking upon impact. Before either of them had a chance to react, the man reached his right hand toward Florian, aiming the pistol he had been concealing underneath his blanket straight at him.

"Surprise!" the man exclaimed with a devilish grin.

Keeping the gun trained on Florian, he stood up in one, deliberate motion, his eyes like coal. Meanwhile, Florian rushed to his feet and placed himself directly between the gun and Janelle.

"No, no, no," the rascal said, his voice like gravel. "She stays within my sight."

Florian stood his ground, refusing to move. The scoundrel approached him slowly, taking one, deliberate step after another. He raised the barrel of the gun to Florian's head, daring him to be a hero.

"It's okay, honey," Janelle said, trembling. "It's not worth it."

Reluctantly, Florian heeded her advice. The man, whose gun was still pointed at Florian, looked Janelle up and down and swooned, "Damn! You banging that hot piece of ass? You know, I'm not usually into chocolate, but I could run my tongue up and down you all day long."

Janelle cringed as the rascal approached her, circling her like a lion stalking its prey and running his hand along her backside. Once behind her, he took his left hand, ran it up her torso and felt her up. At the same time, he slid the head of his pistol under her skirt and up between her thighs. Florian's jaw clenched so tightly that he could feel his teeth press into his gums as he watched Janelle writhe in horror. He began to list in his mind all of the different ways that he would sever each of the man's limbs if given the chance.

"You know, I was only going to rob you," the scoundrel said before whispering in Janelle's ear, licking it with his tongue. "But now that I have you in my grasp, I can't help but imagine all of the gorgeously nasty things I could do to you."

Florian made eye contact with Janelle, assuring her that

everything was going to be alright. For the moment, the man was distracted by his libido, and that gave them the perfect opportunity to gain the upper hand. He watched as the man slid the pistol out from under Janelle's skirt. For a brief second, the gun rotated ever-so-slightly, causing the barrel to point outward. It was at this moment that Florian nodded at Janelle, who simultaneously elbowed the man in the stomach and locked her thighs together, trapping the gun in place. As the thief doubled over, Florian bolted over and swung his fist into the man's chin, sending him crashing into the dumpster.

Then, Florian stood over him, reveling in the moment, and said, "No one touches my girl!"

{}~{}~{}~{}~{}~{}~{}~{}~{}~{}

After dropping Janelle at home, Florian returned to the club to close up. He cleaned up the bar, locked the doors and shut off the lights. Then, before leaving, he descended the stairs into the basement and watched the world around him fade into darkness. The sound of his own breathing echoed off the cement until it was all he could hear. As he turned the handle to Lena's office, the door creaked. A single lamp shone from Lena's desk, and she looked up from her paperwork, her gaze falling on him.

"How did it go with Janelle tonight?" she asked.

Before Florian could respond, he felt two, dirty hands wrap around his neck. He didn't flinch, nor did he waver. Once again, he stood his ground.

Warm, moist breath fell on the back of his neck, and a gruff voice whispered in his ear, "Did you miss me?"

*That voice, I know it.*

Quickly grasping the hands that encircled his neck, separating them from his jugular, he spun around to face the scoundrel. They stared at each other for a moment, their eyes throwing daggers, before their scowls suddenly changed into fits of laughter.

"Izzy!" Florian exclaimed, embracing his friend. "That was the performance of a lifetime tonight! I got chills!"

"Who was performing?" Izzy laughed. "That fine-ass bitch gave me chills in all the right places! Though, you didn't have to hit me so hard."

Florian shrugged. "I had to sell it."

"The two of you can chat on your own time," Lena said. "I take it Izzy performed well?"

"He performed admirably," Florian answered.

"I always perform admirably," Izzy interjected, motioning demonstratively to his crotch.

Ignoring Izzy's comment, Lena asked, "And when can I expect Janelle to be joining us?"

"Soon. Very soon."

# 6

## OFF-FEED

NEW YORK, NEW YORK

*T*he life of a "warehouse girl," as they were often called, was enough to destroy even the strongest of women. It was a suffocating existence, full of darkness and pain. Over the years, Natasha had seen, without fail, every girl that walked through the warehouse door, save for the occasional female client, meet one of two fates; they either succumbed to the darkness or met the grim reaper, whether by choice or by punishment. No one escaped, although many tried. It turned out that fate could be tempted but never defeated.

In an existence so dim, even a pure thing can become like a drug. You crave it. You need it, and you will do whatever it takes to get it. One night of Natasha and Blair sleeping beside each other became two, and two became three. Soon, it was a nightly ritual. Even though they knew that, if they were caught, Alexei's wrath would be swift and excruciating, Natasha believed the risk to be worth it. Their late-night talks, the warmth of human touch without expectation or desire, the intoxicating feeling of belief and trust became increasingly addicting. It was her painkiller, and she could never get enough.

A couple weeks later, Natasha awoke the same way she did every evening. As the light descended beneath the curtain's crest, she yawned, stretching her arms and legs as far as they could go until every muscle in her body was tense. Then, she rolled over to give Blair one, final hug before their night began. That evening, however, Blair wasn't in bed. Instead, she was standing at its edge, putting on the same, black, lace half-top and mini skirt she wore every night.

She turned to Natasha and smiled, chuckling, "Evening, sleepyhead."

"Did I oversleep?" Natasha yawned.

"He'll be here any minute," Blair said.

"Why didn't you wake me?" Natasha asked as she got out of bed and got dressed.

"You looked so peaceful. I didn't want to rip you from your dreams any sooner than I must."

"I'd rather spend my time with you."

Blair giggled, "What do you think you're doing right now?"

"I've been thinking," Natasha said excitedly, taking Blair's hands in hers. "We should run away, finally get out of here."

Blair's face fell. "You know that's not possible."

"Don't you want to?"

"More than anything, but he'll find us. And things will only get worse."

"But we can get away," Natasha said. "I know we can. We can live a good life and be happy, but we have to do it together."

Blair sighed, "I'm sorry, Natasha…"

Suddenly, a voice down the hall screamed, "No, no, no! Not today!"

Like a flash, Blair was gone, sprinting down the hall toward the source of the noise. Natasha quickly followed, and soon, they were standing in Jasmine's room, ankle-deep in bile. Blair knelt beside Jasmine, who was curled up in the only clean spot left on the floor, sobbing silently.

Typically, Jasmine was the most fiery, vivacious spirit in the room, an enchanting, Latina princess with hair that cascaded in beautiful curls down her back like a chocolate fountain. Her eyes were always so full of life that they overflowed like a boiling pot, but that evening, she looked like she had one foot firmly planted in the grave. Her flawless, tan skin was almost translucent, and her hands, feet and face were covered in retch. She was in no shape to work the streets.

Blair put her hand on Jasmine's shoulder while Natasha stripped the sheets from the bed and began to clean the floor and her feet as best she could. As Natasha bent down to clean, the putrid stench of what could only be described as the horrifying combination of curdled milk, stomach acid and freshly steamed rat fur invaded her nostrils. She quickly stood up to keep from retching herself. Then, taking one, final breath of fresh air, she held her breath and rushed to clean the floor before her air ran out.

"What happened?" Blair asked.

"I felt fine when I woke up," Jasmine choked through her tears. "But, as soon as I sat up, it felt like something was burning inside of me. At first, I thought I could walk it off, but that only made it worse. So, I tried to hold it all down, but you can see how well that went for me."

"Do you think you're...?" Natasha asked hesitantly, afraid to so much as utter the word they were all thinking.

"Oh God, I hope not!" Jasmine gasped before shaking her head. "I don't think I am, though. Last night, there was this one pair of ripped jeans. He came in, hacking, coughing and looking like death. I tried not to kiss him, like I usually do, but he insisted. So, I just grinned, beared it and hoped I wouldn't catch anything, but obviously, hope doesn't get you very far. I can't afford to miss my quota today. Alexei will kill me. I've already been short two days this week."

Blair looked back at Natasha with a look that could only mean that they were both thinking the same thing. Natasha nodded in approval.

"Natasha and I will take care of it," Blair said.

"I can't ask you to do that," Jasmine replied.

"You need to rest," Natasha insisted.

Jasmine reiterated, "I can't."

"This isn't a negotiation," Blair said. "We'll take care of Alexei. You take care of yourself."

"Thank you so much. Both of you. I don't know how I'll ever repay you," Jasmine replied.

"Well, then it's a good thing you don't have to." Natasha smiled. "We 'warehouse girls' have to stick together, right?"

Thankfully for them, Alexei was a creature of habit, more so due to being an uneducated brute who ruled through intimidation and force as opposed to being the least bit organized. He took roll call twice per day: once as the sun set, when everyone awoke, and again as it rose, when he collected that night's earnings before bedtime. During the nights, however, there was too much commotion in the warehouse for him to notice one girl who wasn't around. This meant they could stash Jasmine away in one of the storage rooms out back, and she would be a ghost, providing they could earn enough to match both their quotas and hers. The first step, however, was to make sure Alexei saw her at roll call.

Once they cleaned Jasmine up, they hoisted her onto their shoulders and carried her into the hallway. Carefully propping her up between them, they secured their hands firmly to the small of her back for extra support. The strain on Jasmine's face was excruciating to watch, as there was hardly enough strength in her bones to stand, much less look like nothing was wrong. Likewise, it took all of Natasha's strength just to keep Jasmine standing, as she kept slipping down from the constant buckling of her knees. As the last rays of the sun disappeared from behind the warehouse windows, Blair looked over at Natasha and smiled. That was all it took to let her know that everything was going to be okay.

Alexei entered the warehouse the same way he did every day, with a crash and a shout. Then, he strutted demonstratively onto the warehouse floor but stopped immediately upon seeing the girls waiting for roll call, a puzzled expression sweeping across his face. Admittedly, it was out of the ordinary for any of the girls, especially Natasha and Blair, to be anywhere but in their rooms before he arrived. However, the look in his eyes wasn't one of confusion; it was suspicion, as though he had spotted a robber inside his house. Walking toward them slowly, he scanned them for anything he deemed out of the ordinary. Natasha looked to Blair for reassurance again but, this time, received none, as Blair looked as nervous as she felt.

Reaching them, Alexei said, "You're up early."

"We wanted to get an early start today," Natasha gulped, fighting through the beads of sweat that were forming on her brow.

"Hmmm," he pondered, his eyes focused on Jasmine. "You look pale."

Blair piped in, "I let her try on my makeup this morning. She wanted to try a different look. I think it suits her. Don't you?"

"It makes her look like nightmare. I will allow, for now. But, if this affects quota, she will be made to fix. You may get to work," he replied as he made his way past them to continue roll call.

Once he was gone, they quickly deposited Jasmine in a back room and got to work. Each of them took turns, alternating between bringing clients back to their own rooms and Jasmine's room, in case Alexei grew suspicious. After a few hours, they had earned enough to cover Jasmine's quota and began to work on their own. Natasha had never worked so hard or so quickly in her life. She was exhausted, but every time she felt like giving up, Blair was nearby to lift her up and remind her that she could do it. So, she pressed on.

Even then, Natasha was seventy-five dollars short with fifteen minutes to go, which meant she would either have to service two clients in that time or raise her price. She was growing desperate, and desperation never bred anything good, much less normal.

Most of the suits, crew necks, and wife-beaters she saw in a given night came in one of two flavors. They were either all about the sex, which was simple enough to drown out, or they came for the companionship they weren't getting from their wives. Thankfully, since most suits were self-absorbed at their core, they only ever wanted to speak of themselves, which was also rather easy to ignore, apart from the occasional head-nod or horrified gasp at some trivial detail about their lives. Occasionally, however, Natasha ran into a suit with desires that were a little outside of the mainstream. Most of these were harmless eccentricities, such as foot fetishes, blindfolds or a preference for light bondage. Sometimes, however, the special requests she received verged on the sociopathic, and regretfully, free will was not allowed in the warehouse.

That night, it was an Armani suit with white gold cufflinks and a matching tie that took the prize for most memorable lay.

He parked his silver Range Rover across the street and walked toward her with a casual confidence that, along with his striking features, would have typically drawn the eye of every woman for five miles. To Natasha, however, he was just another mark, a mark with a black briefcase, which could only mean one thing; he brought tools, a lot of them. That was the first red flag.

The Armani smiled as he approached her and asked with the same sultry tone he had likely used to pick up countless women at the local bars, "How much for a little fun?"

"For you?" Natasha asked with a wink as she raised her finger to her mouth and nibbled at her nails more out of nervousness than foreplay. "I'll do it for a hundred."

"You've got yourself a deal, sweetheart," he said, taking her by the hand and leading her into the warehouse.

That was the second red flag; she had doubled her usual price, expecting to barter, but he didn't even blink.

Once inside her room, the Armani looked her up and down and ordered, "Take everything off, sit on the bed and do whatever I say."

"Yes, sir," she replied.

Whipping her hair gently to the side with a sensual flare, she reached her hands behind her back to unhook her bra. When she looked over at him, however, instead of watching her, like a typical client, he was bent over, carefully rifling through his briefcase. She stood there for a second, dumbfounded, before nonchalantly throwing the rest of her clothes on the floor and plopping onto the bed. At this point, even the air raid sirens were going off as a third red flag was raised.

"Close your eyes," the suit said.

As she did, her mind started to toggle through the worst things she could imagine coming out of that briefcase: whips, nipple clamps, full body restraints, knives. He sat down beside her, and her palms began to sweat. Every horror story she had ever heard in passing played on repeat in her own, private cinema. Then, taking her hands in his, he placed something large and rubbery in them, like a heavy-duty, unrolled condom.

"Someone's a bit overconfident," she thought.

"Open your eyes," he said with an air of boyish excitement.

When she opened her eyes, the Armani Suit was in his birthday suit, holding a blue balloon in his hand. She looked down at her own hands, and sitting in them was a matching, pink balloon. She blinked. It was still there. She blinked again. Still, nothing changed. Meanwhile, the suit sat there, staring at her expectantly.

"Aren't you going to blow it up?" he asked.

"You want me to... blow it up?" she floundered.

"That's what you do with balloons," he said, matter-of-factly.

"You know this isn't what they mean when they call it a blowjob, right?" she smirked, entertained by her own wit.

"Less talking. More blowing."

Natasha held the shaft of the balloon between her fingers and brought it to her lips. The suit groaned pleasurably as he slid his own balloon over his manhood, stroking it tenderly with his hand. She placed her lips around the head of the balloon, caressing its opening with her tongue while choking back every pang of laughter that tried to escape. As she blew, the suit began to pleasure himself vigorously. Usually, she closed her eyes at these sorts of moments, trying to drown everything out as if her body was simply on loan. However, for a reason she couldn't explain, she found herself unable to look away, even to blink. As the balloon neared its breaking point, she began to slow down, wondering whether he expected her to stop or keep going until it burst.

Curious, she took her mouth off the shaft and asked hesitantly, "Do I keep going, or-"

"Don't stop. Please don't stop," he answered, clearly out of breath.

So, she took the balloon in her mouth once again and continued blowing until...

*Pop!*

As the sound echoed like a gunshot throughout the warehouse, the suit threw his head back and sighed asthmatically, nearly shaking with pleasure. Meanwhile, Natasha remained frozen. There were no words for the utter confusion that coursed through her veins. She watched as the suit donned his clothes, paid her and left. Finally, she blinked. For some reason, she felt oddly festive as she collected her earnings and helped Blair get Jasmine ready for roll call.

They had done it. They had earned enough to meet all three of their quotas, and Alexei was none the wiser.

Later that morning, Natasha and Blair lay together in bed. Blair's head rested on Natasha's chest as Natasha ran her fingers through Blair's silky locks, which were cast in a glorious glow from the rays of sunlight that streamed over the tops of the curtains. In that moment, there wasn't a thing in the world that could bother Natasha. Usually, she spent her final, few, waking moments in dread, fearing what was to come after her dreams. That morning, however, instead of feeling cold and alone, as she usually did, a warmth emanated from deep inside her, like a tiny, glowing star. It was a feeling she hadn't come close to since she was a little girl. If she hadn't known better, she could have sworn it was joy.

She turned her head to Blair, saying, "Thank you."

"For what?" Blair asked, her eyes shining like the sun.

"For what you did for Jasmine," Natasha answered. "And showing me that I can still matter, even in this place."

Blair shook her head, insisting, "I should be thanking you."

"Why?"

"You were the one who inspired me to do it."

Finally, Natasha couldn't hold in her laughter any longer. It worked its way from her stomach to her throat and forced its way out in the form of a girlish giggle.

Blair looked at her, confused. "What's so funny?"

"I'll tell you," Natasha said. "But you're not going to believe me."

As Natasha recounted the happenings of her night to Blair, the two of them fell asleep with smiles on their faces and laughter on their lips.

# 7

# BULL

INDIANAPOLIS, INDIANA

*K*ayde sat in the lobby of the Indianapolis Police Department, waiting for Detective Stanbridge to get out of a briefing. For all intents and purposes, Detective Stanbridge was the lead detective investigating Blair's disappearance and, according to the Chief, the "Best Detective in Greater Indiana." As far as Kayde was concerned, however, he was an incompetent clown who couldn't find his glasses if they were resting on his nose. After a year of searching, the only sign of Blair that Stanbridge had managed to dredge up was a drunk, homeless man who swore up, down and sideways that he had seen Blair on the highway billboards, advertising a new line of perfume. Needless to say, Detective Stanbridge wasn't everything he was cracked up to be. Television painted detectives as heroes, giants among men, but Kayde was quickly becoming convinced that the giants were nothing more than monkeys on stilts.

As he waited, Kayde tapped his finger anxiously on the armrest of his chair. After countless hours spent waiting in that lobby, he had grown to hate everything about the police station, from the old, leather seats that stuck to his skin like duct tape to the smell of stale potato chips that seemed to fester all around him. He didn't want to spend so much as one more second in that place. However, even though everything in him was pulling him out the front door toward The Eclipse to look for Blair himself, prudence said to stay put, that Stanbridge was his best option for finding her.

Stanbridge had to listen. He had to, especially now that there was a lead.

Finally, Detective Stanbridge entered the lobby looking like a grizzled soldier off to fight yet another battle, his lips fluttering violently behind the forced exhale that escaped his mouth. The disdain that exuded from his very being was so tangible that Kayde could almost taste it, and, fortunately for him, the feeling was mutual. Kayde leapt from his chair, determined to say what needed to be said before Stanbridge had the chance to dampen his thunder.

However, before Kayde had a chance to speak, Stanbridge interrupted him, "It's been three days. We have nothing new on Blair."

"Well, I do," Kayde announced proudly. "I found her! Or at least, I found out where she *was*, which was at The Eclipse, worki-"

Stanbridge looked away and tapped his fingers twice on his thigh, which, as Kayde had long since figured out, was what he did whenever he was about to lie.

"You already knew," Kayde said, his voice lowering dramatically.

"For eight months now," Stanbridge replied.

"Am I your beast that you think it best to put blinders on me?"

"And what would you have done if you'd known? Would you have gone after her? By the time we got to The Eclipse, she was long gone. And we can't devote department resources to chasing a runaway prostitute across the country."

"But she didn't choose this! I have a-"

"You have a what? A witness? A girl who told you she was forced into 'the life?' We scoured that place, inspected every inch, looking for anything we could use as evidence. There was nothing. There *is* nothing. Just a teenage girl who finally had enough of her home life. You need to accept that, Kayde."

Kayde couldn't listen to another word. In that moment, he wanted nothing more than to put a massive dent in the side of Stanbridge's smug face, but his equally strong desire not to go to jail for assaulting a police officer won out. So, instead, he went home, believing that surely his parents would take his side.

After all, there was no way they could believe what Detective Stanbridge had said about Blair. It was inconceivable.

Blair had always been the responsible one, the one with a moral compass, who did what she knew was right no matter what anyone, including her parents, thought. And everyone knew it. There was one time, when Kayde was still driving her to and from school, that he took her to her favorite, frozen yogurt place for a "sibling date." As they walked out of the shop, fortune smiled upon him in the form of an unmarked envelope, lying open on the ground with two, hundred dollar bills inside, waiting for someone to take claim of them.

Of course, being the broke college student that he was, he tried to pocket it, but Blair wouldn't have it. She snatched the envelope from his hands and spent the rest of the day searching high and low for its owner, even bringing it to the police station when she couldn't find to whom it belonged. Then, once thirty days had passed with the money still unclaimed, it was hers. However, instead of keeping it for herself, like most would have, she donated it to a local Boys and Girls Club because she didn't feel right keeping someone else's money.

That was the kind of person she was: generous, responsible and upright. He couldn't understand why he and Theresa were the only ones who seemed to still believe that.

The next few hours, as Kayde waited for his parents to get home from work, were unbearable. At first, he tried to wait patiently. He turned on the television. He picked up a book. He even tried to listen to the radio, but nothing could get his mind to settle down. After all, patience was never his strength. He was the type of person who would rather show up at your front door to tell you something important than wait an hour for you to return a text. However, the last time he showed up at his father's work unannounced, his father made him repaint the living room, even though Kayde had only come to tell him that he had been cast in the senior musical. He couldn't afford a repeat performance, and this was news that had to be handled delicately, for his mother's sake.

Since Blair's disappearance, his mother had been a mess. For days, she refused to eat. For weeks, she couldn't sleep. The news had wrecked her inside and out. Only recently had she managed to return to a semblance of normalcy, and, while it would be good news to know that Blair was still alive, it could kill her to know what she had been forced into. So, after a few minutes spent deciding how to best break the news, Kayde started cooking, frying up a plain cheeseburger and fries for his dad and baking a balsamic-glazed chicken for his mom: their favorites.

As he set the final plate on the table, his parents walked through the door. Before the door even had the chance to close, he bolted over to help them with their jackets.

"Welcome home, you two," he said. "After a long day at work, I know the last thing you want to do is have to worry about dinner. So, I took the liberty of worrying about it for you. I made your favorites!"

"Well, isn't that sweet of you?!" his mother exclaimed. "It's been so long since we've had a family dinner together."

"What's the occasion?" his father asked suspiciously.

"Can't a son do something nice for his parents just because he loves them?" Kayde deflected.

His father blew past him and took his seat at that table, saying, "A couple years ago, maybe, but ever since you went off to college, you've hardly said two words to us unless you wanted something."

"Aaron!" his mother exclaimed. "Let's not turn this into a fight. Our son did something nice for us. Can't we be thankful?"

"If you must consider it something, consider it an apology for not spending enough quality time with you," Kayde said as he pulled out his mom's chair for her.

She smiled and curtsied playfully at Kayde as she sat down. Meanwhile, his father merely grunted at him through a mouthful of cheeseburger.

Despite everything that everyone else had said throughout his life, Kayde was never good enough, never driven enough, for his father, at least not in the ways he was supposed to be. He never wanted the "right things" out of life, specifically to play football or go into accounting, and Blair's disappearance had been the final nail in the coffin. Blair had always been the perfect child, the spitting image of her mother in every way. Kayde, however, wasn't much like either of his parents. Where Blair was adored, Kayde felt reviled. After she went missing, it all fell apart. Their mother retreated inside herself, riddled with despair, and their father became angry at everyone and everything, especially Kayde.

Kayde hoped this dinner would change all that.

After several moments of silent eating, his mother broke the silence. "How was your day, Kayde?"

"Pretty good," he replied, still trying to figure out how to break the news.

"Did you do anything special?" she probed further.

He replied, "I went down to the police station."

"Again?" his father said with a definitive eye roll. "Haven't you tortured that poor detective enough?"

"But this was different. I found something, a lead. I couldn't just sit on it," Kayde explained.

"And what could you have possibly found that Detective Stanbridge couldn't?"

"I went to The Eclipse. Obviously, she's not there now, but they know her there. Apparently, whoever took her had been forcing her to work there as a prostitute. I tried to tell Stanbridge, but-"

His parents shared a pained, knowing look.

"You have to be kidding me!" Kayde yelled, finally reaching the limit of his patience. "Is everyone determined to keep me in the dark?"

His mother tried to keep the peace. "We didn't want to upset you."

"What's upsetting is finding out that your parents have been keeping secrets from you, secrets that could've actually made a difference," he said.

"And what difference would it have made?" his father asked condescendingly.

"I could've done something about it!" Kayde screamed, slamming his hands on the table.

"Bull!" his father shouted, matching Kayde's intensity. "She was long gone by the time Detective Stanbridge caught up to her. Get it through your head, Kayde; she doesn't want to be found."

"You think you know what she wants? You obviously don't know her at all if you think she would choose this," Kayde yelled.

"And how would you know?" his father shot back. "You were barely here long enough over those two semesters to remember what your sister looked like, much less what she would have chosen. After you *abandoned* her, she abandoned us for some college student she met at the park, quickly becoming irritable and defiant. On several occasions, she even threatened to run off with him. It seems she finally did, and, when he inevitably dumped her on the side of the road, she decided to sell herself instead of come home to her 'stupid' parents and non-existent brother."

That was the last straw. First, the police had given up on Blair. Now, her own parents had thrown in the towel. It was clear that Kayde was the only person left who had any faith in her. So, without another word, he left, storming out of the house toward the only place he could think to go: The Eclipse. Once again, he planted his feet on the cold blacktop that overlooked the parking lot, but this time, he had a purpose. Carefully scanning every face in the crowd, he looked for Violet's pimp, Eric. Finally, after a moment, Kayde found him standing beside Violet.

Suddenly, a torrent of emotion, consisting of equal parts turmoil and peace, certainty and uncertainty, washed over him. The road before him, which had previously been fraught with darkness, was now illuminated, and he was standing at a fork in the road. Two paths lay before him, both of which led to despair, but only one to salvation. And he was done being prudent. So, he marched, determinedly, toward Eric, as if drawn by something outside of himself.

"Eric!" Kayde called out, still twenty feet away. "I want in."

"In? You'll have to pay double if you want penetration," Eric laughed.

Violet, who was next to Eric, soliciting a client, turned to see what was going on. She took one look in Kayde's eyes, and hers grew wide.

With an air of realization, she said, "Don't do this."

Ignoring her plea, Kayde set himself inches from Eric's face and answered, "The business. I want in."

Eric scoffed, "Then bring me a girl."

# 8

## DAMAGED

DETROIT, MICHIGAN

"*P*lease, don't! No! NO!" Anna screamed, her voice echoing through the upstairs hallway of Bradie's new home.

Bradie awoke suddenly, as though a million volts of electricity had surged through his body. He shot up in bed and immediately went into crisis mode. Grabbing his gun from the night stand, he flew out of bed, darted toward the door and tried, as quickly as he could, to assess the situation.

*Is someone inside? Are they trying to hurt Anna? Did he follow her all the way here?*

The door opened slowly and silently as he entered the hallway. In the distant darkness, he heard a whisper, though he couldn't make out its source or content. Carefully, he slid along the wall, muffling his footsteps as he walked. After a few seconds, he reached Anna's door, which was cracked open a couple inches. As he took the door handle between his middle and ring fingers and placed the back of his hand against the door, every muscle in his body tensed, preparing for a fight.

That was when he heard the whisper again but this time, more clearly. It was Stacy.

"It's okay," she whispered. "Anna, I'm here. You're just dreaming."

Instantly, the tension in Bradie's body dissipated, and he breathed a deep sigh of relief. Cracking the door open a little more, he listened. As he brought his ear to the door, he heard a sudden, loud crack, like the sound of bone meeting flesh. Stacy grimaced audibly.

Anna gasped, "Oh my God! I - I'm so sorry, Mrs. Lam! I didn't mean to hit you! I was having a nightmare. I - I thought you were *him*."

"It's okay," Stacy said. "You're okay. Why don't you tell me what happened in your dream?"

"It was terrible," Anna sighed.

"I know."

"I couldn't breathe."

"I know."

"It was so peaceful at first," Anna began. "I was in the middle of a lake, floating on my back. Beautiful, high mountains surrounded me on every side beneath a clear, blue sky as a cool breeze blew around me on every side. It was so serene. I was finally at peace, and I felt safe. Then, suddenly, the sky grew dark. Storm clouds crept over the peaks of the mountains until they filled the sky, lightning flashing between them. I looked into the water, which had turned to cold, black tar.

"That's when I saw *him* - well, his face - glaring at me beneath the water's sludgy surface. I tried to scream, but no sound came out. Suddenly, the mountains started to close in on me, and, when I looked back down to where his face was, it was gone. In its place, a giant, black hand, even darker than the tar, raced toward me. I tried to swim away, but it was too late. The hand took hold of my ankle and pulled me underneath the water. I flailed my arms. I kicked my feet and gasped for air, but nothing worked. As the last thread of life drained from my bones, I felt you tugging at me. That's when I woke up. It was so horrible, Mrs. Lam."

"I know, but you're okay now. You can always come to me for anything. I'm here for you. You're safe with me, and please, call me Stacy."

"Thank you, Stacy."

After that, Bradie tried to go back to sleep, but he couldn't. His mind wouldn't allow it. Instead, he was overcome by worry and doubt. He had thought that distance would grant Anna freedom, but it was clear that she was still chained to her captor in a way that Bradie couldn't understand. By the time the clock struck five that morning, he couldn't take it anymore. He had to do something. So, he picked up his phone and called Loman, hoping to hear that some progress had been made in finding Anna's keeper. After four rings, there was nothing but silence on the other end. He hung up and dialed again, but still, there was nothing. Running out of options, Bradie did the only thing he could think to do; he left. He left, and he went to the only place he could think to go: work.

That morning, he walked into the Detroit Police Department in a daze. Everything around him blurred together into a haze of black and grey. The giant, glass doors that marked the entrance, the officers coming and going from their daily duties, the clamor of police radios all around him, even the hysterical, young blonde at the front counter just blended into the haze. His body was there, but his mind was a thousand miles away. Before he knew it, he was in the back of the building, sitting at a desk with his name on it. With nothing to do, his mind continued to race.

*How could someone have such a hold on another person? Maybe she was right. Maybe he will always find her. As long as he's out there, no matter how far she runs, he will always be there, in her dreams, waiting for her to let her guard down. Maybe it's not distance that will break her free of him but justice. If she knows he's gone, that he can't hurt anyone ever again, maybe then she'll be free. Maybe that's it!*

*Justice...*

After what only seemed like seconds, two, large shadows crept onto Bradie's desk, breaking his trance. Quickly, he turned around and found two men standing behind him. On the left stood a tall, grey-haired man of about sixty, who Bradie recognized immediately from pictures on the internet as Chief Huntsman.

According to his biography on the department website, Chief Huntsman had been with the department for thirty-five years, which was long enough to build up quite the reputation. Under his leadership, the department had seen the highest arrest and conviction rates it had in decades, but, over that same period, its officer transfer rate was also the highest in the nation. In Detroit, it seemed that an officer either flourished or folded. Despite his reputation, however, the Chief carried himself with a friendly, relaxed manner, his soft face making him look more like the crazy, but favorite, uncle who gets unbelievably drunk at every birthday party than a hard-nosed, police chief.

Next to him stood a much younger, fresh-faced officer who wore a smug expression that told Bradie all he needed to know; he was a pretty boy, know-it-all, who thought he was top dog because he graduated at the top of his class.

Chief Huntsman smiled and offered a welcoming hand to Bradie, saying, "We weren't expecting you for another few hours."

Taking his hand and shaking it firmly, Bradie replied, "I thought it best to get an early start on my first day. You know, brand new city, brand new start. Might as well hit the ground running."

"That's what I like to hear!" the Chief beamed. "It's great to meet you, Bradie. I've heard so much about you. Especially about what you did for that poor girl in L.A. I trust she's adjusting well to your family."

Bradie nodded.

Chief Huntsman continued, "Good! Now, I'd like to introduce you to your new partner. This is Shepard Wilcox. I have a feeling big things are in store for the two of you!"

"Nice to meet you," Bradie said, extending his hand toward Shepard as the Chief returned to his back office.

Shepard looked at Bradie's hand, scoffed and sat himself right on top of his desk. Then, resting his foot on the padding of Bradie's chair, he studied Bradie intently as he stroked the faint patch of stubble he was trying to pass as a beard.

Finally, Shepard said, "I give it six months."

*What? Until you're finally old enough to grow a real beard?*

"Until you finally break a damn smile!" Shepard exclaimed, breaking out in a fit of laughter. "Quit being so serious about everything! My god, we're detectives, not morticians! I've got just the thing to cheer you up. Let's go!"

Suddenly, Shepard vaulted up from the desk and flew past Bradie, who, dumbfounded, stood there, trying to figure out what exactly just happened.

Then, tapping Bradie's shoulder in drum-like rhythm, Shepard sang lightly, "Dead body by the lake. It'll fit right in with your whole macabre, death-of-the-party vibe."

Bradie found the ride to the lakeside to be exceedingly unbearable. For the entirety of the forty-five-minute drive to the other side of Belle Isle, Shepard tried incessantly to figure out which movie detective duo the two of them would inevitably become. Bradie had never been so happy to arrive at a crime scene in his entire life. However, when they opened the doors and stepped foot on the bank of the lake, something in Shepard changed. His cultish enthusiasm vanished, replaced by absolute professionalism.

"If you canvas the scene, I'll start interviewing the witnesses," Shepard said, but not before giving Bradie a wink to remind him that aliens had not, in fact, taken over his body.

Before surveying the scene, Bradie took a look across the lake, which shimmered with a glorious shade of orange under the setting sun that hung just above the tree line. A few feet from the lake's edge, there sat a shadow, lying as if a force field surrounded it for five feet on either side. Inside that bubble, time was frozen. Outside, a frenzy of crime scene tape, forensic analysts and police officers ran at near hyper-speed. However, nothing dared pass the five-foot barrier. As Bradie entered the field, the air changed, as though death still hovered over the black, body bag.

Slowly, he pulled back the zipper, revealing what once was the victim's face. However, now, it looked completely unrecognizable as a human being. Its skin was an unsettling combination of emerald and bronze. The flesh appeared to have been peeled away from the bone, like a serpent after shedding its skin, damaging it beyond recognition. Pulling the zipper back even further, he quickly discovered that this was not a typical drowning case. Although the torso was bloated to approximately three times its original size, he spotted a four-inch slit in the abdomen, which indicated that the victim had been stabbed, bled to death and dumped in the lake postmortem.

Although the smell that exuded from the body was putrescent, he knew this would be his only chance at identifying this John Doe. So, holding his breath to avoid the stench, he searched through the victim's pockets until he pulled out a wallet. As he opened it, he quickly found that most of the victim's credit cards and other forms of identification had long since eroded, making it impossible to read with the naked eye. However, there was a small pocket of cards in the center that remained relatively undamaged. One of these was a student ID from Wayne County Community College for one, Nicholas Maselo.

# 9

# BRED

NEW YORK, NEW YORK

*W*hen Natasha opened her eyes, she was met by the imposing figure of Alexei, looming ominously at the edge of the bed. Immediately, the breath left her lungs. As she shot out of bed and onto her feet, the floor itself seemed to warp underneath her, bending and swaying at an unnerving rhythm. Awoken by the commotion, Blair also leapt to her feet on the opposite side of the bed. Alexei, however, didn't budge. He didn't even blink. Instead, his steady, steely gaze cut through Natasha's chest, momentarily stopping her heart.

*This is it… The bells are finally tolling for me.*

Desperate, she made one, final plea. "Please, this is all my fault. I asked her to stay."

"What have I told you about curfew?" Alexei asked.

With that, the final knife plunged into Natasha's heart. She could take another beating. She could withstand another violation, but the one thing she couldn't survive was knowing she had caused Blair pain as well. She would sooner die.

Alexei approached Natasha, raising his hand to strike her

again. Lowering her head, she grimaced and awaited the blow, but it never came. Cautiously, she opened her eyes, only to find Alexei's hand hovering inches from her face and a smile spreading devilishly across his face, as though a fiendish plan was formulating deep in the recesses of his apish mind. Natasha's heart began to beat again, but this time, it thumped at a break-neck pace. Turning suddenly, Alexei planted himself directly in the center of the aisle outside of the room.

He bellowed, his voice echoing through the warehouse that was already in full swing, "Fifty dollars to watch hot, lesbian sex."

Natasha froze, unable to comprehend what she had just heard. Instantly, her lungs forgot how to breathe, and her head grew dizzy. In that moment, as her body was swallowed up by the floor beneath her, she did something she had vowed to never do again; she prayed. She prayed that every man in the warehouse that day was deaf and for time to freeze. She even prayed that she would drop dead, anything except for what now seemed inevitable.

But, her prayers went unanswered.

One by one, every man in the warehouse flocked to Alexei, eagerly handing over the money he demanded. In fact, the crowd grew so large that Alexei had to remove the curtains from the two, adjacent rooms to fit them all.

As every eye in the warehouse now trained themselves, expectantly, on them, Natasha gazed helplessly at Blair, looking for some sort of reassurance. She hoped that Blair would tell her to run, that, come hell or high water, they would run away together, even if that meant death. However, Blair shook her head sullenly.

Running out of options, Natasha looked to Alexei, praying that he would relent, but his resolve did not waver. She tried to run but was frozen solid. Her feet melted to the floor. Slowly and carefully, Blair approached her, grabbed her hand and placed it gently on her breast as she placed her own hand on Natasha's cheek.

Leaning in, Blair whispered in her ear, "We'll get through this like we always do, together."

Natasha closed her eyes as their lips met, slow and sweet, like the gentle caress of a Georgia peach. In that moment, she felt safe, more loved and cherished than she had ever been. Her clothes fell to the floor in a heap, slipping from her skin like silk, as Blair ran her hands from Natasha's stomach around to her back before lowering her onto the bed and climbing on top of her.

When Natasha finally opened her eyes, Blair was straddling her, removing her own bra. As it fell behind her, Natasha saw what looked like tar begin to ooze out of the crown of Blair's head. Starting as a single droplet, it dripped down her temple and cheek, but soon, it morphed into several streams of black, oozing sludge that ran down every side of her body. Horrified, Natasha closed her eyes as Blair laid across her body and kissed her on the lips again. Then, she felt tender kisses run down her neck and chest, like soft, cool snowflakes falling on her skin, only to melt shortly after contact. As Blair lowered her head between her thighs, Natasha opened her eyes again.

When she did, like leeches draining the life from her, she saw the seething, bubbling remnants of the tar that now resonated from Blair's body in every spot that she had kissed her. Then, looking down at her best friend, who now appeared to have been completely consumed by the mire, she watched helplessly as it devoured the only innocence she had left inside her. Although she closed her eyes again, she could no longer escape the torment. She could taste the dirt and feel the darkness creep through her bones, infecting her very blood. Everything in the world that was sacred to her had been taken away. She now knew; there was no God in this wretched place.

> *These four walls surround my flesh.*
> *Day and night, they give me no rest.*
> *Cold, black tears run down my cheeks.*
> *This all-consuming darkness has been here for weeks.*
> *A lonely sign hangs, solemn, above my head.*
> *Five ugly words are all that it says.*
> *"Freedom comes to the dead."*

Natasha sat alone on the edge of her bed, holding her head in her hands and rubbing her wrist furiously against her cheekbone in a desperate attempt to remove the black stain that seemed to inhabit her soul. Even in her dreams, it followed her, growing darker with each passing day. Like Prometheus, she was being torn apart, limb by limb, every day, simply for trying to find light in the darkness.

Alexei had quickly discovered that live, lesbian pornography was even more lucrative than prostitution. So, three times a day, he thrust Natasha and Blair center stage to pleasure the eyes of dozens of suits, sweatpants and sweaty palms. With every kiss, every touch of the hand, the black sludge grew and grew until it was the only thing Natasha could see. After a while, even the suits and sweatpants wore Blair's tar-covered face. The only solace left in her world was hidden in the pages of a small, ashen notebook she kept tucked underneath the back corner of her bed, next to her necklace. As she turned to the last page of her notebook and began to write, Blair cautiously pulled back the curtains to her room and sat on the far edge of the bed.

For what seemed like an eternity, they sat in silence, neither of them so much as breathing. Usually, Natasha found this sort of shared silence comforting, as though someone was standing with her in the eye of a hurricane, bearing her fear and pain with only the touch of their hand. This silence, however, was different. It was a quiet that burned deep within the soul, like discord between lovers or a sibling's betrayal. A hundred-foot chasm stood between them, and there was no bridge to cross. At the same time, Natasha wanted nothing more than to remain there forever but also to run away, never to return.

Suddenly, she felt the familiar feeling of Blair's soft, gentle arms wrap around her neck and hold on tight. In an instant, the distance between them closed. Every fear, every hurt melted away inside her embrace. Natasha wrapped her arms around Blair's waist and held on for dear life because, somewhere deep inside, she knew; if she let go, she would lose her forever. So, she closed her eyes, breathing in the sweet, vanilla scent of Blair's silken hair, and prepared to plunge into the depths.

Softly, Blair said, "We can face anything they throw at us, as long as we're together."

And for a moment, Natasha believed it.

Their embrace ended far too soon, like a cup of hot cocoa on a frigid, winter night. Natasha kept her eyes closed for a moment longer out of fear of what might come when she opened them. As she sat there, eyes locked shut, she told herself that the darkness wasn't real, that it was her mind trying to cope with a reality she didn't want to face. She told herself that, if she tried hard enough, she could tear it away, piece by piece, and find Blair smiling underneath.

When she first opened her eyes, that was exactly what she found. Everything was normal, and Blair was smiling at her with that bright-eyed smile that could light up a dark street corner. A wave of relief began to wash over Natasha. However, as soon as it crashed against her shore, she noticed a dark glow beneath her line of vision. She looked down, and Blair's arm was covered in dark, watery tendrils that wrapped around her skin.

In that moment, the darkness that exuded from Blair was nothing like the oozing sludge Natasha had seen before. It was as though all light within its reach simply disappeared, engulfed in a blackness unlike anything she had seen. When Natasha gazed into the streams that now covered both of Blair's arms, she saw nothing, not even a trace of existence. There was no hope, no life and soon, there was no Blair. She was completely consumed by it, and there was no tearing the darkness away. It was all there was.

Slowly, the darkness spread, enveloping the sheets that Blair sat upon. Then, it moved toward Natasha like a virus that wouldn't be satisfied until the whole world was sick. Jumping from the bed, Natasha retreated to the farthest corner of the room, hoping to escape the heaviness it put on her soul, but it followed her, consuming the bed frame and the floor in front of her. From the darkness, a black hand emerged and inched toward her, threatening to suck her into the darkness to be lost forever to the void. The dark figure that used to be Blair stood up and started toward her.

Natasha yelped, "Don't come near me!"

But the shadow didn't listen. Instead, it stepped toward her, opening its black mouth wide, and spoke in Blair's voice, "It's okay. Don't be afraid."

"Get out," she stammered.

It reached out to her and took her by the arm. Its grip was gentle, but its touch burned like an icy fire.

Natasha screamed, shaking free from its grasp, "Get away from me!"

The shadow backed away, putting its arms in front of it, and said, "You can't let them win, Natasha."

As the shadow disappeared behind the curtain, taking the

darkness with it, Natasha breathed a sigh of relief. However, the relief was short-lived because, along with the darkness, it took the only thing she ever cared about in the world. So, she sat on the edge of the bed, feeling the weight of isolation press against her chest. Instinctively, her hand moved to the place where the shadow had held her. It was cold to the touch. Looking down at her arm, she saw black tendrils in the shape of a hand, bubbling and festering from inside her skin.

In that moment, every atom in her body dedicated itself to a single purpose: survival. Like a feral cat on the brink of death, she clawed desperately at the blight, trying to rip it from her skin, but it remained. Even as her skin began to burn, it remained. Even after her fingertips bled, it still remained. Finally, her strength depleted, she collapsed on her bed, defeated. She closed her eyes and tried to let herself drift off into slumber, hoping that her dreams would grant her reprieve from the darkness.

But they did not, for the darkness followed her, even into her dreams.

∼

*Indianapolis, Indiana*

KAYDE COULDN'T MOVE. HE STARED OUT THE WINDSHIELD AT THE world outside his car that seemed to be nothing more than a faint blur, with his hands glued to the steering wheel and his back fused to his seat. In that moment, nothing about his existence seemed to make sense. Though he was on the verge of hyperventilation, he couldn't breathe. Even as his body felt like it was racing at a hundred miles per hour, he was unable to move, frozen in solid ice. He was a living, breathing contradiction.

"What do I do?" Kayde asked.

"You run," Violet replied, her head, again, in his crotch. "You forget any of this ever happened, and you run."

She was right; he could run. However, he knew that, if he didn't take the leap, if he didn't descend into hell to go after Blair, no one would. Then, she would be forever lost to the depths. But, at the same time, he also feared that the underworld would swallow him whole, damning them both to an eternity of torment. Like Orpheus, he hovered above the precipice of hell itself, contemplating whether or not to begin his descent.

*If I don't do this, will I be condemning her a second time?*

"I will bear her away from Hades," Kayde whispered, his voice trembling. "For she was taken before her time."

"You don't have to do this," Violet said.

However, Kayde remained entranced, unmoving, unspeaking, simply staring ahead as though he was hypnotized.

Determined to break his trance, Violet sat up, took Kayde by the shoulders and, shaking them, repeated, "You don't have to do this."

"Why do you even care?" Kayde asked as he continued to stare out the window.

"To be honest, because I like you. There aren't a lot of people left in the world I can say that about, and I don't want that to change. I don't want to see you be here long enough to become something you're not. This life has a way of turning decent people into monsters."

"But she's my sister."

"You know what? I changed my mind. Let's go to the cops. Together. Maybe I was wrong. Maybe they can help."

Kayde shook his head. "No, you were right. They won't do anything but sit on their asses, like they have for the past year, and tell me, again, that she ran away. They didn't believe me before. Why would it be any different now? Someone else has to find her."

"But why does it have to be you?" Violet asked, her tone growing desperate.

"Because it's my fault!" Kayde exclaimed, finally fixing his eyes onto Violet.

As he did, his eyes burned with a fire so hot that it could have melted the gates of hell itself. He had never been so determined about anything in his life, and nothing was going to get in his way. Looking into his eyes, Violet's resolve melted away. Then, she closed her eyes, took a deep breath, and told Kayde everything he needed to know.

*He dared to go down to Styx, through the gate of Taenarus, also, to see if he might move the dead.*

Fort Harrison Park used to be the place Kayde would go to clear his mind. He often took walks there, inspired by the beauty and grandeur of the natural world around him. He could spend hours by the water, reading poetry, stories or whatever was currently stimulating his creative mind. It was one of the few places where he could escape, finally feel free to be himself.

However, this time, everything was different. It was as if Persephone had returned to the underworld, taking nature's joy with her. The trees that once glowed with brilliant jade were now pale and grey. The water that, before, flowed with a grace and majesty that aroused his imagination now seemed to be stagnant and diseased. Everything that usually filled him with awe and wonder now filled him with dread. As he overlooked his wooden cage, Violet's instructions echoed through the canyons of his mind.

*First, you'll need to pick your target.*

Kayde stood with the rising sun to his back and surveyed everything that lay before him. Fort Harrison Park was often a frenzied place when the city was awake, but few ventured out early enough to see the sun pass the tree line, making it the perfect time to strike. As he gazed across the water, one girl in particular caught Kayde's eye. She was ravishing, with all the features of a supermodel: long, blonde hair, flawless skin, legs as long as the Empire State Building and a tight, pink shirt and white miniskirt that cleverly towed the line between fashionable and flirtatious. She was perfect.

*But make sure she's not too pretty. That's how you get caught. You have to find the kind of girl who's pretty but doesn't know it.*

Moving on, he searched the area again, trying to locate another target. On the edge of the water, he saw a young girl with her head buried in a book, her hair pulled back into two, girlish pigtails. Her face was speckled with acne, and she wore a pair of large, turquoise glasses. At first, Kayde was tempted to dismiss her as a lost cause, but, studying her for a moment longer, he began to see those features for what they truly were: distractions.

So, piece by piece, Kayde stripped away the surface and looked deeper. There, he saw hair that shone with brilliant amber, contrasting beautifully against her fair skin, and underneath her sweatshirt and baggy sweatpants, he saw gorgeous curves. She was the type of girl who would spend her whole life being told she was Medusa when, in fact, she was Aphrodite in disguise. Discreetly, he made his way toward the water's edge, eventually sitting in the grass a few feet away from her. As he looked out across the water, waiting for the right moment to speak, his nerves crept up on him. His throat became dry. His muscles grew tense, and sweat dripped from his brow. Finally, he turned to her.

*Take an interest in her.*

"What are you reading?" he asked.

It was as if, at the exact moment he opened his mouth to speak, a swarm of butterflies flew into his mouth and made their home in his stomach. Suddenly, words, which were usually his bread and butter, became harder to find than common sense in a high school auditorium.

Aphrodite lowered her book, looked at him, tilted her head to the left and blinked three times in rapid succession. "Just a book on aerospace engineering," she replied.

He opened his mouth to speak, but no words came out.

*Compliment her.*

"I like your eyes," Kayde stammered. "They're very... green."

He could feel the water pouring through the grapefruit-sized hole in his boat, but he wasn't about to abandon ship yet.

*Gain her trust.*

"I'm a police officer," he said.

*But most importantly, be yourself.*

At this point, Aphrodite's head was tilted at a perfect, right angle, her eyes blinking at a furious pace. Without taking her eyes off of Kayde, she closed her book, stood to her feet and backed away cautiously until she was gone.

That did not go according to plan.

*You're a nice guy. Use that to your advantage.*

As he continued through the park, trying to regain his confidence, a faint, whimpering sound caught his attention. Atop a nearby bench, a girl sat with her head in her hands, sobbing. Though she tried to remain unnoticed, the sorrow that exuded from her very being, escaping through her whispered cries, made her impossible to ignore. Sitting beside her on the bench, Kayde attempted to console her.

"Hey, what's wrong?" he asked.

"Leave me alone!" the girl replied, her voice muffled by the hands that still covered her face.

"But I'd hate to leave such a sad, beautiful girl all alone," he said. "Why don't you tell me what's wrong, and we'll see if I can't wipe those tears off your face?"

"What do you care?! All you men ever do is make a girl feel like she's on top of the world so you can knock her back down again, hoping she breaks from the fall."

"Is that why you're crying? Did someone hurt you?"

She nodded sadly.

"I bet that guy," he continued. "The one who hurt you, is sitting at home right now, all alone, drowning his sorrows in a bowl of Chunky Monkey because he realizes that he had a precious ruby in his hand but let it slip away."

At this, the girl lowered her hands and looked up at Kayde. She wiped the river of tears from her eyes and finally cracked a smile. "You mean it?" she asked.

"Now, there's that beautiful smile!" he exclaimed. "Of course I mean it! That guy doesn't know what he's missing. I, for a fact, know plenty of guys that would pay for the chance to get in bed with a girl as beautiful as you."

Open mouth, insert foot.

*Smack!*

Kayde felt like he got hit by a runaway train as her hand collided with his cheek. She left in a huff, smacking him in the other cheek with her purse as she left.

His journey to the underworld was quickly becoming harder than he had imagined. He thought Orpheus must have had it easy. At least he had been blessed by the gods with the gift of music, a song that was able to sway the heart of the Lord of the Damned. Kayde couldn't even talk to a girl without hitting a sour note. He was getting desperate.

*If all else fails, abduction is always a valid option.*

So, Kayde sat in the bushes along the jogging trail, like a hunter in his blind, waiting for the perfect opportunity to strike. After a few moments, a lone, female jogger made her way up the path. She was the perfect target: tall, brunette and most importantly, not paying attention to her surroundings. Instead, her eyes were focused straight ahead, and the loud, rock music that blasted from her noise-cancelling headphones would serve to mask his movements beautifully.

As she passed, Kayde sprung out from behind the bushes. Wrapping both of his arms around her neck, he dragged her into the woods, where he thought he would easily overpower her. However, as soon as their feet hit the leaves, she regained her balance and elbowed him firmly in the stomach. Then, she grasped him by the wrist, and, in one, smooth motion, flipped him over her back and flat onto his. Hitting the ground with a dramatic crash, he let out a whimper and a cough, and he heard what he was convinced was the sound of his spine breaking from the impact. As he writhed in pain on the ground, the jogger grabbed her headphones, which had fallen during the struggle, and bolted off, heading for what he assumed was the nearest police station.

Once the pain subsided, Kayde limped back to where he had begun, on top of the bridge. Immediately, doubt and despair overtook him. He was running out of options. Although he had done everything Violet told him to do, nothing had worked. Distraught, he rested his head on the bridge railing, locked both hands behind his head and prayed that someone would come along and put an end to his misery.

Just then, he heard a voice whisper, "Hey man, you look like you could use a pick-me-up."

Kayde lifted his head off the railing just in time to see a young man in a black hoodie and sunglasses slide him a small, plastic bag, which held a small needle and a pile of snow-like powder.

"This, here. This be magic sugar," the man continued. "One hit of this shit, and all your worries will fade away. You could literally be on fire, and it'd be like a frickin' day at the beach."

Taken aback, Kayde stuttered, "No, I... Uh - I'm not interested."

"Listen, man," the hoodie whispered, peering around him anxiously. "I'll tell you what; take this as a free sample. If you like it, I'll be here tomorrow. Same time. There's plenty more where that came from."

Before Kayde could respond, the man was gone, without a trace. As he looked down at the "magic sugar," surprisingly, it began to tempt him. Never in his life had he thought there would be a time when he would think about using, but in that moment, the thought seemed moderately enticing. However, thinking better of it, he took the bag and placed it in his pocket, as to not pollute the water supply or leave temptation for someone else. He figured he would simply throw it in the trash when he got home.

After all, he was already going to hell. Why should he offer the Devil a handbasket too?

That night, he couldn't sleep. Every time he closed his eyes, all he could see was Blair, engulfed in flames and screaming his name. It was unbearable, like his own, personal hell. Even when his eyes were open, he could hear her screams echo in his ears, accusing him, questioning him, torturing him.

*Are you even trying?*

*Do you want to find me?*

*You're a failure.*

*You're worthless.*

As the clock struck three, he couldn't take it anymore. He needed a distraction. Thankfully, Theresa never went to bed before four in the morning and was always up for a late-night stroll. So, he called her, and they met at the site of his failure, which was only a few blocks from her house.

Any other night, the park would have looked magical, inspiring even. The moon, which hovered high above the tree line, cast a dim glow on the canopy above them, like a heavenly shadow. Under the bridge, the lake shimmered brilliantly, reflecting the radiance of the clear, starry sky as fireflies danced above the surface of the water, basking in the moonlight. It was a beautiful sight, but Kayde couldn't help but feel a sort of mockery in its audacious beauty, like it was marking the entrance to a glorious, new world that could be his, with Blair, if only he wasn't such a failure and a coward. For the entirety of their two-mile-long walk, he didn't say a word. Instead, he stared off into the darkness, drowning in his guilt and doubt. Finally, Theresa broke the silence.

"What's got you so damn chatty this evening?" she teased. "Do you do this a lot? Call a girl at three in the morning, only to go all Silence of the Lambs on them?"

"I found out what happened to Blair," he replied sullenly, his eyes fixed on the horizon.

"Shit..."

"No, it's not that. She's alive."

"Seriously? Did you tell the cops?"

"They already knew. They already knew everything."

"You're shitting me," she said.

"She was working as a prostitute at The Eclipse," he explained.

"Blair wouldn't do that," she fumed.

"I tried to tell them, but they didn't believe me. And when I went there to find her, she was already gone."

"Where the hell is she?!"

"I don't know," Kayde sighed.

"Then find her and bring her back!" Theresa snapped.

He didn't respond. The truth of the matter was that he didn't know if he could do what was necessary to find Blair, and he was scared, scared of who he might hurt, of what he would have to do and who he would have to become. And even if he wanted to, he didn't know if he could do it. It wasn't in his DNA. Entering that world required bravery and strength, two things he didn't have. The lot had fallen to him, but he couldn't shake the feeling that it was meant for someone else, someone better.

Theresa stopped in her tracks. Turning to Kayde, she slapped him across the face, causing him to double back in pain and shock. Then, she grabbed him by the face and stared him in the eyes.

"Quit being such a pussy!" she said. "No one else is going to find Blair, so it has to be you. Don't you dare hesitate! If a wall rises up in your path, knock it the hell down. If someone gets in your way, take them the hell out. Obstacles aren't put in your path to keep you from moving forward. They're put there to test your resolve. If you give two shits about Blair, you will find her and bring her back, whatever it takes. Do you understand?"

Her words struck like lightning inside his soul, illuminating the path that lay before him. Suddenly, everything became crystal clear. He turned to Theresa and wrapped his arms around her neck, holding her in his embrace as tears began to stream down his face.

"I think I do," he whispered in her ear. "I think I finally understand what I have to do. Thank you, Theresa. Thank you for everything."

Then, he took the needle he had been concealing in his palm and plunged it into Theresa's jugular, injecting a mixture of cocaine and sleeping pills into her bloodstream. Instantly, her eyes grew wide. She looked up at Kayde in confusion as a glossy film covered her iris.

"Wh-what are you doing?" she gasped as her knees began to buckle, sending her crashing into his arms.

He looked her in the eyes, as she began to fade into unconsciousness, and replied, "Exactly what you said: whatever it takes."

# 10

# CORNERED

## DETROIT, MICHIGAN

"So, what do you think?" Shepard asked as he pulled his car along the curbside. "Tough guy detective from the Bronx who's spent one too many years undercover or clean-cut, good guy with a hint of playboy swagger?"

Bradie rolled his eyes. "Is this really the right time?"

"It's always the right time for character exploration," Shepard said, giving Bradie a playful shove. "Come on! Lighten up a bit, will you? We're living the dream!"

"The dream" was certainly not the way Bradie would have described their investigation of Nick Maselo's death to this point. So far, it had been almost exclusively made up of crying family members, old, high school friends who hadn't seen him in years and middle schoolers he occasionally played Call of Duty with. The only workable lead, albeit a long shot, was that two of Nick's acquaintances had heard from a friend that he may have been friends with or, at least, had occasionally been seen in same general vicinity as Los Hermanos: a local street gang known mostly for growing the best weed in Detroit. For all intents and purposes, that was their only chance at finding Nick's killer.

The old house they pulled beside, the den of Los Hermanos, looked as though an earthquake had shaken its foundation to the core before tornadoes and lightning had simultaneously torn through its frame. Its fence gate had been ripped from its hinges, leaving behind an empty space that had yet to be filled, and the front steps were littered with tiny craters where water damage had caused the wood to warp and creak under a person's weight. On both sides of the house, its once chestnut exterior was faded and cracked, leaving its bare wood exposed. Even the roof had succumbed to the elements as nearly half of its shingles were either missing or out of place. It was a wonder that the house could manage to support the weight of the seven tattooed, Hispanic thugs who were smoking on the front porch. Bradie was convinced that if a butterfly was to land on one of their noses, the whole thing would likely come toppling over.

Stepping onto the asphalt, Shepard yelled at the thugs in a horrendous, New York accent, "Hey assholes! Detroit PD! Any of you know-"

Before Shepard could finish, they were gone, leaving behind only a cloud of smoke. Running in every direction, they leapt over fences and bounded around the house.

"Come on, guys!" Shepard exclaimed. "My accent was bad, but it wasn't that bad!"

Leaping back into the driver's seat, Shepard started the car while Bradie took off on foot. As Bradie rounded the right side of the house, he saw a thug struggle to hoist himself over the back fence. Immediately, Bradie sped up, determined to make up ground. Reaching the back corner of the yard, he hopped slightly to the left, planted his foot on the center bar of the side fence, grabbed the top of the back fence with his hands and launched himself well over the clearing.

When he landed, he was fifteen feet behind his target. Then, the chase began. The runner darted left, hopping another fence and darting across the neighbor's yard before ducking under a clothesline and flinging its contents into the air as he passed. Following, Bradie dodged to and fro, weaving past each airborne projectile with ease, but by the time he regained line of sight, the man had vanished. Bradie zipped around the nearest corner, trying, to no avail, to locate him. It was as if he had evaporated into thin air.

Just then, Bradie heard a faint rustling from the bushes behind him. Half a second later, the gangbanger leapt from his hiding place and struck Bradie in the back of the skull, sending him face first into the sidewalk. He got up as quickly as he could, but it was too late. The thug was already thirty yards away, crossing the intersection onto the next street over. By the time Bradie would have been able to cross that street, the runner would have been long gone. He watched helplessly as the man crossed the street, looking back with a devilish smirk. Then, he turned his head back to make his escape, and...

*Slam!*

He ran headfirst into the open door of Shepard's car. Somehow, whether by premonition or analysis, Shepard had predicted exactly where the path of their chase would lead and arrived precisely at the right time to open his car door into the thug's face. Shepard exited his car, looking as though he had just won Olympic gold.

"That was sick!" he said as he stood the thug up and sat him on the hood of his car. "I can't believe that actually worked!"

Bradie chuckled, shaking his head as he made his way across the street, "Good work. You're cleverer than they give you credit for."

"I'm a regular Sherlock Holmes," Shepard said with a smile.

"I wouldn't go that far," Bradie laughed before turning his attention on the thug. "Now, as for you..."

"Don't shoot me, cerdo," the gangbanger mocked in a thick, Hispanic accent. "I ain't done nothing wrong."

"Then why did you run?" Bradie asked.

The man smiled with a cocky sort of smile that made Bradie want to knock the teeth out of his mouth, not that he had any left worth keeping. Most of his teeth were yellow, verging on dark brown from plaque and decay. He was the sort of guy that thought he was all that because he had done a few sit-ups at the local penitentiary while doing time for possession. Below his left eye, he bore three teardrop tattoos, supposedly signifying the number of people he had killed, but his hands told a different story. They were delicate, well-manicured and looked like they had never seen dirt or a hard day's work in their lives. In the end, this thug was all bark and no bite, like a Chihuahua at a dog kennel. He talked a big game. However, once the big dogs came out to play, he was the type that would inevitably run into a corner and hide.

"Hey!" the Chihuahua yipped. "What you want me to do when esta puta comes up in my business, yelling like he's some badass? You can't be too careful as a minority these days with you pieces de mierda. Never know when you gonna get shot."

Bradie puffed out his chest and stared furiously at the thug with a glare that would have raised the hairs on a snake. He pulled Nick's ID from his pocket and shoved it in the Chihuahua's face.

But, the Chihuahua shook his head. "Hermano, if you think I'm gonna rat on Little Nicky, you got the wrong cholo."

"Little Nicky's dead, hermano," Shepard said. "We were thinking you might've done it, seeing how squirrelly you're acting."

Immediately, the Chihuahua's head dropped. The news

came as a shock to him, and it broke through his resistance. After crossing himself in mourning, he sighed and told them everything they wanted to know. "Little Nicky," as they called him, had run with Los Hermanos on and off for a couple of years. He was never really into the gang scene, but he stuck around because he enjoyed hanging out and having a few smokes with the guys. As far as any of the Hermanos knew, he was a friendly guy who never had any enemies.

Then, one day, as they were on the front porch, smoking a few joints as usual, a woman approached them with a job making deliveries for her small business. Past that point, the details were extremely vague, except that Nick had jumped at the opportunity.

"I ain't heard from Little Nicky since," the Chihuahua continued. "Except that, 'bout a week later, una chica bonita showed up on our front porch as a gracias for our cooperation."

"What do you mean?" Bradie asked.

The thug smirked. "Es tu estupido, puta? You know, una gracias. A thank you. A gift. Una chica to do whatever we wanted with."

There it was: his breakthrough. After weeks of hearing nothing but bad news from Loman, he finally had his first bread crumb on the trail he hoped would lead to a way to keep his promise to Anna. He had to press for more information.

"Where did she come from?"

"No se, hermano. She didn't tell. I didn't ask."

"You have to know something!" Bradie yelled. "Just think!"

But, the gangbanger shook his head, insisting, "That's it, amigo. All I know."

*Did his eye just twitch?! He's hiding something.*

All of a sudden, everything was red: the Chihuahua's face, the car, the sidewalk. Even Bradie's hands were stained with scarlet. He felt like a bull in a china shop, and he was about to demolish the Great Wall itself with the fury that now consumed him.

"What are you hiding?!" Bradie growled, slamming his fist into the car hood.

At this point, Bradie was two inches from the gangbanger's face and one word away from removing his head from his neck. Before he could, however, Shepard grabbed Bradie by the shoulders and pulled him away, motioning for the Chihuahua to leave.

Furious, Bradie broke from Shepard's grip. "What the hell are you doing?!" He barked.

"Saving you from months of lawyers and paperwork," Shepard answered. "What's gotten into you?"

Suddenly, Bradie snapped back into reality and said, "Nothing. His story just reminded me of something. That's all."

Another promising lead led to another dead-end, and they were back where they started.

That night, Bradie couldn't sleep, which was beginning to seem like a pattern for him. So, instead of lying in bed for the whole night, he sat on the couch, intently studying the remaining contents of Nick's wallet. It wasn't much, but it was the only evidence he had: a school ID, a subway card, a health insurance card, some loose change and a laminated picture of a blonde, bikini model lying seductively on a sandy beach.

As he continued to stare blankly at the evidence, Bradie felt like a car door had just been slammed in *his* face, sending him back to square one with nothing but a name and nothing solid to prove that Nick Maselo was anything more than a normal, college student.

He was about to head back to bed when Anna came down the stairs. As she turned toward the kitchen, the light from the living room caught her eye.

"What are you still doing up?" she asked.

"I could ask you the same question, young lady," Bradie replied.

Leaning against the kitchen counter, she giggled, "Don't change the subject on me. What were you doing?"

"Working on a case. No matter what I do, I can't seem to figure it out."

"Can I help?"

Walking over and placing Nick's effects on the counter, he sighed, "I got these off a body some fishermen found in the lake. It's not much, but it's all I have."

She studied the cards for a moment before picking up Nick's student ID. Tilting her head to the left, she intently studied his half-faded picture on the front. Then, as if she was simultaneously grieving his loss and trying to understand the contents of his soul, she ran her thumb slowly along the curvature of his face. After repeating the process three more times, she set the picture down and began the procedure all over again with the picture of the model. Her thumb carefully mapped the outline of the model's slender body until it reached her thigh. Then, after stopping for a few seconds, Anna squinted as she brought the picture to her eye.

"This name," she said. "I've heard it before."

Bradie leaned in and looked at the spot where Anna's thumb had stopped. In speckled, gold letters so faint that they almost blended in with the sandy beach behind the model were written the words:

Leon Tarsus Modeling.

Anna continued, "One of the girls I was kept with, Ebony, always wanted to be a model, but her parents never supported her or her dream. They said modeling was nothing more than a glorified sex trade, and she hated them for that. One day, when she heard about a casting call down the street from her apartment complex, run by a man named Leon Tarsus, she begged her parents to let her go. But, they refused, even going so far as to ground her to her room so she couldn't leave. But, when has that ever stopped a girl from doing what she wanted? However, that casting call earned her nothing but a one-stop ticket into 'the life.'"

Suddenly, something clicked, a vague memory that was crammed in the recesses of Bradie's mind came flooding back into his consciousness. Only this time, it was completely clear. He closed his eyes and tried to remember.

*A couple weeks ago, I was walking into the precinct on my first day, my mind running in circles. Officers passed on every side, but I paid them no attention. Instead, my head was down, and my mind was blank. Everything faded away, except for one thing. At the front desk stood a young girl with hair that shimmered like gold and legs like two, marble pillars that rose majestically out of the earth. She looked like Helen of Troy but without the fabled poise. Instead, she was frantic, and her words were jumbled. Despite this, three words rang out above the rest.*

*Modeling. Kidnapped. Tarsus.*

A quick Gaggle search confirmed what Bradie already knew; Leon Tarsus Modeling had held a casting call in Detroit at the abandoned, Goddard and Gafley warehouse two days before his first day. There was no time to waste. Before he had a chance to tell his legs to move, he was out the door and inside his car. As he turned the ignition, Anna hopped into the passenger seat.

"I'm coming too," she said.

"It's better if you don't," Bradie replied. "I don't want to make you relive anything you'd be better off forgetting. I just want your nightmares to end. Your counselor said-"

"I don't care what the counselor said. Neither you nor she can protect me from the nightmares; I already lived them. They're a part of me. I can't live as though the past never happened, especially when there's a chance I can help. Besides, like you said, you can't do this without me."

"I don't think those were my exact words."

"They were, and I plan to hold you to them."

Bradie laughed. Looking at Anna for a moment, he marveled at her resilience and strength. She had walked through the fires of hell, but the flames had not consumed her. Instead, they had refined her, like gold.

*Maybe this is her justice. Maybe the nightmares only continue because she feels helpless, unable to do anything for the others who have lived through the same horrors she did. This could be her way to end the nightmares, once and for all.*

"Alright, let's go," he replied.

As they approached the Goddard and Gafley warehouse, Bradie thought it looked like the kind of place kids would dare each other to so much as step foot inside. On either side of the main entrance, its window panes were shattered, and large chunks of its dirty, mold-ridden brick façade were torn away from the building and lying on the ground below. Even the street lamps outside the building refused to shine in fear of the monsters that might loom in the shadows.

Cross your heart, hope not to die.

The rusted, metal door's banshee-like scream careened off the damp, cement walls, filling the entire space as they entered the main room. Throughout the warehouse, the air smelled rotten, like the cold, wet breath of a beast, sending shivers up and down Bradie's spine as they lit their torches. Though they saw no monsters in the darkness, the two, small streams of light that danced throughout the empty room did nothing to alleviate the pounding inside his chest.

After thirty minutes, it felt like he had reached another dead-end. The warehouse was empty, apart from a generous collection of mold, mildew and dead rats in every corner. As he leaned against the wall, frustrated and exhausted, an overwhelming wave of hopelessness rushed over him. He was about to give up for good when he heard Anna's voice break through the silence.

"I think I found something."

Immediately, Bradie rushed to her side. In her hands, she held a small piece of paper. Its edges were jagged and its surface crumpled, like it had been hastily torn and then tossed to the side. On its front, there was only a name and an address written in large, sloppy letters:

PAUL CROSS: 19503 LYNN ROSE RD.

Though it wasn't much, it was something, something they could use.

# 11

# BRIDLED

DETROIT, MICHIGAN

*S*aturday mornings were Paul's favorite part of the week, when he and Elle finally had the chance to spend some quality time together. Between work, school and early bedtimes, they hardly managed to see each other during the weeks, but Saturday mornings meant freedom. They meant creativity, and, most of all, they meant puppet shows. At precisely 7:45 a.m., every Saturday, Paul was required to be front row for Crossroads: A Week in the Life of Eleanor Cross.

That Saturday's episode was a brilliant blend of drama, action, comedy and music, which, as always, starred Elle as the self-proclaimed "most amazing six-year-old in the universe." After narrowly escaping after rescuing Thomas Pencilson from the hands of Little Suzie Rotten, Elle now found herself imprisoned at the dining room table by the villainous Mommy, who was attempting to kill her by force-feeding her broccoli.

"Ha, ha, ha!" Mommy cackled. "I have you now! Now you will be forced to eat broccoli and perish!"

"No!" Elle screamed. "I won't do it, and you can't make me!"

Just then, when all seemed lost, the heroic Daddy appeared. Standing directly between Elle and the dastardly villain, he stared Mommy in the eyes and dared her to make a move. Paul gripped the edge of his seat. Could Elle be saved? Could Daddy finally gain the upper hand against the evil Mommy? He had never won a battle against her before. Would this finally be his day?

As they approached the climax of the story, Rebecca appeared in the doorway behind Paul and asked, "How come I always have to be the villain?"

Paul turned around and whispered, "Because she's going for realism. Come on, can you honestly picture me being the bad guy?"

"Plot twist," she chuckled. "By saving her from Mommy, you doom her to a life of poor nutrition. Who's the bad guy now?"

"Oh, I'll show you just how bad I can be," he said with a wink.

Elle, who, during their brief intermission, had stepped out from behind the stage and stood in front of them, both hands on her hips, cleared her throat emphatically and announced, "Excuse me, but there is no talking during the show!"

Rebecca apologized silently and sat down next to Paul. Bringing her hand to her mouth, she zipped it closed and threw away the key.

Then, taking him by the hand, she leaned in close and whispered softly in his ear, "You better."

Once the audience finally settled down, Daddy continued the show in a dramatically low voice, "Have no fear, young lady! I will eat your vegetables so you don't have to!"

"No!" Mommy screamed as she withered away. "You can't! Think about the nutrition!"

"My hero!" Elle exclaimed, wrapping Daddy in a giant, bear hug.

Finally, the curtain fell, and the crowd roared with applause. As the performers came out from behind the stage to take their final bows, the audience whistled and cheered with exuberance. Rushing the stage, Paul hoisted Elle onto his shoulders and ran her around the room for a victory lap. Rebecca cheered wildly as Elle waved to all her adoring fans, her face glowing with joy. In that moment, Paul thought nothing in the world could be better.

Saturday mornings were made of pure magic.

Saturday afternoons, however, were made of something different. They were gritty, dirty and held together by cheap glue, a sobering blend of gratitude, accomplishment and pain when Paul and Elle helped out at Rebecca's homeless shelter. Every week at the shelter, Paul was hit smack-dab in the face with a reality he was grateful his family would never have to endure. The hardest part of it all was having to watch families with young children walk through the shelter doors with nowhere else to turn, knowing there was nothing more he could do for them except give them a hot meal and hope for the best.

The shelter itself was a beautiful place, a safe haven for the less fortunate. Rebecca had done a phenomenal job turning what used to be a notorious crack den, scheduled to be demolished by the city, into a place where the destitute and downtrodden could feed their bodies, minds and souls. It was something Paul had always admired about Rebecca, one of the things that made him fall in love with her in the first place: her uncanny ability to see things that others couldn't. Where others saw despair and hopelessness, she saw a phoenix, destined to rise from the ashes. For every criminal, for every delinquent, for every "too-far-gone," she saw a story that had not yet been finished.

Every inch of the shelter reflected that theme: a story yet unfinished. Throughout the building, the walls were painted the brightest of blues to represent the open sky, an endless field of opportunity that lay before them. She wanted, above all else, for everyone who entered to feel like they were walking on air. That way, when they re-entered the real world, they knew they were destined to soar. On the center wall, written in flowing, white cursive, as the only clouds in the otherwise clear sky, read these words;

---

"And I am sure of this, that He who began a good work in you will bring it to completion."

---

Every day of the week, excluding Sundays, on top of the plates upon plates of food that were passed out, every person who walked through the shelter doors, no matter what they were looking for, was offered a free class so they could gain a knowledge or skill they could use to better themselves. This particular Saturday, as a testament to the transformation Rebecca had brought to the shelter, the building that was once a place for druggies to score was now a place where they could come to be set free from their addictions.

The Narcotics Anonymous group was led by a man named Georgie. He was a frail, grey-haired man with a long, scraggly beard, and he was another of the infinite examples of how Rebecca never gave up on anyone. Back when he was still running the crack den, she had tried to befriend Georgie. At first, she failed spectacularly. In fact, he couldn't stand her and resisted every attempt she made to reach out. However, when the den was shut down by the city, his entire life crashed around him.

A few weeks later, Rebecca found him in the alley behind the shelter, half-dead and shaking from withdrawal. Never one to give up on anyone, though, she brought him inside and nursed him back to health, spending several nights at his bedside to make sure he wanted for nothing. Although getting clean hadn't yet found him a home or a steady job, it had given him joy. Those days, George couldn't even walk into a room without bringing a smile to everyone's face.

"Paulie boy!" Georgie said as he entered the shelter that day.

"My man!" Paul replied, grabbing Georgie by the hand and wrapping him in a friendly hug. "Where have you been all my life? I haven't seen nearly enough of you lately."

"Well, who's fault is that? You know my door's always open for you, buddy," Georgie said with a smile.

Paul laughed, "You don't even have a door."

"That's why it's always open!"

Once everything was set up for the meeting, Paul nuzzled up next to Rebecca, who was sitting on the far end of the room by the kitchen door. Kissing her on the cheek, he held her hand as she rested her head on his shoulder. Then, one by one, struggling addicts came forward to tell their stories.

After each person finished their story, Georgie wrapped them in a tight, bracing hug and made it a point to remind them of how brave they were for sharing their story. This went on for about thirty minutes until a nervous, young woman, no older than nineteen, hesitantly opened the doors to the shelter, her clothes tattered and torn.

The mascara bled from her eyes from the beads of sweat that dripped from her forehead. As she raised her hands to her face to, once again, wipe the dead skin from under her nose, her long sleeves pulled back, revealing cuts on her wrists. Even tough she looked like she was hanging onto her sanity by a single, loose thread, there was something uniquely beautiful about her, like a lonely, black rose in the field of lilies. Her eyes darted nervously around the room as she hunkered down in the corner, hoping to simply remain a fly on the wall.

Paul leaned over to Rebecca and whispered in her ear, "Who's that?"

"I don't know," Rebecca replied. "She's come here every day for the last two weeks but never says a word, refusing to even make eye contact. Georgie says he sees her occasionally by the underpass, looking for a score. I can't even imagine the kind of pain it would take for someone to shut down like that."

A few moments later, Georgie called out to the dark wall-flower, inviting her to talk to the group. Instantly, her eyes grew to twice their normal size. Standing up, she took two, cautious steps toward the group as though she wanted to open up. However, when she looked at the dozens of eyes that were now set on her, panic set in, the doors flung open, and she vanished, leaving behind only a faint memory that she was there at all.

*Interesting. Very interesting.*

{}~{}~{}~{}~{}~{}~{}~{}~{}~{}

"Once you're sure you have everything you need for the job, you need to pick your target," Paul explained to Izzy as they pulled their van to the side of the road.

Looking out across the street, Paul thought that Grand River Avenue was the perfect portrait of fast-paced, American society. All along both lanes, cars flew by with no regard for their surroundings, their drivers glued to their cell phones, and across the way, every storefront and restaurant operated like well-oiled machines. People buzzed along the sidewalk in a frenzy, making it difficult to pick any one face out of the crowd. Which is exactly what made it the perfect training ground for Izzy.

It didn't take long for Izzy to find his preferred target: a leggy blonde with perfect hair, gorgeous curves and yoga pants that were one size too small or, as Izzy referred to her, "that damn, sexy bitch." Not even five seconds after he had singled her out, however, her boyfriend showed up, with take-out in tow, took her by the hand and whisked her away.

"That," Paul said. "Is precisely why 'that damn, sexy bitch' is never the target. There is always someone who will miss her."

After six more attempts, Izzy finally chose wisely: the lonely, young brunette sitting alone on the curb, simply staring into nothingness.

"Now you're getting the idea!" Paul congratulated. "If you play your cards right, she's exactly the kind of girl who might be desperate enough to take the bait."

"You want me to nab her?" Izzy asked impatiently.

"No," Paul answered. "I've got a different target in mind, someone I picked especially for today. If I'm right, she should be here any second. She'll be the lone storm cloud in the sky."

As if on cue, the Black Rose from Rebecca's shelter emerged from amidst the chaos. She stumbled across the concrete, looking just as weathered and beaten as she had at the shelter. In her hands, she held a small bag of food, which she clutched to her chest as though it was her only child. Peering around each shoulder sheepishly, she sat down on the curbside to eat. Within seconds, Florian and Izzy picked her out of the crowd. It was obvious that they saw the same thing Paul did, an allure beyond explanation.

He had to have her.

"Which game are we running?" Florian asked.

"The Kingpin," Paul answered.

Izzy said, "I take it I'm the king?"

"No," Paul said, shaking his head. "That's Florian's job today."

"How is that different from any other day?" Florian said as he stepped out onto the street with a playful salute, requiring no further instructions.

"In order to run the Kingpin," Paul explained. "Your target has to be a recovering drug addict, but you have to be careful. If she's too clean, she won't take the bait. However, if she's too dirty, the bait won't be tempting enough. So, she has to be on the mend, but at the point where her body still needs the drugs to feel normal, which is why you need to do at least two weeks' worth of research before running this con."

They watched from the car as Florian sat down next to the Black Rose. Immediately, she turned away from him and clutched her meal to her chest, guarding it as a mother lion guards her cubs. Sensing her fear, Florian reached into his jacket pocket and offered her a bag of assorted nuts. Cautious, she looked over at him, then, at the nuts, then, back at him. Finally, her hunger won out, and, quickly snatching the bag from his hand, she turned back to the street and continued with her lunch.

Paul continued, "You always start by gaining their trust. No matter what game you're running, your target will be suspicious, which means you should never show your hand until you are absolutely sure they'll take the bait."

After a moment, Florian reached into his jacket pocket again, this time, pulling out a small bag of cocaine. He showed it to her, keeping it concealed from the rest of the world behind his palm. Black Rose looked at it longingly out of the corner of her eye. With shaking hands, she set her food on the curb, her entire body drawn to her vice, but suddenly, she stopped. Then, closing her eyes, she took three deep breaths, stood up and walked away.

"It didn't work," Izzy lamented.

"Set the bait, cast the line, let the water settle," Paul whispered.

Not even a minute passed before Black Rose returned, standing behind Florian like a woman fighting a mountain. Though she fought with everything she had, she was powerless against the overwhelming urge that compelled her to stay. Florian looked up at her and smiled.

"And reel her in," Paul said.

After lifting himself off the curb, Florian grabbed Black Rose by the hand and whispered softly in her ear. Her eyes shot downward as she bit her bottom lip. She was hooked.

Paul continued, "Once she's taken the bait, you take her somewhere discreet. Thankfully for us, we have an arrangement with some local motels. We feed them extra business; they look the other way."

"Is it my turn now?" Izzy asked.

"Not yet," Paul replied. "I've got something special planned for you."

Paul patched his phone into a camera feed from the motel room he set up earlier that day so he and Izzy could observe. When the picture came into focus, Florian was getting down to business, with his tongue so far down Black Rose's throat that it looked like he was trying to pollinate. As she lifted her arms over her head, he ripped off her shirt, grabbing her roughly by the breasts. Then, he ran his tongue down her chest and stomach, nibbling gently at her belt buckle as he knelt to the floor. With one hand, Florian stripped off her belt and unbuttoned her jeans while his other hand latched onto a small briefcase under the bed skirt. Placing it on top of the bed, he opened it, and inside, there were two, identical needles and two, small tourniquets neatly packed inside.

Paul explained, "This is why you double and triple check all of your equipment before you leave the club. Both needles look exactly the same, so your target won't get suspicious. However, they couldn't be more different. The needle on the right contains a harmless concoction I mixed up at the club while the needle on the left contains the real stuff, along with a special, sleeping potion I added to it. Make sure you're one-hundred percent confident which one you have before you do anything. If you choose the wrong syringe, it could turn into a long night for you. Once you're sure, tighten the tourniquet around your arm first, so everything looks legit. Then, inject yourself with the needle on the right."

After injecting himself, Florian half-closed his eyes and fluttered them rapidly, turning his body toward Black Rose so she could witness his performance.

"Everything you do must be focused on helping her feel as safe as possible," Paul continued. "As long as you do that, she should be putty in your hands. Once you've sufficiently sold the idea that you took a hit, take the other needle in your hand and check in with your target. This is the most important part. If you don't check in, she still has a chance to cut tail and run. She has to agree to everything, or it's all for nothing."

Florian followed the formula immaculately, taking the other syringe from the briefcase and looking to Black Rose for her consent. She nodded and allowed him to wrap the tourniquet around her arm. Checking in with her a second time, to which she, again, consented, he took the unused needle and, after carefully finding the right vein, stuck it into her forearm. As the drugs entered her system, her eyes rolled back in her head. Then, she crashed down onto the bed.

"Once she's out, you throw her in the back of the truck and

ship her off to Vegas, where we have a buyer who will pay good money for someone like her. No one will even know she's gone. But, before we do any of that, there's one more, loose end to tie up. That's where you come in," Paul said.

"What do you want me to do, boss," Izzy asked.

"Her," Paul answered. "While you do anything and everything you can imagine to her, Florian and I will be putting together a special, video package as insurance for the buyer. If the drugs aren't enough to keep her hooked, he can threaten to send the video to anyone and everyone she's ever cared about. That way, she'll think twice before running away."

Without a word, Izzy dashed out of the van with his pants at his knees. Once the door shut, Paul kicked his feet up on the dash and watched as Izzy deflowered the Black Rose.

# 12

## WEEDY

NEW YORK, NEW YORK

*N*atasha lay in bed, flat on her back, awake, but with her eyes fused shut. She didn't sleep much anymore. In fact, she no longer wanted to because her dreams were filled with demons and dark visions that gave her no rest. The only solace that remained in her world was found in the darkness behind her eyelids, where she had painstakingly built an entire world and painted it pitch black. In her world, there were no people, no light and no joy, but there was also no pain and no heartache, only emptiness. Though she had once feared the darkness, she now embraced it. There was only brokenness to be found in the light, and the darkness made her feel whole. She only wished that she could stay there forever, existing only in a state of perpetual, waking sleep.

Regretfully, the moon always rose with nightfall, and with it that night, came Alexei's voice, billowing through the warehouse with an angry, ominous tone that could only mean one thing; they had brought in a new girl, which also meant that Alexei would use this moment to instill fear and dominance in his new recruit. As always, he would force all of the girls to stand, motionless, outside of their rooms with their curtains closed. If anyone so much as moved, they would be met with a severe, public beating. Occasionally, he would even pick a girl to give a beating to for no reason, simply to prove that he could.

In that moment, Natasha wanted nothing more than to remain hidden in the darkness, but she knew the light would always find her out. So, she opened her eyes and prepared herself for the night ahead. As soon as her feet hit the floor, her stomach tied itself up in knots.

*Not today. I can't be sick today.*

She tried everything she could think of to shake it off, but the knot would remain in her gut for the rest of the night.

When she made her way into the hallway, she saw Alexei standing in the middle of the aisle like a prison guard at roll call, waiting for someone, anyone, to step out of line. Behind him stood a girl who looked like she already had one foot in the grave, only proven to still be alive by the fact that she was breathing. She had been stripped of her clothes, though she hardly seemed to notice due to the glossy film that covered her eyes, which were inflamed and looked like they were bleeding scarlet. Her raven-colored hair was tangled and knotted, and her thighs bore numerous, deep-set bruises. If a breeze had flown through the warehouse door in that moment, Natasha was sure the girl would have fallen headfirst into the concrete, dead upon impact.

The last girl to emerge from her room was Blair. Natasha tried not to notice; in fact, she tried to forget that Blair even existed. Over the past, several weeks, they had hardly spoken to or seen each other, outside of their three, daily rendezvous. Despite the loneliness, however, Natasha could no longer imagine things being any different. It had simply become too painful for her to see Blair as anything more than another mark, a lace top and mini-skirt, but, in that moment, Natasha felt weak. She missed her friend. So, her gaze shifted to Blair, whose eyes were already fixed on her. For a brief second, their eyes met. Blair smiled, and for that second, Natasha's heart felt warm again. However, as quickly as that warmth had come, it disappeared, replaced by an ache that was stronger than ever. She looked away, unable to breathe.

"Girls," Alexei announced. "This is Angelica. She will be working streets with you from now on. Katrianna, I trust you will show her ropes. Get her ready for work."

As soon as she heard the name "Katrianna," Natasha looked at Blair again, who now looked like she had been run over by a steamroller. She didn't move. She didn't blink, and she didn't breathe. It was as though time itself had frozen around her. A despair had settled inside her eyes, the likes of which Natasha had never seen there before. Blair's eyes had always contained the bright glimmer of hope that broke through the darkness, but now, they were an empty void, overtaken by darkness and despair.

As soon as Alexei left the warehouse, Blair grabbed Angelica by the hand and dragged her into her room. Natasha followed, making her way into the empty room next to Blair's, which was to be Angelica's. Sitting on the far edge of the bed, she placed her ear to the curtain and listened. She had to know what had taken the light from Blair's eyes.

"Terry?" she heard Blair whisper.

Silence.

"Theresa?!" Blair whispered again.

After a brief pause, Theresa replied, "Blair...?"

All of a sudden, Natasha was overcome by the same despair she had seen in Blair. When they were still friends, Blair often told Natasha stories about what life was like before the warehouse. It was her way of reminding herself that she had an identity outside of what "the life" was trying to turn her into. More often than not, those stories included Theresa. As kids, they were inseparable, the kind of friends that could weather any storm, the type of friends that, for a time, Natasha had thought her and Blair to be. In that moment, emotions began to flood through Natasha's veins that she couldn't explain: loneliness, sadness and rage. It was as though her most prized possession in the entire world had been stolen from her. She felt replaced.

"How did you get here?" Blair asked.

"It was terrible," Theresa sobbed.

"I know."

"I couldn't breathe."

"I know."

Blair repeated, "How did you get here?"

Theresa took a deep breath before answering, "Kayde…"

"Kayde?" Blair choked.

"I couldn't believe it either," Theresa said. "He was so desperate to find you. And when he told me that he'd figured out what happened to you, that he had a way to find you but was afraid of what he would have to do, I should have known. I told him that he needed to find you, whatever the cost. It was so stupid of me. If I had only known what he was planning…

"He hugged me, and the next thing I knew, I was in a dark room with a needle in my arm, being pumped full of shit. God, you wouldn't believe how dark it is, Blair, when you're that high. I always thought it looked so damn cool when we were in school. I thought it would bring you to a world full of awesome color, but there's nothing. My body's gone, and all that's left is darkness. I don't even know what's happening to my body when I'm in that place, which I guess is a good thing. But it's so damn lonely, Blair. I don't know if I can do it again. I hate being that alone."

"You're never alone. I'm here now."

*And all that's left is darkness.*

{}~{}~{}~{}~{}~{}~{}~{}~{}~{}

Natasha stood on the street corner as the moon reached the apex of its climb, settling directly over her head. Theresa's words played over and over again in her mind, as if they were calling out to her, echoing through the canyon of her soul and growing steadily louder with each repetition until they began to change everything. Suddenly, her sadness was replaced with anticipation, her rage with yearning. The Black Hand had devastated the only escape she had from the pain, but now, it was reaching toward her, offering something new, something permanent. An eternal escape. She just had to take hold of it.

On the other side of the street stood her harbinger of freedom. Every night, while the suits and wife beaters stole their escape from her purse, others bought theirs across the street from the hoodie who lurked in the shadows. He was like a phantom, only appearing once the light had disappeared and only visible to those who knew he was there. For him, business was always steady, but even phantoms need to rest from their weary work. The moment that happened would be the moment Natasha would strike.

All life seemed to stop along the street as the moon halted halfway up its ascent. Neither person nor car passed her line of vision for what seemed like an age, meaning it was time. As she crossed the twenty feet of concrete that stood between her and freedom, an overwhelming mixture of confidence and joy swept over her. She had found her way out, and all she had to do was enter into the shadows.

Natasha approached the hoodie, who was seated against the dirty, brick wall. Hovering over him, she bent forward, placing her breasts directly in front of his face.

"I hear you're the man to go to when a girl wants a good time," she said in a breathy tone.

"Ain't you one of them whores from across the street?" the hoodie scoffed. "Do I look like a damn charity? I don't give nothin' to bitches who can't pay."

"Well, that's a shame," she replied as she grabbed his hood and pulled him to his feet. "'Cause this bitch knows how to make you feel things you ain't never felt before."

Natasha grabbed him firmly by the jaw, guiding him up off the ground, and slid her tongue down his throat as she slipped her hand down his pants. In that moment, something wild and incredible began to course through her veins. For the first time in her life, she was in control.

As his pants fell to the ground, she dropped to her knees, rubbing her body against his. Lifting up his shirt, she ran her tongue down his abdomen and began to test his manhood. She clenched her jaw tight, and he struggled for air. Then, she pulled back, causing him to shake. As she pushed him even further, his knees buckled. She could feel his strength falter, so she gripped him even harder. Then, with a sudden release, he fell back to the floor, barely able to breathe. She stood over him, victorious, and claimed her prize.

When the night was over, Natasha returned to her room. Kneeling at the edge of her bed, she took out her prize from underneath her bra. Spreading it out in seven, even lines in front of her, she smiled. It was finally over. In a few, short seconds, she would finally be free. She bent forward so she could finally take in the sweet scent of freedom. As she breathed it in, the freedom burned, rising through her nostrils.

Then, it hit her: ecstasy, release. She opened her eyes and welcomed the darkness.

*Months pass by, but death doesn't come.*
*And all I can hear is this infuriating hum.*
*My body survives on the despair that it breathes,*
*A self-loathing poison the only food that I eat.*
*The voice of my guard is filled with such hate.*
*These prison bars show the reflection of my face,*
*But all I see is an empty space.*

Blair walked toward her room at the end of yet another long night, feeling like the sky itself was pressing down on her shoulders. She couldn't understand anything that had happened that day. In an instant, her whole world had been flipped on its head, leaving her angry and betrayed, confused and dismayed. She felt the heavy weight of despair and the rush of every emotion she had worked so hard to cut from her life.

As she passed Natasha's room, she grazed her fingers across the curtain. It was so lonely without her best friend, the only person left in the world with whom she could be vulnerable, who could steady her ship in the storm. Theresa couldn't be that for her. She was damaged and broken, and it would take every bit of strength left in Blair's bones just to keep Theresa afloat. She needed Natasha now, more than she would ever know. Blair just wished that Natasha could see things the way she saw them, but she also understood what had been keeping Natasha so distant; Blair had seen the darkness too. From the moment they first kissed, it flooded her entire world until it was all she could see. However, when she looked into Natasha's eyes, she knew she wasn't alone in the darkness.

And that made all the difference.

For a moment, Blair lingered outside Natasha's room, wanting nothing more than to lie next to her and melt into her arms. Even if all they did was cry, at least they would be crying together. But, she knew it wasn't meant to be, and she couldn't cause Natasha that kind of pain. As she turned to walk away, however, she heard a faint, gurgling sound from behind the curtain. Immediately, she pulled back the curtain and found Natasha flat on her back, unconscious. Her body convulsed as thick, tan liquid bubbled inside her mouth, causing her to cough uncontrollably.

Blair sprinted to Natasha and turned her onto her side. As she did, vomit spewed onto the floor.

"Natasha?" Blair whispered urgently. "What happened? Are you okay?"

Natasha didn't respond. She was catatonic. Though her body was still alive, her mind was gone. Moving quickly, Blair propped a pillow behind Natasha to make sure she wouldn't roll onto her back. Then, slowly peeking through the curtain to make sure no one was around, she scurried to her room and ripped the sheet off her bed. Returning to Natasha's room, she knelt down on the floor to clean the retch that now festered on the floor. When she placed her hand on the bed to steady herself, she felt a strange, powdery substance lightly layer her palm. She raised it to her mouth and knew immediately what it was: cocaine.

As quickly as she could, Blair cleaned the floor with her bed sheet and snuck into the side alley to toss it in the dumpster. As she walked toward the street, a single question filled her mind; where could Natasha have gotten cocaine? It wasn't as though drugs were in steady supply in the warehouse, other than those meant for Theresa. So, Blair stood on the curbside and looked out across the street. When she did, she saw a man exit the alley across the street, clutching nervously at his jacket pocket.

Reaching the door to his car, he looked over both shoulders three times. Then, he sat in the driver's seat and gripped the steering wheel with all his might before pulling out a small bag, the contents of which he dumped into his hand. Finally, he held his hand to his nose and inhaled.

And Blair had her answer.

# 13

# REARED

INDIANAPOLIS, INDIANA

*K*ayde had done it. He was in.

       Let the descent begin.

It was Kayde's first official night on the job, or at least his first night alone. For the past, few weeks, he had only been allowed to shadow Eric on the slow nights, but now, he was in charge of the south entrance for one of the biggest concerts of the year, DC and the Moonlight Band. The task was daunting; he had to keep his girls on task, track the number of clients per girl, collect all payments and, most importantly, according to Eric, dole out punishment if necessary. So, there he stood, an unwilling slave driver, grasping hesitantly at his whip and praying he was never forced to use it. It was a brave, new world he lived in, and everything in this world was unbearably dark.

Everything, that is, except for Violet.

She was his saving grace, his guardian angel, his muse. Every night, he couldn't help but watch as she floated from client to client like a beautiful, well-oiled machine. Her technique was flawlessly poetic. Once she marked her target, she glided over to them and walked her fingers up their chest. Then, reaching their shoulders, she leaned in close, inches from their ear, and whispered softly. As the night wore on, Kayde found himself transfixed by her every movement to the point where he could feel her warm breath tickle the back of his neck, causing shivers to run up and down his spine. When he closed his eyes, he could feel her hands run up and down his body and her lips press against his.

What he wouldn't have given to take her away from that place and spend all night enjoying her caress. It would have been a dream.

Just then, a voice broke through his slumber, "What the hell are you doing?!"

Suddenly, Kayde jolted back to reality, only to find Eric staring him down like a lion, ready to pounce. He stammered, "I'm just – I'm doing what you told me to do."

"You aren't doing shit," Eric scoffed. "And you haven't been paying attention long enough to notice that your girls aren't either. Sure, Violet's working, but she's the only one. Vanessa's smoking in the parking lot. Tatianna's been in the same client's car for thirty minutes now, and Sasha's sitting behind the transformer, not even pretending to be busy. Get your shit together, or we're going to have a very different conversation at the end of the night."

As Eric watched, Kayde tiptoed toward Vanessa, who was leaning against a handicap sign in the parking lot, halfway through a lit cigarette. She took in each hit slowly as though she was trying to savor every last hint of tobacco. Only once her lungs had completely filled with its vapors did she let the smoke escape in a river's torrent of smoke.

Vanessa was the type of girl who kept those around her guessing at every turn, never sure if she was about to die of boredom or fly off the handle. Everyone who met her walked on eggshells when she was around, knowing that chances were, her reaction could simply depend on which way the wind blew. As he approached her, Kayde gulped, his palms growing sweaty. Immediately upon meeting her eyes, his pulse became as rapid as the beating of many hooves. He tried to fight off the anxiety that filled him, but he couldn't help but still feel as though the world around him was shaking.

"What the hell are you doing?" he asked in a rough, harsh tone that felt quite unnatural.

"Working," Vanessa answered, blowing a thick cloud of smoke in his face.

He tried to hold his breath as he fought through the large, grey cloud that obscured his vision. However, upon entering the fog, it felt like a hand reached out of the cloud and clawed him in the eyes. Suddenly, pain seared through his retinas and into his skull, causing him to gasp for air. When he did, the smoke entered his lungs, only to be expelled seconds later by a fit of vigorous, involuntary coughing. Once his coughing had calmed down, Kayde tried to regain his composure. Snatching the cigarette from Vanessa's hand, he flicked it to the side.

"You aren't doing shit," he said. "We are way below quota right now, and you need to get your ass moving."

"And what are you going to do if I don't?"

"You don't want to find out."

Raising her eyebrows at him, she looked him up and down. Then, lighting another cigarette, she rolled her eyes and, once again, delivered a thick cloud of smoke in his face before half-heartedly returning to work.

"At least she's working," he muttered to himself.

Before he made it halfway back to the other side of The Eclipse, a strong but pudgy hand grabbed him by the shoulder. Kayde whipped around to see a pig-faced man staring him down, his nostrils flaring back-and-forth as if he was trying to expel an evil spirit from his body.

"What kind of shithole operation are you running?" the pig huffed.

"What do you mean?" Kayde asked.

"Is that your whore?" the man replied, pointing his stubby finger at Vanessa, who looked like she had only made it to the next handicap sign before stopping to enjoy yet another cigarette.

"I guess you could say that."

"Well, someone needs to knock some sense into that bitch. When I asked her how much it cost for a ride, she nearly spit in my face, saying she didn't screw ugly bastards like me. Now, are you going to do something about that bitch, or do I need to knock that damn smirk off her face myself?"

"I'll take care of it."

"And while you're at it," the man said, pushing Kayde back. "I want you to find me another one of your whores, and I want her for free. I don't care how ugly she thinks I am. She better treat me like I'm damn Brad Pitt, or it'll be your face I'll be knocking in."

The pig wound his hooves back again to give Kayde another shove. But, as he was about to let loose, Violet's small, delicate hand took hold of his wrist, locking it in place. Her fingers strolled from the pig's hooves to his neck like a spider constructing its web. Then, taking hold of his chin, she turned him around before running her index finger down his torso.

"What kind of horrible girl would call such a beautiful man 'ugly?'" she said in a sultry tone. "Let Violet take care of you. I'll make everything better."

Taking the man by the hand, she led him toward his car, flashing a sly wink at Kayde as she left. He smiled, and in that moment, he knew that he could have never dreamed of doing this without her.

Later that night, Kayde and Violet sat alone in her room in the basement of one of the houses across from The Eclipse. Her room wasn't much to look at, consisting of only a dirty, twin mattress and a dresser full of clothes in a dark, musty room that was lit by a single, pull-string light bulb, but she had one thing the other girls didn't: a place where she could be alone. In fact, she had chosen that room, over all the others, for that very reason. The only other relief she had was found in her books, which she kept hidden under a pile of clothes in the bottom drawer of her dresser.

Over the years, she had made it a point to collect books and magazines from anywhere she could find them, even stealing them from the backs of her clients' cars on occasion. It was her way of escape. When the pressures of life weighed her down, she always had something to take her away. She could go anywhere and be anyone simply by turning a page. Story was her salvation.

"You know," Violet chuckled, after reading the closing lines of Paradise Lost. "I never liked reading before. Always thought it was boring. Now, it's the only thing that keeps me sane."

"I know how you feel," Kayde sighed.

"What's on your mind?" she asked as she closed the book and returned it to its hiding place. "You've barely said a word since I started reading."

"Nothing. I'm just thinking."

"About...?"

"Why do you do it?"

"And what is it that I do exactly?" she chuckled.

"Everything," he said. "You're always there when I need you, and you always help me, no matter what. I just can't understand why."

She shrugged, sitting back down beside Kayde. "Because you're a nice guy. In this place, that's like getting struck by lightning. Call me crazy, but I like a little electricity in my life."

"I just wish Sasha and Vanessa saw me the same way. I can't seem to get them to do anything."

"What do you see when you look at me?"

"I see an incredibly strong woman who has been through more than I could ever hope to endure and somehow, has not been broken by it. I see someone who-"

"That's it, right there!" she exclaimed. "You see me as a someone. For everyone else, I'm a something. Something to be used, abused and thrown away. You treat me like a person, not a thing. When you talk to them, you don't do that. Instead, you try to be Eric, but you're not him. You're a nice guy who would never hurt them, despite the character you try to portray. You have to be you."

"But what if I'm not a nice guy?" he asked.

Knowing that he was referring to Theresa, she answered the question he was really asking, "You did what anyone would have done."

"I'm not sure she would agree."

"There's nothing more important than family. She would understand that."

"Can you live in this world and still be a nice guy?"

"You do it with me, so it can't be impossible."

*Contradiction. Contrast.*

*Could white paint, when applied to the right canvas, appear to be black?*

Then, a realization hit him, a discovery buried deep beneath the pages Violet had just read to him. They were refrains he had read many times before, but never like this. It was a revelation.

The Tree of the Knowledge of Good and Evil, in and of itself, was a contradiction. He had always assumed that mankind's demise came solely from their knowledge of evil. However, he now understood that the knowledge of good was just as responsible. For, to know good is to also know evil. Consequently, in order for Kayde to fit in with the demons, he needed to become an angel.

{}~{}~{}~{}~{}~{}~{}~{}~{}~{}

A few days later, Eric once again put Kayde in charge of the south entrance. As he arrived, Kayde got out of his car, with six bags of Farmer Ron's burgers and a lawn chair in tow. Setting the lawn chair by the transformer, he placed the bags on top of it before calling his girls to him.

After they gathered around him, he addressed them, "We had a rough start to our relationship, and I take full blame for that. After careful thought, however, I decided you don't need another slave driver. You already have plenty of that to go around. So, I'm implementing some new rules. First, you are no longer allowed to work on an empty stomach. Tonight, regretfully, you'll have to suffer a bit.

"Since I didn't know what everyone wanted, I brought Farmer Ron's. Next time, however, if you want something else, let me know, and I'll get it for you. Second, you are required to take ten-minute breaks every two hours, no exceptions. I don't care what you do during your break. I just want you to take one. We will rotate breaks so there are enough girls working at all times. Lastly, if anyone feels threatened by a client, come to me, and I'll take care of it. You have enough to worry about every night without having to worry about your safety. New rules will be instituted as I deem necessary. Now, eat up! Work starts in twenty minutes."

Dumbfounded, the girls stared at him for a moment, unmoving, until Violet took a step forward. Kissing him on the cheek, she reached into one of the bags and pulled out a burger. Then, one by one, the girls came forward, took their meals and began to eat.

That night, they doubled their quota.

~

*Detroit, Michigan*

THE DAY HAD FINALLY COME. IT WAS THE CULMINATION OF MONTHS of hard work and preparation: Janelle's interview with Lena. Florian had meticulously crafted every, last detail to ensure that everything was perfect. Even a single, wrong move could spell disaster, but he was confident. It wasn't his first time performing this particular piece, and so far, everything had gone according to script.

Pulling his car into the parking lot at Illuminate, fifteen minutes early, as always, he began to put the finishing touches on his masterpiece. That morning, the rising of the sun had seen him penning the final lines of the monologue he had prepared specifically for this occasion. It was a beautiful blend of love and encouragement, with a light touch of fore-shadowing.

Placing his hand on Janelle's shoulder, which was trembling with anxiety, he began, "She's going to love you. I promise. I know I said that Lena can be a little rough around the edges, but you're going to blow her away, just like you did to me. You're amazing."

"You mean it?" Janelle sighed.

"Of course, I mean it!" he said. "From the moment I first saw you, I knew you had to be mine. The way you walk is angelic. The sound of your voice, hypnotizing, like a heavenly chorus. None of our girls perform with the passion you do. She has to give you the job based on your singing talent alone. But, beyond that, you're the complete package. She'd be a fool not to see that, and Lena's no fool."

With that, he kissed her tenderly on the cheek, and she smiled weakly, looking at him with wide, longing eyes that could have melted the heart of a gargoyle. Her mouth opened to speak, but no sound came out.

Suddenly, she turned away from him. "Do you love me?"

"I love you with every thought in my head, every molecule of breath in my lungs, every beat of my heart," he answered.

"But, do you love me with every minute of your hours, every hour of your days, every day of your life? Is it the kind of love that endures, no matter what, or is it the kind you only remember fondly as what used to be?"

"It's the type of love that can't be qualified, contained, or measured. It is as much a part of me as my blood. I would cease to exist without it. It will endure as long as I do."

With those words, the anxiety evaporated from her face, as though a crushing weight had been lifted from her shoulders. She smiled like a kid on Christmas morning who had received everything they ever wanted. Florian smiled too, though it was more out of self-adoration than genuine affection, believing that was the best piece of theater he had ever put on, a performance so touching that he had almost convinced himself of his sincerity. At this point, the interview was merely a formality. There was nothing that could stand in his way now.

As his hand grasped the door handle, she announced, "Florian, I'm pregnant."

A millennium passed before he mustered up the strength to take another breath. He released his grip on the door handle, his stomach in knots, like he had been hit in the gut by a George Foreman punch and grill at the same time. Nothing like this had ever happened to him before, but he knew the situation could be salvaged, somehow. He just needed to buy some time while he figured out exactly how.

"That's fantastic!" Florian exclaimed as excitedly as he could manage. "You know what, screw Lena. We are going to dinner, and we are going to celebrate!"

Those were the last words, besides "table for two" and "Chicken Caesar Salad," that he uttered for the next hour. Though his body was running on auto-pilot, his mind flew by at warp speed. Every, last synapse in his brain was pulsating at a furious pace, dedicated to a single purpose: to play out every angle, rehash every look, every word, and rewrite his masterpiece so this new plot twist didn't turn his triumph to tragedy. In that moment, he couldn't help but feel jealous of Shakespeare. At least his actors followed the script.

His options were few: cut bait and run, wait out the pregnancy or pray that it wasn't too late to bring her in. Failure, however, wasn't an option. Above all, Lena expected results. If he failed, he feared he would be cut into a million pieces and fed to his closest relatives. His mind was spinning. He couldn't think. He couldn't move, and he couldn't breathe.

"Are you sure you're okay with this, babe?" Janelle's voice echoed faintly in the far reaches of his mind.

Slowly, reality came back into focus, like waking from a terrible dream. He stared at his half-eaten plate of salad for a moment, contemplating his next move. The problem was that he didn't have one. Looking up at Janelle's eyes, however, Florian felt something behind their deep, dark waters that he had never experienced before: genuine concern and affection. Every other girl he had been with looked at him with awe and desire, like he was their paragon of perfection, their knight in shining armor who had come to whisk them away from their troubles. Their eyes were always full of need, but not Janelle's. Instead, she looked at him with eyes that knew, despite everything undoubtedly going through her mind, that in that moment, she didn't need him; he needed her.

"I'm sorry," he said. "It's a lot to take in at once, and there are so many things to figure out. But, I'm all in. Don't worry."

"You don't have to have it all figured out right now," she said. "We have plenty of time. What do you say we get out of here and do something fun? This place is too stuffy. It's making me all fidgety."

Janelle stood up and took Florian by the hand as he laid the money on the table. After leading him to his car, she removed her half-sweater and wrapped it around his eyes. Then, she slid her hand into his back pocket and grabbed his keys, but not before giving his ass a slight squeeze. Everything after that was darkness. She ushered him into the passenger's seat, and a moment later, the driver's side door opened and slammed shut quickly. A seatbelt clicked. The ignition fired, and the engine roared like a lion before settling into a quiet purr. Apart from his own breathing, that was the only sound he heard for the duration of the ride. Fifteen minutes later, the car stopped, and the engine settled down for a cat nap.

"Don't make a move unless I tell you to," she ordered.

He didn't move a muscle. There was no way he was about to disobey a direct order, especially when it was accompanied by a firm grab of his crotch. His heart began to flutter as the sound of footsteps approached his door. The door creaked open, and a soft hand inched across his shoulders, taking firm hold of his collar. Then, warm breath gently caressed his ear.

"Get out," the breath whispered.

A shiver ran down his spine as the hand pulled him out of the car and into the night air. In that moment, he didn't know whether the shiver was caused by the tickle of Janelle's steamy breath or the cool, wet breeze that encircled the car, but he didn't care. Releasing its grip on his collar, her hand slid down his arm until it latched onto his hand as she led him into the great unknown. The ground shifted beneath his feet with every step he took as a familiar, yet intoxicating, aroma filled the night air. It was the perfect blend of water, sand, strawberries and moonlight. He was hypnotized by its scent and completely under her spell.

"Stay here and don't open your eyes until I tell you too," she said.

Quickly obliging, he stopped, and the ground once again shifted beneath his feet, this time, wrapping them in a welcoming embrace. After a moment, he heard Janelle's voice beckon for him to open his eyes. When he did, he saw her standing, thigh-deep in the water, with all of her clothes sitting on the sand in front of him. Her skin glimmered in the moon-light, as though pure light emanated from within her. In that moment, Florian was convinced that she must be the goddess of the moon, Selene, herself. She turned her head toward him and reached out her hand, calling for him to journey with her into the depths.

He knew that he shouldn't, that he was losing control, but he didn't care. There was something about her, something behind her caramel eyes he couldn't explain that drew him to her. He didn't know if there would ever be a girl who could hold him in her clutches forever, but damn, if she didn't come close.

## 14

## ALPHA

DETROIT, MICHIGAN

*P*aul crouched nervously behind a rose bush with gun drawn, praying that he remained unseen. Time was quickly running out on what he knew would be his last chance. Carefully pulling the bush's thorny branches apart, he surveyed what lay before him. On both sides, two, monstrous trees stood sentry before a warped, wooden prison that was guarded by a merciless mercenary. The mercenary paced back and forth in front of the prison gates, her eyes scanning the field. His window would be short. As she turned away, Paul made a break for it, diving behind the nearest tree. He checked around the corner. Thankfully, she hadn't noticed him, and he breathed a sigh of relief.

This was it: make or break time. Paul knew he only had one chance, and they couldn't both make it out of this alive. It was either him or her. Closing his eyes, he took what he knew might be his final breath. The gun cocked, and he waited. His timing had to be perfect. In that moment, time slowed to a standstill, like the final seconds of a high-noon shootout. Turning the corner, he raised his gun to fire, but she was waiting for him.

Before he could pull the trigger, two, silver bullets hit him in the center of his chest, sending him plummeting to the ground. As he took one, final look at the bright blue sky above, the darkness closed in on him.

As he faded into the void, he heard a disappointed voice say, "You didn't save me."

The cold hands of death latched onto his shoulders, and suddenly, there was nothing, no light at the end of the tunnel, only blackness.

Suddenly, everything shook, as though some outside force was beckoning him back to life. The light returned to his eyes, revealing a tiny angel who stood above him, covered in glorious light.

"Why didn't you save me?" the angel asked.

"I'm sorry," Paul responded. "I wasn't fast enough, but I promise; I'll save you next time."

Finally, the world around him came back into focus. Overhead, the sun shone through the myriad of clouds that littered the sky, creating a tapestry the likes of which even Michelangelo couldn't have captured on canvas. Beneath the skyline, tree branches danced in the wind like woodland nymphs, creating a leafy halo around the head of his angel, his daughter. She looked down at him with doe eyes and smiled.

"It's ok, Daddy. I still love you!" she exclaimed, wrapping her arms around him.

As Paul held Elle in a tight embrace, another figure appeared above him, sporting a sinister grin that every man knows: the smug smile of a victorious wife. Rebecca looked down at him, her gun resting on her shoulder.

"You hesitated," she chuckled. "How many times do I have to tell you? You'll never save Elle if you hesitate."

Paul turned to Elle and begged, "'What do you say we go again? Daddy could use a chance at redemption."

Elle frowned, her brow furrowing.

She huffed, "But, you said we could go to the station after we finished playing for my birthday present!"

Every year since Elle turned three, she had only wanted one thing for her birthday: a visit to the police station. It was her lifelong dream to follow in the footsteps of the greatest female detectives of all time, Nancy Drew and Velma Dinkley, and Paul was not the type of father to squash his little girl's dream. So, every year, a week before her birthday party, they went down to the precinct, and every year, they were met by a familiar sound.

"Ellie Vanellie!"

Elle had made many friends at the precinct over the years, but none loved her more than Officer Wilcox, or "Shep," as she affectionately called him. Shep was the department's loud-mouthed, perpetually baby-faced mascot with an equally child-like personality. Every year, he would whisk Elle away into some forbidden corner of the station and show her all of their hidden treasures. It was her favorite part of her birthday. As soon as she heard Shep's voice, she let go of Paul's hand and leapt into his open arms.

"Shep! I missed you!" Elle exclaimed.

"I missed you too, Ellie," Shep replied.

"Where are you taking me today?" she asked.

"Patience, my young grasshopper. Patience. All in due time," he answered with a playful wink.

Then, like the passing of the wind, they were gone, and Paul was alone in the precinct, which meant he had the perfect opportunity to do some reconnaissance. So, he journeyed back to Chief Huntsman's office, reacquainting himself with his surroundings on the way. After Paul had begun working under Lena, the Chief was one of the first people Paul befriended. After all, as his father always said; friends in high places keep one from falling too low when the ground crumbles underfoot. Around the precinct, Chief Huntsman was known as a hard man, tough on crime and even tougher on his officers, but Paul found him to be strangely naïve with regard to the people he chose to trust.

Which was something Paul intended to use to his advantage.

"You busy, Chief?" Paul asked as the door to Chief Huntsman's office creaked open.

"Paul Cross!" the Chief exclaimed. "I'm never too busy for you! Where's the beautiful birthday girl?"

"Shep already scooped her up."

Chief Huntsman shook his head with a chuckle. "Of course, he did. Sometimes, I think he's more excited to see your daughter than he is to see his own. He has her birthday circled on his calendar and everything. What can I do you for, Paul?"

"Elle demanded that I tell you," Paul said as he laid a handmade, birthday invitation propped open on his desk. "That she worked for ten quintillion hours on this card, just for you, which means you have to keep it forever in a place where you'll see it every day so you can always remember your favorite, soon-to-be-detective."

The Chief picked up the card and looked inside as a childish grin enveloped the entirety of his aspect.

"Tell Elle, of course I'll come!" he exclaimed, placing the card delicately on the edge of his desk. "And tell her that her card is going to stay right here, next to the pictures of my own kids, for the rest of eternity."

Just then, there was a knock on the door. Its clanking sound reverberated through Paul's ears as though bare knuckles were striking his own eardrum in painful rhythm. Suddenly, his spine grew cold, and the hair on the back of his neck stood up as straight as a bed of nails. Something in the quiet "rap-tap-

tap" of the door felt ominous, like the last few grains of sand descending to the bottom of the hourglass, but he couldn't put his finger on why.

The Chief called for the door to open. As it did, a stern-faced detective, who looked like he was only a few months removed from breaking up street fights and investigating petty grievances, entered the room. He was the picture of professionalism, from his wrinkle-free suit, which was practically steaming from its daily appointment with a hot iron, to his perfectly groomed face. Even his haircut, which was a simple, military buzz-cut, added to the picture he wanted the world to see, that he had it all together, but all it took was one look in the detective's eyes for Paul to know the truth; he was hiding, trying to keep up appearances. Everything on the surface was a façade designed to conceal how lost he truly was in this new world.

"I don't believe the two of you have had the pleasure of meeting," Chief Huntsman said. "This is Bradie Lam, just transferred here from the LAPD. Bradie, this is Paul Cross."

As he heard Paul's name, Bradie's expression grew deadly serious. His mouth locked shut, his right eye twitched and his head tilted to the side.

*He knows my name.*

*Curious. How could a detective from over a thousand miles away have heard my name?*

*And why does it make him angry?*

Paul extended his hand toward Bradie. "I take it you've heard my name before, Detective. You seem surprised to hear it."

"Sorry, yes," Bradie responded, shaking his hand firmly. "I stumbled across your name last night while I was working on a case."

"What case would that be, if you don't mind my asking? Is there anything I can do to help?"

"One thing; do you know a man named Nick Maselo?"

"He used to work at the nightclub I help manage. Regretfully, we had to let him go a couple months ago and haven't seen him since. Is he in some sort of trouble?"

"You could say that. We found his body in the lake a few weeks ago."

*Redd disposed of Nick's body in a lake?! Is he trying to get caught?!*

*Wait a second...*

*Where did he hear my name?*

"Do you mind if I ask you a question, Detective? You said-"

Before Paul could finish, he felt a familiar thud against the back of his leg. Turning around, he found Elle clinging to the back of his leg, excitedly thrusting a flimsy piece of paper toward his face.

He took the paper from her as she yelled, "Daddy! Daddy! Look what Shep gave me!"

"A requisition form," Paul chuckled. "This must be the best birthday ever!"

Elle grinned wider than the Cheshire Cat on Halloween, and Paul wondered what he had done to deserve such a wonderful, little bundle of joy. He picked her up, her little arms wrapped around his neck, and he found heaven. In that moment, he thought that if he could only bottle the joy that came from a daughter's sweet embrace, he would be the richest man alive. She was his light in the darkness. The whole world could have been burning around him, and it wouldn't have mattered at all.

Before they left, Paul turned to Bradie and said, "Nick was a good kid. Feel free to stop by the club anytime you want to talk. The doors are always open. I really hope you find your man."

Those were the last words Paul said until they got home. It wasn't for lack of trying, however, as Elle hardly stopped speaking long enough for him to get in a word. So, he listened

with bated breath as she described, in impeccable detail, everything she saw on her fateful journey to the evidence room. She
was nearing the end of her tale when the final, plot twist hit
him like a bullet to the chest.

"And you were there too!"

Paul nearly swerved the car into a tree from the shock.

She continued, "Well, I mean, you weren't in the evidence
room. But, as we were walking out, I saw a piece of paper with
your name and our address scribbled in really messy handwrit-
ing, like it was written by a four-year-old."

*Redd. It had to have been him. Only Redd could be so damn
stupid.*

At that exact moment, whether by coincidence or prophecy,
Paul noticed, as he pulled into his driveway, a mahogany pick-
up parked on the street outside of his house. Complete with a
"PUMPED" license plate, a black, "Ride or Die" bumper sticker
above the tailpipe and a pair of giant, steel balls hanging from
the exhaust, it was unmistakably Redd's, the kind of truck
made especially for a man who was obviously overcompen-
sating for something. At least, that was the best explanation
Paul could come up with for why someone would need to
display that much machismo.

*Why the hell is he here?*

Grabbing Elle by the hand, he rushed to the front door,
trying his best to remain calm and breathe easy, but inside, he
was seething. His stomach turned inside out. His cheeks
burned as though there were flaming coals resting behind them,
and his mind flashed with images of Redd, tied to a chair with
a large, silver dagger protruding from his chest. Paul could put
up with a lot of things, but his family was off-limits. As they
approached the front door, he couldn't help but fear the worst;
Redd had taken Rebecca captive or, worse yet, told her
everything.

*Close your eyes, breathe deep, raise the curtain.*

He opened the door, and surprisingly, everything was exactly how he had left it. Not a picture frame was the slightest bit out of place. Crossing the threshold into his house, the appetizing aroma of onion, garlic and tomato assaulted his nostrils with a barrage of culinary ecstasy. He stood in the doorway, frozen in his confusion, still gripping Elle's hand. A moment later, Rebecca appeared from the dining room and greeted both of them with loving kisses on the lips. Everything seemed normal.

A little too normal.

"How was the station?" Rebecca asked.

"It was amazing!" Elle exclaimed. "I got to go in the evidence room!"

Just then, Redd's deep, resounding voice echoed from the kitchen, asking, "Is that Elle Belle I hear?"

As the echo of his voice finally settled, Redd emerged from the kitchen, garbed in Rebecca's egg-white, flowered apron and matching pair of oven mitts that barely fit over his ape-like hands, like a masculine, muscular Martha Stewart. Paul thought it was a wonder that he had been able to get any cooking done at all, considering his overall lack of useful skills, but surprisingly, his apron was clean, except for a large, spaghetti sauce stain conveniently located in front of his crotch. Any other day, Paul would have paid good money to see this sight, but that day, it simply infuriated him.

"Redd!" Elle exclaimed, letting go of Paul's hand and bolting over to Redd.

Dropping to a knee, Redd held his arms outstretched as Elle leapt into his arms. He lifted her high into the air and spun her around. On the back end of their final turn, he grinned mischievously at Paul, winking at him before setting Elle back on the ground.

"I didn't realize you two knew each other," Paul said, trying to fake a smile through gritted teeth.

Elle said, "Redd comes to the library when Mommy and I go and reads with me."

"I volunteer at the library on my day off," Redd chuckled. "You've got a very smart girl on your hands, Paul! I think she reads even better than I do."

"I'm sure she does," Paul muttered.

"Redd decided it would be fun to surprise us by cooking a homemade, Italian meal for all of us! Isn't that nice of him?" Rebecca said.

"Absolutely!" Paul exclaimed, clapping his hands twice in an attempt to feign excitement. "And I have an idea to make this even better! Why don't the two of you sit at the table while I help Redd get everything ready to eat?"

Rebecca nodded, leading Elle into the dining room as Paul and Redd retreated into the kitchen. The noise that escaped Paul's mouth in that moment, once they were safely out of Rebecca's earshot, was unearthly, sounding as though he was trying to summon demons out of the mouth of hell. As he poured every ounce of hate and every murderous urge into his words, it took everything he had to keep from exploding.

"What the hell do you think you're doing?!" he growled.

Redd chuckled, "Probably making a thousand Italian grandmothers roll over in their graves, but the packaged lasagna is so much more convenient."

"Cut the shit, Redd."

"I think we got off on the wrong foot the other day. So, I thought I'd come and smooth things over."

Paul's hand gripped the edge of the kitchen island so hard that it felt like they might bleed.

"This is no time for a damn vendetta," Paul said. "We have more important things to deal with right now, like the fact that the police are investigating Nick's murder because of *your* dumbass mistake."

Without a word, Redd waltzed over to the refrigerator and stood in front of it for a moment, running his hand across the pictures of friends and family that littered its face. Stopping on a picture of Elle on her first day of school, he removed it from the fridge and ran his thumb across its front.

"That girl of yours is a smart one, Paul," he said, his voice dropping to a low hum. "Real smart. I bet she's top of her class at Thurgood Marshall Elementary. You should be careful with her, though, because that's the thing about smart girls; they trust their guts too much. All it takes is a little dose of kindness for the wrong type of person to get far too close."

"Don't you dare threaten my family."

"Threaten? Who's threatening? Just a friendly warning. Get your shit in order, Paul."

# 15

# OMEGA

DETROIT, MICHIGAN

"*B*radie, this is Paul Cross."

*What are the odds…?*

Bradie hadn't been inside the walls of the precinct for five minutes before he was face to face with the man he had come to talk to the Chief about. The mere sound of Paul's name burned him to his core, welling up a deep sense of anger and hatred, but also destiny, inside his bones. He tried to shake off their meeting as mere coincidence, but it wouldn't fade. It was too profound, too unlikely, to be mere chance. He took a moment to study his foe.

*Average build. Clean-cut. Rounded face. Friendly smile. Well-groomed.*

Making him look more like the young, local bartender that everyone inherently trusted with their problems than a criminal mastermind, Paul's appearance wasn't exactly what Bradie had expected from someone so apparently connected with these cases. But, even the devil masqueraded as an angel of light. There had to be a connection, something that tied him to the case, some reason his name had been in that warehouse.

Paul extended his hand toward him and said, "I take it you've heard my name before, Detective. You seem surprised to hear it."

*Perceptive, bold.*

*Interesting.*

"Sorry, yes," Bradie responded, shaking his hand firmly. "I stumbled across your name last night while I was working on a case."

"What case would that be, if you don't mind my asking? Is there anything I can do to help?"

"One thing; do you know a man named Nick Maselo?"

"He used to work at the nightclub I help manage. Regretfully, we had to let him go a couple months ago and haven't seen him since. Is he in some sort of trouble?"

"You could say that. We found his body in the lake a few weeks ago."

Bradie looked closely at Paul for his reaction to this piece of information, but there was nothing: no surprise, no sadness, no shock. The only perceptible change in his expression was buried deep beneath the earthy, brown surface of his eyes. It was the same expression Bradie saw whenever Stacy came home to a full dishwasher, like something was supposed to be done but hadn't been.

*He already knows.*

Paul asked, "Do you mind if I ask you a question, detective? You said-"

However, before he could finish, a small, pigtailed girl burst into the room and latched onto his leg. Excitedly, she thrust a requisition form in Paul's face that she had gotten from Shepard. As he picked her up and held her gently in his arms, the love that emanated from his countenance was almost tangible. It seemed that getting a clear read on this new adversary could prove more difficult than Bradie had estimated. Regardless, it was clear; Paul was hiding something

Before leaving, Paul turned back to Bradie and said, "Nick was a good kid. Feel free to stop by the club anytime if you want to talk. The doors are always open. I really hope you find your man."

"Me too," Bradie whispered under his breath, convinced he already had.

Once Paul left, Bradie turned to the Chief and asked, "How do you know him?"

"Paul and Illuminate have always been good friends of the department," Chief Huntsman answered. "He brings little Ellie around every year, a week before her birthday party, and every year, I bring as many officers to her party as I can. Anything for my favorite, Junior Detective."

There wasn't any time to waste. Since Paul was out for a day with his daughter, it was the perfect time for Bradie to do a little leg work. So, he left the precinct, parked his car across from Illuminate and waited. During his short time in Detroit, he had heard many stories, from cop and criminal alike, about the bright, shining star Paul's nightclub supposedly was. They said its presence was a sign that things were finally looking up for a desolate part of the city. As he sat outside of it, however, the daylight revealed the club's true nature, exposing its apparent light for what it really was: fool's gold, a mirage in a desert wasteland. It also brought to light every spot where the building's stark white exterior was beginning to fade, uncovering the layers of dirt and grime that had simply been painted over. Even its neon sign, which had been said by many to be a beacon in the night, looked like a tacky, Vegas imitation as it flickered dimly under the noonday sun.

While Bradie studied his surroundings, a young girl across the street caught his attention. Wearing little more than a blue tank top and jean shorts that were hardly long enough to cover all the parts that mattered, she glided across the sidewalk with long, deliberate strides, her eyes trained on a singular target. As she approached a tan station wagon on the opposite side of the street, her long, thick locks, which flowed like a chocolate river so rich, so tempting, that one could easily find themselves as lost as Augustus Gloop inside, blew gloriously in the breeze, aided by her hands, which ran smoothly through them. Once outside the station wagon, she leaned into its open window, being intentional to show as much cleavage as possible. After a moment of flirtatious banter, the driver handed her a small wad of cash, and she led him behind the nightclub. As she turned the corner, her eyes met Bradie's with a seductive wink.

*Bingo.*

After two and a half minutes, they returned from behind the club, the man's face stuck in a perpetual, wide-eyed smile, like a hippie after an hour at Woodstock and her face blank, as though she had already forgotten all about him. Leaving the man behind, the girl made her way toward Bradie, her gaze now trained intently on him, as she slowly undressed him with her eyes. He shifted uncomfortably in his seat, trying to remain focused. Winking at him, she bit her lip as she, once again, ran her hands through her hair and leaned into Bradie's open window.

*If she's being forced to do this, she's doing a damn good job.*

"Hey there, sexy," she said in a breathy tone. "Oh, you look so tense! Relax, baby. Erica will loosen you up."

"I hear you're the best," Bradie replied.

"You heard right. I'll grind every last knot out of that sexy body of yours."

"How much?"

"Usually, fifty. But for you, forty."

"Done deal."

As Bradie opened the door and handed her a pair of twen-
ties, Erica took him by the hand and led him away, following
the same path she had taken moments earlier. They disappeared behind the nightclub, through the back door and down
the stairs into the basement. As their feet hit the dusty, concrete
floor, the air grew cold and damp around them. The sounds of
groans and heavy breathing echoed off the basement's
cavernous walls from all directions, through the numerous
doorways on each side of the hallway that opened like cave
tunnels into utter blackness.

It was clear that they had entered the underworld.

Suddenly, Erica took a sharp, right turn down the third
corridor. As Bradie followed, darkness enveloped him. He held
his free hand in front of his face, but it was no longer there, lost
in the shadow. After a moment spent traversing the darkness, a
small light appeared in the distance, and the world slowly came
back into view. Against the back wall, a small, electric candle
sat beside a lonely, twin mattress in the otherwise empty space.
The noise that had once filled their ears at a deafening level
now sounded like white noise in the background as she laid
him gently onto the bed and climbed on top of him.

"What brings a guy like you to a place like this?" Erica
asked as she removed her top. "You don't look like the type of
guy I usually see around here."

Grabbing Bradie's hands, she ran them slowly up her
exposed body until they were resting on her breasts. Her skin
was immaculately smooth, like velvet to the touch. She swayed
her body rhythmically, accentuating every inch and every curve
of her flawless frame. She was intoxicating in every way.

Bradie said, "You came highly recommended by a friend of
mine - Paul Cross - he said this was the place to come for a
good time."

At the sound of Paul's name, Erica's left eye twitched. After quickly shaking off the surprise, she slid her hands down Bradie's torso, sending a cold shiver down his spine. As she unbuttoned his pants and caressed his crotch, he lost himself in her touch. At this point, she could do no wrong. He wanted nothing more than to lose himself in her body and drink of her wine.

Erica chuckled, "Someone's excited! I might just set a new speed record with you."

Suddenly, Bradie shot back into reality. Realizing how close he was to the edge, he pushed her off and jumped to his feet. She tumbled back onto the bed, confused.

"I'm sorry," he fumbled. "This was a mistake - my wife - I'm married. Keep the money. It's yours. I'm sorry."

Stumbling back through the dark corridor, he rushed up the stairs and darted to his car as adrenaline flowed violently through his veins. Closing his eyes, he took three, soothing breaths, but his heart was still doing the forty-yard dash.

She knew Paul, and she feared him. Paul Cross was a dead man walking, and all Bradie had to do was find a way to prove it.

# 16

# DOWNER

INDIANAPOLIS, INDIANA

*A*fter stumbling through the first few steps in his devil's dance, Kayde had finally found his rhythm. The tempo became engrained in his body, and soon, the steps were second nature to him and his girls. Over the weeks that followed, there was hardly a night that they missed their quota. In fact, most nights saw each girl handily surpass theirs.

Even though Kayde got most of the credit for his team's success, he knew that he would be neck-deep in a rising tide without Violet. She was his secret weapon, his go-to girl, his shelter in the storm. Whenever they were under their quota, which seemed to rise higher with each night that passed, she picked up the slack. If any of the girls were having a rough night, she was the first one to pick them up, dust them off and send them back into the field. Often times, she would take care of a problem before Kayde even knew there was one.

That night, they were more than halfway through a Pan concert, which was surprisingly one of their biggest events of the year, before Violet took her first break. Kayde stood nearby, trying to look like he was keeping an eye on the other girls when, in fact, he couldn't keep his eyes off of her. After being around her for so long, he thought that her glow would have died down, but somehow, she radiated even brighter than when he had first laid eyes on her.

Everything she did dragged him deeper under her spell: the way her hair fell in front of her face, the way she smiled to herself when she thought no one was looking, even the way she yawned so vehemently that her eyes nearly shut. Despite everything that told him he couldn't afford attachments, everything inside him that screamed that his focus needed to remain on Blair and Blair alone, he was drawn to her, and soon found himself beside her, smiling at the pair of black heels that lay on the ground before her feet.

He joked, "Are the heels really that bad?"

"I'd like to see you walk in these spawns of Satan for an hour, much less the whole, damn night," Violet laughed as she set her heels back on her feet.

"Then it's settled," he said with a smile. "I'll have to wear heels next time we have a big night."

She stood up, patted him mockingly on the shoulder and shot him a playful wink. "As much as I'd love to see that, I care about you too much to watch you put yourself through that kind of pain. Now, if you'll excuse me, good sir, I have been sitting here for far too long."

"But you've only been on break for two minutes. You have another eight minutes still," he said.

"Don't be silly, hun," she laughed as she walked away. "You know you can't keep this ass out of the game for more than three minutes without starting a riot. And we can't have that, now. There are quotas to hit."

"How are you so perfect?"

"I guess that's just how God made me."

Violet didn't make it far, however, before Sasha limped by,

favoring her left ankle. She walked barefoot, cradling a pair of jet black heels in her arms. It was apparent from the defeated grimace that was painted across her face that something was seriously wrong. Usually, Sasha wasn't the type to show emotion easily, whether you told her that her dog died or she won the lottery. Regardless of circumstance, the blank expression she bore remained constant, which was a large part of her allure. So, for her to show any indication of pain was cause for concern. Quickly, Violet and Kayde huddled around her like foxes to a sick pup as she collapsed into the grass. Breathing a sigh of ecstatic relief, she immediately began to massage her ankle as she looked at Kayde apologetically.

Kneeling down in front of her, he placed a comforting hand on her shoulder, asking, "What happened?"

"These damn, cheap, knock-off heels broke!" she exclaimed as she chucked her heels, one of which was cracked at the heel stem like a chipped wine glass, across the lawn. "I'll be fine. Just give me a minute or two."

"Not a chance," he said. "I'm going to get you some ice, and you're going to rest. I don't need you working yourself out of commission."

"But I'm eight tricks off my quota," she said.

"Eight? Is that it?" Violet shrugged nonchalantly. "That'll barely take me an hour to cover. I'll just tell my boys that prices are up today. You stay right there and rest."

"Thank you," Sasha replied.

As Violet turned to leave, Kayde chased after her, placing his hand on her shoulder. As their skin touched, a surge of electricity crackled in the space between them. He could tell that she felt it too because, when she turned to face him, her visage was glowing like moonlight. For a moment, he got lost in her eyes, exploring the endless fields behind them. All he wished he could do was lay with her in an empty field and read her poems and write ballads in her name. If only circumstances had been different, he would have done just that.

"Thank you," he said. "Seriously."

"What would you do without me?" Violet sang with a dramatic hair flip as she skipped back to the parking lot.

In that moment, Kayde certainly hoped he would never have to find out the answer to that question.

With Violet on double duty, the last few hours of the night went off without a hitch. Sasha was able to take her time on the bench, resting her ankle, and they managed to squeak by their quota for the night. On the way back home from The Eclipse, there was no fanfare, no crowds screaming their names, but the atmosphere was one of victory nonetheless. Every face bore a smile, even the ones that had long since forgotten what one was. It felt like a major win for everyone, like things were finally starting to come together. In that moment, Kayde even entertained the passing thought that maybe, just maybe, he could actually do it; he could find Blair.

That feeling evaporated quickly, however, as they walked into the house across the street. On the other side of the door was Eric, standing tall and strong with his arms crossed and chest puffed out. His face was granite, like an executioner in front of the guillotine. Instinctively, the girls circled around him and Kayde, who now stood dead center, frantically trying to figure out what was going on. Meanwhile, Eric scanned the crowd. Then, without a word, he entered the circle, returning a second later with Sasha by the scruff of her hair. As he dragged her along the ground, she tried to keep her balance. However, her ankles soon buckled, causing her body to fall to the floor, and her bare back slid along the unpolished, wood floor. As they reached the center of the circle, Eric threw her down, and she fell headlong across the floor.

Eric addressed the crowd, "How many times do we have to

go over this before you get it? Your quotas are not negotiable. They are not optional, and they are not a group effort. They are individual quotas that every one of you must meet every night. No exceptions."

"You can't punish her for that!" Kayde exclaimed. "She twisted her ankle, so I told her she could have the night off."

"That was your mistake," Eric said.

"I figured it didn't matter who brought in the money, as long as it got in," Kayde replied.

"Well, you figured wrong, and she should have known better. But, since you insist it's your fault, you can have the honor of giving her the beating. Consider that your punishment."

Immediately, Kayde froze as massive waves of guilt and regret raged inside his soul. He thought what he had done was a merciful, good deed, but he saw now that no good deed done in hell goes unpunished. He looked at his hands, which shook with fear. Then, he looked at Sasha and saw that she was shaking too. Stepping toward her hesitantly, he tried to take a deep breath, but his lungs remained locked. His mind tried furiously to find another option, a way out, but there was none to be found. As he lifted his fist into the air, preparing to strike, Sasha braced herself, looking away. Kayde did as well. When he did, he caught sight of Violet standing in the crowd, tears welling up in her eyes. From where he stood, he could see her mouth the same words she had said to him weeks before.

*You have to be you.*

"No," Kayde said as he lowered his hand to his side. "We've both learned our lessons. This isn't necessary."

Eric looked at Kayde quizzically as he slowly circled him. "See, I don't think you have," he said. "You still think this is about her. Sasha already understands how things work around here; what we say goes. You can't blame a dog for obeying its master's command. Sometimes, it's the master who needs to be trained."

"But, why does every punishment have to be a beating?" Kayde argued, his voice raising in frustration.

"Because that's how we do things!" Eric exploded before immediately returning to a calm, confident tone. "Look around you. These whores are not your equals. They're your bitches, and bitches need leashes."

"Then leave Sasha out of this. If I'm the one who screwed up, I should be the one who's punished. She doesn't deserve a beating."

"You know what? I think you might be right, Kayde. We don't need to beat a bitch every time she does something wrong. Maybe there is another way. Stand her up."

Kayde bent over and placed his hands under Sasha's shoulders, lifting her to her feet and whispering in her ear, "See, everything's going to be okay."

Once she was standing, Eric looked her in the eyes and asked with a hint of condescension, like a third-grade teacher at the end of a particularly frustrating lesson, "Now, what have we learned today?"

"That we - that I have to hit our - I mean - *my* quota every night, no matter what," she stammered.

"Very good," Eric said as he walked around her, forcibly removing her clothes. "And what are we going to do next time?"

"Tough it out," she answered, looking to Kayde for support.

"What are you doing?" Kayde asked, feeling the first, bitter pangs of regret sweep across his chest.

"Exactly what you said, Kayde," Eric replied with a wicked smile as he backed Sasha against the wall. "Finding another way."

"I didn't say to do this," Kayde said.

Eric shrugged. "Eh, tomayto, tomahto."

Grabbing Sasha's arms, he pushed her against the wall. She winced as her bare back pressed against the cold plaster of the wall. Kayde watched helplessly as Eric forced her arms and legs apart into a spread-eagle position. Once she was perfectly still, her eyes still shut tight, he stood in front of her, looking back at Kayde just long enough to shoot him a mischievous wink. Then, he dropped his pants and, taking hold of his manhood, let loose a stream of urine that soaked her bare stomach. She grimaced as the stream split in two and ran down both her legs, forming small puddles at the base of her feet. With nothing left to expel, Eric put his pants back on and walked determinedly toward Kayde.

"Make sure she doesn't move a muscle for the next hour, let her soak in it," Eric ordered. "If she moves or anyone helps her in any way, I will know. Oh, and Kayde? You *are* the one being punished."

# 17

# LOCOED

NEW YORK, NEW YORK

*N*atasha looked over the bridge's edge at the water below. From that height, the river that flowed freely beneath her looked cool and inviting. As she looked down, a warm breeze wafted across her face, gently encouraging her to take a step forward. She closed her eyes, feeling as though she was floating above the clouds, swaying to the rhythm of the wind. In that moment, she was free, resolving that she would welcome death with open arms.

"Wait!" a voice screamed in the distance. "Please."

Turning around, Natasha saw Blair thirty feet away, reaching out to stop her. A heavy knot formed in her stomach and began to work its way up her throat as her breathing became labored.

"Leave me alone!" Natasha pleaded, turning desperately away.

"Please!" Blair yelled. "Don't do this. I need you."

"I'm not that important."

Natasha's heels lifted off the ground as she moved toward her descent. Closing her eyes again, she awaited the end.

Suddenly, however, her arm was jerked back, and she fell into the open arms of Blair, the force of her fall sending them both tumbling to the ground.

Taking Natasha's hand, Blair stared lovingly into her eyes and said, "You are that important. To me."

"Even still?" Natasha asked. "After everything I've done?"

"Always. I love you."

"I love you too."

Blair placed her right hand on Natasha's cheek. Then, gazing into Natasha's eyes, she leaned in until her welcoming breath caressed Natasha's lips. Blair's lips parted, and her eyes twinkled like the North Star, drawing Natasha into the passionate embrace of her kiss.

"Cut!" a voice sounded from the other side of the bridge. "That was perfect! Let's move on to the bedroom scene."

The wild success of Natasha and Blair's "Live, Lesbian Sex Shows" had prompted Alexei to explore other such profitable exploits, specifically pornography. Over the weeks that had followed, they had been forced to play everything from school girls to sisters, even venturing into the realms of bondage and torture. This particular day, they were filming the culmination of a three-part "erotic romance series" about a girl who fell in love with her brother's girlfriend. After a few, casual encounters, Natasha's character sabotaged her brother's relationship so she could be with her lover forever. Soon, however, her lover found out, which led to a horrible fight, and instead of having to live the rest of her life apart from her true love, Natasha had decided to end it all.

After all, if it has a storyline, you're not watching pornography; you're watching art.

Natasha stood to leave, not wishing to be there one second longer than she had to, but Blair grabbed her by the arm. Fuming with anger, Natasha whipped around to face the person who now represented everything she hated about the world she lived in. At this point, Blair was nothing more to Natasha than a fallen tree, blocking her path to freedom, and Natasha was holding a chainsaw, doing everything she could to cut Blair out of her life, piece by piece. After all, it was far better to feel lonely while alone than to feel lonely with someone else, especially when that someone was supposed to be her best friend.

"We need to talk," Blair whispered.

"About what?" Natasha scoffed, finally wrenching herself from Blair's grip.

"I know about the drugs."

"What do you care?"

"I care about you."

"Well, maybe you should stop."

> *I built this place*
> *With ice cold rage.*
> *I can't escape*
> *This stone soul cage.*

That night, after a day's sleep, Natasha sat in her room, finally alone. A deep aching resonated within her bones, like her heart was made of the heaviest kind of steel. Its massive weight pressed on her rib cage, making it harder and harder to breathe. She held her hands in front of her face. In them were held the means of her escape, the drugs she had, once again, earned from across the street, and the thought of it consumed her.

Inhale.

Natasha stared blankly at the scarlet curtain in front of her. Suddenly, a small, black spec appeared in the curtain's center, bringing a relieved smile to her face. Slowly, the spec grew in all directions, creeping like a shadow and spreading like a cancer until it enveloped the entire curtain; only, this cancer was her cure. Once it had devoured the curtain, the darkness spread to the floor, the ceiling, the walls, multiplying until everything around her succumbed to the darkness.

Until she was all that was left.

She stood to her feet, watching the bed disappear into the abyss beneath her, which appeared to go on for an eternity. And so, she stood, existing, but at the same time, not.

In the void, there was nothing: no air, no sound, no feeling. She was alone with the darkness. At first, the sensation of no sensation, complete and total numbness, was startling. It was unlike anything she had ever experienced, but now, it was her drug. She didn't crave the cocaine; she craved the emptiness. For hours, she could remain in the void without ever wanting for anything.

As she gazed into the darkness, there was a sudden flicker of light in the distance. Then, there was another, but this time, it was closer and brighter. This continued for several moments, with each flash of light growing progressively brighter and larger until what once was darkness was now as blinding as the sun. She tried to shield her eyes from the blast, but it penetrated her defense, settling like a deep pressure inside of her, which could only mean one thing; she was coming back to reality.

She screamed, "No! Not yet! It's too soon!"

With a sudden burst of color, the world around her returned. A large, greaseball of a man was hunched over top of her, his naked body slamming over and over again into her fragile frame.

The Greaseball smirked. "Are you going to cum already? Damn, that's hot."

Suddenly, his eyes rolled back into his head from the sudden rush of blood and ecstasy as his body gyrated at a spastic pace, nearly throwing Natasha off the back of the bed. At the same time, her body tightened, trying to stop the vicious flow. Screaming in pain, she locked her hands onto the sides of her mattress and dug her nails into her bed sheets. Then, seconds later, it was over, and he lay motionless, flat on top of her for much longer than was comfortable. Finally, just before Natasha thought she might suffocate under his weight, the Greaseball stood up to get dressed.

Winking at her, he said, "I'll have to come see you again sometime."

As soon as he left, Natasha leapt off the bed and checked under the back corner of her mattress, where she kept her salvation. However, there was nothing there. Suddenly, panic set in. She needed to return to the void, to escape. Frantically, she scoured every inch of her room, looking for even a single grain of white powder, but still, there was none to be found.

With the determination of a leopard going in for the kill, she marched over to the alley across the street. Zeroing in on her prey, she, in one, fluid motion, knocked the cigarette from the hoodie's hand and planted her lips on his. Forcing his hands against the brick wall behind him, she ran her leg up the back of his calf. Then, as before, she worked her way down his torso and unbuttoned his jeans.

*Smack! Crash!*

In an instant, Natasha's prey fell to the ground with a loud thud. Above her, Alexei stood, fuming, with his left arm outstretched and hand clenched into a fist. He looked at her with a glare that sent shivers down her spine as she recoiled against the wall, quaking with fear.

*How did he know?*

He yelled, "Stupid whore! Your body is mine. Do not give it away for free."

His clenched fist fell viciously and without mercy onto her

temple again and again, slamming her head into the pavement and causing blood to pour down her face. She tried to absorb herself into the pavement to avoid another blow, but it did nothing to alleviate the punishment. In that moment, fear consumed her, but it was not a fear of death. She did not fear death; instead, she feared that she would be forced to endure.

Her beating finished for the time being, Alexei took her by the hair and dragged her across the street. She fought to regain her balance and lift herself to her feet, but she could not. Instead, her body bounced along the pavement. Concrete tore into her skin, sending searing pain up her back and down her legs. As he forced her inside the warehouse, Natasha looked up and saw Blair, standing outside the warehouse and looking down at her with sadness and horror, but also guilt. Suddenly, Natasha came to a terrible realization; she had been sold out.

There could be no forgiveness for this betrayal.

∽

*Detroit, Michigan*

AFTER A LONG DAY OF WORK, FLORIAN LIKED NOTHING MORE THAN to return to his quiet, Metro Detroit apartment and be alone. There was no other place where he was able to remove his mask and just be. Playing a role all day, no matter how enjoyable it could be, was exhausting work. As he walked through the doors to his apartment building, he left his mask at the door, not planning on picking it up again until the weekend was over.

Then, he rode the elevator to his apartment, which sat on the corner of the top floor of a twenty-seven-story high-rise. After months of searching, he had chosen this particular unit specifically for its privacy and, most of all, for the view. From his living room, he could see the entire city, stretched out as far as he could see. Sometimes, he would sit for hours by the window, watching the city move. It was like he had the world's largest ant farm at his fingertips, which made him feel powerful, yet simultaneously reminded him of how insignificant he was. That kind of perspective was worth the extra two-hundred dollars a month.

At the end of that day, Florian was running on fumes. As he walked down the hallway with his eyes fixed on the handle to his door, he saw nothing else. The sound of his own footsteps was the only noise he allowed to tickle his eardrum. Its rhythm soothed his mind. As he got closer to his apartment, however, another sound fought for his attention: the faint sound of sobbing. With every step he took, it grew louder and louder until it became the only thing he could hear.

Below his door handle sat Janelle, curled up in an upright fetal position with her head buried in her knees, muffling the sound of her despair. To her left sat a small suitcase, which been propped haphazardly against the wall, causing it to teeter precariously on the edge. Even the slightest breeze looked like it could knock it flat on its face.

For a moment, Florian stood over her, attempting to reapply his mask. This new development was unexpected, and unanticipated problems always meant danger. As he stooped down to comfort her, he quickly ran through every scenario he could think of in his head. He was treading in deep waters. He had to act carefully, lest he risk drowning.

"What's the matter, baby?" he asked, placing his hand cautiously on her shoulder.

"I'm sorry," she said, looking up at him as she nervously tried to wipe the tears from her eyes. "You're home earlier than - I'm sorry - I shouldn't have come."

Quickly, Janelle stood up to run away, but before she could,

Florian grabbed her by the hand and pulled her back to him. Wrapping his arms around her, he held her until she melted into his arms. Then, he wiped the tears from her face and looked in her eyes.

"What happened?" he asked.

"They kicked me out," Janelle answered.

*Shit...*

"That's horrible!" he exclaimed, opening the door and ushering her inside. "Why don't you come in so we can talk about it?"

Functionally, Florian's apartment was little more than a bachelor pad, measuring six-hundred square feet and consisting solely of the bare necessities. The only non-essential items in his apartment were a large bookcase, which held his vast collection of scripts and sonnets by playwrights ranging from Shakespeare to Moliere, and his mask collection, which hung on the walls throughout the apartment and spanned across both era and continent.

There was something about masks that held a special place in Florian's heart and soul. He was fascinated by the ability of a simple mask to change the way the world viewed a person and even how a person viewed the world. He believed that to wear a mask was to become a chameleon, a shapeshifter who could morph into anyone, or anything, he wanted.

"What happened?" he asked again as they sat down on his couch.

"I knew they'd freak if I told them," Janelle said. "But I figured they'd be, you know, less upset if they heard it from me before I couldn't hide it anymore. I was wrong. We got in a big fight, which ended with my dad saying that I either had to get rid of it and you, or I wasn't welcome in his house anymore. Obviously, I can't - I'm sorry for showing up like this. I didn't know where else to go."

"No, don't apologize," he said. "It was an unexpected surprise, but not an unwelcome one."

"Thank you. I don't know what I'd do without you."

"What are you going to do about school?"

"I don't know," she sighed. "Fall classes are starting in just over a month. I guess I'm going to have to drop out."

"Don't do that!" he exclaimed. "You only have two years left. You can't let this stop you."

"But, I can't even get there. The bus doesn't stop at any shelters."

"Don't be ridiculous! You're going to stay here. There's a bus stop around the corner. Hell, I'll bring you to school myself if you want!"

"You don't have to do that."

"I want to," he promised.

"How are we going to fit both of us and the baby in this apartment?" she asked, looking around the living room. "I'm getting claustrophobic just thinking about it!"

*Eureka!*

It was in that moment that Florian thought of the perfect way to salvage everything. He couldn't believe he hadn't thought of it before.

He smiled. "It's funny you say that because I was just asking myself the same question. But, you know, I have a little money saved up. I figured I had a couple more years until your eighteenth birthday so I could ask you. However, considering the circumstances, now seems as good a time as any. What do you say we start looking to buy a house?"

She almost jumped out of her skin out of sheer shock and delight. "You mean it?!" she exclaimed.

"Absolutely!" he replied. "There's nothing I want more."

And so, the chameleon changed his colors yet again.

# 18

# HEAT

DETROIT, MICHIGAN

*a* s was their Saturday morning tradition, a ritual which had quickly become Bradie's favorite part of the week, he and Anna sat across the table from each other at TT's diner, sharing two, double-stacked plates of Belgian Waffles. Nothing gave him more pleasure than having the opportunity to witness, firsthand, the strength, maturity, and resilience that simply exuded from her pores. The way she faced her past, head-on, unafraid to tell her story, was something to behold. He could hardly believe she was same girl he met on that rooftop, the one who was ready to end it all in one leap. However, he was beginning to understand that, in fact, she hadn't changed.

This was always who she was. The true courage on the roof that day hadn't been in the detective who had talked her off the ledge; it was in the girl who, despite everything that told her to jump, stepped off the ledge and entered the unknown. In the end, he hadn't saved her; she had saved herself.

That day, however, Bradie couldn't focus on anything. All he could think about was the case. It was as if he was right there, on the precipice of victory, with the key in his hand but with no way to convince anyone it would open the door. Despite everyone else's doubt, he felt it in his bones; Paul was guilty. He just needed a way to prove it. The pressure weighed so heavily on his mind that he didn't even notice the full plate of waffles that had been sitting in front of him, untouched, for fifteen minutes.

Finally, Anna looked up from her own, half-eaten plate and joked, "If you're not going to eat those, I'll gladly take them off your hands for you."

Suddenly, Bradie snapped back to reality. "Sorry, I'm a little distracted today," he said.

"Did you find out anything about Paul Cross?" she asked.

"Yes and no," he sighed. "I'm still trying to wrap my head around it."

"Okay. So, tell me about it. Maybe fresh ears are just the thing you need."

Bradie sighed. Ever since their night at the warehouse, Anna's nightmares had worsened, and he couldn't help but feel it was his fault for letting her go with him in the first place. Her therapist said it was something called "re-traumatization," that, by entering that world again, her mind was forcing her back inside that reality, even if only in her dreams. Only within the last, few days had she returned to having peaceful night's of sleep. He couldn't bear to make her go through that again. It wasn't fair to her. This was his weight to bear, not hers.

Noticing his apprehension, she looked him in the eyes and repeated, "Tell me about it."

Searching her eyes, he tried to find a reason to refuse but found none. Beneath their surface, he saw a blazing inferno, as if a phoenix lay resting behind her irises, waiting to be released. Its heat melted away his apprehension and brought him to a realization; hellfire doesn't only destroy. It also strengthens and empowers. Like a refiner's fire, it could either turn her to ash or make her stronger than before.

So, he took a deep breath and told her everything: about Paul, about Illuminate, about the darkness of the basement and the groans and echoes, and that, despite all he had seen, he still had nothing but circumstantial evidence.

"And what aren't you telling me?" she asked, nodding expectantly.

"What do you mean?" he asked, perplexed.

"Everything you've told me so far is pretty much par for the course," she said. "Bad guys are good at being bad. They make connections and weave tales. They build a cover so bulletproof that even the most confident of detectives can't put a dent in their armor. But, there's something else, something you've thought about mentioning but didn't think it was important enough. So, what's different about this one? What is it about Paul Cross that seems out of place?"

"The party," Bradie whispered under his breath.

*How didn't I see it before?*

He continued, "Paul has a little girl, a pigtailed, wannabe detective. Her birthday is today, and there's a party. That's why Paul was at the precinct, to drop off an invitation for the entire department."

Without hesitation, Anna stuffed the last, two bites of waffle into her mouth, stood up and put on her coat.

"Where are you going?" Bradie asked. "I haven't even touched my waffles."

"Get it to go," she ordered. "We have a party to attend."

∽

A PRINCESS–POLICEMAN PARTY WASN'T EXACTLY EVERY NORMAL girl's idea of a birthday bash, but Elle had never been accused of being a normal, little girl and for good reason; her mother wasn't normal either. She was exceptional. Like everything decorating related, Rebecca had a knack for birthday party planning. In fact, if she hadn't been so intent on helping the homeless, she had always considered party planning a viable career option. She had the innate ability to take any theme, or combination of themes, and find a way to make it make sense. This party was no exception.

As was always the case with a Rebecca Cross production, the party started in the driveway. Beautifully drawn in sidewalk chalk, a pink drawbridge extended from the fence gate to the edge of the driveway. In the middle of the drawbridge was drawn an elaborate, blue police badge with the words "Detective Eleanor Cross, Detroit PD" written across its face. Along the edges of the drawbridge were four stanchions with pink and blue, crime scene tape stretched between them. Beyond the stanchions, the chalk outlines of four, little girls holding lollipops lay motionless on the asphalt. Then, to complete the grand entry, Rebecca had positioned a giant, bouncy castle in perfect view of the drawbridge, with a banner that read "Happy Birthday Elle" hung between its peaks.

Once past the gate, the world transformed into a medieval, carnival crime scene. On the right were classic party games, such as: pin the badge on the officer, castle piñata, handcuff toss, princess dress-up and an obstacle course, complete with dragon slaying at the end. To the left, tables were set up for the parents to sit at, all centered around the present table, which was placed on a large, center stage and decorated with tiaras, police badges, pink and blue cupcakes to match and crime scene tape. The pièce de résistance, however, was the cake. It was a triple-tiered, pink, purple and blue castle, ornately decorated with candy pearls, diamonds and princess figurines lying flat across the opened drawbridge. Candied crime scene tape was strung across the posts that marked the beginning of the drawbridge, behind which stood Sherlock Holmes, who was bent over, investigating a set of sugary footprints that led into the castle.

From the moment the party started, Elle insisted that Paul shadow her everywhere she went. She told him that it was a very special day, and on very special days, it was *very* important that he be with her at all times, playing all of her favorite games, especially the obstacle course.

As Elle began the obstacle course, Paul lay helpless beneath the terrible dragon, whom the villagers had named Florian. The dragon roared fiercely, threatening to tear him limb from limb. Paul's only hope was that a brave and daring knight, or knightess, would save him.

"Help me!" he cried.

"Have no fear!" a voice yelled in the distance. "Eleanor Cross: princess, policewoman and dragon slayer, is here!"

As Elle began her rescue, many, harrowing obstacles stood in her path. After vaulting over the mountains, she crawled through the swamp, traversed the Fiery Bridge of Death and even fought off three, giant ogres in the Forbidden Valley. Finally, only one obstacle stood between her and Paul: the dreaded, Foggy Maze of Destruction. Fear filled Paul's heart as she disappeared into the mist. No one had ever survived its peril, meaning it would take a miracle for Elle to survive. As the dragon opened its mouth to devour Paul whole, its fiery breath charring his face, anxiety took hold of him.

He prayed that his demise would be swift and painless.

Just then, like a flash of lightning, Elle emerged from the maze, victorious. She drew her sword and in one, fell swoop, cut the head off the dragon, causing the kingdom to erupt with cheers and applause, for Paul was finally safe. Planting a grateful kiss on her forehead, he thanked his elegant hero for risking her life to save his.

With the danger finally averted, Paul decided that he deserved some time to rest. After all, being rescued from dragons was exhausting work. Sitting down at one of the tables, he watched Elle as she ran the obstacle course with her friends, her bright pink, police uniform shining in the sun, and her lilac tutu twirling majestically with every swing of her sword. As she ran, the bedazzled tiara that crowned her head bobbed and bounced, held in place only by her pigtails. She was having the time of her life, living out her dream of being a royal detective, and the beaming smile on her face lit up his whole world.

Paul loved seeing her so happy, but he couldn't help but worry. For the last, several nights, he had awoken in cold sweats from horrible dreams about Elle being kidnapped, hurt or beaten. Redd's veiled threats played over and over in his mind, enraging him to his core. His fist clenched and unclenched nervously. He was about to finally lose it when Lena and Rebecca joined him at the table, laughing and carrying full plates of food.

It was a startling sight to see Lena smiling, laughing and having a good time. Around Rebecca, it was as though she was an entirely different person altogether. Her shoulders were loose, and her face appeared softer. Even the icy blue of her eyes became like gentle streams of water, like maybe there was a real person under that stony exterior after all.

"I'm glad to see you having a good time. You should smile more often. It becomes you," Paul said.

Lena chuckled, "Don't get used to it. This smile comes out once a year for Elle's birthday, and that's it."

"Didn't I see you smile the other day when we were out at lunch?" Rebecca asked.

"He doesn't need to know that," Lena shushed, playfully shoving Rebecca aside.

At that moment, Florian sauntered onto the stage and planted himself firmly in the center. He stood up straight, held his head high and clapped three times in rapid succession, immediately drawing every eye in the kingdom to him. He smiled. This was his element.

Lena rolled her eyes. "I'm going to need another drink."

"I think we all will in a minute," Rebecca groaned in agreement.

Clearing his throat, Florian announced in a loud, theatrical voice, "Ladies and gentlemen, boys and girls. It is time for this evening's entertainment, hosted by yours truly."

Led by Elle, the children charged the stage, knowing exactly what was to come. Every year, without fail, Florian put on a one-man, Shakespearean play for Elle and her friends, and every year, the show became more absurd. For the previous year's party, he had performed Romeo and Juliet, complete with a passionate scene in which he made out with himself. This year, he endeavored to expand his cast by using puppets and masks to perform his all-time favorite play, Hamlet, which was sure to be an awe-inspiring show, complete with shocking twists and an award-winning performance. Regretfully, however, Paul would have to miss it. He had an appointment in the kitchen with a leftover platter of deli spirals.

As he rounded the corner toward the back deck, his eyes met those of the Detective Bradie Lam, who stood, jaw clenched, at the entrance to the kingdom with a young blonde beside him. Despite Bradie's every attempt to play it cool and appear relaxed, it was obvious that he was working. With stiff shoulders, his hands fidgeted with loose change in his pockets, and his eyes darted back and forth in their sockets, studying his surroundings.

Without breaking stride, Paul made his way over and greeted him with a firm handshake, "Detective! It's so good to see you! Bradie, right? I'm so sorry I didn't think to invite you when we met the other day."

"Oh, it's no problem," Bradie said. "You were busy. We had just met."

Paul shook his head. "Regardless, I should have thought to invite you. This is your girlfriend, I presume?"

Bradie opened his mouth to speak but closed it again just as quickly. He paused. The blonde looked up at Bradie, chuckled and extended her hand to Paul.

"More like his daughter," she said. "My name's Anna."

"Well, it's nice to meet you, Anna. Feel free to-"

Paul stopped abruptly, his gaze drifting to the gate, where Redd was crossing over the drawbridge and into the kingdom. In his hands, he held a small present. Their eyes met, and Redd smirked, like a hyena about to cheat its way into a meal. Suddenly, a quiet, crackling sound resonated in Paul's ears, like blood rushing fiercely through his veins. In that moment, his fist clenched so tight that his fingernails dug into his palms. Then, he remembered; Detective Lam and Anna were still standing there.

"I'm sorry," Paul said, trying feverishly to appear calm. "I got distracted. Feel free to enjoy the festivities. Cross Kingdom is glad to welcome you as its guests this afternoon. If you feel that you are in the need of some 'adult' beverages, I believe the Chief may have managed to smuggle a few past our guards. I would love to stay and converse with you both, but the court jester has just arrived. He and I have some important business to attend to."

He didn't even give Bradie a chance to respond. Instead, he sped off, like a cheetah, toward Redd.

"Redd, buddy!" Paul announced with contrived excitement.

"Good to see you! Can I speak with you for a moment in private?"

Clamping his fist around Redd's arm, Paul forced him against the fence.

Then, he whispered, "I told you to stay away from my family."

Unfazed, Redd replied, "Elle invited me, and I couldn't exactly say no. We wouldn't want to disappoint the birthday girl on her big day, would we?"

"I want you to leave. Now."

Just then, Elle yelled from across the yard as she galloped toward them, "Redd!"

"I guess we'll have to finish this conversation another time," Redd said.

"Come on!" Elle said, taking Redd by the hand. "Come on! You're missing the show!"

It was all Paul could do not to explode. His entire body shook with rage, and sweat trickled down his brow. Trying to get away before someone, particularly Bradie, noticed how unhinged he was becoming, he scurried to the kitchen and grabbed a bottle of beer from the fridge. Then, popping the lid, he downed it in a single gulp. Its taste was bittersweet and biting, quenching his thirst but only serving to remind him of how far behind he was in the game Redd was playing. None of it made any sense. It felt like he was still reading the preface while Redd was nearing the final chapter.

Leaning against the sink, he watched the party from the window. The children were still sitting in front of the stage, watching Florian's "masterpiece," including Elle, who sat on Redd's lap, laughing and giggling. She looked like she was having the time of her life, but that only made Paul feel worse.

"Are you uncomfortable with all this too?" Rebecca asked, joining him at the window.

Never in Paul's life had he wanted so badly to tell her everything. All he wanted to do was forget about the party and lay in bed for the rest of the day, with her head on his chest, and tell her everything about the club, Redd and Bradie, but he couldn't do that. She would never understand.

So, he played it off. "With what? Redd and Elle? What makes you say that?"

"I don't know," Rebecca sighed. "Something about the way he acts with her isn't normal. Last week, before you got here, he kept asking questions about her, saying how beautiful our daughter was and wanting to know what kind of things she likes. I don't know. I thought he was okay at first, and normally, I wouldn't worry about it. But... Maybe I'm being silly. I just have a weird feeling about him."

"Don't worry, honey," Paul said. "Redd's harmless. He really loves kids, talks about it all the time. He has a daughter around Elle's age, but her mother won't let him see her. I think Elle is the closest thing to her that he has right now."

*If only that were true.*

"I guess," she sighed. "He still makes me uncomfortable, though. I'm not sure I want him coming over to see her anymore."

"I'll talk to him. I'm sure he'll understand."

"Thank you," she said, still unsure. "Can I talk to you about something else too?"

"Of course!" he replied.

"Do you remember that girl from the Narcotics Anonymous meeting? The wallflower who ran out when Georgie tried to talk to her?"

"Yeah, I remember her," he answered, shifting his body curiously toward Rebecca.

"I'm worried about her," she said. "I was at the mall the other day, picking up a few things for the shelter. And when I was leaving, I noticed a group of prostitutes standing by the corner. So, I went to my car and grabbed some of the gift cards that I keep in my glove box, in case I run into somebody who could use them. But, when I got back to give them the cards, I saw her. She was one of the prostitutes!"

*Shit! Redd was supposed to ship her off to Vegas, not leave her in our own, damn backyard!*

She continued, "I tried to say something to her, but she was so high that she didn't even recognize me."

"That's awful!" Paul exclaimed, trying to keep his hands from shaking.

"I know! So, I was thinking; what if the shelter held a special dinner for local prostitutes? It's horrible that some of these women are so addicted to drugs that they feel they have to sell themselves in order to get more. I've also been reading a lot lately, and people are saying that some of these women are literally being forced into prostitution! Can you believe it? I feel like we have to do something. What do you think?"

*That's a horrible idea!*

"That's a wonderful idea!" Paul exclaimed. "Of course, I'll do it!"

Leaning in, Rebecca planted a grateful kiss on his cheek before returning to the party. By this point, he could no longer control the rage inside of him. It felt like the walls were closing in on him. Enraged, he clenched his fist, forgetting that he was still holding his beer bottle.

*Crash!*

Suddenly, the bottle shattered into dozens of microscopic pieces that fell to the floor like rain. Paul hurried to the pantry to grab a broom and dust pan. But, when he wrapped his fingers around the door knob, a sharp, stinging sensation shot up his forearm. Stepping back, he turned his hand over, revealing a large, jagged chunk of glass sticking out of his hand.

Frantically, he rushed to the sink and ran the water, slowly and carefully placing his hand underneath the running faucet and pulling the shard of glass from his palm. As it exited the wound, intense, burning pain shot up his wrist, accompanied by a deluge of crimson blood that poured down the drain, turning the water pink.

After wrapping his injured hand in gauze, Paul took the shard in his un-injured hand and held it in front of his eyes. He turned it from side to side, gazing at it as it shimmered under the fluorescent light, creating an auburn glow on the ceiling above. Kneeling on the floor, he placed it in front of him. Then, taking a knife in his hand, he smashed the chunk over and over again, with calculated blows, until it was nothing but slivers.

Finally, once there was nothing left to destroy, he stood up, looked out the window and smiled.

*19503 LYNN ROSE ROAD. DETROIT, MICHIGAN.*

Despite seamlessly blending in with the houses that surrounded it, Paul's two-story Tudor was hard to miss with a party underway. In fact, the sea of multi-colored balloons that covered the entire length of the driveway and the quarter-mile long row of cars parked along the street side was so noticeable that Bradie spotted it as soon as he turned onto Paul's street.

As he pulled his car into a spot along the curbside, he wondered how Paul managed to afford this house solely off of a night club manager's salary. When Bradie had looked at houses before moving to Detroit, every house in that section of the city fell well outside of his price range, even on a detective's salary. Either something fishy was going on, or he had gone into the wrong line of work.

Bradie became even more suspicious as they made their

way up the driveway and into the backyard. He couldn't believe how much money Paul had spent on a six-year-old's birthday party, no matter how mismatched the party's theme may have been. The balloons alone had to have cost upward of a hundred dollars, not even accounting for the giant, castle-themed bounce house, the immaculately decorated cake and the plethora of activities strewn about the yard, which included several princess-police themed games and a large obstacle course on the far end of the yard.

As they entered the backyard, passing through several crime scenes on the way, all was relatively quiet by party stan-dards. Everyone at the party, including the children, was in the middle of the yard, encircling a stage, where a well-groomed, young man was preparing for a show.

Within five seconds of entering the backyard, Bradie met eyes with Paul, who was only a few feet away.

"Is that him?" Anna asked.

"It is," Bradie replied.

Without so much as breaking stride, Paul hurried over and greeted him with a firm handshake, "Detective! It's so good to see you! Bradie, right? I'm so sorry I didn't think to invite you when we met the other day."

"Oh, it's no problem," Bradie said. "You were busy. We had just met."

Paul shook his head. "Regardless, I should have thought to invite you. This is your girlfriend, I presume?"

Bradie opened his mouth to speak but closed it again just as quickly. He paused.

*What do I call her? What does she want to be called?*

Before Bradie could decide how to respond, Anna extended her hand to Paul and chuckled, "More like his daughter. My name's Anna."

"Well, it's nice to meet you, Anna. Feel free to-"

Paul stopped abruptly. His eyes widened, drifting toward the gate, where a brutish man had just entered. Immediately, his fists clenched, his pupils dilated, and his cheeks turned bright red. Then, he paused. His eyes darted back and forth for a moment before returning to Bradie and Anna, as though he had only then remembered they were still there.

"I'm sorry," Paul stammered. "I got distracted. Feel free to enjoy the festivities. Cross Kingdom is glad to welcome you as its guests this afternoon. If you feel that you are in the need of some 'adult' beverages, I believe the Chief may have managed to smuggle a few past our guards. I would love to stay and converse with you both, but the court jester has just arrived. He and I have some important business to attend to."

Before Bradie could even offer a simple "thank you," Paul was gone, speeding off like a cheetah toward the man and ushering him out of sight.

Bradie looked at Anna. "Daughter? Did you mean it?"

"I wouldn't have said it if I hadn't," she said. "Now, let's split up and take a look around."

"Are you sure you're okay with that?"

"Don't get all 'over-protective-parent' on me, Dad," Anna joked. "I'll be fine. Plus, even here, you're still a cop. If anyone at this party is connected to either the murder or the brothel, you'll spook them. It'll be better if it's just me."

Regretfully, she was right. In this setting, Bradie stuck out like a leopard amongst gazelles. One wrong move would scatter the herd, leaving him with nothing. He posed a threat, but Anna didn't.

While she made her best effort to blend in with the peasants, Bradie sat back and observed. She grabbed a plate of food from behind the stage and sat at one of the adult tables, next to a woman of ambiguous descent, who was attempting to drown out the overly dramatic show with a few shots of whiskey.

Upon seeing Anna, the woman tried her best to smile and greet her warmly, but her eyes remained as cold as liquid nitrogen. Immediately, she looked Anna up and down, as if she were assigning a monetary value to her appearance. Quickly becoming uncomfortable, Bradie shifted in his seat, resisting every urge to intervene. He had to trust Anna, even if he didn't exactly like it.

Just then, a kind-faced woman in a policewoman's costume took a seat across from him and handed him a full plate of food.

"I didn't know what you like, so I brought a bit of everything," she said.

Taken slightly aback, Bradie stammered, "I-I'm sorry. You didn't have to get me any of this."

"What kind of hostess would I be if I didn't make sure everyone was well-fed?" she giggled, offering her hand. "Rebecca Cross, proud mother of the birthday girl."

"Bradie Lam. Nice to meet you."

"Oh, my husband was just talking about you the other day. You're the detective that's looking into what happened to Nick. Poor kid. It breaks my heart that somebody did that to him. He was a good guy, deep down."

"You knew him?" Bradie asked.

"Not well," Rebecca answered. "I saw him occasionally, here and there, but one time, Elle was feeling a little sick. She had a high fever, and Nick heard about it. So, he brought over a homemade batch of chicken noodle soup. It was very sweet of him. I really hoped things would turn out better for him, considering his background. Let me know if there's ever anything I can do to help. I'm surprisingly resourceful when I need to be."

"Thank you, Rebecca."

"Now, if you'll excuse me, I think I saw my husband sneak

away to nab some deli spirals. I'd better stop him before there's none left for later."

With that, she waved goodbye and scurried into the house through the back door, leaving Bradie even more perplexed than when he first arrived. Rebecca didn't seem like the type of person who would approve of the things Bradie believed Paul to be involved with. She was genuine, friendly and perceptive. Was it possible that Paul was a trafficker, and she didn't know? It was one thing for him to fool his co-workers or a cop, but his wife, who he sees twenty-four, seven? That was another thing entirely.

*Did someone plant his name at the warehouse to throw me off, or is Paul more complicated than I thought?*

Bradie pondered these questions and more until the party came to a close. He had hoped that the party would afford him some answers, but all it did was raise more questions. His only hope was that Anna had been able to find something.

After the party, when they got back into the car, Bradie asked, "Did you find out anything?"

"Nothing concrete," Anna replied, shaking her head. "Just observations."

"What did you think about Paul?"

"Honestly," she sighed. "If we hadn't found his name in that warehouse, he wouldn't be my first choice for a trafficker."

"So, you don't think he's hiding something?" he asked.

"See, that's the tough part," she explained "Everyone is hiding something. You are. I am, and so is he. He was definitely playing a character, working hard to come across as the nice guy, but it was too convincing for it not to be a part of him."

For every answer, there were two more questions, waiting around the corner.

"What about everyone else?"

"If anyone at that party is connected to what you saw at the nightclub, I would bet money on it being either the court jester or the woman, the one I first talked to. She was playing a character too, but hers was far less convincing. She tried to talk to me like I was a real person, but all she saw was a price tag. It was like I was on display. She looked at me with the same look I got from every pimp, every madam I ever worked for. It's undeniable.

"The one you really have to look out for, though, is the court jester. I've met a lot of men like him over the years: enforcers with a short fuse, basically human time bombs. Guys like him demand authority and will do anything to acquire power, including screwing with the lives of anyone who's ticked him off by planting their name and address at a crime scene for the police to find."

## 19

# ROUNDUP

### INDIANPOLIS, INDIANA

*Sometimes, I dream in color...*
*Now, I know what you're thinking;*
*Isn't the nature of dreams to exist beyond the natural,*
  *which is, to radiate with glorious color?*
*You would think this,*
*But you'd be wrong*
*Because, you see, dreams are mirrors held up to*
  *our souls*
*That reflect the deepest subconscious,*
*And my soul is often dark.*
*And my dreams are full of half-lit streets and*
  *Cimmerian Shadows, where neither sun nor moon*
  *light the skies,*
*Where everything is black.*
*But sometimes, I dream in color.*
*Sometimes, I dream, and the world explodes with*
  *technicolor.*
*Sometimes, I dream, and the sun shines green.*

*Sometimes, I dream of bright yellow castles and fields*
      *Speckled with silver.*
*I dream of colors never before seen.*
*And in those dreams,*
*I feel alive, like the dream is reality, and reality is*
      *the dream.*
*And sometimes, even after I wake, I still dream...*
*And sometimes, those dreams are in color too.*

*K*ayde lay amongst a field of yellow lilies on a hilltop with nothing but jade grass and blue sky for miles. He stared up at the clouds as they whisked by, leaving light, feathery trails of smoke in their wake. The sweet aroma of lavender tickled his nostrils, leaving him breathless from its essence. In the distance, he could hear the sound of songbirds echo melodiously across the hilltops. As he closed his eyes, he felt more at peace than he had ever been.

Suddenly, a warm breeze wafted across his face, soothing him, like a lover's caress. His whole body leaned into its warmth. He was enraptured, captured by the moment. As he stared into the clouds, they danced above him, singing together in beautiful harmony. In the center of the sky, three clouds came together to take the shape of a beautiful woman with a flow-ered crown atop her head. Around her flew butterflies of various sizes, and in her hands, she held a vine of grapes that wrapped itself around her as a frame envelops a painting. It was the most beautiful sight he had ever seen.

Kayde wished he could stay in that place forever, but regret-fully, every dream must come to an end. When he awoke, only one thought was on his mind: Violet. He looked at the clock. It read 7:00 a.m., which gave him plenty of time to get dressed, shower and make it to The Eclipse in time to spend an hour with Violet before he had to work.

When he was with her, everything else faded away, melting into oblivion. She laid her head on his shoulder, and he was in heaven. Her voice was like the sweetest of balms, reaching into the deepest, darkest depths of his soul and healing everything that was broken. She was the only person left he could confide in, in whom he could trust, who knew about Blair and could help him find her.

"We have to get into the Manager's office," Violet said emphatically, yet apologetically.

"How do we know it'll be there?" Kayde asked, pacing nervously around Violet's room.

"It'll be there," she assured him. "The Manager keeps meticulous records. He's quite OCD about it. When they first brought me here, he brought me into his office, sat me down, and went through all his files on me, which included everything, even my Social Security Number. Trust me, wherever they moved Blair, you'll find it in his files."

"How do I get in?"

"You don't. I do."

"I can't let you do that. If they find you, they'll hurt you."

"And if they find you, they'll kill you. They'll only beat me. I'm far too valuable as a product for them to kill, and your sister needs you alive."

"No, enough people have been hurt. I can't risk you too," he said, sitting next to her on the bed.

Violet smiled, brushing her hair behind her ear. "Why are you so perfect?" She asked with a girlish giggle.

"I'm not," he answered, turning away in shame.

"No, really," she said, grabbing him by the chin and turning him back to her. "No one's ever treated me the way you treat me. Not even my own parents. I didn't even know there were guys like you in the world. Now, I'm not naïve. I know you're not perfect in a purely objec-

tive sense, but I don't care about that. You're perfect
to me."

Leaning in, she kissed him on the cheek, her lips soft and wet
on his skin. Her scent was magnetic, her touch, hypnotic. He
closed his eyes and leaned into her warmth. As she pulled away
from the kiss, her breath caressed his ears like a warm, summer's
breeze. In that moment, he was drawn to her by a feeling he
couldn't describe. It was like he lost all control of himself. He was
drunk on her presence, intoxicated by her very soul, and he
couldn't get enough. So, as if pulled by some mysterious force, his
hand reached out and grabbed hers. She smiled, her fingers inter-
twining with his. His palms grew sweaty as he looked into her
eyes. Finally, the dam burst forth, releasing tidal waves of desire.
Pressing his lips fervently into hers, he sank into her sweet waters.

As they kissed, Violet placed her hands on his shoulders
and thrust herself into him. Then, she threw him onto the bed
and climbed on top of him, leaving him breathless. Her hands
climbed slowly up her thighs until they took hold of her shirt.
Kayde was hard-pressed to look away as it rose above her head
and fell to the floor. In that moment, he thought that she was
the most perfect human being to ever have existed. Her body
was flawless, radiating with the purest beauty he had ever seen
as her hands loosened the buckles of his jeans.

She smiled and bit her lip as she lowered his zipper. "Oh!"
She chuckled. "Don't get too excited now! We want to make
sure this lasts."

In that moment, Kayde wanted nothing more than to find
himself knee-deep in the depths of her beauty. It was what he
had wanted from the moment he first saw her.

"Wait," he said, taking Violet by the hand.

"Isn't this what you want?" she asked, puzzled.

"I do," he answered as he laced his fingers with hers. "More than anything, but I don't want to be like all the other guys, the ones who see you as just another object to be used. I want this to be special, to make sure that *this* lasts."

"How are you so perfect?"

Laying down next to him, she rested her head on his shoulder as he wrapped his arm around her and kissed her gently on the forehead. Then, without a word, they simply lay there because there was nothing in the world that needed to be said. Being together was all either of them needed, like a beautiful, perfect dream.

He wished he could stay in that place forever and hold her until the world ended around them.

But, every dream must come to an end.

Suddenly, there was a knock on the door. Jumping out of bed, Kayde rushed to open it while Violet quickly got dressed. As it opened, the door creaked ominously, revealing Eric standing behind it. Looking curiously around the room, he smirked at Kayde.

"Did I come at a bad time?" Eric chuckled, winking slyly at Violet before taking on a more sinister expression. "Your girlfriend will have to wait. The Manager would like to see you now."

*How quickly moments can change.*

The Manager's office looked exactly how Violet had described. As the door swung open, Kayde felt as though he was entering the lair of Polyphemus himself, who, instead of a pile of bones, was hoarding the remains of his many victims in a cacophony of cabinets. He only hoped the Manager to be as blind to his deception as the mythical cyclops was to Odysseus'. Regretfully, there would be no wine or strong drink to save him this day, only his own wit. After squeezing himself through the tiny openings between the cabinets, he finally found his way to the Manager's desk, which was empty, apart from a single, open file in the center: Kayde's.

Panic set in as he waited for the Manager to arrive. His chest tightened, his throat closing tighter than a boa constrictor's hold on its prey. He tried to swallow, but he couldn't. If the Manager was as detailed as Violet had described, he must have known about Blair, possibly from the beginning. He had to. After all, he had Kayde's file.

Then, Kayde realized something; he was alone with the files. If he could find Blair's transfer file, he could take Violet, run to wherever Blair was and never look back. His eyes darted furiously around the room, trying to spot the right drawer. That turned out to be no easy task, however, as it was like trying to find one's way through a labyrinth. Finally, after a moment of searching, he spotted it, at the bottom of a crimson cabinet in the left-hand corner of the room: a drawer labeled "TRANSFERS."

Before he could take a step toward it, however, the door opened. His heart sank as he turned to meet the Manager, only to realize they had already met. It was the ticketing agent he had accosted regarding Blair when he first came to The Eclipse. By this point, Kayde's heart had settled nicely inside of his pinky toe. He couldn't imagine feeling any lower. There was no coming back from this. Walking past Kayde, the Manager sat down in the leather seat on the other side of the desk.

After browsing through Kayde's file for a moment, the Manager fidgeted with his glasses, studying Kayde intently, and said, "Kayde Meade. It's a pleasure to officially make your acquaintance."

Taking a deep breath, Kayde replied, "I would say the same, but it's difficult to make yourself acquainted with someone you only know as 'The Manager.'"

"That is by design." The Manager smirked. "Anonymity is a

priceless commodity in this business. It's an idea you would do well to learn."

"What exactly does that mean?"

"It means that you should be careful to whom you allow access to your information and emotions. It makes it difficult to remain unnoticed."

"I take it you're referring to my sister."

"Smart boy."

"I don't see what that has to do with anything," Kayde said.

The Manager laughed, "Oh, but that has everything to do with it, my boy! I can't be expected to turn a blind eye when a young man so adamant about finding his sister, who just so happened to have been one of my girls, decides to work for me. Do you think me a blind beggar on the street corner? And, you know, I almost let it go. I almost did because I assumed that someone so emotional, so naive, would crumble quickly, but you haven't. So now, you've got my full attention, Kayde. I'm intrigued."

"I don't mean to come off as rude, but there's really nothing to it. I saw a business opportunity, and I took it."

"What about the passion and intensity, the sheer audacity in your eyes when we first met? You were so enraged!"

"Sure, I was upset," Kayde answered. "But the truth is; I'm nobody. What could I do to stop any of this?"

"Said Odysseus to the monster he was moments away from slaying," the Manager mused.

"And how exactly, would you say, I intend to slay you, sir?" Kayde asked.

"By going to the police with what you know," the Manager answered.

"And lose any chance I might have had at finding my sister? Hypothetically speaking, of course, emotional doesn't necessarily mean naïve."

"So, it seems."

"So, do you plan to kill me over mere speculation?"

"Kill you?!" the Manager gasped facetiously. "My friend, if I intended to kill you, you would already be dead. Besides, what fun is there in killing you before the drama has a chance to play itself out? I would much rather watch it unfold. Just know, Kayde, you must be careful. Not everyone you encounter in this business is as sporting as I am. Some would much rather watch you burn than squirm. And don't forget, you're not the only person you endanger by your actions."

"What's that supposed to mean?" Kayde asked.

"Your relationship with Violet has not gone unnoticed. I advise you watch your step before she finds herself in danger as well."

# 20

# RATAQUE

NEW YORK, NEW YORK

*N*atasha awoke in a panic, unable to breathe. A rancid, sour liquid stewed at the base of her mouth, burning like liquid metal in her esophagus. Shooting up in bed, she tried to force it down, but as she did, her stomach flipped upside down. She clenched every muscle in her body, trying to keep herself from throwing up all over the floor, but it was no use; she erupted like Vesuvius, spewing lava across every corner of the room. The scene before her looked like it came straight out of a second-rate horror film. She was certain that, somewhere in her room, a small village of dust mites was cursing her name.

*Not again. I can't feel sick again.*

Immediately, she ripped the blanket from her mattress and knelt down clean up the mess. As she scrubbed the floor clean, it felt like a hundred, tiny dwarves were swinging their pick-axes to the beat of "Heigh Ho" in her stomach. She rocked anxiously on her knees, trying to keep herself from puking again.

Once the floor was clean, Natasha took the dirty blanket in

her hands and held her breath. After a mad dash to the dumpster behind the building, she tossed the blanket inside and began to leave. It was at this moment she finally gasped for air. When she did, she was instantly assaulted by the horrifying combination of spoiled food, vomit and feces, as though a hundred sewer rats had died inside her nostrils.

She heaved again.

*That's strange. I've been by this dumpster a thousand times, and I've never-*

A horrifying thought entered her mind. There was no time to waste. Bolting back into her room, she shut the curtain behind her. Then, she grabbed the only three things Alexei allowed the girls to keep in their rooms: plain, white toothpaste, a toothbrush and a cup. Frantically squeezing the toothpaste into the cup, she took a deep breath and dropped her panties to the floor. With a nervous gulp, she placed the cup between her legs and closed her eyes before releasing a torrent of urine. Once the cup was filled, she placed it on her bed and stirred anxiously with the handle of her toothbrush. Then, it was a waiting game.

The minutes passed like a snail on the highway. Natasha couldn't stand the anticipation. Her head was on the chopping block, and she was waiting for the guillotine to fall. It was unbearable. After a few minutes, the mixture began to churn and bubble, slowly shifting from yellow to blue as the blade fell. She slammed her face into the mattress because she knew that could only mean one thing;

She was pregnant.

Somehow, over the course of the four years she had been in the warehouse, Natasha had never been pregnant. Sure, she had seen other girls get pregnant, but she assumed that pregnancy would be the one curse God would not bestow upon her. Obviously, she had been wrong.

And now, she had to get rid of it before anyone found out. Over those same years, she had seen every pregnancy in the warehouse, without fail, turn out the same way. First, Alexei would force the women to carry the child to term because there was a lucrative, niche market for everything, especially pregnant women. Then, once a girl's glow faded, he would take them into the back alley and shove a metal clothes hangar inside them, forcing them to deliver their now deceased offspring. After all, a baby in the warehouse only meant more mouths to feed and extra noise Alexei could never hope to control. This was not an existence that Natasha envied, and she would do anything to avoid it.

In the moments before Alexei took roll call, most of the girls either spent their time sleeping or enjoying the final, few moments they got to spend with their own thoughts before their bodies and lives were no longer their own. That evening, Theresa was doing the latter. As Natasha entered her room, Theresa was seated on the edge of her bed, stationary, staring at the scarlet screen, her eyes glazed over as her hands shook involuntarily on her lap. Natasha knew this look well; Theresa was at home in the darkness, which meant that this was the perfect opportunity to extract some information.

Sitting next to Theresa on the bed, Natasha adopted the friendliest tone she could muster up, placed her hands on Theresa's shoulders and exclaimed, "Oh, honey! You look awful!"

Theresa turned her head toward Natasha, her pupils as small as mustard seeds, and mumbled, "Natasha?"

"What did they do to you?" Natasha asked in an attempt to deflect attention off of herself.

"Blair is worried about you. She - she says you've grown distant."

"I know, but right now, honey, I'm worried about you. What happened?"

"She says you can't let the darkness win."

"Have you seen the darkness?"

"It's all I see, all around me, in my blood," Theresa answered.

"When did it come?" Natasha prodded.

"Right before you," Theresa replied.

"Does the darkness come at the same time every night?"

"The darkness always follows last light. That's when *he* comes, always at the same time, and the darkness comes with him. He holds it in his hand. I can feel it as it penetrates me, enters me, infects me. It consumes me, and then, I - I am one with the darkness. I *am* the darkness. I need it, but I don't want it."

Having learned everything she wanted to know, Natasha stood to her feet and started toward the hall. Theresa was teetering on the edge between insanity and reality, and Natasha had no interest in playing therapist. After all, she had a date with the darkness. Before Natasha could exit the room, however, Theresa took her by the arm and pulled her back so violently that Natasha only managed to stop herself a few inches from Theresa's eyes, which seemed to flutter between blinding light and utter darkness, between fire and ashes, as though she was fighting for control of her own body.

"You can't let the darkness win," Theresa implored before fading back into her trance.

*But, my dear, it has already won.*

Over the next, three days, Natasha spent every free moment studying Alexei's every move, from when he entered the warehouse to the moment he left. Thankfully for her, this was a relatively easy task, considering he kept to a strict, military-like routine. Moments after last light, he entered the warehouse, carrying a small, blue duffel bag. Then, he walked the length of the warehouse, checking in every room to make sure no one was missing, his bag always by his side. Once his inspections were complete, he went to Theresa's room. Setting the bag on the floor outside her room, he opened the top pocket and pulled out a single syringe. Then, he held it up to his right eye, tapping it precisely three times before heading inside. Exactly twenty-five seconds later, he emerged from the room, took the bag and exited through the front door. It was like clockwork.

She had to strike within those twenty-five seconds.

On the fourth day, Natasha peered through the break in her curtain, waiting for her opportunity. Her heart was racing. The time had finally come, and now, nothing could stand between her and the darkness. After that day, she could finally make the pain end. As the final rays of light escaped the warehouse, leaving only darkness in its wake, Alexei walked through the doors with her salvation atop his shoulder. She couldn't take her eyes off of it. Hunger consumed her. She was a wolf stalking its prey, saliva dripping from her fangs as Alexei set the bag on the floor.

*One.*

She flew through the curtains of her room.

*Two.*

She raced down the hall like a hare, her footsteps light and quick, as to not draw attention to herself.

*Three.*

The bag was almost in her grasp. She reached out to take it.

*Four.*

A warm, soft hand wrapped around her forearm and pulled her back.

*Five.*

"What are you doing?" Natasha asked as she whipped around, only to find Blair holding onto her arm.

"We need to talk," Blair answered.

*Eight.*

"There's nothing to talk about," Natasha said, trying to break free of Blair's grip.

"I'm worried about you."

"Now is not the time!"

*Thirteen.*

"I miss you."

Natasha demanded, "Let me go!"

"Not until you talk to me," Blair insisted.

"I don't want to talk to you," Natasha said. "I don't want to see you. Hell, I don't even want to think about you. It would be better for both of us if you just left me the hell alone!"

Blair's hand released from her arm.

*Twenty-one.*

"What happened to you?"

"You did."

Natasha turned back toward the bag just in time to see Alexei exit Theresa's room, take the duffel bag and leave through the front doors. Immediately, her heart sank. She had missed her chance.

"You're dead to me," Natasha huffed under her breath.

*Twenty-five.*

That day, Natasha didn't sleep. She couldn't. The withdrawal wouldn't let her. Every time she closed her eyes, her body would shake and soak her sheets with sweat. Her mouth was as dry as the Sahara Desert, making swallowing a luxury she could no longer afford. As she lay awake in bed, her mind raced with questions, anxiety and doubts. She couldn't understand why Blair seemed so determined take the one, good thing she had left in her life.

*Why can't she just let me be happy?*

After what felt like an eternity, Natasha finally saw night fall from under her curtain. Leaping out of bed, she rushed toward the hall in time to see Alexei set the bag down outside Theresa's room. She had to act quickly. This time, nothing would get in her way. Within five seconds, she was on her knees next to the bag, unzipping the top pocket and rifling through its contents. After twelve seconds, she held three syringes in her hand and closed the bag up again so there would be no sign she was ever there. By twenty seconds, she was back in her room, carefully hiding the syringes under the folds of her bed sheet. Once daybreak came the next morning, the darkness would finally be hers forever.

As the sun rose that morning, she sat on the edge of her bed, staring at the single syringe she held in her hand while the remaining two sat on the bed next to her. The room may have been filled with light, but the plastic casing around the needle glowed even brighter than the noonday sun. For the first time, Natasha held her destiny in her hands. For the first time, she had a choice. She had never truly imagined death before. It never seemed like an option she had been given. She had always assumed that her destiny was to barely exist, trapped in a state of perpetual torment.

Her mother always told her that God was the only one who could choose who lived and who died. There had even been a time when she had believed it. However, her mother had also said that God was merciful. If that were true, Natasha would have already been dead. In that moment, as she looked upon her salvation, she knew that, in fact, she had become God.

Either way, whether she died that day or simply relieved herself of her burden, she was in control, for the first, and hope-fully the last, time.

Her finger ran across the smooth surface of the cylinder, which was cold to the touch. She brought the tip of its needle to her arm, and it penetrated her flesh. Her breathing quickened.

Her eyes closed, and she sighed. It was orgasmic. As salvation entered her, an icy coldness crawled up her arm and settled in her shoulder. She pulled the needle from her arm. A tiny speck of darkness began to grow on the curtain in front of her. Grabbing the second syringe, she plunged it into her veins, causing her legs to burn. Her heart raced. Her breathing slowed as the darkness continued to grow, consuming everything around her, save for one thing: the final syringe. Taking it in her hand, she drove it inside her. Then, she fell back onto the bed. From the darkness above her, a black hand reached toward her. She raised her own hand to meet it. As they touched, darkness, like many, tiny vines, crept up her arm. Soon, it enveloped her. She gasped for air, and then, there was nothing.

Only the darkness.

> *Sleepless nights too many to count,*
> *My vision so faded that I start to doubt.*
> *Am I alive or in a dream?*
> *Or is this place not the horror it seems?*
> *I look again at the sign above my head,*
> *But it's words no longer fill me with dread.*
> *"Freedom comes to the dead."*

A strained, gasping sound echoed ominously throughout the warehouse, waking Blair from her slumber. She shot out of bed, fearing the worst, that Natasha was using again. Dashing out of her room, she sped down the hall to Natasha's room. When she arrived, Natasha was comatose, her body as stiff as a board on her bed. Lowering her ear to Natasha's mouth, Blair found that she was barely breathing. Then, she checked under the bed and found three, used syringes beside a cup of blue, frothy liquid.

*She's pregnant...*

Wasting no time, Blair darted back to her room. Reaching under the back corner of her mattress, she pulled out her own syringe, which was filled with Naloxone. When Theresa first arrived at the warehouse, she told Blair everything, including the one time she nearly overdosed, only to be saved at the last minute by a dose of Naloxone. Since that day, she said that all her keepers, Alexei included, kept some with them at all times, just in case. Considering Natasha's new-formed habit, Blair figured it was only a matter of time before she succumbed to her hunger and stole some for herself. So, a few days after she confronted Natasha about her drug use, Blair took a single syringe of the antidote to protect Natasha against her own avarice. The day before, when she caught Natasha making a break for the duffel bag, Blair's fears were confirmed.

When Blair returned to Natasha's room, Natasha was no longer comatose. Instead, her body seized and gyrated as though she was possessed. Her mouth opened, gasping for air, but it was no use. Her lungs had forgotten how to breathe. Pinning Natasha's forearm to the bed so it couldn't move, Blair plunged the needle into what she hoped was a vein. Within seconds, Natasha's body settled into a deep sleep, and her breathing returned to normal. Then, Blair reached under the bed and took the three syringes, along with the Naloxone, and threw them in the dumpster around back. With Natasha in stable condition and the evidence disposed of, there was only one thing left to do.

Blair crossed the street, praying that Natasha's dealer was still there. Alexei wasn't what anyone would consider a smart man, but eventually, he would notice that much missing cocaine, which meant Blair needed to replace it, lest she risk him giving Natasha yet another thrashing. As she entered the alleyway, the dealer was standing in the shadows, counting his money.

His eyes fell on Blair, and he said, "I didn't think I'd be seeing any more of you whores around after that Russian prick knocked that other bitch's head in."

Walking slowly past him, she swung her hips from side to side and ran her index finger across his collarbone as she whispered in his ear, "He's not around tonight, and my friends and I want to party. Name your price."

"Depends." He smirked. "How much do you bitches want?"

"Oh, I don't know. There are three of us, so maybe three hypes of H."

"Three hypes? That'll cost you."

"Like I said, name your price."

"Price gotta match the product. Your friend blew me for some blow, so for injection, how about you let me inject my dick into your ass?"

Without hesitation, Blair placed her left-hand against the dirty, brick wall in front of her, and, taking her right hand and sliding it sensually down her body, she dropped her skirt and panties to the floor. Then, she looked at the dealer, licked her lips and motioned for him to come closer. As he approached her, she saw his hands excitedly fumble at his belt and felt his rough, greasy hands force her cheeks apart. Although she tried to relax the best she could in an attempt to dull the pain, the intense, burning that followed was more horrible than she could find words to describe. However, after a few minutes, it was over, and the dealer handed her the three hypes she needed, which she carefully hid underneath the back corner of her mattress until the next evening, when she could discreetly slip them into Alexei's duffel during his inspections.

But, it was quickly becoming clear; Natasha wouldn't give up easily, meaning Blair needed to think outside the box if she wanted to protect her friend.

~

*Detroit, Michigan*

FLORIAN'S HEART PULSED VIOLENTLY INSIDE HIS EARDRUM. HE took a deep breath, though he didn't know why he was so nervous. It was just dinner. It was only Vinny's. They had been there countless times before, but somehow, this night felt different. Living together had made their nights out much more difficult. Before, whenever he and Janelle went to dinner, there was always a plethora of things to talk about. The days they spent apart held countless tales to be told and vast amounts of new information to be shared. Now, however, it had been only hours since they had seen each other last, and those hours held even fewer stories.

At the start of the night, he endeavored to re-create, as best he could, the finest parts of their relationship in an attempt to remind Janelle that romance did not, in fact, die the moment they moved in together. So, he picked her up outside of his apartment building, taking a few moments to relish in her beauty. As always, she looked like a dream, garnished with sapphire, like the rarest of gems. She was the one thing that had remained unchanged since they moved in together. With every day that passed, she grew more beautiful, if that was even possible.

At Vinny's, Florian ordered the same meals they had gotten on their first date and tried his best to keep their conversation fresh and invigorating, with a hint of anticipation. However, as the night continued, he felt his focus wane like the descending of the tide.

After finishing her meal, Janelle looked up at Florian and asked, "Hey, honey, is everything okay?"

"Of course!" Florian answered. "I'm sorry. I've been a little aloof, haven't I? I'm a little distracted, but I'm happy. I promise. Would you mind taking a walk with me? I could use the fresh air."

"I would like that," she replied.

The air that night was cool and clear. It was the type of night that made one want to sit under the stars and fall in love, but that night, there were no stars. Instead, Florian and Janelle stood under an infinitely black sky, like a blank canvas, full of endless possibilities, that was simply waiting for someone to grab a paintbrush.

They walked hand-in-hand by the Fisher Theater, discussing topics ranging from art to architecture. It was almost time. The night was coming to a close, and Florian knew they would have to return home soon. Sensing his anxiousness, his palms began to sweat, so he let go of Janelle's hand, hoping she wouldn't notice. As they passed by an alleyway, he stopped and placed his hands on her shoulders.

"Wait right there," he said. "I want to see you the way I saw you before."

"You aren't setting me up to get mugged again, are you?" she joked.

"No," he chuckled. "I just want to try to recapture the magic of that night. You know, I never really got to say what I wanted to say."

"Oh really?"

It was time to put the final touch on his masterpiece, his Mona Lisa.

"I'm going to try to keep myself from giving a big speech this time," Florian said.

"But that sounds so unlike you," Janelle teased.

"Don't mock," he chuckled before clearing his throat dramatically. "When I met you, I couldn't have imagined where we would end up. And honestly, I still can't believe we're here.

You have made my life immeasurably better. You have brought light into my darkness, color to my grey. I love you more than I ever thought possible."

With those words, Florian dropped to a knee. Then, reaching into his pocket, he pulled out the ring he had spent hours picking out, especially for her. It was the most beautiful ring he had ever seen, an intricately designed masterpiece that took on the shape of a vine and wrapped all the way around the finger. In its center stood the centerpiece: a flawless, princess diamond. As he held it out to her, trying to keep his hands from shaking, the ring's silvery luster gleamed underneath the light of the street lamps.

"I was going to wait until you turned eighteen," he continued. "And originally, this was supposed to be a promise ring. But, over the last few weeks, I realized that I don't want to wait. I know that I want to be with you for the rest of my life. Will you marry me?"

For what seemed like an eternity, Janelle didn't speak. Instead, she stood in silence, completely frozen. Then, she beamed with joy before furrowing her brow. Over the next thirty seconds, her expression vacillated rapidly between joy, shock, worry and uncertainty. She opened her mouth to speak. Then, she closed it again.

Florian whispered, "You know, it's customary to give a man an answer when he asks you to marry him."

Finally, she said, "My dad's never going to be okay with this."

"Why does it matter?" Florian asked. "It's not like you live there anymore."

"It's not like my eighteenth birthday is tomorrow, either. Unless you're planning to wait two years, he's going to have to sign a paper saying that he's okay with this."

"You're telling me you've never forged a signature before?"

"I didn't say that..."

"Then, what's the problem?" he asked.

"Well," she chuckled. "I have to pick my classes this week for the fall semester. I don't know if I can handle having a wedding and choosing classes in the same week."

"We can get married after you choose your classes," Florian laughed. "So, is that a yes?"

"Of course, it's a yes!" she exclaimed.

Thus, Florian masterpiece was all but complete, with only one piece left to fall into place.

# PRIDE

DETROIT, MICHIGAN

*T*hat Monday morning, Paul burst through the doors of Illuminate like a raging bull into a club that, save for Lena, who was at the bar, drinking a glass of whiskey and poring over a stack of paperwork, was empty. The resounding crash of the doors as they smashed into the wall echoed across the club floor like the shot of a cannon.

"Paul," Lena sighed without so much as looking up from her paperwork. "Could you enter a little quieter next time?"

"We have a problem," Paul said, placing his hands on the bar next to her.

"Other than your entrances?" she asked.

"With Redd."

"What's the problem with Redd?" Redd, who had overheard the conversation while walking up the stairs from the basement, asked in a mocking tone.

Unfazed by his entrance, Paul made a beeline across the room toward Redd, slammed his fist on the counter and demanded, "Tell Lena what you did."

Redd rolled his eyes. "I can't exactly do that when I don't know what I did, now can I?"

"You know what you did," Paul said.

"I'm afraid you'll have to enlighten me," Redd replied.

"Will someone tell me what Redd did?!" Lena exclaimed.

"Where do I start?" Paul asked. "First, he dumped Nick's body in a lake - a damn lake! Which, of course, means that the cops found it. Second, instead of shipping my last recruit to Vegas, *like he was supposed to*, he stuck her in the center of town for Rebecca to see. Now, she wants to do a fundraiser for local prostitutes, yet another issue I have to contend with.

"Then, to top it all off, the detective investigating Nick's murder, which, by the way, was also Redd's doing, knows my name. My name! There's a piece of paper at the precinct with my name and address on it. I can only imagine how that got there! Now, he's suspicious of me, which means he's suspicious of Illuminate. I'm trying my best to keep him off our tail, but in order to do that, I had to invite him here so he could interview us. He could literally show up at any time."

At that moment, as if summoned by Paul's very words, the doors opened, and Bradie and Shepard walked into the club. Immediately, Bradie's eyes fell on Paul, who tried frantically to raise the curtain and assume character. Leaving his place at the bar to approach Bradie, Paul placed his hands subtly behind his back and motioned for Redd to return to the basement and get the girls out.

"Detective Lam!" Paul exclaimed as Redd disappeared into the basement. "I'm so glad you took me up on my offer! It's good to see you. I would like you to meet my boss, Lena. Did you two get a chance to meet at the party on Saturday?"

"We saw each other in passing," Lena said sweetly with a smile and a handshake. "It's so good to meet you, Detective."

"You too, Lena," Bradie replied. "I was hoping-"

"Hi, my name is Shepard Wilcox," Shepard, who had been eyeing Lena from the moment he walked through the door, said as he stepped in front of Bradie and took her hand. "It's so good to finally meet the beauty *and* brains behind this night club I keep hearing about."

"And he's as polite as he is handsome!" Lena exclaimed. "It's a pleasure to meet you."

"The pleasure is all mine," Shepard insisted.

"Well," Paul said. "Since the two of you seem to be getting along so swimmingly, why don't you get to talking while Bradie and I go on a short tour of the club?"

"You read my mind," Shepard answered, plopping down on the barstool next to Lena.

"I hope you don't mind multitasking," Paul said as he placed his hand on Bradie's shoulder, leading him toward the center of the club. "I thought this would be a golden opportunity to show you the place. This is a rare treat, you know. Not many people get to see the club when we aren't in full swing."

"I can't wait," Bradie replied. "Shall we work our way up from the basement or work our way down?"

Paul laughed, "You can't start a tour in the basement. That's like starting a concert with a ballad. You have to start with a bang."

"I thought you were supposed to 'end with a bang.'"

"Only if you want to wake your audience from the coma you put them in."

Bradie shrugged. As they walked, he ran his index and middle fingers along the wall, feeling every bump, crease and indent in the panels. His eyes danced around the room, taking in every molecule of what he saw, but he didn't speak. Instead, he walked and watched with his shoulders held back, like an alpha lion asserting his dominance over the pack.

"Those panels are my favorite part of the club," Paul

explained. "During the day, they don't look like much, just white and plain, but at night, they light up with all sorts of colors. They can do that because, although the panels look solid, they're actually translucent with long rows of colored lights underneath them."

"So, what you're saying is that not everything is what it seems to be," Bradie said.

"You could say that."

"How exactly did you get in this line of work, Paul?"

"Mostly, I was lucky. I was in high school when Rebecca got pregnant with Elle. So, naturally, since I wasn't exactly rolling in money, I went looking for a job. That's when Lena approached me and offered to hire me at her night club. From there, I guess the rest is history. But, enough about me. You're here to talk about Nick."

"We are. I'm getting the lay of the land, making sure I have all the puzzle pieces in place."

With every step he took, Bradie gained more confidence. He held his head a little higher, and his chest puffed out a little further. It was like he was sitting at the poker table with a full house, convinced that his opponent had nothing more than a pair of threes. After a few moments, they had toured the entirety of the top floor and reached the basement door.

"Looks like we've reached the end of the line. Did the show start with a sufficient bang?" A smug smile stretched across Bradie's face as he wrapped his fingers around the handle.

Paul took a look at the clock, reasoning that he'd given Redd plenty of time to clear the basement. "I would say so," he answered.

As they made their way into the basement, there was a distinct change in the way Bradie interacted with the world. His eyes no longer darted around the room. No longer did they study their surroundings. Instead, they stared forward, unmoving, as though they were locked onto a target.

*He's been here before.*

As soon as his foot hit the cement floor, Bradie lit his flashlight and took a sharp, right turn into one of the girls' rooms. Paul followed quickly behind, guided only by the distant stream of Bradie's flashlight, which quickly zipped in every direction in a frenzied attempt to locate a path. Finally, the light stopped, focusing itself on a single spot at the bottom, left-hand corner of the room.

"Now, what's this doing in the basement of a nightclub?" Bradie asked.

When Paul got close enough to see clearly again, he found Bradie kneeling on the ground with his flashlight trained on a single, twin mattress on the dirty floor and his right hand tucked discreetly under its back corner, searching for a clue.

*Bradie thinks he's the alpha lion in this encounter, but little does he know, he's encroaching upon territory that's already been claimed.*

"We try to view this place as a place for girls, who are hard on their luck, to get back on their feet," Paul explained. "Since we mostly give jobs to former drug addicts, runaways and the homeless, sometimes they need a place to stay. These rooms are our way of giving back to the community that supports us so generously, something I learned from my beautiful wife, who I believe you already met. Speaking of which, I've been meaning to ask you. When we met, you said you came across my name during an investigation. I was curious; did that happen to have anything to do with Monica Hatfield?"

Bradie cocked his head slightly to the left and stammered, "Uh - yes, actually. She - I was looking into something for a friend of hers, Alice Harper, about a modeling casting call. "

"Ah, so you heard my name from Leon Tarsus. That

explains it. See, Leon discovered Monica at a local casting call a few months ago. Regretfully, however, she wasn't the only thing he discovered that day. He also found out that Monica was being beaten severely by her father. That's when Leon contacted me. You see, Monica wanted to get away from her abusive home, but she didn't have anywhere to go. And she couldn't afford professional headshots or tuition for the modeling classes she needed to take. So, Leon sent her here to earn what she needed for her classes."

"Would you mind if I talk to her? If her father really was beating her, that's something I'd like to look into right away."

"Of course! I can take you right to her. She's out to lunch with some of the other girls."

"You have other girls living down here?" Bradie asked.

"Yes," Paul answered. "I think we have nine or ten right now."

*Well, seventeen, but who's counting?*

"I've heard a rumor going around that this is the place to go if you want some private, *adult* entertainment. Do you know anything about that?"

"Where did you hear that?" Paul asked, feigning concern. "That's disappointing to hear because I thought we were done with that. I really did. You see, sometimes, when you take in the kind of girls we do, you're bound to uncover a few bad eggs. A couple years ago, we found out, after the fact of course, that some of our girls had been using our rooms as a sort of mini-brothel to earn enough to fund their drug habits. Obviously, we don't stand for that sort of thing here, so I put an end to it and started doing enough background on the girls we brought here in order to avoid that sort of thing happening again. But, if the rumors are swirling again, maybe a few slipped through the cracks. Thank you, Detective. I'll look into this. If you find anything concrete, please let me know. I don't want our business connected to anything like that."

DAMN, HE'S GOOD.

Bradie waited by the back door of the club while Paul left to get Monica. A million questions raced through his mind, and doubt settled itself comfortably beside those questions.

*Is there even a case here?*

For every question he asked, Paul had a convincing answer.

*Was the whole basement humming with the sounds of prostitution, or was I hearing what I wanted to hear?*

*Could it really be only a few girls selling themselves in that basement?*

Paul had an explanation for everything: for Monica, for the paper at the warehouse, even for what he had seen with his own eyes in the basement.

*Or, could an entire operation be going on underneath the club, and Paul doesn't even know?*

When Monica rounded the corner, Bradie couldn't believe she was the same girl Alice Harper had told him about. She had described Monica as a pauper, a nothing, the type of girl that wouldn't get a second glance on a city street, but this girl didn't fit that description in the least. Instead, she was stunning, brimming with sensual confidence as she pivoted her hips demonstratively from side to side. Every step she took lit the sidewalk with bright flashes of blue and green, which beautifully complimented the tight, red dress that emblazoned her with a fiery beauty. Her hair was silky, smooth and curled to perfection, like Galatea, as though new life had breathed into what once was stone.

"Pleasure to meet you, Detective Lam," Monica said unconvincingly.

Bradie held out his hand to greet her, but she paid him no attention, walking past him as though he wasn't there.

Then, noticing that he wasn't following her, she turned her head back and shouted, "Cars make for better places to chat than street corners, don't you think?"

*This day keeps getting stranger.*

Quickly, he doubled back to open the passenger's side door of his car for Monica, who rolled her eyes and lowered herself into her seat. As he made his way around the front of the car, he looked at Anna, who was waiting in the backseat. She nodded, but it wasn't a nod of acknowledgment or readiness. It was as though she was answering the questions that circled through his mind with a resounding yes.

*How could she know?*

As he entered the car, Bradie struggled to find the right question to ask. Everything he could think of was either too personal or too impersonal to start a conversation. So, instead of jumping into a question and answer session, he decided to look at Monica for a moment, trying to see what Anna saw.

First, he looked in her eyes, which were as bright as a clear, blue sky. However, just beyond the horizon, storm clouds flashed with thunder and lightning, lighting her eyes with immense color. It was an incredible juxtaposition of light and darkness, of freedom and fear, of beauty and pain. She was holding a great hurt inside of her, but its source was still uncertain. One thing, however, was clear from the scowl painted across her face; she didn't want to talk to him.

"How are you?" Bradie asked, trying to make her feel comfortable.

"I haven't got all day," Monica sighed. "So please, ask me your questions so we can get this over with."

"What's the rush? I was hoping we could get to know each other," he said.

"What's there to know?"

"Well, what's a young girl like you doing living in the basement of a nightclub?"

"What do you really want to know, Detective: what it felt like when my father touched me, how many times a week he hit me? Do you want me to tell you about my last birthday, when he got so drunk, and I was so scared that I hid under my bed the whole day to avoid him? You want to know why I live in the basement of a nightclub? Because anything is better than that."

In that moment, words completely escaped him. Even if she was the victim he thought she was, there was nothing more he was going to get out of her. The fires of hell could have been burning around her, scorching her skin without end, and she still would have considered it an improvement over where she had come from.

Sometimes, hell isn't the worst fate that can befall a person.

'That's all the questions I have for you," he said. "I'm sorry for-"

"Are you happy?" Anna asked, leaning forward so her head rested between them. "With your life now that you're away from him?"

Monica paused. As she did, a single drop of rain fell from the storm clouds behind her eyes. It plummeted to the earth, landing just beneath her eyelid and lingering there for a fraction of a second before evaporating.

The sadness hadn't ended when she left home; it had merely been replaced by a duller kind of ache.

Quickly regaining her composure, Monica replied, "I've never been happier."

And that was the honest truth.

After Monica left, Bradie turned to Anna and asked, "So?"

"She didn't choose this," Anna answered, wiping a stream of tears from her eyes.

"How do you know?"

"I knew it from the moment I looked in her eyes. I know you saw it too, though you didn't know what it was. It was the same look I saw in every girl I met while I was trapped in that life. It's not just pain, not only hurt. It's not that the storm clouds are creeping up on you; it's that you're trying to force the clouds back so no one can see, except you can't hide them completely. They're always there. Most people just don't look deep enough."

"If you knew from the beginning, why did you ask if she was happy?"

"So you could see what I see. I know you can't prove it yet. I know we have nothing to go on except for suspicions and circumstantial evidence, but someone is pulling those girls' strings. We just need to find the puppet master."

THERE WAS ONLY ONE THING FLORIAN NEEDED IN ORDER TO complete his masterpiece: final approval from Lena. Of course, this was merely a formality because he had forgotten nothing. Every piece was in place, and the last lines had already been penned. It was perfection.

As he parked his car across from Illuminate, a deep sense of satisfaction and pride washed over him. He had always thought of himself as a playwright extraordinaire, but considering recent events, he thought that he might have to start thinking of himself as a master manipulator of marionettes instead. Crossing the street, he held his head up high, walking past Monica, who was exiting a jet black car that was parked along the club.

"Looks like someone's getting a head start on the day. Or, should I say, giving some head to start the day?" Florian joked as he passed.

"Living the dream," Monica replied unenthusiastically.

She was more agitated than usual, but Florian chalked it up to waking up on the wrong side of the bed that morning. That all changed, however, with one step inside the club. As soon as the door opened, a chill enveloped the air. The club's usual, relaxed nature was gone, replaced by a tension that was so thick, so tangible, that the compiled works of Shakespeare could have fit inside.

Paul and Redd sat on opposite ends of the club, staring furiously at each other, the space between them lit with an unsettling shade of crimson. The other end of the club was unsettling too, albeit for a different reason. There, Lena sat at the bar, talking with what appeared to be a detective. She was smiling, laughing and twirling her hair with her index finger. Surprisingly, she almost looked like a normal person, and in that moment, Florian actually found her attractive, which may have been the most disturbing part of all.

"It was *very* nice to meet you, Shepard," Lena said. "I hope I was able to help in some way. If you have any more questions for me, you have my number. Call me."

The detective bit his lip and replied, "Don't worry, ma'am. I will."

Lena smiled and waved at the detective until he was out of the doors. Then, as soon as he left, the warmth and softness left her instantly, leaving behind a familiar, cold shell.

Calling for everyone to meet at the bar, she announced, "From this moment forward, I want all your time and energy focused on making sure this investigation goes away quietly. There is far too much heat on us right now. Until then, I am halting all operations outside of what is necessary to run the club. The girls will be kept in the basement, except during business hours, and will only service clients outside the walls of this building. I am also putting a halt on all current, acquisition projects. Florian, this especially applies to you. You are to make no effort to bring Janelle in until I say so."

With that, the world stopped. Florian couldn't move. He couldn't breathe. It felt as though a vice grip had taken a hold of his chest. He didn't know what to do. Every possible option ran through his head at the same time, but they were all so incomplete that any one of them would turn his masterpiece into a farce. So, he did the only thing he could think to do; he asked Paul. Paul always knew what to do. Florian had been a first-hand witness to Paul's genius. If anyone could find a way out of this situation, he could.

Discreetly, Florian took Paul by the arm and led him to the far corner of the room, where he said, "I need your advice."

"This really isn't the best time," Paul replied.

"I know, but I wouldn't be asking if it wasn't dire," Florian pleaded.

"OK. Shoot."

"I've really backed myself into a corner with Janelle. First, she got pregnant. Then, her parents kicked her out of her house, and she wound up living with me. I figured the only way to salvage the whole situation was if I asked her to marry me and buy a house together. That way, I could use the marriage, the house and the baby as reasons why I would need her to work as a prostitute for a while until we got our feet under us. It's the perfect plan. At least, it was. See, the wedding's supposed to be next Friday, and I was going to bring her in tomorrow."

"Well," Paul said. "You have a couple options. You can-"

"I know. Dump her, stall her or marry her," Florian said, listing the options on his fingers.

"Do you want to marry her?" Paul asked.

"No, of course not."

"Well, do you love her?"

"What do you mean?" Florian asked.

"You listed marrying her as an option," Paul explained. "You wouldn't have done that with any of the other girls you've been with. Since you asked for my advice, here it is; if you don't love her, you wouldn't even think of marrying her. And if you love her, you have to marry her. Forget the job. Forget what you think you're supposed to do. Do you love her?"

*No, I couldn't love her.*

*Could I?*

～

"Hey, Paul, can I talk to you about something?" a voice called out from behind him.

*I seriously don't have time for this!*

Paul turned around to find Erica standing behind him, shuffling her feet nervously against the floor.

"Sure thing," he sighed. "What do you need?"

If there was one girl at Illuminate that Paul wanted to ensure stayed as happy as possible, it was Erica. Not only was she their top earner, but she was also Paul's right-hand girl, who was responsible for training new girls, in-house supervision and occasionally doling out punishment for minor infractions. Since putting her in charge, profits had grown fifteen percent, and the street corners were routinely painted with every color of the rainbow. Special arrangements weren't often made in this business, but for Erica, they could usually come to some sort of understanding.

She looked down, placing both hands behind her back, and said, "I was thinking; I've been here for some time now. I've put in extra time over the last year training the other girls. Probably paid off my debt five times over by now. I just thought that, maybe, it was about time I... moved on?"

"Is it because of something we did?" Paul asked, feigning concern. "If it is, I'll get to fixing it right away. We'd really hate to lose you."

"No, no. It's nothing like that," she answered. "Actually, my mom's back in town. She came to see me, even, last night at the club and told me that she's really sorry for everything that happened - before I ran away. She wants me back."

"Well, I'm sure your debt's paid off by now. I'll check the books and see what I can do."

From the main floor, he led Erica through the basement and into Lena's office, where the files were kept. Pulling Erica's from the cabinet, he plopped it open on the desk and rifled through it until he reached the page that tallied every last cent of her debt over the year and a half since she came to Illuminate. As usual, the page shone bright red.

"Looks like you're still short a thousand," he lamented.

"How is that even possible?!" she shouted in disbelief, crowding over his shoulder to read the numbers. "I've earned twice that amount a week since March."

"What about tips?" he asked.

"We both know tips are bullshit," she said. "Half my clients assume I'm bringing home four figures a night while the other half don't give a shit."

"I'm sorry, but there's not much I can do about that."

"What about my base rate? When I took over as bottom, you said I'd get twenty percent a night to go toward the principle."

"Well," he said. "Once you take into account rent, make-up, clothes, your performance fee, and DJ fee, among other things, you're still only breaking even every night."

"Performance fee?!" she protested. "Why do I have to pay in order to work?"

"What can I say?" He shrugged. "It's a competitive business."

"That's a load of shit, and you know it."

*When you can't keep them happy, at least keep them working.*

# 22

# EUTHANASIA

INDIANAPOLIS, INDIANA

*L*ong car rides have the potential to be either the paragon of all things good, filled to the brim with meaningful conversations and a deeper understanding of what makes your ride mate tick, or the bane of one's existence, consisting only of awkward silences and even more uncomfortable attempts at small talk. Regretfully for Kayde, car rides with Eric were fully and completely the latter option. After several of these excruciating trips, which started immediately after his meeting with the Manager and existed only as a means of testing and evaluation, he found that they, without fail, followed a very specific, three-phase pattern.

First came the silence, when Kayde would feel the insatiable urge to talk about something, anything, but was always far too self-conscious to actually speak. Then came the small talk, which usually consisted of Eric talking at length about a topic he was interested in, such as sports or hunting, but Kayde had absolutely no interest in or knowledge about. During this phase, Kayde would spend half the conversation debating whether or not he would rather walk to their destination. This inevitably led into the final phase, which was a silence even colder than the first, once they both remembered they had absolutely nothing in common except for the air they were breathing.

*Phase one.*

Kayde opened the door to Eric's car and sat down. After buckling himself in, he squirmed uncomfortably for a few moments, attempting to find a position that was even moderately comfortable. Though the leather seats he sat upon may have once been second only to the thrones of gods, like satin against the skin, after years' worth of beer stains, as well as sinkholes and divots from unmentionable activities, they felt more like freshly microwaved, cafeteria turkey. Once he finally found a position that didn't make his skin crawl, he nestled his head against the window and tried to get some shut eye.

Moments later, as Kayde was reaching the precipice of slumber, Eric opened his mouth and asked, "Who was she?"

Phase two was coming much earlier than usual.

Shaking the sandman's dust from his shoulders, Kayde sat up and replied, "Who was who?"

"The girl you brought when you first joined," Eric answered. "I've been meaning to ask you about her. The look in your eyes that night was nasty, man, like you'd just run over someone's dog. You knew her, didn't you?"

Kayde gulped, wishing they could go back to talking about sports, hunting, the weather, anything but Theresa. Anything but the albatross of guilt that shadowed him everywhere he went, waiting for the chance to dig its talons into his shoulders once more.

"She was my sister's best friend," he said in the most ineffectual way he could muster up.

"Your sister?" Eric laughed. "You mean the sister you came here to find in the first place? Shit, that's cold, Kayde. Liquid nitrogen cold. To take some rando is one thing. That's nothing, but your sister's best friend? That's a whole different level of desperate, man."

"Desperate?"

"The least you could do is level with me. I know you think of me as some kind of idiot, but even I know the only reason you joined in the first place was to find your sister. You're not exactly James Bond, dude. Honestly, between you and me, I think the only reason the Manager lets you stick around is because you're some sort of social experiment for him. So, be careful. I certainly wouldn't want to see what happens if you fail."

With those words, they quickly moved on to phase three.

For the remainder of the trip, Kayde sat in silence, frustrated, pondering what Eric had said. For a time, he thought he could simply sing his song to Hades and convince him to release Blair, but it turned out that Hades already knew the tune and was simply dangling Blair in front of Kayde for his own entertainment. It was difficult to tell whether that fact made him feel angry or hopeless.

An hour later, the car stopped in front of a small, abandoned warehouse in downtown Indianapolis that they were using to house the girls who Eric deemed weren't pretty enough or confident enough to work events at The Music Center. Kayde had been there a few times with Eric before, mostly for inspections and general threatening, but something felt different this time. Usually, Eric borderline-sleepwalked through these trips, only waking to give the occasional instruction or threatening glare. It was always the same: get in, get out, get on with your life. This time, however, he seemed jovial, like an elephant in a peanut factory. As he exited the car and started toward the entrance, he shot Kayde a sly wink.

*That can't be a good sign.*

Bursting through the warehouse door, Eric marched into the center of the large, open area between the entrance and rows upon rows of blue curtains that separated the girls' living quarters.

Then, planting his feet squarely on the dirty, concrete floor, he shouted, "I need everyone out here, now!"

Suddenly, the curtains rustled, sending the warehouse's three dozen girls, like a school of fish driven to shore, into the center of the room. Soon, Kayde and Eric were surrounded by a circle of terrified faces, all of which were looking at Eric.

Once all the girls were gathered, Eric nodded authoritatively at a vicious-looking, tattooed man, who immediately disappeared into the crowd, only to return a moment later with a pale, ruby-haired girl by the scruff of her hair. The tattooed man then threw the girl to the ground in front of Eric. She looked up at him in tears, shaking uncontrollably, like an abused dog that knew it was about to, once again, face unfathomable punishment. In an instant, Kayde's heart grew heavy, and he turned away, unable and unwilling to watch.

Stepping past the girl, Eric addressed the crowd. "I've got to say; I'm disappointed. I thought we had an understanding here. You do as we say, and nobody gets hurt, an arrangement in which I think we've been more than fair. Unfortunately, this only works if everyone is on board, and, also unfortunately, it appears that not everyone is. You see, Sylvia decided she no longer appreciated everything we've given you, figuring instead that it would be a good idea to escape. Of course, we found her, thanks to Hadassah, who all of you should thank because, had she not come forward, this punishment would apply to everyone. Now, in case you don't all get the picture yet, I want you to watch what happens when you run away."

Then, he turned to Kayde, took his gun from its holster, and offered it to him, saying, "The honor is all yours, mate. Make it short and sweet. Right to the head."

With shaking hands, Kayde took the gun and stared at it for a moment as sweat fell from his palms and forehead like a raging monsoon. The rapid pounding of his heart reverberated through his body and echoed in his ears. Suddenly, he felt every eye in the room fix on him, wondering what he was going to do. He even wondered the same thing. In one hand, he held the life of the girl on the floor, and in the other, he held Blair's. Although he knew it was just another test, another experiment, he couldn't help but wonder.

*Does saving one life justify taking another's?*

*And another's?*

*And another's?*

The body count was quickly rising, with no signs of stopping, but another refusal could mark the end of his journey into the underworld and his chances of finding Blair.

As he looked out over the crowd, at the sea of frightened faces, one girl stood out. Unlike the others, she didn't look afraid. Her lips weren't trembling, nor was her brow shrunken with worry. Instead, she looked dead, as if no life existed behind her pale eyes. Curious, Kayde looked at her, and for a split second, he saw Blair, staring at him coldly, her frozen eyes boring through his soul, and instantly, all doubt and fear faded away. He finally understood. In the grand scheme of things, Blair's life wasn't more important than this girl's. Sylvia was also somebody's friend, somebody's daughter, somebody's sister, but another truth rang just as loud; she wasn't *his* sister. Finally resolved, he walked determinately over to Sylvia, held the gun to her head, and calmly pulled the trigger.

*Click.*

*Click.*

Placing his hand on Kayde's shoulder, Eric took the gun

from his hand and said, "Good work. I didn't think you had it in you."

With blistering speed and precision and without warning, Eric turned and slammed his fist into Sylvia's cheek, sending her crashing to the ground. Then, climbing on top of her, he continued to land blow after blow onto her skull.

And though Kayde tried to close his eyes and drown it out, her screams painted a picture more vivid than his eyes ever could.

{}~{}~{}~{}~{}~{}~{}~{}~{}~{}

Later that night, Kayde lay motionless on Violet's bed, staring at the dim, flickering light that hung above his head. Next to him, Violet rested her head on his chest with her arms wrapped around him. Since leaving the warehouse, he had hardly said two words to anyone, including Violet, instead choosing to run on auto-pilot and shut out the voice in his head that simply circled around the same thought over and over again in an endless loop; in order to journey into hell and sway the heart of the devil, did he have to become a demon himself? He wondered if Orpheus had failed to rescue his beloved because he tried to hold onto his humanity within the horrors of hell. Maybe Kayde was doomed to make the same mistake unless he became something different, something monstrous.

"It's not your fault," Violet said.

"You heard what happened?" he sighed.

"I overheard Eric talking to the Manager," she replied. "You can't blame yourself. Nothing even happened. It was just a test."

"And if it hadn't been a test?" he asked.

"Then you would only be guilty of trying to protect your

sister," she answered. "If it wasn't you, it would've been Eric. And you would be left with no chance of finding Blair."

"But it still would've been me... Blair wouldn't want any of this. She would hate me for what I did to Theresa. Sure, she's still alive, and I fully intend to get her out. But, I don't even want to imagine the pain she's going through on account of me. Then today, I barely hesitated at the thought of killing that poor girl. How many lives am I willing to sacrifice on the devil's altar in exchange for her life? And at what point does it become not worth it anymore? Given the choice, though, I would do it again and again, as many times as it took. At what point do I descend so far that I become just like Eric?"

"You could never be like him."

"What makes you so sure?"

"Because you have the most beautiful soul I've ever seen. There isn't a thing in the world that could tarnish it."

"You're too sweet." Kayde smiled. "But regardless, I need to get into the Manager's office and find out where they sent Blair before his experiment goes too far."

"Why don't you let me take care of that?" Violet offered.

"I can't let you do that," he said.

"But if they catch you, they'll kill you. And all of this would've been pointless," she replied.

"I can't."

"Why not?"

"No!" he barked. "I can't let you get hurt. Not you. Not on account of me."

She smiled, biting the bottom corner of her lip, and asked, "Why are you so perfect to me?"

"Because I care about the people who are important to me."

Violet kissed Kayde on the cheek. Then, pressing down on his shoulder, she pushed him onto the bed and hoisted herself on top of him, and their lips met in a passionate embrace. As he slid his hands up her leg and placed them on her waist, she raised to her knees and, taking his hands in hers, slid them up her shirt.

As she lifted her shirt above her head, he stopped her, once again, saying, "Wait."

She smiled and said, "This is special. Because *you're* special."

Kayde could hardly believe it, but Violet was even more beautiful with her clothes off. Every inch of her was more perfect than he thought possible. Her velvet skin illuminated the entire room with its radiance, and her curves couldn't have been shapelier if they had been imagined by the likes of Da Vinci himself. She was Aphrodite in the flesh, equally beautiful and sensual. He had always been led to believe, whether by his parents, his friends or the boys in the locker room, that sex was purely a physical act, nothing more than animal instinct, but being with Violet was so much more. Every touch was poetic. Every movement was art, every sensation, spiritual. He had never felt so close to another human being in his life, and in that moment, he could feel their souls being welded together by something he couldn't explain.

It was all over far too soon. Kayde wished it was possible to make that feeling last forever. Though try he would, three more times that night to be precise, he knew it never would. When it was all over, Violet fell back onto the bed next to him, wrapping her arm around his chest. She sighed pleasurably, her body against his, and in that moment, they didn't need words. Their souls spoke in a way that was much more profound.

# 23

# ORPHANED

DETROIT, MICHIGAN

"*D*addy, look! I did it!"

Elle's small, yellow and white-striped Frisbee glided across the clear horizon as smoothly as Paul had ever seen. Its motion was so fluid, so perfectly singular, that it appeared to have been drawn onto the bright blue canvas above. In an instant, the entire universe froze. Even the air stood still, allowing the Frisbee to fly calmly across the playground. In that moment, the reservoir of fatherly pride that sat deep within him welled up to overflowing and cascaded furiously through his veins. After dozens of failed attempts to make the Frisbee fly the ten feet that stood between father and daughter, Elle had finally done it. She had performed the perfect throw.

*Like father, like daughter.*

Following Bradie's visit to the club, the ground underneath Paul's feet had finally settled. The Black Rose had been express-shipped out of state as to safely evade any suspicion from Rebecca. Police pressure had all but subsided due to a lack of new evidence or activity, and he hadn't seen hide nor hair of

Redd since their confrontation. Lena's freeze on new acquisitions had even afforded him a few extra days off, which allowed him to spend some much-needed time with his family, especially Elle. His strategy had played out to perfection, turning rough waters into smooth sailing.

As Paul reached out to take hold of the small, spinning projectile, a strong breeze rushed past his shoulder. Sliding across his outstretched arm, it grazed the right edge of the disc, causing it to flutter like a canary with a crippled wing. For a moment, it appeared as though the Frisbee would be able to muscle its way to its target, but soon, its fluttering turned into a free-fall, depositing the disk a foot from Paul's fingertips.

He took two, small steps before bending over to pick it up. Taking it in his hand, he exclaimed, "Awesome job, honey! That was a great throw!"

Elle tilted her head to the side and replied, "But Daddy, I didn't do it. It fell before it got to you."

Paul smiled. "You can't control which way the wind blows. Sometimes, you can do things perfectly and still fall short because of circumstances you can't control."

Then, after looking around him for a second, he asked, "Now, tell me something; do you happen to remember what Daddy did with his water bottle? You're wearing this old man out, and I need a drink."

"Daddy!" Elle laughed. "You're not old. My teacher says you're not old until you're at least thirty, so you can't be tired yet."

"You're stalling," Paul teased. "You don't remember, do you?"

"I remember, Daddy! You put it under the picnic table with the rest of our stuff after we finished our lunch."

Sticking his tongue out at Elle, Paul turned to make his way toward the picnic table. As he did, she smiled at him giddily, flipped her hair to the side and shifted her weight rapidly from side to side, dancing to a rhythm all her own. In that moment, Paul wished he could shut her off from the outside world forever. She was so innocent, so perfect, like an ice cream sundae on a Sunday afternoon or the feeling of sand between ocean-drenched toes. The world didn't deserve her.

Placing his hand on the table's bench, he peered underneath in search of his water bottle. He moved their bags around, rifled through the cooler they had kept their lunches in and looked under, around and inside everything they brought with them, but the bottle was nowhere to be found. Even after double-checking, there was still nothing. Frustrated, he stood up and placed his hand on top of the picnic table. As he did, he felt something cool and metallic graze momentarily across his fingertips.

"You little turd," Paul laughed, wrapping his hand around the bottle and taking a swig of warm, yet refreshing, water. "It wasn't under the table. It was on top."

"But, you said you were going to put it under the table because it would stay cooler in the shade," Elle said, perplexed.

She was right. He had said that.

He must have forgotten to do it.

"I hope you're ready to run!" Paul announced as he downed one last drink of water. "Because I'm going to send this one into the next postal code!"

He locked the Frisbee in place by his left hip and cocked his shoulders back. Taking aim at the peak of the tree line behind Elle, he reared back and fired. The Frisbee soared viciously through the air like a falcon in pursuit of its prey. Elle's head shot to the sky as it zipped overhead. Then, she took off after it as though a white wolf nipped at her heels. Within seconds, the disc was several yards beyond her. Though her little legs churned and churned, with every step, she grew further behind.

"It's going too fast!" she cried out in desperation. "I can't get it!"

Suddenly, Paul felt the ground quake beneath him, sending shockwaves through every inch of his body and turning his sinews to gelatin. Even the air itself seemed to shake. His vision blurred, as though he was peering through pure static. Then, there was nothing. The vibrant colors around him melted away, blended together and turned to the pitchest black he had ever seen. A terrifying coldness, like liquid nitrogen coursing through his veins, filled his being. In that moment, though he wasn't a religious man, Paul felt the overwhelming urge to cry out to a god he never believed in, but he couldn't. His mouth wouldn't move.

If these were to be the final moments his lungs held breath, he only hoped that, if there was a god, he would see fit to overlook his momentary muteness and help Elle remember how to call 911.

Then, he felt something he didn't expect, weightlessness, as though he was floating through the vast emptiness of space with nothing around him for miles and no one to hear him scream. The overwhelming emptiness he felt in that moment was simultaneously freeing and excruciating, like morphine laced with sulfuric acid. As he hung lifeless in the darkness, slowly descending toward the earth, two, stone-like arms temporarily halted his descent.

"What was that you said?" a gravelly voice whispered, its ominous hiss echoing through the darkness. "Sometimes you can't control which way the wind blows."

With those words, Paul plummeted to the ground. The collision felt like a shot to the heart, but even that was mere child's play in comparison to the terror that gripped him. That voice was undeniable; it was Redd's. Though Paul fought with every fiber of his being to get back up, it was useless. He would have had more luck if a ten-ton building had been sitting atop his shoulders. As he reached his hand helplessly into the abyss, his vision returned in time for him to see Redd lead Elle toward the road.

Then, there was nothing.

Only darkness.

The next thing Paul knew, he was lying face down in a sea of emerald as the sun disappeared over the horizon. Around him, the air had grown cold. His face and arms dripped with dew as he rose to his knees. He had lost the entire day. As he stood to his feet, a rage unlike anything he had ever felt before boiled inside his veins. With every step he took, it grew until he was consumed.

Redd had crossed the line this time. It was one thing for him to puff out his chest, stamp his feet and bellow like a ram fighting for dominance amongst the herd. It was another thing for him to go after his daughter. That was when Paul's horns came out.

He wasted no time. Within seconds, his car barreled down Detroit's city streets at uncomfortably dangerous speeds, headed toward Illuminate. As he reached the club, the gearshift hardly reached the park position before the keys left the ignition.

It was moments before the club was set to open. College students from every walk of life stood in line outside the club, brewing with an excitement that seemed to light the glow sticks they held in their hands with every color of the spectrum. Usually, Paul saw this sight as beautiful: a stunning portrait of humanity coming together for a shared celebration of life. People who otherwise would never speak to each other had joined together in this place to form a single entity that was greater than what they were apart. That day, however, he simply saw it as a nuisance. He pushed and shoved his way through the crowd until he finally made it to the door. Then, the door burst open like the cork of a shaken Champagne bottle as Paul zipped past the bar and entered the basement.

Once down the stairs, he planted his feet on the damp, cement floor and called out, "Redd!"

The sound of his voice echoed through the halls of the basement, its volume compounding and escalating until it grew into a deafening wail. It was high noon at the O.K. Corral, and Paul was waiting for his opponent to step out of the shadows. Finally, on the far end of the hall, Redd entered the arena. He walked slowly, with his shoulders held high and loose like a prizefighter who knew the match was already rigged in his favor. His heels drug on the ground behind him in a show of dominance.

"How does it feel?" Redd asked. "To be in the passenger seat for a change?"

"You have no right," Paul said.

"I have the right to anything I can take."

"That does not include my family!"

"Then maybe you shouldn't let them out into the wild, where the animals prowl. Or maybe you should do a better job protecting them."

With a swift, sudden movement, Paul's forearm drove into Redd's throat, forcing him into the wall. He pinned him there like a bear who had cornered its prey, his eyes burning like fire. His hair stood on end, and the rage that, until this moment, had been bottled up now oozed from his very pores.

*Redd better be careful what he says next.*

Redd sneered, "You're not going to hurt me, Paul."

"Lena will do a lot worse when she finds out what you've done," Paul said.

"But Lena's not going to find out, is she?"

"Then you better have a damn good reason why I shouldn't tell her."

"Because this is my game, which means we play by my rules. If you hand me over to Lena, you'll never find out where Elle is. Same goes for if you try to tail me. Hell, if I so much as smell your scent outside this building, she dies. In my game, you have two options. Option number one, you do whatever I say, whenever I say, for however long I say, and maybe, just maybe, I let her go. Option two, you kill me with your own hands and bring my body to the docks. If you do that, my guy will tell you where to find your daughter."

"How will he even know I'm the one who kills you?"

"Because I brought some insurance," Redd snickered as he pulled out his phone and handed it to Paul. On the screen, Paul saw himself. Redd was live streaming every second of their interaction from a button camera on his shirt.

"You bastard," Paul whispered.

"Now you're getting the idea!" Redd exclaimed. "You see, if I die at the hands of anyone other than you, I have friends watching, with strict orders to tie weights to Elle's ankles and throw her into Lake Erie. I'd choose wisely if I were you because, once you deliver my body to the docks, my guy is also under orders to bring my body straight to the cops. I'm sure your detective friend would love to find the body of yet another person connected to you."

Paul's forearm tensed, pushing deeper and deeper into Redd's throat. His breathing quickened. His hand began to shake, but Redd didn't move. He simply stared Paul dead in the eyes and smiled. In that moment, Paul saw the flicker of something that frightened him to his core: desire. Redd wanted Paul to kill him. Death wasn't the roadblock; it was the destination. Option one was nothing more than a smokescreen that inevitably led to option two. While Redd still breathed, Paul would never get Elle back. And Redd's death almost certainly led to Paul's incarceration. Either way, he would never get to hold his daughter again. He would never hear her laugh as he read her another story or watch another puppet show. His grip on the Redd's neck loosened, and Redd dropped to the floor.

"I'll let you think about it," Redd said as he patted Paul condescendingly on the back and retreated to the club, leaving him alone.

That was when the panic set in. Paul's chest tightened, leaving him unable to breathe. His knees grew weak. It felt like the walls were closing in on him as the air around him became light and dizzying. His pulse quickened. His fist tightened. Then, as though he was being controlled by some, outside force, he slammed his fist repeatedly against the concrete wall. At this point, he couldn't even feel pain anymore. Though he could see his knuckles bruise and bleed, he couldn't feel a thing. He was pure instinct, unfettered adrenaline. With every pound, the voice in the back of his head grew louder and louder.

It screamed, "Fight!"

It screamed, "Win!"

And with every dent he made into the immovable object before him, one truth became clear; there had to be another way.

{}~{}~{}~{}~{}~{}~{}~{}~{}~{}

That night, the homeless shelter looked hardly recognizable. Every inch had been polished to pure perfection. It was a special night: Rebecca's benefit dinner for local prostitutes. She had been planning for weeks, making sure everything was perfect so she could give every girl that walked through those doors the VIP treatment. The way she saw it, they spent the majority of their lives being treated like either commodities or cast-outs. They deserved a chance to have everything revolve around their needs for once, from food to decoration.

Starting at the service counter, a red carpet ran across the center of the room, extending out into the street. On either side of the aisle, from front to back, were gold stanchions, connected by red velvet ropes, and beside the stanchions stood long tables with solid black tablecloths and eggshell chairs. Each place at the table was set with beautiful, handmade plates and bowls that had been made from scratch by Rebecca's great-grand-mother, seventy years earlier. They were extraordinary, covered with white, like porcelain, and shining brilliantly underneath the fluorescent lights.

In the center of each plate was a hand-painted array of intri-cate flowers and birds, each with its own, special design, and their rims were embroidered with solid gold. Finally, the icing on the cake of the whole affair were the centerpieces, the actual statues made for the Screen Guild Awards, which Rebecca had acquired from a friend of hers who worked for the prestigious R.W. Oscar and Company. It was their own, special awards dinner.

Rebecca and Georgie were just finishing up with the final preparations for the night when Paul stumbled into the shelter. Walking up to Rebecca, he said, "I'm so sorry I'm late. Some-thing came up last minute."

"It's all right," Rebecca replied. "At least you're here. Where's Elle?"

Thus rose the curtain.

"My parents didn't tell you?" Paul asked. "They called and said that they missed their Ellie so much that she had to stay with them for the whole week. I figured they wouldn't have called me unless they'd already asked you, so, I took her over. I'm sorry. Should I have told them she couldn't?"

Rebecca sighed, "No, it's fine, I guess. I just wish your mom would give us some notice before she did something like this. This is an important night, and I was planning on Elle being here. I bought a really cute server's outfit for her and everything."

"Look at the bright side. Now, we'll just have to have her serve us a fancy dinner one of these days."

"You have an answer for everything, don't you?"

"Just not for how I landed a girl as wonderful as you."

"Alright, Casanova," she said with a playful wink. "The girls will be coming any second. You'd better get dressed."

After kissing Rebecca on the lips, Paul was off, dashing to the back room where he had hung up his best suit. Throwing it on as quickly as he could, he darted back up front. By the time he made it to the dining hall, the girls were already streaming in. He looked over at Rebecca, who was smiling ear to ear with pride over the turn out. There was little else in the world he enjoyed more than to see her light up with joy. That was why he had insured that this night, of all nights, would be a success. While Rebecca provided the décor and location, Paul provided the girls. It was a win-win scenario for him. Rebecca was able to have her big night, his girls got a morale boost and a night off, and he knew that none of them would so much as think about letting anyone know they knew him, at least not as long as he was there.

From that point on, the benefit dinner went exactly as planned. Dinners were served, and Rebecca and Georgie made sure to spend time with each girl before the end of the night. Meanwhile, Paul spent the night surveying the room, taking mental notes on which girls connected best with Rebecca so he knew who to send back after a few days. After all, a night like this with zero follow-up would either break Rebecca's spirits or raise suspicions.

Two hours later, the night was over. The girls filed out, and Paul, Georgie and Rebecca tore everything down. Once it was all put away, Georgie went back to his room, and Paul leaned up against the wall, exhausted. So far, he had managed to bury his despair six-feet beneath his soul's soil, but over the course of time, it had risen like a phantom, breaking through each layer of rock and dirt that stood in its path. The vice grip it held on him was almost tangible as it wrapped its icy fingers around Paul's heart and slowed his blood. Soon, every beat became labored. As he tried to break from its hold, even if only for a moment, Rebecca leaned against the wall next to him. He frantically tried to bury it all back down again in fear that she would see right through him, but one look at his wife showed that she was fighting her own phantom too.

"What's wrong, my love?" he asked.

"Nothing," she answered. "It's silly."

"Nothing's silly if it bothers you this much," he insisted.

"I guess I was hoping she'd be here tonight."

"The girl from the NA meeting?"

"Yeah…"

"I'm sorry, honey," he said, wrapping his arm around her shoulder. "I know how badly you wanted to reach her, but you can't save them all. Sometimes, there's too much standing in the way."

"You're right. I just can't shake the feeling that something awful happened to her," she sighed. "I could use something to take my mind off all this. What do you say we catch a late-night movie? Since Elle is with your parents, that means we can stay up late."

"Absolutely! That sounds amazing! I just have to talk to

Georgie about something really quick. Do you mind waiting in the car for me? I'll only be a couple minutes."

"Don't keep me waiting too long, stud."

A kiss so sweet it could make him an addict.

Georgie's room was buried in the back of the shelter. It was small and dark, lit only by a single light bulb that hung above his bed, and was comprised only of a twin size mattress and a set of shelves, where he kept an assortment of pictures, Bibles and snack foods. Rebecca, on many occasions, had tried to convince him to move out of the former utility closet and into one of the bigger rooms. After all, he deserved it for the immeasurable number of hours he spent helping around the shelter, but Georgie always refused. He said it was important to keep the larger rooms open in case someone came to the shelter who needed it more than he did. As always, he was thinking of others before himself.

That was why Paul came to him that night. There was no one else to whom he felt he could entrust this kind of information while also trusting them to do everything within their power to help. Peering around the corner, Paul tapped on the door post three times.

Georgie exclaimed, "Paulie boy! What brings you to my humble establishment?"

Paul took a step forward, placing himself in the center of the doorway, and asked, "You said your door was always open, right?"

"For you? Always!"

"I need your help."

"What do you need?"

"Someone's taken Elle. I need you to help me get her back."

# 24

# CARRION

## THE VOID

*T*hey say that, when a person dies, their whole life flashes before their eyes. However, Natasha never anticipated that saying would be so literal. Deep down, she always expected it to be more of a re-living, like experiencing life for a second time in order to truly understand how the pieces fit together. For most, she believed that to be a blessing. But, if she was honest with herself, she always feared the re-living more than death itself. Since she didn't believe in an afterlife in any sort of tangible sense, she always considered the re-living to be one's heaven or hell, depending on the life they lived. Once it was over, she believed true death to be emptiness, a cessation of existence. Compared to the life she had lived, that was almost something to look forward to.

However, as her body faded into darkness, she was surprised to find herself transported into a strange, new realm. Everything around her was black, but somehow, she could still see. She shifted her gaze downward, curious to see what form she had taken, only to see herself in her own body, except different.

Her hands and feet were covered in a thick layer of dirt and grime, and her fingernails appeared to have been completely torn away, replaced by bloody husks where they used to reside. Then, she looked at her arms, which were bruised and bloodied with track marks running up and down the length of both. Beyond her arms, she saw that she was dressed in a white nightgown that was torn beneath her waist. Unlike the rest of her, however, the nightgown wasn't dirty or covered in blood. Instead, it was clean, shining with a bright, white light that lit the world around her. It was as though she existed in this place simply as a metaphor.

Suddenly, tiny, white lights started to dance around her, taking the form of images that flashed and flickered in front of her just long enough for her to remember everything, even the moments she had long since forgotten. She quickly found that, if she fixated on a specific memory, that moment would play back like a home movie, complete with surround sound. Tears fell from her eyes as she heard her mother's voice for the first time in years. She had forgotten how strong and reassuring her voice had once been. Quickly, Natasha found herself replaying years of bedtime stories and nightly prayers so she could stare into her mother's hazel eyes and remember the sweet, vanilla scent of her golden hair. Everything melted away in those moments: every fear, every hurt, every feeling other than peace.

She spent what felt like years watching every family Christmas and listening to her father play every song he had ever written for her on his guitar by a blazing fireplace. His voice was like that of an angel. It had the power to light every dark place in her heart and move mountains. She marveled at how strong he was. Though she could see him get weaker and weaker with every memory that passed, he refused to let anyone know how much brimmed beneath the surface. Eventually, he could hardly muster the strength to lift himself out of bed, but he always made time for his little girl. She only wished she had inherited the tiniest bit of that strength. Even though it wouldn't have made things easy, maybe it would have made them bearable.

Then, she saw the hospital room. Choking back the tears, she tried frantically to move the images along. Instead of passing, however, they grew until she was completely surrounded by them. Soon, she found herself sitting by her father's bedside, gazing painfully at the shell that lay before her. The color had left his skin, leaving him pale. Even his deep, blue eyes were colorless. Tubes and wires ran in and out of his body. At this point, he appeared to be more machine than man. Natasha remembered this day; it was the day he died. As she sat there, dreading being forced to relive this moment, her father struggled to turn himself to his side.

He whispered in a low, gravelly voice, which was all he had left, "Hey, honey, could you come closer to Daddy for a minute? I want to tell you something."

She rushed to his side and said, "Don't, Daddy. You need your strength."

"No, this is important," he sighed. "I don't know how much longer I'm going to have."

"Don't say that!" she rebuked. "You're going to get better. Mommy and I have been praying that you get better. That means God's going to heal you, right?"

"I don't think so, sweetheart. I think maybe God has a different plan for me. But, no matter what happens to me, never forget how much light shines within your heart. The darkness is going to try to take you, honey, but don't let it. Keep fighting. Promise me you'll shine, Grace."

"I promise, Daddy," Natasha sobbed as her father's eyes closed for the last time.

That was the moment she stopped being Grace, though she wouldn't be given her new name for some time. It was also the moment she realized there was no God.

Suddenly, the hospital room faded away, and the glow from her gown started to dim. Slowly, the light around her grew dark with each set of images that followed. She watched reluctantly as her mother sank into depression. As a child, Natasha never understood what drove her mother into the arms of asshole after asshole. Now, however, she understood; without her father, life was unbearable for her mother. For a while, the assholes came and went without spending enough time to impact either of their lives. Some of them didn't even earn an image in the cosmic story of her life. Then, there was Jerry.

Jerry was a lawyer from Detroit who her mom had met at the diner she worked at one summer's eve. He seemed decent enough at first: handsome, successful and charming. On the surface, he was just like Natasha's father, which was why they packed up two weeks later and moved into his fancy, Detroit loft. Moving from Kansas City to Detroit was rough for a twelve-year old girl, but her mother was "in love," as she said. Natasha insisted it was all moving too quickly, but she was just "holding on too tightly to the memory of her father" and needed to "let him go."

After all, what does a little girl know about love?

Natasha had only lived at Jerry's for two months before he first touched her, which according to him, was "a mistake." Her mother was working late at her new job, and he was lonely. Besides, she was "asking for it" because she was watching a movie in the living room, dressed in "basically nothing," which meant she was wearing a camisole and shorts, like she did every night. Soon, however, one mistake became a ritual every time her mother didn't make it home by nine o'clock, and there was no fighting it. He was too strong. Then, one night, touching turned into penetration, and Natasha had enough. She told her mother but was only met with anger and denial. Her mother yelled at Natasha, telling her over and over again how horrible it was to make up stories just because she didn't like Jerry.

That was the moment Natasha decided to run away and never come back.

Once again, the images grew and swirled around her until she found herself walking the busy streets of Detroit with everything she owned in a backpack. Across the horizon, the sun was setting, filling the sky with an orange glow. Her stomach growled. She spent the whole of the day wandering the streets, searching for food and shelter, yet finding neither. Suddenly, the aroma of freshly cooked burgers invaded her nostrils. Immediately, she scoured the street like a bloodhound on the hunt, looking for the source of the scent: a homeless shelter at the end of the street.

Quickly shuffling inside, she grabbed two burgers from the old man behind the counter and sat down, alone, in the back corner of the room. The grease dripped seductively from the six-ounce, store-bought patty as she brought it to her mouth. Her first bite was as though she was tasting from the nectar of the gods. It was angelic, which seemed strange, considering she had never liked burgers before. In fact, she considered them dry, tasteless and an insult to the culinary arts, but, in that moment, hunger spoke far louder than principle. Within moments, her plate was barren, and her stomach was finally satisfied.

As she stood to leave, a kind-faced woman, who looked like she couldn't have been older than twenty, sat across from her and extended an invitation. "There's no need to rush out the door, hun. You can stay as long as you want. I hear the conversation alone keeps people coming through those doors for weeks."

Hesitantly, Natasha sat down.

The woman continued, "Where are your parents, honey?"

"Gone," Natasha answered, both out of bitterness and pain.

"I'm so sorry, sweetheart," the woman said, placing her hand on Natasha's. "Do you have anywhere to sleep tonight?"

Natasha shook her head.

"Well, there's a room here for you if you want it, and there's always good food on the menu," the woman said as she reached her hands behind her neck and clasped the gleaming, silver necklace she wore around her neck. "You know, when I was your age, I didn't have the best home life. My father was a mean drunk, and my mother was so scared of him that it was almost like she wasn't there at all. I was afraid all the time. Then, one day, my aunt stopped by to visit. She knew how hard it was for me there, so, she put her arm around me and gave me this necklace, saying that as long as I wore it, I would always walk in light, no matter how dark the world around me got. Over the years, the world didn't get any brighter, but my heart did. Soon, I realized that it wasn't the necklace that had changed me but what it symbolized. I hope one day it does the same for you."

She held the necklace toward Natasha with a loving, reassuring smile. Thanking her, Natasha took it in her hands and placed it in her pocket, knowing that, although she wasn't sure how, one day it would be the only thing she had left to hold onto.

That was the moment her faith in humanity was restored, only to be shattered the next afternoon by the man that would start her down the path toward becoming Natasha.

All at once, the glow around her dissipated, leaving everything dark, except for the staticky flicker of the images blurring together into a wash of grey. She stood in complete darkness for what seemed like an eternity, like she was standing inside a black hole. Around her, there was no sound, no light, no feeling except for emptiness. For a moment, she wondered if she had finally died and was trapped in hell, an eternity devoid of anything resembling existence. Then, suddenly, her gown glowed for a few micro-seconds before burning out once more.

One by one, like fireflies filling an empty field, the lights swirled around her, playfully rubbing against her skin as they passed and sending waves of pure light up her arms and legs. As each surge rippled across her veins, she felt something warm pulsate inside her chest. When she looked down, she saw that her gown was glowing as steadily and radiant as ever. All at once, the lights blew past her and congregated in front of her, swirling like a hurricane. Then, blinding light exploded all around her, driving the darkness away.

Instinctively, Natasha shielded her eyes from the glare. When she lowered her guard, she was lying in her bed at the warehouse. At first, she thought that perhaps she had woken up, that she was alive, but there were no track marks on her arms, no syringes on the floor. This was a memory, but of what?

Curious, she searched for a clue that would separate this day from all the others in that wretched place, but everything looked the same, except for the vase of violets she had been given by that one, obsessive pair of slacks, who came by at least once a week to see her, usually bearing some sort of gift. That is, he used to come every week until his wife found out he wasn't really out bowling with the guys. Actually, she hadn't seen him or that vase of flowers since around the time...

The time she met Blair.

Almost on cue, Blair burst into Natasha's room in a frenzy, scanning the room feverishly like a wounded fox trying to evade the hunter's keen eye.

Finally, in desperation, her eyes met Natasha's, and she pleaded, "I need to hide!"

"Wait, slow down," Natasha said. "Why do you need to hide?"

Blair shook her head. "Talk later. Hide now."

The ominous echo of furious footsteps reverberated down the hall, which could only mean one thing; Alexei was coming. There was no time to waste. Tilting her head intently to the side, Natasha motioned toward the bed. Blair nodded and dove headfirst underneath, pulling the sheet halfway down to the floor. Seconds later, Alexei came storming through the curtain, his face as red as a boiled lobster and his fists wound so tight that it looked like he might just punch Natasha in the face for so much as existing.

"Where'd she go?" he asked.

Natasha looked around nervously for a way to escape as she backed slowly away from him, trying to keep out of the reach of his right hook.

"Where'd who go?" she stalled.

"I saw her. Tell me where she went, and I won't hurt you," he said in a harsh tone that was less than reassuring.

It was quickly becoming clear that reason would not win this day. So, she reached out behind her, clawing desperately for something to fight back with, and ran her hands across the surface of her nightstand. As he took a determined step toward her, she felt the cold, smooth sheen of glass across her fingertips. He took another step toward her, and she slowly wrapped her hand around its curvy, grooved surface. Then, he took another step, leaving him within arm's reach.

As he did, she glanced over at the bed. From where she stood, she could see Blair's feet creep out from behind the edge of the sheet. In an attempt to do something, anything, to keep Alexei from spotting Blair, Natasha did the only thing she could think to do. Tightening her grip on the vase, she hurled it at his head. Then, she ran. She ran and didn't look back to see the damage she had done. She ran as though the fate of the world depended on it, only hoping the distraction would give Blair enough time to escape.

She didn't even make it to the front door, however, before Alexei's calloused fingers wrapped around her neck. In an instant, she was thrown back, and her head rattled against brick, causing her to slump to the ground. As her vision blurred, an intense, throbbing pain shot through her skull, leaving her hands numb. As her eyes refocused, she saw the menacing scowl of Alexei looming inches from her face. Blood dripped from the jagged, three-inch-long shard of glass that protruded from his cranium, and his eyes were red with rage.

"You bitch," he whispered threateningly.

Grabbing Natasha by the throat, he lifted her until her feet were a foot off the ground. He looked at her with a gaze that usually filled her with fear, but instead, she was overcome by something vaguely resembling happiness. A smile crept across her face, which only served to further fan the flame of his fury. As he threw her to the ground, he took hold of the back of her hair, tearing out a large chunk from the root. The gravelly floor beneath her felt like knives slicing through the backs of her thighs. He threw her onto the bed and climbed on top of her, forcing her legs open.

She closed her eyes and forced reality behind bars. The world around her faded into a blur.

Later that morning, Natasha and Blair lay together in Natasha's bed for the first of what would shortly become a countless number of times. They stayed in silence, staring up at the ceiling, but the silence wasn't awkward or unwanted. In fact, it was the relaxing, beautiful sort of silence that came from simple, human connection, the kind Natasha hadn't enjoyed since a time beyond her memory.

Finally. Natasha turned to her side facing Blair and asked, "Why was he after you?"

Blair looked over at Natasha and chuckled softly as she mirrored Natasha's position, placing her face inches away, "He may or may not have caught me making a break for the nearest police station."

"It's a good thing he never figured out it was you." Natasha smiled.

"I guess we're all due a lucky break every now and again," Blair laughed before settling into a joyous grin. "You're different from the others."

"I'm really not."

"You are. All the others carry death in their eyes, everywhere they go, but not you. Your eyes shine with life. You try to hide it so they can't see. But, I see it, and it's beautiful. You're beautiful."

Suddenly, the world around Natasha flickered like a candle being blown out, and something tugged at her feet, trying to pull her away. In an instant, she was thrown onto her back and dragged across the sheets. Instinctively, she threw her arms in front of her, trying to grab onto anything she could. Her hands gripped the bedpost with all her might, but it wasn't enough. Like a baby bird in a hurricane, she was thrown into the darkness as everything around her turned to pitch black, leaving her falling.

And falling.

And falling.

～

*Detroit, Michigan*

FLORIAN ALWAYS KNEW THIS DAY MIGHT COME: STANDING BEFORE A

judge, about to be sentenced to life for the job he chose to perform. He just never imagined that day would also be his wedding day. Paul's words had played on repeat since that detective's visit to the club.

*Do you love her?*

How was he supposed to answer that question? Love was merely a concept, a theory that had been planted, like inception, in the minds of the masses by artists and politicians. It was a clever means of distracting simple minds and focusing their energies on an endless chase so they wouldn't try to wrap their minds around ideas and policies they couldn't possibly understand. Love wasn't something that affected the clever, the powerful or the transcendent.

That was the truth that was passed down to Florian at an early age by his mother. She wasn't weak or simple-minded like everyone else. She was powerful, and she used the concept of love to take whatever she wanted from men who were too blind to see through her charade, a power Florian aimed to emulate in everything he did.

*Do you love her?*

He had read sonnets and soliloquies about love but always believed them to be willfully false, mere fabrication. However, from the first moment he saw Janelle, all those preconceptions faded away. Something about her was different. Something about her was special. She had reached into his soul and stolen the key, a key he didn't even know was there. Everything she did made it harder to imagine a world in which she wasn't his. He didn't want to go back to waking to anything other than her scent, but his dependence on her essence scared him to his core.

*Do you love her?*

So, he tried everything in his power to break free of her. As they looked at house after house for their new home, Florian forced himself to grow cold and distant. He tried to make himself deplore every second of their search, but the girlish glee that filled her eyes with each house they saw melted the icicles around his heart. When they sat in the doctor's office, watching the tiny flicker that represented the life they had created together, he tried to remain unmoved. Soon, however, Janelle's dainty fingers wrapped around his, and he was moved to tears. Every day while she was at summer school, he tried to imagine his apartment the way it used to be, untouched but by his sole presence, but it was empty and hollow. The watercolor had run off the canvas, leaving it blank. His life was grey without her to liven it with glorious color.

He was empty without her.

"Do you take Janelle West to be your lawfully wedded wife?" the judge asked.

Florian had always told himself he would never marry, that marriage was a doomed institution he refused to take part of. In that moment, however, staring into her chestnut eyes, he realized that the reason he had sworn off love was not principle. Instead, it was fear, fear that love would leave him helpless, like a wounded gazelle in the savanna. He was afraid that a single moment of genuine affection would leave him on the side of the road, holding the tattered fragments of his heart in his hand and wishing he had never known the word "love."

But her eyes...

Her eyes felt safe. They felt warm, like home, and for the first time in his life, Florian wasn't afraid. In her eyes, he found love, genuine love, but he also found shame, which slithered up his spine like a serpent and planted questions in his mind.

*What makes you think you deserve her?*

*What could you possibly have to offer her after all you've done?*

*After what you tried to do?*

*Wouldn't she be better off without you?*

But, above all the questions that rang in his ears, one tolled even louder.

*Do you love her?*

"I do," Florian answered with a smile that ran the lengths of the Pacific Ocean.

When they kissed, it was as if the Northern Lights danced above their heads. Her lips were roses, wet with the morning dew. The space between them pulsed with electricity like a summer storm. He could hardly get enough of her cherry, sweet kiss all the way from city hall to their apartment, which now felt more like their home. The masks had been taken off the walls, replaced by pictures of their love. His windows, which had once been left perpetually open to the world, were now covered by gold and mahogany curtains. There was even a side table next to his bookcase, which now included the complete sets of all of Janelle's favorite books. A couple months earlier, Florian would have counted these changes as tragic, but now, he wouldn't have had things any other way.

The door to the apartment had barely closed for a second before Florian had Janelle backed up against the wall. Running the back of his fingers up her side, he lovingly caressed the soft skin under her blouse. His lips were drawn to hers like Romeo's to Juliet's, as though there was no other place that the stars had fated for them to be. He took her right hand, carefully interlacing his fingers with hers, and pressed it against the wall as his right hand took hold of her thigh. A second later, she broke from his kiss. He leaned in, pressing his body into hers, longing for her sweet, supple lips. She tilted her head to the side and kissed his neck just below the ear, causing his hair to stand on end. He closed his eyes, and he was standing on her shore. The water was calling his name.

Her warm, moist breath grazed across his ear as she whispered, "Take me."

Taking her by the hand, he led her into their room. Once inside, he set her down on the bed and knelt over top of her, placing his knees on either side and running his hands through her hair. She leaned back, sighing, as their lips met in one more passionate embrace. His hands slipped down her back and lifted her blouse over her head. Her skin shimmered like garnet underneath the lamplight. She had always had a glow about her, but that night, there was something uniquely special about her: a beauty that transcended time, space and reality.

"In all my life, I've never seen a sight more beautiful," Florian said.

Janelle giggled, "I bet you say that to all your wives."

"There is, and only ever will be, one girl for me," he replied.

All at once, the stars dimmed. The entire universe went dark, save for a single beam of moonlight, which penetrated the skylight above their heads and fell in front of Florian. Within seconds, he was knee-deep in her ocean, bombarded by her waves, and with every thrust, he fell deeper and deeper. Closing his eyes, he stared out at the horizon. In the distance, he heard a moaning melody that sounded like sirens beckoning him to let go of the ground beneath his feet and float out into the ocean. Then, he was pulled under the surface, drowning beneath her waves, but he didn't fight. He didn't hold his breath.

Instead, he breathed her in.

# MAD-COW

## DETROIT, MICHIGAN

*B*radie stood in the center of his living room with his hand over his mouth, stroking the half-inch of stubble that he had neglected to shave over the past week. In front of him stood a six-foot high, cork board that held every scrap of evidence he had in his case against Paul. The board's corners and edges were filled with photos, names and news clipping he had printed from the internet. Held in place by pushpins, multi-colored strings ran across the entirety of the board, grouping the pieces together into categories. Out of everything on the board, the center, on which he'd placed the scrap of paper from the Goddard and Gafley warehouse, with Paul's name and address, had the least connecting points attached to it, a fact that Bradie couldn't wrap his mind around.

"What am I missing?" Bradie muttered to himself.

Anna, who was sitting on the couch behind him, said, "There does seem to be a gap in the evidence, but what does your gut tell you?"

"That it's him," he answered. "But, at best, the evidence says he has a passing knowledge of the prostitution going on under the club. At worst, it says I've been following a trail of red herrings this whole time."

"Where there are red herrings, there's usually somebody placing them there," Anna said as she stood up to take a closer look at the board.

Then, she paused for a moment, her eyes darting back-and-forth across the board and taking everything in before continuing, "You're right though. There are too many coincidences for there to be nothing going on. Have you gotten anything off the bug?"

He had nearly forgotten. When he was in the basement of Illuminate, he planted a bug on the bottom corner of the mattress he had been on with Erica. For the first week or so, he was faithful to monitor it every day, but after time and time again of nothing but silence on the other end, it felt like a fruitless endeavor. So, he neglected it in favor of other pursuits. However, since other pursuits were also leading nowhere, it seemed only reasonable to listen in.

Anna pulled Bradie's computer from underneath the couch and set it on the coffee table in front of her. Sliding next to her on the couch, he plugged in two sets of headphones so they could both hear. As the volume in the headphones clicked on, he heard a faint, rhythmic sound in the distance, like the slow gallop of a colt. He turned the volume louder, and the gallop was joined by the percussive chorus of creaking and heavy breathing. Soon, a melodic anthem of groaning in tenor and soprano joined in, making the subject of this symphony abundantly clear.

The male voice moaned, "Oh my God! You're so damn hot."

*That voice. Why does it sound so familiar?*

With each successive beat, the rhythm grew louder. Bradie grimaced, turning to Anna for confirmation, but she didn't move. Instead, her eyes were glued to the computer screen as she watched the sound waves ascend and descend like a volcano about to erupt.

"Do you like it when I pound the shit out of you, baby?" the male voice asked.

"Just like that!" the female voice screamed with a voice that also seemed familiar, although it certainly wasn't Erica's. "Oh my God, don't stop! Oh! Oh, Shepard! You're so hard!"

Furious, he ripped the headphones out of his ears and flung them forcefully across the room. Then, springing up from the couch, he stormed toward the front door, unable to believe how completely he had been duped.

"Where are you going?" Anna asked, taking her own headphones out of her ears and following Bradie.

"The only place left with answers," he huffed as he walked out the door.

"Well, then I'm coming too."

{}~{}~{}~{}~{}~{}~{}~{}~{}~{}

They sat in his car along the curb across from Illuminate. All was quiet. In that moment, as he stared out onto the empty street, hopelessness, the likes of which he had never felt before, weighed heavily on his heart, mind and soul. He had worked for months to find something, anything, that he could use against Paul, but for every lead he thought he found, another dead end lurked around the corner.

*Another dead end. Another damn dead end! At this rate, it'll be a miracle if I don't get sent back to L.A. by the end of the week.*

Just then, there was a knock at the passenger's side door, which nearly caused Bradie to jump out of his skin in surprise. Turning to see who was behind the knock, he saw Erica, who was motioning for him to open the door, which he did, allowing her to slide quickly inside.

"Drive," she demanded, looking nervously over her shoulder to make sure no one was following her.

"Why?" he asked in befuddlement.

Anna leaned forward, tapped him sternly on the shoulder, and whispered, "Shut up and do as she says."

He turned the ignition, the engine roared to life, and he drove, only later realizing that he had no idea where he was actually going. Essentially, he drove in a straight line until he felt the urge to turn, all the while resisting the urge to make Erica talk before she was ready.

After a few moments, Erica took a deep breath and said, "I'm sorry for freaking you out. I couldn't risk anyone seeing me talk to you."

"You had no problem talking to me the other day," he replied.

"That was before I realized you were a cop," she said.

"How did you know?" he asked.

"I may be a lot of things, but stupid isn't one of them."

"What made you come forward?"

Erica looked away sullenly, staring out the window and biting the bottom corner of her lip. Anna leaned forward and placed a comforting hand on her shoulder.

"What happened?" Anna asked.

Taking one, last look out the window, Erica sighed, "I guess I finally realized there's no other way out. I'll be stuck here forever if I don't do something."

"I'm sorry," Anna said, squeezing Erica's shoulder gently.

"Does management at the club know about the prostitution?" Bradie asked.

"Know?" Erica laughed. "Honey, they make us do it. That's why I came to you. I know you're trying to help, and I want to help you stop it, once and for all."

Sometimes, all it takes is one word, and Jericho begins to crumble.

~

PAUL SAT NERVOUSLY IN THE DINING ROOM AT REBECCA'S SHELTER, waiting for Georgie to go on lunch. After a week of looking for Elle, of trying to find even a trace of where Redd had taken her, they had found nothing. Since then, the nightmares had left him unable to eat or sleep. Every time he closed his eyes, he saw her: cold, hungry and scared. As he waited, he looked at his hands; they were shaking. It was as though, even though the real world around him was still, his was spinning. Even the seat underneath him trembled from the tremors his legs were creating underneath him. With each moment that passed, the intensity of the earthquakes grew and grew until they were uncontrollable. He closed his eyes, trying to quell his anxiety and anger.

When he opened his eyes, however, he saw Redd sitting across the table from him, smiling at him with an unnerving aura of pure joy. At this point, Paul was reeling, barely able to keep his head above water, and Redd knew it. Immediately, Paul's fist clenched so hard that he could feel his nails dig into the skin on his palms. His chest tightened, and his heart raced, the blood in his veins boiling almost instantly, which only served to widen the smile on Redd's face. In that moment, it felt as though Redd could see right through Paul, all the way down to his soul, as though he had been there the whole time.

Redd laughed, "You're not strong enough to get Elle back. You never were. You know what you have to do, but you won't do it. In fact, you can't. You don't have it in you to be an animal like me."

Just then, Paul's phone rang. Turning to his jacket pocket,

he reached inside, pulled it out and checked the screen. It was Lena. He turned back to Redd, but he was gone, vanished in an instant, almost as if he had never been there in the first place.

Bringing the phone to his ear, Paul answered, "Lena, what's going on?"

"I think we can officially say that one half of our crime-fighting duo is officially off our scent," she said.

"What about Bradie?" he questioned.

"He heard everything," she replied. "It was good thinking to link that bug you pulled from Erica's bed to my phone so I could see when he was listening in. And it's about time he did. I swear, if I'd heard that detective yell out one more movie reference, I think I would've killed him."

"That should keep them off our tails for a while. Thanks for the update."

"Are you alright? You sound tense."

"I'm fine, just hashing out a personal matter."

After hanging up the phone, he sat there for a moment, tapping his fingers anxiously on the table at a tempo matching the beating of his heart. With every second that passed, it grew faster and faster until he couldn't stand it anymore. So, standing from the table, he marched straight toward Georgie, who was working behind the serving line. Without a word, Paul grabbed Georgie by the arm and dragged him into the back hallway.

"Paulie," Georgie said, a pained grimace stretching across his face. "I know you're upset. I understand."

His hands still trembling, Paul reluctantly let go of Georgie's arm and paced around the room, muttering, "Sorry. I-I'm sorry. I didn't mean to…"

Georgie sighed, placing his hand on Paul's shoulder, "I can't imagine how hard this must be for you."

"You're certainly right about that," Paul scoffed, shaking him off.

"I'm sorry I kept you waiting," Georgie said.

"Did you find her?" Paul asked.

"I'm sorry, Paul."

Paul took a deep breath and pleaded, "Tell me you found something. A clue, anything."

Georgie shook his head. "He hasn't done anything but eat, sleep and work since I started following him."

"Did he notice you?" Paul questioned.

"No one notices someone like me. But, if he did take Elle, he's not keeping her with him."

*His friend at the docks. He's keeping her there as insurance, leaving me with no other choice.*

Without another word, Paul stormed out of the shelter. He had wasted too much time tiptoeing around the issue, trying to find a way to outwit Redd and circumnavigate his ultimatum. He had been afraid of crossing the line and becoming like Redd, but this was his daughter who was at stake. There was no more waiting, no more plotting to be done. He needed to find Redd and kill him. Nothing could get in the way of what he had to do.

As he turned the corner, however, a figure far in the distance raced toward him with determined speed, soon coming into full view.

*You've got to be shitting me.*

It was Bradie, and he was heading straight toward Paul with a fiery confidence in his eyes. Paul didn't understand. Bradie should have been thrown off their trail for at least a couple of weeks. That had been the whole point of Lena seducing Shepard, to give them time to either figure out a way to clear suspicions or find a road out of town. This was not part of the plan.

*Why is he here?*

*He can't be here to arrest me. There's not enough evidence for that. Planting that bug was a desperate move, and he didn't get anything from that.*

*Maybe he's just pissed that we found his bug.*

*No, it can't be that. The look in his eyes isn't hopeless anger. There's a glimmer of hope there. He has something, or at least he thinks he does. Since we've been in lockdown ever since he showed up at the club, it can't be new evidence, which means someone must have talked. Could it have been Redd? No, that's not his style. He already plans to turn me in. So, it has to be someone else, but who would do that now? It doesn't make any sense, unless...*

*Erica. That little bitch.*

"I seriously don't have time for this today!" Paul yelled from fifteen feet away.

"Then you'll have to make the time," Bradie said. "Because you're coming with me."

Paul rolled his eyes. "You're not seriously telling me you believe anything Erica says, are you?"

"What reason would she have to lie?"

"I don't know. Maybe because she's been using my club as a den for her whoring, which, by the way, is illegal. And then, she finds a bug underneath her mattress, which is also extremely illegal, considering I don't remember you having a warrant the day you stopped by. What's a girl supposed to think? She was afraid to go to jail, so she did the only reasonable thing; she made up some shit story about how she didn't have a choice and how she was being forced to prostitute herself so you wouldn't pay attention to her. And, let me guess, she didn't name any names, did she? Or give you any actual details?"

Bradie's eyes fell to the ground. "Not exactly."

"I didn't think so," Paul chuckled. "Now, quit wasting my time."

As he turned to leave, Paul spotted something out of the corner of his eye, just over Bradie's shoulder. It was Redd, staring at him with the same villainous smile as before. Paul's fist clenched, his hands once again beginning to shake. Then, Redd raised his middle finger to his neck and, in one, fluid motion, slid it across his jugular as he mouthed the words, "She's as good as dead." Then, with a deadly cackle, he vanished, leaving behind nothing but the overwhelming rage that now resided in Paul's heart.

Bradie looked at Paul expectantly, asking, "Aren't you going to say something?"

In his anger, Paul hadn't even realized that Bradie had spoken.

"I'm sorry. What did you say? I didn't quite catch that," Paul said.

"I said, 'I guess you're right,'" Bradie repeated. "It's a waste of time to talk to you now when I'll be seeing you tonight anyways. Hearsay or not, Erica's testimony was enough for a judge to grant me a warrant. So, go home, kiss your wife and daughter because, in a few hours, you'll be in handcuffs."

*Shit. Shit. Shit!*

As soon as Bradie was gone, Paul raced to his car, leaping inside and speeding halfway down the street before the door closed. The whole way to Redd's home, his mind raced faster than a jet engine, playing out every way his next, few hours could run. In the end, Bradie was right. There was no way out. One way or another, jail was inevitable, but Paul also knew one other thing; if he was going to jail, he had better damn well make sure he got Elle back before that could happen, which could only mean one thing.

He had to kill Redd.

Moments later, he found himself sitting in his car outside Redd's apartment complex in the heart of downtown, waiting for his opportunity to strike. He reached into his glove compartment and pulled out a gun and silencer. If he was going to do this, he had to do it in the quickest and least conspicuous way possible: one, quick shot to the head. He even parked next to Redd's truck so he could throw his body in the trunk and leave with as little fuss as possible. It was the perfect plan. Well, as perfect as a plan could be in this unfortunate of a situation. Now, all he had to do was wait for the perfect moment.

Of course, waiting is a whole lot easier when you're not as pissed off as a gorilla protecting its young.

Finally, after what felt like forever, Redd exited the building, walking with his usual, overconfident, meathead strut and stopping every five seconds to check out every hot chick and sexy set of wheels he passed. As Redd walked by Paul, fumbling in his pockets for his truck keys, Paul slowly opened his car door, leaving it ajar as to not alert Redd to his presence. In that moment, it was tempting to just shoot him in the head and get it over with, but he wanted to look Redd in the eyes before taking his life, to watch the life drain from him. He wanted Redd to know who it was that killed him, but most of all, he wanted to smile for the camera as he pulled the trigger.

Sneaking up behind Redd, Paul grabbed him tightly by the collar, shoving him against the side of his truck and glaring into his eyes with an intensity that could have rivaled the heat of the sun itself.

Redd smiled. "So, today's the day, huh? You're actually going to do it. I've got to say; I didn't think you had the balls."

"You should never underestimate me," Paul said as he raised the gun to Redd's head.

Quickly, Redd's smile turned to a scowl. He sighed, "A gun? Really? I'm disappointed, Paul. I thought you were better than that."

"It's the best way the kill a man," Paul said.

"Sure, if you're a bitch."

"You better shut your damn mouth, Redd."

"Or what? You'll crochet me to death? You know what? Fine, shoot me. I guess I should've known you wouldn't have the balls to kill me like a real man."

"Stop," Paul ordered. "Right now."

"I should've known," Redd said. "Because if you weren't so weak, you wouldn't have let me touch your daughter in the first place."

"Don't talk about Elle. You don't have the right!"

"I have the right to whatever-"

Before Redd could finish his sentence, the butt of Paul's gun slammed into Redd's temple, sending him plummeting to the ground. Redd threw his arms out in front of him to brace himself, but the force of the fall was too much. His head hit the cement with a resounding crack, like the sound of a home run blast. Paul watched with anticipation as Redd scrambled to a seated position and raised his hand to his wound, which was now dripping with scarlet. In that moment, a strange warmth rose through Paul's bones, starting at the bottom of his feet and working all the way to the tips of his fingers, like he was finally thawing out after a lifetime in cryogenesis. In that moment, as he stared at the beaten man whose life he now held in his hands, he was no longer sure whether he was playing the role he was forced to play or taking the costume off and seeing himself for the first time.

Maybe it meant he was a monster, that he was as bad as Redd. Maybe it meant Redd had won, but the truth in that moment was that Paul no longer gave a damn.

Redd smiled, seeing the light in Paul's eyes fade to darkness, and mocked, "Deep down, we're all nothing but animals."

The curtain fell.

Paul dropped his pistol to the ground, the midday sun glimmering off its surface as it fell in what seemed like slow-motion. His fist clenched, this time with determined purpose. With timing so precise it almost seemed planned, the gun ricocheted off the ground at the same time his fist hit Redd's skull, landing with a crack so thunderous that Paul wasn't sure if the sound came from his hand or Redd's jaw.

Redd fell onto his back, and Paul climbed on top of him, grabbing him by the collar and continuing to strike with vicious blow after vicious blow. With each hit, the lines between skin, tissue and bone became blurrier. After a minute, the only thing recognizable about Redd was the wide, ugly smile that still adorned his bloodied, disfigured face. His eyes dropped wearily, and Paul watched the life drain from them. Then, with his own, wicked smile gleaming across his face, he struck one last time to the center of Redd's forehead before letting his body fall limp to the ground.

Victorious, he stood over Redd's motionless body, wiped the blood from his mouth and repeated, "I told you to shut your damn mouth."

## 26

# ESCAPED

### INDIANAPOLIS, INDIANA

*A*n eerie silence hung over the ghostly parking lot of The Eclipse as Kayde approached the front doors, completely covered in darkness. That night, neither moon nor stars hung overhead. The only light for miles shone from the dimly lit street lamps along the sidewalk, which cast a haunting glow on the building's exterior. Shivers cascaded down his spine as he stepped foot onto the sidewalk, half-expecting a serial killer or ghoul to pop out from behind a bush to skin him alive. If he listened closely enough, he could almost hear a symphony play the soundtrack of his demise.

The plan was simple: get in, grab Blair's transfer file and get out as quickly as possible. While getting in and out was easy, considering he had a key to the building, the info grab required a little more finesse. Over the weeks preceding his caper, he spent the majority of his free time consuming a sickening number of lock-picking tutorials on the internet and receiving "in the field" training from Violet, who had picked up that particular skill as a teenager, a story Kayde promised himself he would uncover as soon as this was over. It was a simple plan, a good plan.

Regretfully, not all plans forged in the underworld pan out the way they're imagined.

As Kayde reached the doors, fumbling in his pockets for his keys, a voice called out from behind him, "Kayde!"

Immediately, Kayde whipped around, only to find Eric standing behind him with Violet by the scruff of her hair. Though she struggled to fight against him, trying with all her might to stay on her feet, his vice-like grip and intense determination forced her to her knees. She looked up at Kayde, her face sullen, like a sheep being led to the slaughter. Furious, Kayde's hands began to shake. In that moment, he wanted nothing more than to rip Eric's, smug, little head from his shoulders for so much as daring to touch her. His blood boiled so hot that it felt like he was breathing fire.

He was going to make Eric pay for this.

"Get your damn hands off her," Kayde ordered, his voice taking a near demonic tone.

"I'd like to see you try," Eric laughed, pulling his gun from its holster and pointing it at him.

"Why are you doing this?" Kayde asked.

"Because you've reached your final test!" Eric answered. "And boy, has this played out better than we anticipated! You see, we figured you'd come running over here soon enough so you could have a look through those transfer files you saw to figure out where we sent your precious Blair. And, you know, we were going to let you have them. No gimmick. No punishment. Because your real test was to see if you'd choose to run after family and let your sweet, sweet love rot, or whether you'd choose to stay for love and forget your brotherly responsibility. But then, things got so much more interesting. What the

Manager never accounted for was just how much this whore cared for *you*.

"I was checking the footage of the office, waiting for you to burst in, and imagine my surprise when I saw Violet break in to find the info herself, risking her life to save you. Then, I got to thinking. You see, I really enjoyed our test at the warehouse the other day, but there was one thing it was missing: stakes. Some random girl's life was never going to compare with your sister's. You proved that when you told me about what you did to your sister's bestie. But Violet's? Now, that might cause you to hesitate. So, this is your test; kill Violet, and I'll tell you where Blair is. Refuse and I'll kill you, and neither Violet nor your poor sister will ever see freedom again."

"Sounds fair." Kayde shrugged. "Give me the gun, and we'll see what I choose."

"You still think I'm an idiot, don't you? You want me to give you the gun so you can turn around, shoot me and run off with the girl? I don't think so. If you're going to kill her, you're going to do it with your bare hands."

Kayde looked down at Violet, whose eyes now flowed with tears. Kneeling on the ground in front of her, he placed a hand on her cheek. She smiled weakly as she leaned into his caress. He kissed her on the lips, lingering for an extra second so he could always remember her taste, at least for the few seconds of life he had left. His decision was made; if his choice was between hurting Violet and death, he would welcome death with arms wide open.

As he pulled away, however, she took his face in her hands and leaned in for one, last kiss to his cheek. Then, she whispered, "Blair's in New York City. Now, run."

With a final burst of strength, she lunged at Eric's arm. With both hands, she latched onto his forearm, pulling it toward the ground before he fired. The resounding blast from the gun echoed so loudly throughout the empty lot that it sounded like cannon fire. The bullet flew into the darkness, rattling the leaves of a nearby bush. As she sunk her teeth into his flesh, Eric tried to shake her off. But, he couldn't. Even after he slammed her head into the ground, she wouldn't let go. He tried to pull her off, but this just made her sink her teeth deeper, almost taking a large chunk of his arm with her.

Violet looked up at Kayde, blood streaming down her face from the quarter-sized gash above her eye, where her head hit the ground. Her eyes pleaded for him to leave, to run before she couldn't hold on anymore. However, when he looked into the distance, only darkness and uncertainty lay in the shadows. The path before him stretched into the unknown, and he didn't know to where it led, whether to Blair or destruction. In that moment, however, he did know one thing; he could save Violet.

With a single, swift motion, Kayde punched Eric in the jaw. Then, before Eric could react, Kayde slammed his opposite hand into Eric's wrist, dislodging the gun. As the gun hit the ground, Kayde picked it up, cocked it and pointed it at Eric.

"This test is over," Kayde said as he crooked his head to each side, cracking his neck. "Now, let her go before I put a bullet in your skull."

As Eric let go of Violet, a faint, rhythmic, beating sound suddenly echoed out of the darkness, slowly growing louder and faster until it felt as though it came from every direction. A moment later, a dark figure emerged from the shadows. As it entered the orb of light that emanated from the street lamp above their heads, Kayde saw the figure clearly. It was the Manager, clapping with enthusiastic vigor. He had been watching from the darkness the entire time, observing his lab rats as they ran the maze he had constructed for them. Immediately, Kayde whipped the gun to the side, looking down its sights at the Manager, his finger resting on the trigger, ready to fire.

He asked, "What the hell's going on?"

Stopping beside Eric, who subsequently vanished into the darkness, holding his arm, the Manager removed his glasses for a split second to wipe a single, small tear from his eyelid. Then, he said, "Never in my wildest projections could I have predicted such a tremendous display of resilience from the two of you. I expected that Kayde might risk it all for his beloved, but for Violet to risk her own life so he wouldn't turn into the monster he so feared becoming? Think of the odds! You two have vastly exceeded my expectations, and for that, I congratulate you. You moved me, and that is no small feat."

"So, what does that mean for us?" Violet asked.

"For you, my dears," the Manager said. "It means your freedom."

"You can't be serious," Kayde remarked.

"I most certainly am," the Manager replied. "I was prepared to walk out of this day without one or both of you. This was your final test, pass or fail, and you passed with flying colors."

"What's the catch?" Kayde asked.

"Only that I'll be paying close attention to what your next move will be. This particular experiment has run its course. I couldn't devise a greater test if I tried, but the tests are far from over, particularly if you decide to continue the chase for your sister. You might want to move quickly, though. You never know how much time she might have left."

With that, Kayde took Violet's hand, and they escaped into the darkness, unable to fully understand why they had been granted their freedom or where the road ahead might lead. But, if there was one thing Kayde had learned from his time in the underworld, it was this;

When the devil grants you reprieve from the fires of hell, you sure as hell had better not look back.

∾

*New York, New York*

NATASHA OPENED HER EYES, AND THAT, IN AND OF ITSELF, WAS more than she expected to happen that evening. At first, she was confused, wondering if she was still in the void, reliving another formative memory, but that couldn't be. In the void, she felt a tangible disconnect from everything physical, as though she was living a dream, and this was no dream. Everything about the world around her was unbearably real, which meant it had to be something else. For a moment, she wondered if she hadn't taken enough to overdose. But, that didn't make sense either. She had taken three times her usual dosage and of a much stronger substance, which should have been enough to turn her blood acidic. An ounce of her blood should have been able to send a vampire back to his coffin with the shakes from just a taste. There was no reason she should have been alive, much less feel normal, rested even.

As she checked her arms, everything seemed to be in order. She even counted the track marks on her forearm from the syringes from the night before: three marks for three syringes. Maybe she had become more tolerant than she thought. That just meant she would have to double the dosage. If she moved quickly, she could join herself to the darkness before Alexei realized he was missing any of his stash. At least this time, he would kill her if she got caught. Either way, it would be over at last.

As she planted her hands on the edge of the bed to hoist herself up, an intense, burning pain shot all the way up to her bicep, which she thought was strange. She had expected the pain to stop at her forearms, where she shot up, not her bicep. Inspecting her arm one last time, she spotted a fourth mark on the inside of her upper arm, a spot she had left untouched, which meant that someone had given her an antidote, and Natasha had no question in her mind as to who that person had been.

After all, Blair was the only person in the world stupid enough to believe Natasha still had a life worth living.

Just then, as if Natasha's thoughts had summoned her through some, unwanted, black magic, Blair entered the room. She looked at Natasha with eyes that were both relieved and pained to see her, two sentiments Natasha did not share. The only emotion that filled her was rage.

"I don't want to talk to you," Natasha said.

"I know I'm the last person you want to see right now," Blair said.

"What gave you that idea?" Natasha asked.

"I wanted to make sure you were okay."

"I'd be better if you'd left me alone."

"I know," Blair sighed.

"Then why the hell didn't you?" Natasha asked. "I'd finally be free if it wasn't for you."

"Yours wasn't the only life you were trying to end last night."

"That was not your decision to make."

"I know," Blair said, looking anxiously over her shoulder, as though she was looking for something. "I only came here to tell you not to worry about what happens to me."

"Why would I worry about you?" Natasha scoffed.

"Because I know you," Blair answered. "Despite what you think, I know you better than anyone. So please, don't worry about me. Live a good life. You deserve all the good in the world, Natasha."

As the words rolled off Blair's tongue, a commotion brewed outside the room. Natasha darted out to see what was happening. Peeking her head between the folds of the curtain, she saw Theresa sprinting toward the door with Alexei in close pursuit. Though she ran as fast as her legs could take her, regretfully, she wasn't fast enough. As she was about to reach the front doors, Alexei grabbed her by the back of her collar, his muscles coursing with pure adrenaline, and flung her like a rag doll into the wall. Her body hit the wall with a thunderous crash, and she slunk helplessly to the ground.

As he stood over her, raising his fist behind his head to strike, Theresa's eyes peered behind him, her mouth forming a weak smile. This caught Alexei's attention, causing him to whip around. Immediately, his eyes grew wide, and he bolted down the hallway toward the back entrance. Natasha turned back to where Blair had been standing, but she was gone. Instead, she was running in the opposite direction with Alexei's duffel bag wrapped around her wrist. Within seconds, Alexei pounced on her, lifting her by the shirt and delivering a vicious blow to her face. Defeated, she tumbled to the ground.

In that moment, Natasha forgot how to breathe. Her lungs huffed and puffed, but all they seemed to be able to do was inhale. Soon, they weren't even doing that. Her hands shook uncontrollably. All the anger that she had held toward Blair faded in an instant, leaving behind only fear, fear that Alexei would do the same to Blair as he had done to Natasha so many times before. But, most of all, she feared that she would have listen to it all happen, helpless to do anything. She couldn't understand why Blair was doing this. It was so risky, so unlike her to leap before looking. She had to have known that the chances of her getting away with that bag were slim to none.

Then, as Alexei was dragging her through the curtain to an empty room, Blair looked at Natasha, her left eye so swollen from his blows that it could hardly open. However, despite the pain that she was so obviously in and the pain that was inevitably to follow, Blair looked triumphant, like a general who, against all odds, had won the war. Her eyes shone with a brightness that melted the icicles around Natasha's heart and drove away all darkness within its reach.

She looked into Natasha's eyes and mouthed the word, "Run."

> *I gaze at my guard and what do I see?*
> *The one holding me captive is actually me.*
> *I push at my cage and the door then unlocks,*
> *Creaking open to my amazement and shock.*
> *I look down the hallway at other prisoners in cells,*
> *Each steel cage built by none but themselves.*

Suddenly, everything made sense. Everything Blair had done from the moment the darkness had taken hold and every word she had said had been an expression of a single thought, a solitary idea that she had been trying to convey.

With tears in her eyes, Natasha whispered the words she wished she had said instead of being so cold, "I love you too."

She never thought she would find it difficult to leave the prison she had been forced to exist within for so long, but each successive, quiet step toward the door became increasingly painful. Even the door seemed to triple in weight as every synapse in her brain fired at the same time, telling her to stop. Nevertheless, she persisted. She didn't want to leave Blair behind, but she wouldn't let her sacrifice be in vain. As she opened the door and ran to her freedom, Theresa reached toward her with the last of her strength, brushing her hand against Natasha's.

The air outside the warehouse felt different than she remembered. The street looked different too. Even the sunset felt somehow changed. Before, she always tried to avoid the setting sun because it meant the start of a new day. Now, it meant the same thing, but still, it was different. For the first time in a lifetime, each step she took was her own. The air in her lungs belonged to her, and she was finally in control of her life. The moon was on the horizon, and she was going to follow it, wherever it led. She took one, last look at the life she left behind, and then...

*Crash!*

The next thing she knew, she was lying flat on her back on the pavement as worried faces huddled around her. Above and around her, the darkness closed in, enveloping the sky and reaching its hand out to take her. She tried to fight against it with every ounce of strength she had left in her body, but it wasn't enough. The darkness swallowed the trees, the buildings, even the people around her.

Until darkness was all that was left.

# 27

# BRANDED

DETROIT, MICHIGAN

*T*he docks at Lake Erie weren't the most ideal place to conduct business, especially the kind that involved the exchange of one life for another. At least, it wasn't the place Paul would have chosen, but it was the only place that made sense based on what Redd had said. Everywhere Paul looked, there were potential threats, from the polo-clad yachters to the happy families returning from their fishing trips. There were too many potential witnesses for his taste, but sometimes, the riskiest option is the only option.

After thirty minutes of waiting beside his car, Paul grew impatient. He didn't appreciate being jerked around, especially when it should have all been over with. So, without any sign of Redd's man, he made his way toward the water, hoping to find some sort of clue. From twenty feet away from the water's edge, he saw it, sticking out like a bright, pink flamingo in a field of snow on the dock's bulletin board. In giant, red lettering that contrasted oddly against the pink stationary it was printed upon, a flyer sat in the top right corner of the bulletin board that read:

*Are you at a CROSSroads? Then, the THEATER might be the thing for you! When times get tough, ARTISTS must stand in UNITY*
*-PAUL ELLEanor.*

*Subtle. Very subtle.*

The Artist's Unity Theater Building was once a thriving center of art and beauty, where people flocked in order to enjoy everything beautiful. It had been a marvel of architecture, inside and out. Now, however, the only connoisseurs of the culture left inside its walls were rats and squatters. The derelict behemoth towered over Paul, all eighteen of its stories standing as Redd's final mockery of what his life had become. Even Paul couldn't help but chuckle at the undeniable accuracy of the metaphor.

Stepping into the main theater, Paul was overwhelmed with awe of what used to be and sorrow over what now was. Its monstrous, cathedral ceilings had turned to brown and cracked from the moisture that had built up over the years. The once proud arches that had hovered over both stage and screen were now fragmented and broken, their remains scattered across the floor. Even the color had faded from the floor, walls and seats, turning them a hideous grey. It looked like something out of an archaeological dig, a sight to marvel at for historicity sake, but not to linger inside for fear of the spirits of horror movies long past.

As Paul reached the stage, a man emerged from behind the tattered screen. He was unkempt, dirty and bore a greasy, scraggly beard that could have rivaled that of the fiercest of Vikings. He looked like he hadn't seen a decent meal or new clothes since the theater had been abandoned. His feet were bare. His jeans were torn, and his dirty, white t-shirt was ripped in two well before his beard ended. All in all, he looked like he was made of more dirt than man.

He looked at Paul and chuckled, "Redd wasn't kidding. You look awful."

"Speak for yourself, Shithead," Paul said.

"Whoa," the Shithead laughed, raising his palms mockingly toward Paul. "There's no need for hostility, man. A simple exchange, that's all I'm here for. Just give me Redd's body, and I'll give you Elle."

"I don't think so," Paul replied, shaking his head condescendingly.

"That was the deal, man. Redd was-"

Before the Shithead could finish, Paul pounced on top of him, pinning him to the stage floor. Then, he brandished the jagged, silver knife that he had hidden in the side of his boot and lowered it slowly onto the Shithead's neck. The knife glimmered in the tiny streams of sunlight that filtered into the room through the tiny cracks in the walls as a surge of pure adrenaline rushed through Paul's veins. He felt powerful, and, if he was being completely honest with himself, he kind of liked it. He leaned forward until he was only inches from the vagrant's face.

Then, he whispered, "I'm making a new deal. You tell me where Elle is, and I don't gut you like a fish."

"Okay, okay," the man stammered. "She's in room two-twenty-one. The keys are in my left pocket. Now, please, don't kill me."

Paul chuckled as he took the keys, saying, "Did I say I wouldn't kill you? I'm sorry if I mislead you. I only meant it wouldn't be painful."

All it took was one slice to cut through beard and flesh, releasing a fountain of blood. Paul stood back as to not stain himself. Considering he had already cleaned himself up once that day, he had little interest in doing so again. As he stood there, watching, he couldn't help but feel that there was something invigoratingly beautiful about watching the life leave a man's eyes, especially upon the stage. It was like watching the paint drip from a canvas, leaving it void. Now, the stage, which was painted red with the Shithead's blood, was the masterpiece the world would remember him by. It was haunting, yet poetic.

From that point, it took Paul all of ten seconds to cover the two aisles, three flights of stairs and four hallways that stood between the stage and room 221. He stopped momentarily in front of the door to collect himself before barging in and scaring Elle half to death. She had already been through more terror in the past week than most should suffer in a lifetime. The last thing she needed was to see her father, who was supposed to be her paragon of strength and stability, broken, struggling to tread water in the midst of a squall. She couldn't know that everything was different now, that he had changed. As he turned the door handle, he used every last bit of strength in him to raise the curtain.

Behind the door was a room no larger than a prison cell. In a past life, it had probably functioned nicely as an office space for someone in middle management, complete with enough space for a desk, a couple bookshelves and a small couch for those long nights at the office. Its current incarnation, however, was more akin to a rat's nest, home to little more than two, small mattresses, a couple pails that Paul didn't even want to think about what purpose they served and a dozen cockroaches that scattered as soon as the door opened. The walls, floors and ceilings were covered with cracks, stains and dents from years of neglect and abuse.

Despite this, however, the room was filled with the most radiant light because Elle was safe inside, playing with a pair of old, raggedy dolls in the middle of the room. Hearing the door open, she turned to see Paul and smiled so broadly that the dimples in her cheeks grew as large as craters. Dropping her dolls to the ground, she rushed across the room and leapt into his arms.

"Daddy, you made it!" she exclaimed as she smothered him in a bear hug. Then, with furrowed brow, she broke from the hug and inspected him from head to toe, grabbing his face and turning it from side to side with the intense focus of a surgeon. "How are you feeling?"

Paul laughed, "I should be asking you the same question!"

"Don't avoid my question, mister!" she exclaimed. "I've been worried sick about you! Redd said that you weren't feeling yourself, and I had to stay here until you were all better. So, how are you feeling, Daddy? You're not going to pass out again, like at the park, are you?"

"No, I won't be doing that again anytime soon," he answered.

"Pinky promise?" she asked, holding her little finger toward him.

"I promise," he said, interlocking his pinky with hers. "While we're on the subject of promises, can you promise me something too?"

"Anything."

"Don't tell Mommy about this. You know how she worries whenever either of us gets sick. If she asks, tell her you had a fun time at Gram and Gramps, okay pumpkin?"

"Is this one of those times when you have to do something bad in order to do something good for someone you care about?"

"Yes, baby. You're exactly right, as always."

"In that case, I promise!" Elle said, crossing her finger definitively across her chest. "Cross my heart and hope to die."

"Let's hope nobody's dying just yet," Paul laughed. "Because Daddy's going to have to go away for work for a little while, and it's really important to me that Mommy doesn't have to worry while I'm gone. Do you understand, honey?"

"Yes, Daddy."

Paul smiled as he clutched his little girl tight to his chest, wishing he never had to let her go but knowing that was one wish that regretfully couldn't come true.

After dropping Elle off at home, Paul sped over to Illuminate. It was time to finally end all of the games. He had spent far too much time trying to circumnavigate the whirlwind his life had become, afraid to attack it head on. Every move he had made had been an attempt to buy time or goad the other players into making a mistake, and now, because of that strategy, Bradie was on his way with a warrant. He had played himself into a corner, and he had only one move left: his Queen's Gambit.

After lugging Redd's body from the car, Paul hauled him onto the right-hand stage. Then, grabbing a bundle of rope and a chair from the bar, Paul seated Redd's body against the stripper pole and fastened him to it. If it was a case Bradie wanted, Paul would make sure he got one, tied up in a bow. As he finished tying the last knot, Lena and Florian walked through the front doors.

Taking one look at Paul from across the room, she yelled, "This is not what I meant when I told you two to settle this amongst yourselves!"

"He gave me no choice," Paul answered coldly.

"Did you kill him?" Florian asked before vaulting onto the stage beside Paul.

"I beat the living shit out of him," Paul chuckled. "But no, I didn't kill him."

"And how exactly did he give you no other choice?" Lena asked as she strode casually onto the stage.

"He took Elle," Paul replied. "He said that, unless I killed him, I'd never see her again."

As Paul spoke, Lena's face grew cold, as if every last shred of humanity in her bones vaporized, leaving her soulless. Suddenly, every molecule in her body was dedicated to a single emotion: rage. It was an expression Paul had never seen on her before. He had seen her angry, certainly, but never like this. For a moment, she remained still, simply glaring at Redd. Then, without warning, she darted at him, reached into her black, leather jacket, pulled out a pistol and pressed it into Redd's temple.

Then, she looked at Paul and asked, "Did you get her back?"

He nodded. "Yes, but-"

"Good," she said. "Then we don't need him anymore."

"Wait!" Paul shouted, reaching out and pulling the gun down. "I have a better idea."

"So, WHAT YOU'RE TELLING ME," JUDGE MATHIS SAID. "IS THAT you want me to give you a warrant to search the Illuminate Night Club, a club that has hosted police events and has always been a friend to the community, because you get bad vibes from the people who work there, people who, by the way, have always been friends of your department?"

Bradie stood in front of the Judge's desk anxiously, knowing this was his last chance to stay one step ahead of Paul in their game of chess. He had taken a huge risk by telling Paul that he had a warrant before actually obtaining one, but Bradie had seen something in Paul's eyes when they spoke that he hadn't seen there before: recklessness. With a guy like Paul, this was a once in a lifetime chance, one that may never come around again. He had to act quickly before it was gone.

Bradie stammered, "Yes, but, Your Honor, I-"

"And don't get me started on that whole illegal, wiretapping business you were involved in," Mathis warned. "Even if you had gotten anything from it, it would've been inadmissible in court!"

"But, Your Honor, if you would just give me a warrant," Bradie pleaded. "I know I would find something we could use."

"You still haven't given me a good reason to give you one."

"I have a witness!"

"You mean those prostitutes who claim they were forced to break the law and sell themselves for profit?" the Judge scoffed.

"Erica Johnson and Monica Hatfield, yes," Bradie answered.

"Next, you'll be asking me to admit 'the devil made me do it' as a credible alibi!"

"But sir!"

"I'm going to let you in on a secret, Detective Lam," Judge Mathis leaned in and whispered. "Criminals lie. Especially when you catch them red-handed."

At this point, Bradie had heard enough. It had been one thing to hear it from the Chief an hour before; he at least had a vested interest in the community's perception of the department. Hearing it from a judge, who was supposed to be working on the side of justice, however, was more than Bradie could stand. His eyes lit aflame, and his blood pressure skyrocketed. It took every ounce of willpower to keep his fists from flying at the Judge's jaw.

He opened his mouth to speak, but Mathis interrupted him, warning, "I would be very careful with what you say next, Detective. You're on thin ice. I could have you indicted on more than one charge of improper conduct, but I'm being lenient since this is your first, high profile case. However, if you test me, if you go to that club without a warrant, I *will* come down on you with the full force of the law. Find some real evidence against the club, and then, we can talk about a warrant."

*But by then, it might be too late.*

Bradie wrestled with his options all the way from the court-house to his recliner, unable to decide which was worse, losing his job or his integrity. If he was wrong, rushing in blindly could prove to be the worst, and quite possibly last, mistake of his career. If he was right, though, he would certainly be dooming all of those girls to a lifetime of misery by doing nothing. Everything depended on the answer to one question; was he right about Paul, about Illuminate? His conviction was being tested, and he was the kid in the back of the classroom who was still tapping his pencil, trying to divine the answer to the first question.

"Don't you have somewhere to be?" a voice broke through the glass walls of silence around him.

Snapping back into reality, Bradie found Anna sitting on the couch next to him, with her elbows on the armrest and head in her hands, staring intently at him. An amused smile lit up her face. It was clear she been watching him for a while.

Bradie sighed, admitting hesitantly, "I didn't get the warrant."

"So?" Anna asked, squinting her eyes and feigning confusion.

"So?" he echoed. "Without a warrant, I have no legal right to even be there, much less look for evidence. I could lose my job and still walk away with nothing."

"But, you promised," she said, her face becoming suddenly serious.

*Get the others out.*

"But I can't get anyone out if I no longer have a badge. And if I go in there without probable cause, I'll..."

Bradie trailed off suddenly as his eyes widened. That was it, his way in. If Anna went into the club alone, she could be his probable cause. He could say she was in danger, and he had to go in after her. Anything he found after that would be admissible.

"I'll do it," Anna volunteered, already, as always, three steps ahead of him.

"I can't ask you to do that," Bradie said. "It's too dangerous."

"I think you misunderstand me," she said. "Do you think I walked off that roof because you made me feel safe? Quite the opposite actually. I walked off because I saw someone who was willing to give anything for what he believed in, for what was right. For the first time in my life, I saw that, with you, my life could mean something. I could have a purpose. You know what the right thing is. You saw the same thing in that girl's eyes that I did, that she wasn't lying. Now, I'm going, with or without you, so the real question is; are we in this together or not?"

Standing, she reached her hand out to him, and he smiled. There was such certainty in her eyes, like a boxer stepping into the ring knowing that the odds of winning were a million to one but still believing, despite it all, that they were going to win. It was the kind of confidence that could lead an army against the gates of hell, and nary a soldier would blink. As he took her hand and marched out the door toward what was beginning to feel more and more like his destiny, he didn't blink either.

Pulling up to Illuminate, it felt like walking up to an open casket at a wake. It looked the same, but the soul had been ripped from its body, leaving behind an empty shell. There wasn't a car or person within twenty feet of the front doors. The neon lights that usually flooded the street side with bright light were no longer alive. Instead, darkness exuded from every bulb, encasing the building itself in the purest black. Bradie rolled his window down to listen for a clue, any sign of life, but he was met with a silence as dense as steel. Something was off. He couldn't explain what or how, but he could feel it in his bones.

Anna crossed the street first while he waited in the car. She tried to open the front door, but it wouldn't budge. Her hand reached up to examine a sign that was haphazardly taped to its surface. Then, turning the corner, she disappeared behind the building. After a few more seconds, Bradie followed her path across the street, also taking a moment to inspect the stark white sheet of paper, which, in large, bold letters, read:

PERMANENTLY CLOSED. THANK YOU FOR YOUR
PATRONAGE.

Now, he was sure something was off.

The side door of the club was propped open. He made his way inside and found himself inside a ghost town. The interior of the club mirrored its exterior: empty, devoid, dead. Once the door closed behind him, it became so dark inside that he couldn't see his hand in front of his face. So, he lit his flashlight and scanned the room but found nary a sign of life anywhere around him. Chairs and tables were strewn about the room, seemingly at random. The shelves behind the bar were empty apart from a few, half-drunk bottles, and it looked like a whirlwind of flyers had ripped through the room's center.

"Anna!" he called out.

There was no reply. He whirled around, hoping to catch sight of her with his flashlight, but she wasn't there. Instead, he saw a hunched figure on the stage behind him. Upon closer inspection, he saw that it was the large, angry-looking man he had met at Paul's daughter's birthday party, slouched over in a chair and tied securely to a stripper pole, unconscious with his face looking like it had gone through a wood chipper. His jaw was caved in on the left side. His right eye was swollen to twice it's normal size, and dried blood covered most of his face and neck. Climbing onto the stage, Bradie checked for a pulse. It was faint, but it was still there. A piece of paper was taped to the ropes that bound the man's front. It was a note. He picked it up and read:

---

*Detective Bradie Lam,*

*I sincerely apologize that I am unable to be here when you find this note. Believe me, nothing would please me more than to personally see justice done, but regretfully, current circumstances being what they are, certain matters require immediate attention.*

*When I first heard the accusations you leveled against me, I'll admit that I was quite taken aback, even angry at the mere suggestion. But, after doing some looking of my own, I found that you were right; some of our girls were prostituting out of my club. Understandably, I was horrified, but even worse yet, I came to find out that Redd (the half-dead Cretan tied to the chair) was using threats, intimidation, and beatings to force them to do so. I confronted him about what I found, and he threatened me. Foolishly, I didn't think he was serious, but I found out very quickly just how serious he was. That was why I was so terse with you this afternoon when we spoke; I was in the middle of dealing with the repercussions of my foolishness. I'm sorry if I came off as rude.*

*On the bottom of the chair, you'll find Redd's ledger, which documents the illegal transactions he forced those girls to make.*

*I hope that, along with their testimony, is enough to put him away for a very long time.*

*Thank you for all that you do. I wish we could have met under more ideal circumstances.*

*-Paul Cross*

*P.S. I left you a parting gift. Look in the basement.*

---

Kneeling down, Bradie felt around the underside of the chair. He ripped a line of duct tape from the cushion, and there it was: the ledger, filled with names, dates and transaction prices, going back several years.

As he flipped through its pages, Anna peeked her head from behind the basement door and said, "Bradie, you're going to want to see this."

He kept his flashlight lit as he made his way down the stairs and into the basement. Somehow, the space around his light's beam grew even darker as his feet hit the cement floor. He didn't even know a darkness this intense existed. It was like a black hole. If he looked closely, he could make out the outline of an even blacker hand reaching out of the void.

Quickly, he followed Anna down the third corridor to the right, the same one he had been down twice before. At the end of the hallway, he saw Paul's parting gift, or rather gifts. Huddled in the back corner on the floor, clutching their knees to their chests, were close to twenty girls, including Monica and Erica. They were covered in dirt and were shaking with fear. Anna knelt down next to Monica, who was the youngest of the group.

She wrapped her arms around her and whispered, "It's okay. Everything's going to be okay. You're safe now."

Immediately, Bradie stepped back, took out his phone, and dialed the Chief's number to make the call he had been waiting to make since he first met Anna on that rooftop. They had done it. Those girls had a chance at a real life now.

Because of them, but mostly, because of Anna.

But even still, something felt...

Wrong, terribly wrong.

P<small>AUL SAT AT A BAR DOWN THE STREET FROM</small> I<small>LLUMINATE</small>, <small>TAKING</small> one, last shot of whiskey. As the final drop ran down his throat, the sound of sirens blared in the distance. Their roar quickly grew louder and louder, like a fast-approaching storm. Suddenly, red and blue lightning flashed throughout the bar, causing every eye to turn and watch as police cars whipped by. Every eye, that is, except for Paul's. As the storm passed, he calmly pulled a twenty-dollar bill from his pocket and placed it underneath his glass. Then, he walked out the front door with a mischievous smile.

As he rounded the corner into the alleyway behind the bar, he felt two pairs of strong hands latch onto each shoulder, pulling violently at him. Though he tried to fight them off, they were too strong. As they dragged him toward an unmarked van at the end of the alley, he tried to get a good look at their faces. Regretfully, he couldn't make out much of anything because they were wearing black ski-masks. At the van, a third, masked figure stood, holding the side door wide open. With little regard for his safety, they threw Paul inside and suddenly...

Everything went black.

**THE END**

# AFTERWORD

From the bottom of my heart, I want to thank you for reading Branded, the first entry in the Ebon Sky Series. This was an extremely personal project for me, and I hope the story and characters have become personal for you as well, like they have for me.

While the story and characters I've presented in these novels are entirely fictional and a creation of my own mind, the problem is real and in our own backyard. In the shadows, often times right in front of our eyes, men and women like Paul, Redd, and Lena are selling women like Natasha and Blair for profit, leaving behind family members like Kayde to pick up the pieces. Meanwhile, brave men like Bradie are fighting against all odds to make a difference.

You can help them, and you don't even have to go into law enforcement or write a book to do it. If you've been inspired like I have, you can go to any of the following websites and donate or find out more about the real stories.

http://www.freeinternational.org - F.R.E.E. International

http://www.ijm.com - International Justice Mission
http://www.endslaverynow.com - Project Rescue

Or get involved at the local level. There are countless organizations in our towns and cities that do amazing work to help the women in our own backyards. Do some research in your area and attend their events, get involved.

Contact your local representatives as well. The sad truth is that our judicial system does not do much good for trafficking victims. As it stands right now, prostitution is a criminal act for both buyer and seller. This means that human trafficking victims are getting arrested and fined every day for things they have no choice but to do. Though the authorities do everything they can to identify human trafficking victims, the task is daunting. As you have seen through this book, trafficking victims are often too afraid to come forward, even to the police. I don't know what the answer is at a governmental level, but something needs to be done.

Because of this, law enforcement has to rely on people like us to tip them off to trafficking. If you come across a prostitute, please don't write them off. Even if they chose "the life," they might still be victims. Whether they're at a strip club or the side of the road, they may still be beaten behind closed doors and cheated out of a living. Take a moment, talk to them, and most of all, look in their eyes. If you think someone might be a victim of human trafficking, call the National Human Trafficking Hotline.

1 (888) 373-7888

This also applies to online, pornography profiles and adds online for sex. Be vigilant and speak out. It might save a life.

# NOTE FROM THE AUTHOR:

As is always the case with an author, my success or failure as well as the success of the message, depends almost exclusively on you, the reader.

One of the most important ways you can be of help is by leaving a good review on Amazon. New readers, who are searching for books to read, often base their decision whether or not to buy solely off of the reviews. If you liked this book, if it spoke to you at all, I would greatly appreciate an honest review.

Also, never underestimate the power of word of mouth. A simple recommendation to a friend can often be enough to convince someone to read it. And, since one-hundred percent of all proceeds from Branded goes to fight human trafficking, you won't be padding my pockets. Instead, you'll be saving lives.

Be sure to also follow me on Facebook at http://www.facebook.com/ctdanielsauthor and check out my website http://www.ct-daniels.com.

And keep an eye out for the sequel, Caged, which releases May 11, 2018.

# HUMAN TRAFFICKING GLOSSARY:

**Branding:** A tattoo or carving on a victim's skin that indicates ownership by a pimp/brothel owner.

**Bottom** or **"Bottom Bitch"**: A female appointed by the trafficker/pimp to supervise the others and report rule violations. Operating as his "right hand," the Bottom may help instruct victims, collect money, book hotel rooms, post ads, or inflict punishments on other girls.

**Exit Fee:** The money a pimp will demand from a victim who is thinking about trying to leave. It will be an exorbitant sum, to discourage her from leaving. Most pimps never let their victims leave freely.

**Finesse Pimp/Romeo Pimp:** One who prides himself on controlling others primarily through psychological manipulation. Although he may shower his victims with affection and gifts (especially during the recruitment phase), the threat of violence is always present.

**Gorilla (or Guerilla) Pimp:** A pimp who controls his victims almost entirely through physical violence and force.

**Madam**: An older woman who manages a brothel, escort service or other prostitution establishment. She may work alone or in collaboration with other traffickers.

**Quota**: A set amount of money that a trafficking victim must make each night before she can come "home." Quotas are often set between $300 and $2000. If the victim returns without meeting the quota, she is typically beaten and sent back out on the street to earn the rest. Quotas vary according to geographic region, local events, etc.

**Seasoning**: A combination of psychological manipulation, intimidation, gang rape, sodomy, beatings, deprivation of food or sleep, isolation from friends or family and other sources of support, and threatening or holding hostage of a victim's children. Seasoning is designed to break down a victim's resistance and ensure compliance.

**Stable**: A group of victims who are under the control of a single pimp.

**The Game/The Life**: The subculture of prostitution, complete with rules, a hierarchy of authority, and language. Referring to the act of pimping as 'the game' gives the illusion that it can be a fun and easy way to make money, when the reality is much harsher. Women and girls will say they've been "in the life" if they've been involved in prostitution for a while.

**Traffickers**: Traffickers are people who exploit others for profit. They can be any demographic, individuals and groups, street gangs and organized crime, businesses or contractors.

**Trick**: Committing an act of prostitution (*verb*), or the person buying it (*noun*). A victim is said to be "turning a trick" or "with a trick."

**The Wire**: (1) A pimp hotline, like a phone tree pimps use to get the word around, to find out which city is on/off. (2) Wiring money from victim to pimp in different cities/states ("put it on the wire").

**Glossary of terms taken from:**

https://inpublicsafety.com/2014/07/know-the-language-of-human-trafficking-a-glossary-of-sex-trafficking-terms/

# ABOUT THE AUTHOR

C.T. Daniels is a poet, playwright, and author, who has been writing for more than ten years. He studied the art of story-telling at the University of Massachusetts, Amherst under play-wrights Will Power and Marcus Gardley. Since then, he has turned his attention to giving voice to those in our society who do not have one of their own, particularly those involved in the scourge of human trafficking.

*For more information…*
www.ct-daniels.com
CTDanielsBranded@gmail.com